Black L

BLACK LIST

WILL JORDAN

CANELO

First published in Great Britain in 2015 by Canelo

This edition published in Great Britain in 2019 by

Canelo Digital Publishing Limited
57 Shepherds Lane
Beaconsfield, Bucks HP9 2DU
United Kingdom

A CIP catalogue record for this book is available from the British Library.

Print ISBN 978 1 78863 460 1
Ebook ISBN 978 1 910859 09 4

This book is a work of fiction. Names, characters, businesses, organizations, places and events are either the product of the author's imagination or are used fictitiously. Any resemblance to actual persons, living or dead, events or locales is entirely coincidental.

Look for more great books at www.canelo.co

For Daniel – who makes me proud every day

Prologue

Istanbul – 10 May 2009

This can't be happening.

This isn't me. This isn't who I am.

Strange the things that flash through your mind when you know you're about to die. I'd always hoped to utter something profound or poetic in my final moments, some great insight born from a long and fruitful life. But that wouldn't be the truth.

The truth is that I'm not old, wise or fruitful. I work a boring job, live in a modest house, pay my taxes on time and have semi-skimmed milk on my cereal in the morning. I don't take risks, and I don't go looking for trouble.

In most ways I'm a thoroughly average guy. Safe, dull, anonymous. The kind you pass on the street a dozen times a day and don't remember a heartbeat longer than you see them. And until a week ago, that was how I imagined it would always be.

I suppose everyone's luck runs out sooner or later...

–

Sweating, heart pounding, Alex surveyed the yawning gap stretching before him, the terrible drop below and the cluttered rooftop that was now his only way out. Fifteen feet of open air lay between him and salvation. Fifteen feet that might as well have been fifteen miles. Below, maybe seventy feet down, a narrow service alley ran between the modern office blocks.

It would be a rough fall if he jumped, and there was a fair chance he'd break bones or even fail entirely and rag-doll all the way down to the street below.

But it had to be worth a try.

He backed up a pace, trying to draw on the mental and physical reserves he'd need to make the jump, to put aside the danger and just go for it.

He couldn't do it, he realized straight away. He couldn't do it in London several days earlier, and he couldn't do it now. Even now with his life hanging by a thread, he just didn't have it in him.

A rapid series of muted thumps followed by the crunch of shattered wood behind warned him that his makeshift barricade had just been blasted apart.

'Freeze!'

And just like that, it was over. His one chance to escape, to justify the faith that had been shown in him, to prove he wasn't completely useless; it all vanished in that moment.

'Turn around!'

Letting out a breath, Alex reached up for the little USB memory stick hanging around his neck, and turned slowly to face his adversary.

Just as he'd expected, the man standing a few yards away was dressed in casual clothes that belied his deadly purpose. Jeans, hiking boots that had no doubt served him well on the frantic chase up the stairwell, and a loose blue shirt that didn't quite hide the bulky body armour underneath.

He was breathing a little harder, and a faint sheen of sweat coated his forehead. That gave Alex some small measure of satisfaction, as if he had somehow scored a point by making his opponent work for the kill.

And killing was certainly what was on this man's mind now. His weapon was trained on Alex's head, his finger tight on the trigger.

'Give me the memory stick,' he instructed, his voice cold and commanding. He might have had to work a little harder than usual to catch his prey, but he was firmly in control of the situation now.

Yanking the memory stick free from his neck, Alex suddenly thrust it out behind him, dangling it over the gap by its plain canvas necklace. Such an innocuous little piece of technology – the kind of cheap storage device used by everyone from office workers to teenage music fans. But appearances could be deceptive. The information stored within its digital pathways, carefully coded and encrypted, was what really mattered.

That was what he had travelled five thousand miles around the world for. That was what he had risked his life for. That was what he was about to die for.

'You shoot me, I drop this, the police recover it,' he warned. 'They'll find the Black List. Everything you were sent to cover up. It's all on you.'

His soon-to-be killer smiled. The fierce, predatory smile of one used to taking lives without mercy or hesitation. 'The police? You think we can't get to *them*?' he taunted. 'We can get to anyone. So do yourself a favour. Lay it down on the ground and back away, and we both walk. That's it.'

Alex might have laughed if he hadn't been so crushed by his failure. No matter what he did, no matter how compliant and cooperative he was, only one of them was walking away from this, and it wasn't him.

Alex was just another target to this man. Just another loose end to be taken care of. A stupid, clueless civilian who had only made it this far because he'd had someone far smarter and more capable watching his back. Someone who might well have given her life to buy him time to escape.

You fucked up, an accusatory voice in his mind told him. Just like everything else in life, you fucked this up. You might as well give him what he wants. Just back down and give up like you always do.

2

Then Alex did something; something even he didn't expect until it happened.

'No,' he said, his voice surprisingly calm given the frantic pounding of his heart. 'Not this time.'

Taking a step back, he mounted the low parapet encircling the perimeter of the building's roof. A gaping, terrifying chasm lay beneath him. An armed man intent on ending his life stood before him.

And all around, lit by the orange glow of uncountable lights that glimmered off the dark waters of the Bosphorus Strait, was the ancient city of Istanbul.

Not a bad place to end up, Alex thought as he took a step back into the abyss.

Part I

Conception

In 1983, the hacker group known as 'the 414' break into more than sixty computer systems, ranging from Los Alamos National Laboratory to Manhattan's Memorial Sloan Kettering Cancer Center. It is the first widely reported incident of computer hacking.

Chapter 1

London – Ten days earlier

It was a Friday evening, and Trafalgar Square was bustling with tourists, theatre-goers heading for nearby Piccadilly Circus, and stressed-looking office workers starting the long journey home after a tough week. Cars, taxis and buses jostled for position on the crowded roads that encircled the square, with bikes and mopeds zipping in between the slower-moving traffic, often accompanied by angry horn blasts.

It was a balmy, hazy sort of evening typical of late spring in the nation's capital, with only a faint warming breeze sighing along the busy streets. Overhead, the sun was beginning its long descent through wispy clouds that marred the otherwise pristine blue sky.

Taking a sip of his espresso, Alex Yates surveyed the expansive square with casual interest, his eyes hidden behind a pair of dark sunglasses as he took it all in. Over by the ornate fountains that flanked the square, a group of slick-looking stock traders from the nearby City were heading northwards, probably to one of the trendy wine bars in Soho. They were all swagger and expensive clothes and forced joviality, each trying to convince his comrades that the global financial crisis was just another minor storm, easily weathered before the return to more prosperous times.

Not far from this display of desperate optimism, a harassed-looking middle-aged man with wiry grey hair and an unfashionably cut suit scurried towards the stairs leading underground to Charing Cross station. A hard-working man, probably a civil servant or low-level bureaucrat who had frittered away his life in some dingy office cubicle, prematurely aged by stress and rules and deadlines.

As he went, he brushed past a blonde woman walking slowly away from the National Portrait Gallery. Tall, statuesque and wearing expensive jeans, a black fitted shirt and a stylish brown leather jacket, she was the epitome of effortless sophistication. Her features were strikingly good looking with a foreign air to them, yet there was a hardness about her that made him look a little closer.

Perhaps sensing his restless gaze on her, as attractive women often seemed to do, she glanced his way, and just for a moment their eyes met. Even from the other side of the square, Alex was caught off guard by the pair of icy blue eyes that seemed to bore right through him. No doubt she was wondering if he was a potential stalker.

Knowing that the last thing he needed was to draw attention to himself, Alex looked away, turning his attention back to the newspaper resting on his table. People-watching was a dangerous habit to fall into anyway, particularly for someone like him. Every detail of what he was seeing now would be imprinted on his memory forever, no doubt to intrude on his already crowded thoughts days or weeks from now.

He glanced at his watch. It was five past six. His friend was late for their meeting, and while it was too soon to be concerned about such a minor delay, he nonetheless found himself growing uneasy. Everything about this hastily arranged rendezvous made him nervous.

He resisted the urge to look at his watch again, knowing that less than twenty seconds had passed since his last check. Meeting in such a public place was both unnecessary and risky, and the lack of protection left him feeling exposed and vulnerable.

And yet here he was anyway, sitting at a coffee shop on the south side of the square, nursing his second espresso, which was doing his agitated mind no favours, waiting for a man he hadn't seen in over two years.

Why he'd agreed to the meeting in the first place, he couldn't rightly say. The last time he'd worked with Arran Sinclair, he'd ended up with a twelve-month prison sentence and a life-destroying criminal record for his troubles. If the two of them were even seen together by anyone with access to the Criminal Records Bureau database, it could bring him a renewed attention that he certainly didn't need.

But despite it all, Sinclair was a friend. Perhaps more than that, he was a reminder of a time when Alex's future had held a lot more promise than it did now. A time when he'd believed he had it in him to do great things with his life.

A foolish belief perhaps, but at the time it had felt real enough.

At that moment, a shadow fell across his table, startling him from his reverie.

'How's it going, mate?' a Scottish voice, warm and jovial and familiar, asked him. 'Long time no see.'

Glancing up from his coffee, Alex found himself staring into the face of a man he'd once considered a close friend. Tall and slender yet deceptively strong and athletic, and possessing the pale hawkish eyes of a man who saw everything and missed nothing, Arran Sinclair cut a striking figure that left an impression on virtually everyone who met him.

Alex had known him for nearly ten years, and he'd scarcely aged a day since. His features were still lean and ruggedly handsome, his light blonde hair still worn long and defiantly unkempt, his six-foot-four-inch frame clad in simple jeans, a casual shirt and a comfortable-looking leather jacket.

Just seeing him like that was like stepping back in time, and Alex actually had to pause for a moment as a flood of memories came rushing back.

'Arran,' he said after a moment, rising from his chair to greet his old friend. Even standing at full height, he was several inches shorter than Sinclair, forcing him to look up to the man as they shook hands. 'It's good to see you again.'

'And you. It's been too long.' He paused for a moment, as if wanting to say more but unsure how to phrase it. Instead he glanced at a spare chair at the table. 'Mind if I sit down?'

'Go for it.' Alex lowered himself back into his seat as Sinclair removed his jacket and settled down opposite. Neither man said anything for a few seconds, and the tension that had been hanging in the air suddenly became all too apparent. Now that they were face to face again, Alex found himself strangely at a loss for words.

'You're looking well,' he said, not even sure why he'd said it.

Suddenly Sinclair's face lit up in a once-familiar grin, and to Alex's surprise he laughed in amusement. 'Why do I suddenly feel like I'm on a really shit blind date?' he asked, still chortling.

Alex couldn't help but grin as well, the tension between them suddenly dissipating. 'If you were the best they could find, I'd want my money back.'

Their conversation was interrupted briefly when a waitress came over to take Sinclair's order. Typical of him, he ordered a tall latte with two extra shots of espresso.

'Some things never change, I see,' Alex remarked as the young woman hurried off to fetch his order. In all the years Alex had known him, he couldn't recall Sinclair ever ordering anything different.

'I know what I like.' His friend shrugged dismissively. 'Anyway, what the hell are you up to these days? You certainly weren't an easy man to find, even for me.'

Alex wasn't surprised by that. His address had changed twice since they'd parted company. 'Keeping busy,' he evaded. 'On that subject though, how *did* you find me?'

At this, Sinclair made an apologetic face. 'I had to go through Jill,' he said, bracing himself for an angry response. 'I'm sorry, mate, but you weren't online anymore. I didn't know who else to talk to.'

Alex felt himself wince inwardly. Jill, another reminder of his former life that he knew he'd never see again. Bright, enthusiastic, ambitious and hard-working. Not even thirty years old and already an associate partner with a respected legal firm. The kind of person who knew exactly where she was going in life and how to get there.

The kind of person he'd once been.

To her credit, she'd stuck with him longer than he'd expected. She'd been with him throughout the court case, had waited patiently while he served his prison term and even tried to rekindle their relationship when he was finally paroled. However, it hadn't taken long for them to realize things would never go back to the way they were. Too much had changed, for both of them.

It had almost been a relief when she'd finally admitted defeat and called it off. At least now he didn't have to endure the humiliation of her patient support, her words of encouragement every time he applied for another menial job only to be rejected. Their lives were heading in different directions now, and for her sake he was glad she was rid of him.

'It's all right,' Alex said, his jaw tight as he forced the words out. 'I'm sure she filled you in on the gory details.'

'More or less.' Sinclair was perceptive enough to know he'd hit a sore spot. 'She... mentioned you were working for an electrical retailer now. Selling TVs, that kind of thing.'

There was no point in even pretending otherwise. Alex looked his old friend in the eye. 'There weren't a lot of job opportunities for people with my kind of record,' he remarked pointedly. 'I had to take what I could find.'

Sinclair closed his eyes for a moment, seeing his remark for what it was. 'I'm sorry, Alex. I know that doesn't add up to much, but I really mean it. I can only imagine how hard it must have been...'

He trailed off as the waitress returned with his drink, though his expression made it obvious he was eager to say more. Alex however was glad of the reprieve. He neither needed nor wanted Sinclair's gratitude, or worse, his sympathy.

'I was caught, you weren't,' Alex said simply. 'There was no point dragging you all down with me. Anyway, I know you'd have done the same for me.'

At this, his friend nodded slowly, saying nothing. He seemed relieved somehow at Alex's words, as if he'd been carrying the burden around with him for a long time.

'So what's this all about, Arran?' Alex asked, leaning forward and looking him in the eye. Swapping life stories was all well and good, but what he wanted now were answers. 'You contact me out of nowhere after all this time, I'm guessing it's not to talk about my career.'

That was enough to bring Sinclair back to the present. Meeting Alex's searching gaze, he took a sip of his steaming drink. And then, just like that, he said it.

'I'm reforming Valhalla, Alex. And I want you in.'

Alex was grateful he wasn't taking a drink of his own at that moment, otherwise he might have choked on it. Valhalla 7, the group of highly skilled hackers that both of them had helped to create, and which had long since disbanded, was being reunited. The mere mention of the name was enough to make his heart leap.

He looked at his friend in disbelief. 'Are you serious?'

Sinclair said nothing. There was no need. His calm, almost nonchalant demeanour stood in marked contrast to the gravity of the situation. Based on his body language, anyone observing them would think little of their conversation, but Alex knew all too well how serious this was.

'Mate, maybe you missed the part about me being convicted for computer hacking and going to prison for twelve months, or the terms of my parole. If I even go near anything more complicated than a smart phone, I'm fucked.'

His friend nodded, no doubt well prepared for such an objection. 'I know how this must sound,' he admitted. 'I know this is probably the last thing you're interested in doing now. But before you walk away, just hear me out.'

Alex leaned back in his chair, surveying him for a long moment. He gave no words of encouragement, but neither did he object.

'When Valhalla broke up, I started working freelance,' Sinclair explained. 'Picked up a few long-term clients. One in particular came very highly recommended. I've been working for her for the past year or so, doing smaller jobs.'

Alex raised an eyebrow. 'Her?'

He saw a flicker of a smile. 'Didn't even find out it was a woman until recently. All our communication was through anonymous email addresses. Anyway, a few days ago she approaches me about a new job. A big one. The kind of white-hat job we always imagined pulling, but never did.'

Alex frowned at this. 'Government?'

Sinclair's smile broadened. 'Better.'

Reaching into his jacket pocket, he passed a folded piece of paper across the table to Alex. Intrigued, he unfolded the piece of paper and quickly read the brief outline of the job requirements, then read it again to make sure he'd understood correctly. He had.

He looked up at Sinclair in disbelief. 'You're having a laugh, right?'

He shook his head.

'This is ridiculous. You're talking about...' He forced himself to keep his voice down, suddenly very conscious of the public venue for their meeting. '... hacking the fucking CIA?'

Sinclair couldn't hide his grin now. This was the kind of thing he lived for.

'Have you got a cell reserved at Guantanamo Bay?' Alex asked cynically.

But Sinclair was far from daunted by his pessimism. 'Think about it, Alex; their firewalls have never been breached by anyone, ever. No other group has even come close.'

'And for good reason,' Alex agreed. 'It can't be done.'

'Any system can be beaten,' Sinclair countered, speaking as if he was quoting someone else. 'All you need is skill, planning and patience.'

'Who told you that?'

9

'*You* did, eight years ago.' Sinclair tilted his head a little. 'I'm surprised you don't remember, considering...'

Or perhaps he'd chosen to forget. It sounded like the kind of cocky bullshit he used to spout in a different life, before the court case and the prison sentence and the grim reality that things would never be the same again.

'Anyway, you were right all those years ago,' Sinclair went on. 'Skill and patience we can take care of ourselves. As for the luck part, our client might just be able to help us out.'

'What do you mean?' Alex prompted, perplexed by his cryptic hint.

'Put it this way – she's got connections. I can't go into any details at this stage, but believe me when I say most other hacker groups in the world would kill to get their hands on what she's given us. We have an advantage that nobody else ever has.' He leaned forward, his elbows resting on the edge of the table. 'Now, imagine for one minute that we actually did it. Imagine we cracked their firewall and got inside. It could literally change the world. All those conspiracy theories about the government spying on their own people, kidnapping innocent people, torturing them, staging assassinations and coups all over the world... We'd have the proof at our fingertips. Can you imagine what that would mean? Can you imagine the difference we could make?'

He was staring right at Alex now with those intense, hawk-like eyes as he spoke. All pretence of nonchalant disinterest was gone now. Alex could scarcely recall seeing him so excited.

'All the amazing things we'd planned to do, all the times we used to get pissed together in the pub and talk about doing something important,' he went on. 'Well, this is our chance to make it happen. It's a second chance to finish what we started, and they don't come along very often.'

Alex should have expected this from a man like Sinclair. Always an idealist and a believer in freedom of information no matter the cost, age clearly hadn't dulled his passion. If anything it was more intense than ever. The years he'd been forced to bide his time and wait had clearly made an impression on him.

'That's why you want me involved,' Alex said, realizing that his particular talents would be vital to such a scheme. 'You need me to crack the firewall.'

'Nobody can break encryption codes like you, Alex. You can do things that make the rest of us look like rank amateurs.' Sinclair sighed, looking at his friend across the table. 'I'm asking for your help, mate. I *need* your help. And I'm willing to pay for it.'

Another piece of paper made its way across the table. Unable to help himself, Alex unfolded it to read. Yet again, what he saw left him stunned.

One hundred thousand pounds, payable either as cash or into an account of his choice.

'Half up front, half on completion,' Sinclair said when Alex finally looked up at him. 'Enough to get your life back on track. And believe me, there's more where that came from.'

Alex felt like the world was spinning around him. The sudden arrival of Sinclair had turned his life into a maelstrom of possibilities, of opportunities long since abandoned but now suddenly real once more. One hundred thousand pounds could change his life, could pull him out of the mire he was slowly sinking into, could save him.

But Sinclair's offer carried with it something far more valuable. A chance to get back in the game, to do something meaningful with his life, to be someone he was proud to be.

For an instant, he saw the incredible future that was there for the taking. The accomplishments, the achievements, the power to do things that people all over the world would talk about.

It was all there, just waiting for him. All he had to do was reach out and take it.

'I can't. I'm sorry, mate. But I can't do it.'

The words came out almost before he was aware of them, the rational part of his mind reasserting its dominance over the wild, ambitious young man he'd once been.

'I almost lost everything the last time I tried something like this.' With a trembling hand, he slid the piece of paper back across the table to his friend. 'I can't go through that again. I can't help you.'

'Alex, I know there are risks.' Sinclair's voice was gentle, calming now. 'There are always risks, but sometimes they're worth taking. I know you. I know who you are and what you can do. You're not like all these people around us,' he said, his keen eyes taking in the thronging crowds traversing Trafalgar Square. 'You, me… we were made for something more.'

He sighed and leaned back in his chair, looking sadly at his friend.

'If you want to go back to selling TVs and living in some shitty flat, that's your choice – I can't stop you. But think about what you're giving up. I'm offering you a chance to do what you were born to do, what we both know you want to do. Isn't that *worth* risking everything for?' He let that question hang for a moment, sensing Alex's wavering resolve. 'One way or another there's no going back from whatever answer you give me now. So I'll ask for you for the last time, mate. What's it going to be?'

Chapter 2

'Well, what's it going to be?'

Alex blinked, drawn reluctantly out of his thoughts like a man surfacing from the depths of a murky pond. The memory of that meeting in Trafalgar Square three days earlier receded and reality took over again, however reluctant he might be to let it in.

Glancing up from the TV he'd been staring at absently for an unknown time, he found himself looking at the fleshy, amiable face of his co-worker, Mike King.

A few years older than Alex and a good few stones heavier, Mike, with his dishevelled hair, less-than-designer stubble and perpetually creased shirts, somehow looked like a delinquent student who had been plucked out of high school and thrust unwillingly into adult life. He'd been fighting against it ever since, and in that sense at least, he was winning.

From what Alex knew of him, his life outside of work consisted of sustained bouts of drinking – about which he was always willing to provide a lengthy anecdote – and even longer spells of online gaming. The only reason he was even able to hold down a job as a sales assistant was because of his almost supernatural ability to make people buy things they didn't want. Nothing fazed him and because of that, nothing seemed to stop him.

'Sorry mate, what were you saying?' Alex said, realizing he'd missed most of the conversation as his mind continued to replay every detail of his encounter with his old friend.

Mike rolled his eyes, feigning wounded pride. 'My conversation that fascinating, eh? I was asking where you fancy heading for drinks on Friday – Dirty Dick's or the Witness Box? The beer's not as good in Dick's, but at least the girls make a bit of effort. It's all munters and grannies in the Box.'

Alex shook his head. With everything else going on in his life at that moment, going out and getting plastered with Mike was the least of his concerns. Anyway, the last time Mike had persuaded him to go out for 'a few quiet pints' after work, he'd woken up the next morning on his kitchen floor with a splitting headache, a black eye and a traffic cone sitting in the corner of the room. To this day, he had no recollection of how any of those things had come to pass.

'Not sure I can make it on Friday, mate,' he said apologetically. 'Maybe next time, yeah?'

Mike eyed him suspiciously. He might have been an immature, lazy bum and a borderline alcoholic, but he could be a surprisingly shrewd judge of character at times. Something was up with Alex, and he knew it.

'You up to something on the sly, son?'

'Just busy,' he evaded.

Then, just like that, suspicion gave way to a knowing smile. 'It's a woman, isn't it?'

'No.'

'A man?'

'No!' Alex clenched his teeth, wishing he hadn't said anything at all. Mike was relentless when it came to things like this; Hercule Poirot didn't even come close. Alex leaned a little closer and lowered his voice. 'I'm thinking about doing a bit of freelancing.'

Mike's smile was conspiratorial. 'You planning to move to greener pastures?'

Too fucking right he was, Alex thought as he surveyed the bland, cheaply lit electrical showroom around them; the disinterested customers, the dry, air-conditioned atmosphere, the coffee machine that made a weird noise as it brewed, and the bored employees, most of whom were students working here for drinking money. Just getting through the day, probably counting down the minutes until they could leave this dump behind.

How had he ended up in a godforsaken place like this? He knew the answer even before he'd asked the question. Because they were the only people who would take him on. A university-educated computer expert who knew more about coding than Bill Gates, and here he was selling laptops to kids half his age.

'It's a one-off,' he said vaguely.

Mike was about to reply, but the bleep of the nearby desk phone brought a welcome respite. Alex's relief was cut short however when he saw the caller identity. It was Tim Dixon, known less-than-affectionately as the Dick by those unlucky enough to serve under him.

Dixon's office was scarcely twenty feet away in the back area behind the showroom, yet he always insisted on summoning people instead of simply walking over to talk to them, like it somehow gave him more power.

Sighing inwardly, Alex picked up his phone. 'Yeah, Tim?'

'Alex. Just the man I wanted. We need to have a little chat,' Dixon announced without preamble. 'Would you mind coming into my office?'

Alex's heart sank. Being called into Dixon's office for a 'little chat' meant only one thing – he was about to be chewed out for something.

'No problem. I'm on my way.'

As he hung up the phone, Mike gave him a look of feigned sympathy. 'Remember to lube up beforehand, mate. It'll make things easier.'

'Piss off,' Alex fired back over his shoulder.

Some people in life you just never seem to hit it off with. Whether it's because of differing backgrounds, incompatible personalities or plain old dislike, there are always one or two you can't ever see eye to eye with. And when that person happens to be a middle manager who enjoys throwing his weight around with his subordinates, you know you're in for a difficult time.

Such was Alex's lot with Tim Dixon.

After swiping his way out of the staff-only exit from the showroom and negotiating the warren of bare-brick corridors behind the main shop, he stopped outside Dixon's door and, pausing only to smooth down his tie, knocked once.

'Come in!'

Swinging the door open, Alex found himself facing into a small, cramped office not much more spacious than the average bathroom. The decor was just as cheap and the chair was just as uncomfortable as any other in the building, but it was still a private office. A little privilege that elevated its owner above the rest of the workers. And Dixon was the kind of man who relished little privileges.

Early forties, short, stocky and perpetually fighting against all three things, Tim Dixon was dressed in a shirt that was too small for his bulky frame, the sleeves rolled up to reveal the muscular forearms and bulging veins that came from heavy weight-training.

Pretending to be working, he glanced up from his computer wearing the kind of bland smile Alex supposed a movie star would flash an eager reporter.

'Alex, how are you?' he asked in a tone that made it plain he didn't give a shit. Then, without waiting for a reply, he went on, 'Close the door and take a seat, would you?'

Alex did as he was asked, taking a seat without saying a word. Dixon said nothing either, just sat there looking at Alex with that same bland, soulless smile. The seconds seemed to stretch out into hours as Alex sat there, listening to the hum of the air conditioning and the tick of the clock mounted on the wall.

Finally he could take it no longer. 'You wanted to have a talk?' he prompted.

Dixon leaned back in his chair, surveying him thoughtfully. No doubt he wished it was some expensive, high-backed leather affair, but the company wasn't going to spring for it. 'Alex, I'm going to ask you a question, and I'd like an honest answer. Do we have a problem here?'

He frowned. 'Not that I know of.'

'Hmm,' Dixon remarked, reaching for a sheet of paper on his desk. He slid it across to Alex. 'Do you know what this is? It's an email from the head – the *head* – of customer services, asking why one of our sales agents deleted a day's worth of credit-card transactions instead of filing them. He wants to know why his team are having to waste their time contacting every customer by phone to undo that agent's mistake. He wants to know who's responsible.' He left the paper resting on the desk. 'So, what exactly should I tell him, Alex?'

Straight away Alex felt the colour drain from his face. Normally the mundane task of filing the day's card transactions through the till was a simple one, but he'd been rushed, distracted and tired when he'd done it yesterday, and hadn't bothered to check his work. Since it had always worked fine before, he'd assumed he could easily skip the double-checking and save himself some time.

Clearly he'd been wrong.

Beneath the table, his hands slowly clenched into fists. Of all the bloody rotten luck, this was the last thing he needed right now.

'Tim, that was—'

Dixon held up a hand, silencing his excuse before he could even get it out. It was just as well really, because he didn't have one worth listening to. 'To be honest, I don't want to hear it, Alex. If you'd done your job properly and checked your work, this never would have happened. You were sloppy and careless, and you've been here long enough to know better. And let's face it, with your... *record*, any kind of problems with money and accounting are bound to draw attention. Am I wrong?'

Alex said nothing. No response was expected.

'And that's not to mention your timekeeping,' he went on. 'Arriving late, leaving bang on five, making basic mistakes that cost the company money...' He shook his head in mocking disappointment before fixing him with a hard look. 'Let me ask you something. Do you think you're better than this job, Alex?'

That was the real crux of the matter, Alex knew. The real reason Dixon disliked Alex with such a passion. It was because he sensed in Alex something he didn't possess himself – the ability to do more with his life. And that frightened and angered him.

Dixon wasn't naturally intelligent, didn't have a great understanding of the people working beneath him and probably hadn't done particularly well at school, but determination and the ability to feign knowledge had nonetheless carried him into a position of minor power. In all likelihood he wouldn't rise much further than this, but for now he was higher in the food chain than Alex, and he never let the younger man forget it.

'Do you think you deserve something more than this, that you're special somehow?' he went on, the veil of genial professionalism slipping aside. His years of festering resentment had at last found an outlet, and he wasn't about to let it go now. 'Or do you think the rules shouldn't apply to you because you're so much smarter than the rest of us? Maybe you even think you should be the one sitting in this chair instead of me. But you're not, are you, Alex? For all your fancy university degrees and your high-flying jobs, you're still sitting right at the bottom of the pile now. And that's where you'll always be, because you don't have it in you to work for anything better.'

Alex said nothing, because he could think of no response to such an outburst. Such was the thinly veiled hatred in Dixon's voice and the vitriol in his words, he was left genuinely shocked by it. He'd always sensed it on some level, but to sit there and listen to the man openly berate and belittle him was like a slap across the face.

His boss let out a sigh, his mask of professional detachment returning, and surveyed him for a long moment as if pretending to agonize over what to do. They both knew he'd decided what to say long before Alex had walked into his office.

'There's going to be an official discussion about this,' he said. 'I'll let the people in HR know, and we'll set up a meeting for later in the week.' Already he was typing out an email to start the process. 'I suggest you take some time to think about what you're going to say, because a lot of people will be reading the transcript.'

Alex slumped back in his chair, feeling like someone had just driven a fist into his gut. Official discussions with Human Resources on the case made it pretty obvious where this was heading. Dixon had clearly always resented the fact that he'd been obliged to take on a convicted criminal – even a rehabilitated one – and for some time now had been looking for an excuse to cut him loose. And Alex had handed it to him on a plate.

Alex could almost imagine his glee as the angry email arrived in his mailbox.

Glancing up from his computer, Dixon motioned towards the door. 'You can go now.'

Mike King was waiting for him as he shuffled back to his desk. 'How did it go, mate?' he asked, his expression caught between sympathy and amusement.

Alex didn't even spare him a glance as he picked up his coat from the back of his chair and shuffled out, broken and defeated.

—

That was it for me – the beginning of the end of what was laughably called my life. Burning bridges and all that.

I suppose if I'd been braver, I would have marched back into Dixon's office, pinned him against the wall and told him to shove his crappy job up his patronizing arse, told him that he was a pathetic, narrow-minded prick who was only one step higher up the shit pile than me. I would have told him that, unlike him, I'd at least got to fly before I crashed and burned.

But I didn't do any of those things. I just went outside, smoked a cigarette in gloomy silence, shuffled around the showroom floor until 5 p.m. and slunk out of the building with my tail between my legs.

I'd like to say I did this because I was taking the moral high ground, because I wouldn't stoop to Dixon's level, but that wouldn't be the truth. The truth is, I did nothing about it because I knew deep down that he was right. He was a petty, vindictive arsehole, but he was right about me.

I was at the bottom of the pile, and maybe I didn't have what it took to climb higher.

So I let it slide.

Story of my life.

Chapter 3

Stirlingshire, Scotland

He was running out of time. It wouldn't take more than a minute or so for his pursuer to catch up with him.

Just long enough to do what he had to.

The post office at the edge of the small village of Gargunnock in Stirlingshire had long since closed for the day, its windows dark and its doors locked, but that didn't matter to him. The bright red post box fixed into the wall outside was all he needed. He knew it would be emptied first thing in the morning.

Bringing his car skidding to a halt beside the low building, Arran Sinclair hauled the door open and scrambled out, a crumpled envelope clutched in his hand. He'd barely had time to scrawl the address on the way here.

It was a cool, breezy night typical of late springtime in Scotland, the moon obscured by thick ribbons of cloud. The gentle rustle of tree branches in the night breeze was a deceptively serene counterpoint to the urgent thumping of his heart as he fixed a stamp to the envelope.

Pausing a moment by the mailbox, he looked down at the letter and felt the hard plastic shape within. He had made a mistake taking on this task, he realized now. It was beyond his abilities, and he knew that sooner or later he would pay the price.

His only hope was that the recipient of this letter had more luck than himself.

'I'm sorry, Alex,' he said quietly, stuffing the letter into the mailbox.

That was when heard it. Above the rustling of leaves, the sigh of the wind and the thumping of his heart was another note. A rumble, loud and urgent. A car engine at high revs, heading his way.

It was time to go.

His brief mission complete, Sinclair jumped back in his car. Ten seconds later he was roaring down the twisting country lane out of the village, heading for the main road to Stirling about five miles distant. Overhanging branches crowded in close to the road, forming a natural tunnel of sorts that reflected the bright beams of his headlights.

The narrow, unpredictable road would slow the vehicle following him, the steep river gorge to his right acting as a deterrent to all but the boldest of drivers. Sinclair almost smiled as he pressed harder on the accelerator, knowing there was a long straight coming up. He'd grown up around this area, had learned to drive here and knew every bend and corner of this road like the back of his hand.

He held the advantage over the car following him.

No sooner had this thought crossed his mind than he saw something on the bend up ahead, something that made his heart leap and adrenaline surge through his veins. Straight away he slammed on his brakes and turned the wheel hard over. Tyres skidded on slick tarmac and the low metal crash barrier at the edge of the road swung into view as the car fishtailed.

Sinclair tensed up, bracing himself for what was coming.

The crash barrier at the edge of the road presented little resistance, buckling and shearing apart under the impact as the car slammed into it. Pitching over the edge, the car flipped straight over on its roof, rolling and crashing down the steep brush-covered slope to the fast-flowing river far below.

By the time it hit the surface, the chassis had been reduced to a mass of twisted and buckled metal. With nothing buoyant enough to support it, the wreck quickly filled with icy cold water and disappeared beneath the surface within a matter of seconds, leaving only the wreckage-strewn slope behind as testimony to the violence of its final moments.

And in the post box at the nearby village, unseen and undetected by the vehicle that had passed by less than a minute earlier, a single letter waited to be collected.

Chapter 4

It was raining by the time Alex finally made it home that evening, a heavy ceiling of sombre grey clouds having descended on the capital during the afternoon. Not heavy, drumming rain, but that vague misty stuff that clings to hair and skin, and soaks through clothes more effectively than the average monsoon.

The train station from which he'd disembarked along with all the other weary commuters was about half a mile from his flat, leaving him with the none-too-pleasant prospect of a run through the rain in a jacket that was wholly inadequate for the task. Using the takeaway pizza box he'd picked up on the way home as a makeshift umbrella, he scurried up the street to the grey four-storey apartment block that he called home.

It didn't make much difference. By the time he was done fumbling around with his keys to get into the main stairwell, he was more or less soaked to the skin anyway. The pizza box was also rapidly disintegrating into a sodden mess, which did little to improve his mood as he trudged up two flights of stairs to his landing.

The flat he'd been renting for the past year or so was certainly nothing to look at, he reflected as he pushed the door open with one foot, ignoring the pile of letters that had accumulated behind it. Most of them were circulars anyway — charity appeals and solar panel brochures that he had no interest in.

Typical of low-rent single-bedroom places in the western suburbs of London, it was small and cramped, designed with simple utility and efficiency in mind. A talented interior decorator might have made the modest living space appear cosy and homely, but Alex wasn't such a person. The furniture was mostly cheap Ikea flat-pack stuff that never seemed to go together properly, the kitchen cluttered and untidy, the sink filled with unwashed dishes.

Dumping the pizza box on the kitchen counter, Alex peeled off his jacket and undid his work tie, gratefully discarding both. One way or another, he didn't imagine he would need his work clothes much longer. Not if Dixon had anything to say about it.

Aware that he was dripping water on the carpet, he retreated to the bathroom for a towel to dry himself. As he did so, he caught a glimpse of his reflection in the mirror.

With light brown hair now dripping with rain water, grey eyes that betrayed not a hint of colour, regular features that were neither handsome nor ugly, and a physique that was beginning to lose its youthful vigour as years of junk food and lack of exercise took their toll, Alex's appearance was about as average and unremarkable as they came.

He had seen only twenty-eight years of life, yet he felt and looked ten years older at that moment. His face was drawn, his eyes ringed by dark circles of fatigue, his jaw coated by a light dusting of stubble. He'd barely slept in the three days since his meeting with Sinclair, his restless mind endlessly turning over their tense conversation, wondering what might have been.

He'd refused his friend's offer, of course. As much as he might have wanted to turn back time and reclaim the life that had been taken from him, this wasn't the way to do it. One spell in prison was more than enough for this lifetime.

So they'd parted ways without reaching an agreement, each unhappy and disappointed in the other. Sinclair's parting words, delivered with a hint of pity that had stung Alex deeply, had been to wish him luck with the rest of his life.

Gratefully leaving the mirror, he returned to the kitchen, opened the fridge and helped himself to a can of beer. He'd lost his appetite for the sodden mess that the pizza had become, but the alcohol would serve him better.

Flopping down on the couch, he cracked open the beer and took a long pull on it, grimacing as the gassy mixture settled on his empty stomach. With the rain still pattering off the window and the orange glow of street lights permeating the room, he allowed his head to tilt back and let out a long, defeated sight.

He'd refused Sinclair's offer, done the rational thing and stepped back from something that could land him in prison for life this time. He'd made the only decision a man in his position could, as he'd told himself countless times already. So why did he feel so shitty about it? Why did he feel like he'd just made the biggest mistake of his life?

Not for the first time, his friend's words echoed in his mind.

If you want to go back to selling TVs and living in some shitty flat, that's your choice – I can't stop you. But think about what you're giving up. I'm offering you a chance to do what you were born to do, what we both know you want to do. Isn't that worth risking everything for?

Alex took another pull on the beer, wishing he had something stronger in the flat. If ever there was a time to drink himself to sleep, this was it.

On impulse, he reached down, feeling around underneath the couch until his hand brushed against an old shoe box. Lifting it out, he flipped the lid off and set the box on his lap to inspect the contents.

Alex could hardly call himself the sentimental type. He'd never been one for hoarding keepsakes or mementos, but even he still kept some photographs from his younger days, unsorted and faded but still usable. Forbidden as he was to own a computer, these old photographs were about the only reminders he still had of a time when his life had been very different.

Many were childhood pictures showing him unwrapping presents at Christmas or dressed up for Halloween, and later when he was a school kid with bad hair and a worse attitude. But the one he was most interested in at that moment was sitting on top of the pile. He knew this because for the past two nights he'd gone through the same ritual.

Taken ten years ago, not long after he'd started at university, it showed Alex seated on a worn leather couch in his student flat, bottle of beer in hand, flanked by two other young men similarly armed. The first was unmistakably Arran Sinclair. Even back then, his trademark unruly blonde hair and infectious grin were very much in evidence, and in truth the face staring back from the photograph looked little different from the man Alex had met three days ago.

Things just seemed to come easy to Sinclair. He was tall, good looking and possessed a confident, easygoing charm that was rare in one so young, and men and women alike had instinctively seemed to warm to him. He'd certainly never lacked for female attention during his time at university, which was partly why Alex had first made a point of spending time with him.

The second man was less well endowed. A short, stocky Norwegian with a fleshy face and long dark hair tied back in a simple ponytail, he was grinning at the camera with the unfocussed eyes of a man who had already overdone it. Then again, Gregar Landvik never did know when to hold back, Alex thought with a grim smile.

The three of them had hooked up in that chaotic, frenzied time that accompanied the start of a new term, and despite their differing back-grounds and personalities had quickly become firm friends. Alex couldn't rightly say what brought them together, but somehow they just seemed to gravitate towards each other.

Later the three students had applied their considerable talents to the world of computer hacking, eventually forming a group of like-minded individuals which they named Valhalla 7. Their work brought them great success for a time, but also exposed differences between them that were ultimately to destroy the group.

But in that picture, none of those things had yet come to pass. The three men grinning back at Alex were young and happy, filled with optimism and excitement about the great adventure that lay ahead. He could scarcely imagine what that felt like now, and couldn't help wondering what his younger self would make of his life today.

'Glad you're not here to see it, mate,' Alex said, draining his beer.

He was just getting up to retrieve another from the kitchen when he spotted something over by the front door. A hand-addressed envelope was mixed in amongst the charity appeals, utility bills and marketing crap.

Alex paused, frowning for a moment. Who the hell still sent letters in this day and age? Even his parents were tech-savvy enough to connect with their friends online.

Intrigued, he knelt down to pick it up, and immediately felt his heart-beat quicken. He'd recognize Arran Sinclair's jerky, chaotic handwriting anywhere. The poor quality of the penmanship suggested it had been scrawled in a hurry, but if so, why had his friend chosen such an old-fashioned way of contacting him?

More interesting still was the bulge of something hard inside the envelope. Clearly it contained more than just a missive from his friend, and judging by the weight and dimensions of the object, Alex had a fair idea of what it was.

Wasting no time, Alex tore open the envelope to reveal its contents, and his suspicions were proven correct when a digital memory stick fell into his hand. Smaller than the key fob for a car, the unassuming little storage device was capable of holding up to 50 gigabytes of data. Enough to carry tens of thousands of books, hundreds of hours of high-definition video or just about anything else one could conceivably need to store.

But with no computer, Alex had no way of knowing what this one held.

Slipping it into his pocket for now, he unfolded the crumpled letter, hoping that his friend had imparted some useful information. However, what he saw only deepened his concern.

Keep this safe. Don't tell anyone about it. I'll contact you when I can.

Arran.

Hardly comprehensive instructions, Alex thought with a flash of irrita-tion. Given the timing of Sinclair's letter, it seemed logical to assume it had something to do with the job he'd been offered, but why entrust such a thing to a man who had already refused to help?

And yet, Sinclair wouldn't have done something like this without good reason. The question was, what did the memory stick contain that was so important?

Sinking onto his couch once more, Alex stared at the inconspicuous little storage device as if he could discern its contents simply through focussed determination.

There was only one way he could find out what was so important about it, and that involved breaking the terms of his parole.

He shook his head, frustration at his own impotence mingling with a growing concern for his friend's safety.

'For fuck's sake, Arran. What have you got yourself into?' he asked aloud. Even as he did so, he knew he wouldn't find any answers here.

Chapter 5

Three days.

That's how long I held out. Three days of going through the motions of my daily life, waiting with growing concern for Arran to contact me. Three days of turning over all kinds of possibilities in my mind. Three days of nervous anticipation that found no relief.

The memory stick felt like a lead weight in my pocket, kept with me at all times just in case someone broke into my flat while I was out.

Dixon's threatened meeting with Human Resources came and went. I sat through it more or less in silence, hardly even aware of what was happening around me. All I could hear were words like 'poor performance', 'unreliable' and 'questionable future'.

In truth, part of me was hoping they'd just fire me and save us all the aggravation, but I suppose they had to go through the motions. We all had to.

–

By the evening of the third day, Alex had finally made up his mind. There had been no word from Sinclair, and no indication that his friend would come to relieve him of the unwanted burden of the memory stick. One way or another, he needed to know what was going on.

Returning home from another unfulfilling day at work, Alex discarded his shirt and trousers, slipping on a pair of faded jeans and a Metallica t-shirt he'd owned since he was a teenager. Though not normally superstitious, he'd always worn it back in the day when undertaking a new hacking attempt, as if it somehow conveyed an element of protection or luck. Pulling it on felt like stepping back in time.

'Well, Arran, I hope you're fucking happy now,' he mumbled as he zipped up a black hoodie over the t-shirt. 'I'm about to break my parole, just like you wanted. Wanker.'

Shuddering in the unseasonably cold evening breeze, he left his apartment block and headed east, following the main drag towards Brentford tube station. With his hood up, head down and hands in his pockets, he was about as anonymous as it was possible to be in a place like this. People walked right by him, not paying the slightest notice.

But unknown to Alex, one person did notice him. One person's sole focus was directed at him in fact as they followed him about thirty yards back, sometimes coming closer, sometimes allowing the gap to widen. Once or twice they even appeared to stop and allow him to wander off, but always they stayed with him.

A pair of cold, intense blue eyes followed his every move.

Oblivious to his silent pursuer, Alex continued on his way, passing sad-looking charity shops, boarded-up retail units waiting to be leased and houses festooned with For Sale signs. The global financial crisis was still hammering the UK hard, and an air of gloom and doom seemed to have descended on the entire country. Even the stray cats lurking near takeaway bins looked more grim than usual.

What he was looking for was about a hundred yards distant – he could already see the neon sign above the door, fashioned in the shape of a giant @ symbol.

Internet cafes were by now a thing of the past – throwbacks to the 1990s, when only rich people could afford online access at home. But even in the twenty-first century there were still a few such places dotted around, kept going partly by nostalgia and partly by tourists with no other means of accessing their emails.

Coffee@Once was one such place. Alex had never felt the need to venture inside, particularly with his parole terms hanging over him, but he'd passed by enough times to know the layout well enough. Coffee house at the front, computer terminals lined up in a series of discreet booths at the back.

The decor was like something out of an episode of *Friends*; all domestic couches, mismatching furniture and shabby-chic exposed floorboards. A typical hangout for people with thick-framed glasses they didn't need and hair meticulously styled to look like they didn't care about it, all trying so hard to be unique that they ended up looking like they'd rolled off a hipster assembly line. Still, they had what he needed, and they stayed open until 10 p.m.

Making his way inside, he was immediately assailed by the strong, sickly-sweet aroma of coffee beans. Whatever they brewed there must have been like rocket fuel.

Doing his best to ignore the tinge of nausea that the smell of coffee shops always brought out in him, he caught the eye of one of the staff members and walked over to talk with him.

He was a tall, sparsely built young man with a row of piercings in one eyebrow, and blonde hair shaved at the sides and gelled into a ridiculous quiff on top. Still, at least it made Alex's teenage photos look a little better.

'Evening. What can I get for you?' he asked, eyeing up Alex's appearance with casual disapproval. Apparently branded t-shirts and scruffy hoodies weren't in keeping with the standards expected here.

'I need one of your machines.'

A heavily pierced brow rose with some difficulty. 'No coffee, or food? We're doing a special offer on blueberry and coconut muffins today.'

Alex tried not to make a face. Food was the last thing on his mind, and he was hardly swimming in cash as it was. This place would no doubt happily relieve him of what little he had left. 'No, I just want to check a few things online.'

'It's up to you,' he remarked, not looking as if he cared much either way. 'How long?'

'Half an hour should be enough.'

'Cool beans,' the young man said, inputting some commands into a master terminal that controlled access to the other computers in the room. 'That'll be ten pounds.'

It was Alex's turn to raise an eyebrow. That would have been extortionate even back when places like this were cutting-edge. A cursory tally of the money in his wallet plus whatever loose change he could dig out of his pockets wasn't looking good.

'I've got... seven fifty?'

The young man looked at him like he'd just scraped Alex from the sole of his designer shoe. 'We take card payments.'

A couple of minutes later, Alex was ensconced in one of the booths near the corner of the room, with a glowing computer monitor staring back at him and a cup of overpriced coffee steaming away by his side.

He reached out to place his hands on the keyboard, then hesitated. This was the point of no return. He could still walk away without having technically done anything wrong. He could throw the memory stick and its mysterious contents into the nearest bin, forever consigning it to his past, and live out the rest of his life in ignorance.

The moment of indecision came and, like the passing of a shadow at dawn, it was gone. Taking a breath, Alex reached out and logged into the terminal with the username he'd been given by the none-too-helpful staff member.

It was done. He was committed now. There was no choice but to see it through.

Strangely, he felt less fear now that the decision was made. The knowledge that there was no going back somehow freed him to move forward, there being little to lose.

And as much as he hated to admit it, there was a thrill in finally being connected again. He was online. This was his world. This was what had once given his life meaning.

His first port of call was the message board used by the members of Valhalla 7. If anyone could shed light on what had happened to Sinclair, they could.

The group's five remaining members were physically separated by hundreds, and in some cases thousands, of miles, therefore they needed a place online to meet and plan their activities. And they had yet to find anything better than a good old-fashioned bulletin board.

At least not when he'd been amongst their ranks.

The board was invisible to Google or any other internet search engine. It was safe, anonymous and above all, discreet. To access it, Alex was forced to manually input the IP address from memory – a daunting task for most people, but not for him. Remembering such things had always been frighteningly easy for Alex.

It was forgetting that was the hard part.

Presented with the basic login page, he inputted his old username and password, then held his breath as he hit Enter. Sinclair had once told him that he was welcome to re-join them any time he wanted, and that the door would always be open, but there was still a chance his identity had been revoked rather than risk compromising the group.

Mercifully however his identity was accepted. The login page vanished, and just like that he was once again back in the hub of Valhalla 7's activity. He hadn't laid eyes on this site in over two years. Two years of camaraderie, arguments, jokes, ideas and debates that he'd missed out on.

Straight away he saw the familiar usernames associated with various conversation threads – Loki, Baldr, Vali, Njord and Freyja – and couldn't help but smile.

The names had been Sinclair's idea. Always fascinated by Norse mythology, he had chosen each username, as well as the name of the group itself, to fit with this ideal. It had seemed a little over the top at the time, yet each of them had settled into their new identities surprisingly quickly. Needless to say, Alex's own identity of Odin wasn't present in any of the active threads, and apparently none of the other users was online at that moment.

Seeing the once-familiar message board and the usernames he used to interact with every single day brought with it a wave of nostalgia and melancholy. For a moment Alex almost felt as if he was back in that period of his life again, launching online forays across the digital battleground of cyberspace.

But he wasn't, and the crash of a dropped coffee cup on the far side of the room was enough to remind him of his surroundings.

Forcing his mind back to the task at hand, he quickly scanned through the list of recent discussion threads in search of leads. There was nothing specifically relating to the job Sinclair had referenced, though the frequency of postings had dropped off considerably over the past couple of weeks, suggesting the group was preoccupied with more pressing tasks.

And then, two days ago, it stopped. No more posts of any kind. It was as if communication amongst the group had simply ceased.

With growing unease, he brought up each user's profile one by one, only to meet with the same result each time.

Baldr – Last online: 2 days ago
Vali – Last online: 2 days ago
Freyja – Last online: 2 days ago
Njord – Last online: 2 days ago

Finally he came to Sinclair's profile, though by now he knew exactly what to expect.

Loki – Last online: 2 days ago

Alex leaned back in his seat, unsure of what to make of this discovery. It was possible that whatever the group were collaborating on had required them to cease all other online activity, or perhaps even to come together and work in the same physical location. It had never happened before, but given what Sinclair was suggesting, it wouldn't be unreasonable.

And yet, Alex's mind wasn't eased by these thoughts. There was another, far more sinister explanation behind this.

Leaving the message board for now, he navigated to Google and inputted Sinclair's full name, bracing himself before hitting the Search button.

'Oh fuck,' he gasped, seeing the top news article:

Local Man Missing after Freak Crash

Alex could barely believe what he was seeing as his eyes eagerly devoured the brief article, written for a local paper in Arran's home city of Stirling. The words seemed to leap out of the screen at him yet made no impact on his shocked mind.

> ... Police investigators believe Mr Sinclair lost control of his car...
> ... The vehicle rolled down an embankment into the river Avon...
> ... Search teams are still looking downstream for his body...
> ... no hope of finding him alive...

Alex swallowed, his mouth suddenly dry, his heart pounding as he imagined his friend's car being forced off the road, imagined shadowy men gunning him down as he tried to escape the wreck, imagined them dragging his lifeless body into a waiting van to be disposed of where no one would ever find it.

He imagined it all in the blink of an eye. And he knew he'd never forget it.

Arran Sinclair; his friend, the man who had inspired him to do things he'd once thought impossible, who had opened his eyes to a world of possibilities, was gone.

With trembling hand he reached for the coffee by his side, wishing it was something a lot stronger at that moment. Instead he missed his mark, and gasped as scalding hot coffee slopped over the edge of the cup and onto his hand.

The pain was sudden and intense, but it was enough to bring him back to reality with a start. He was after all in a public place, and anyone who happened to be watching at that moment would have known from his expression that something terrible had happened.

Gritting his teeth and wiping his wet hand on his jeans, he did his best to compose himself and push aside the grief and anger that now raged within him. He had to be rational about this. He had to think.

That crash had been no accident; there was no doubt of that in Alex's mind. Whatever his friend had been looking for within the CIA's secure network, his efforts had been discovered and shut down with brutal efficiency. And judging by the lack of activity online, there was a good chance they had even got to the rest of Valhalla 7.

Were they all dead? Had it really come to that?

Stop, stop, stop, he told himself angrily. You're making wild assumptions without knowing all the facts.

All he knew for sure was that Sinclair's car had come off the road and there was no sign of his body. They could have killed him, but then they would never know how much he'd managed to uncover. It would surely have made more sense to capture him and keep him alive for questioning.

Given the horror stories of torture and interrogation he'd heard over the years, Alex couldn't rightly say whether that was preferable to death, but the mere possibility that his friend might still be alive kindled a spark of hope within him. And already he was beginning to see a possible way out.

They could interrogate him forever, but Sinclair couldn't give them what they wanted; he'd made sure of that when he mailed the memory stick to Alex. The information they needed so badly was sitting now in the pocket of his jeans. He alone possessed the secrets that could mean the difference between life and death.

He wondered, would they be willing to trade Sinclair for it? More to the point, could Alex actually broker such a trade and expect to get away with it?

A warning message on screen told him he only had ten minutes of his allotted time left before his session expired. That was enough to jolt him out of his chaotic thoughts.

Before he went any further, he needed to know what was on that memory stick. This was all for nothing if it didn't contain anything of value.

Retrieving the stick from his pocket, he removed the little plastic cap protecting the pin connector. 'All right, you little bastard,' he said quietly. 'Let's see what you're all about.'

With that, he inserted the memory stick into his terminal's USB port and waited while the machine processed its contents.

Chapter 6

It was mid afternoon in Virginia, and technical specialist Lewis Santiago was halfway through what had so far been a busy shift at the Information Operations Centre. As part of the highly secretive organisation responsible for maintaining the integrity of the CIA's computer network, he rarely found himself with time to kill.

Today alone he had processed four requests for elevated user privileges, two potential security threats and one panicked intern who had lost her access card.

Not exactly the stuff of legend, he thought with a wry smile. In fact, anyone fond of conspiracy thrillers would have been quite disappointed by the reality of the place that served as the nerve centre of the CIA's cyber security division. There were no massive wall-mounted television screens crowded with information, no rows of supercomputers covered with flashing lights, no sinister-looking men in suits surveying the operation from overhead offices.

In reality, the place was a fairly normal-looking workspace within the CIA's vast headquarters building. Three rows of eight desks partially walled off for privacy, a collection of smaller offices and meeting rooms along one wall, and a kitchen area in one corner with really bad instant coffee. This could have been any generic office space anywhere on earth.

The only difference was in the work they did here.

He sighed and took a sip of tea, allowing himself a few moments of quiet before moving on to his next task. The cheap coffee in here made him jittery and agitated, and those were two things that didn't go well with a desk job like this.

He was just about to open a new work request to begin an audit of inactive user identities when suddenly an alert box popped up on his screen. Santiago paused, taken aback by the warning.

Such alerts only flashed up if a major system alert had been triggered. Quickly scanning the details of the warning, his eyes opened wider at the realisation of what he was seeing.

Warning: Code D1 – Unauthorized access detected

The D stood for Disavowed, meaning that the user ID in question had been removed from the Agency's system, while the number that followed referred to the level of urgency. In this case, level 1 represented the highest possible level of severity. So high that even he wasn't permitted to view the user's former identity.

Never in his six years on the job had Santiago encountered a level 1 breach.

Straight away he hit the Assistance Required button – better known as the panic button – next to his computer terminal. This would place a priority call through to his supervisor asking him to come to his desk immediately.

As the automated system went to work, Santiago turned his attention back to the warning message, bringing up a trace program to track down the source of the breach.

–

Whatever Alex had been expecting to find hidden away within the memory stick, this certainly wasn't it. Rather than reports of classified missions, blueprints for some top-secret new jet fighter or photographs of the president murdering his secretary, what he instead found himself staring at was page after page of computer code.

Clearly he was looking at some kind of program in its most elemental form. But for what?

He had no idea as to its purpose, and he certainly wasn't going to discover it in the few minutes remaining on his online session here. To have any hope of understanding it, he would need time to pick apart the code, trawl through it and run it in a controlled environment.

None of which he was able to do here.

'What the hell have you given me, Arran?' he asked, staring at the screen.

–

It took all of thirty seconds for Brad Yorke, the senior officer in the room, to reach Santiago's terminal.

'What have you got?' he asked, his tone caught somewhere between concern and irritation at having to abandon his own work and hightail it over here. The fact that he was a good thirty pounds overweight probably hadn't helped his mood.

'It's a D1 access alert, sir,' Santiago reported, pausing only long enough to glance up at his supervisor. 'Happened less than a minute ago. We're running a trace right now.'

That was enough to cut through whatever reservations Yorke might have had. 'Show me the user ID,' he said, leaning in closer to view the monitor.

'The ID's locked down.' Turning around, Santiago brought up the ID, which displayed as nothing more than an 8-digit code number. 'This is all I've got.'

Straight away Yorke's eyes went wide.

'Shit.' Straightening up, he raised his voice to address the rest of the room. 'All right, everyone, I want you to drop whatever you're doing and listen up. We've got a high-level disavowed ID that's just gone active. Santiago's running a trace right now, and I want him backed up to the fullest extent. All other tasks are to be placed on hold until further notice. From now until I say otherwise, finding whoever's trying to use this ID is the first, last and only priority for everyone in this room. Get on it.'

As the tempo of work in the room increased, Yorke turned his attention back to Santiago. 'How are you doing, son?'

'Trace program's active,' the young man said, too absorbed in his work to look away from the screen now. 'It's coming from an unmasked IP address. United Kingdom, south of England...' He paused as a dialogue box popped up, informing him the trace had completed. 'Yes. Looks like it's coming from an internet cafe in central London.'

'Can you get me the identity of the user?'

Santiago shook his head. 'There are eight sub-terminals on that network. Could be any one of them.'

Yorke thought about that for a moment. 'Okay, contact British security services and have them vector local police units to the scene. Tell them to lock down the entire cafe if they have to.'

Santiago stared at him in shock. 'Sir?'

'Just get on it. If they give you any shit, tell them it's on our authority,' Yorke said over his shoulder, as he fished a cell phone from his pocket and quickly dialled a number. It was answered with typical brisk efficiency.

'This is section leader Brad Yorke in network security,' he began. 'Put me through to Deputy Director Cain's office immediately.'

–

So absorbed was he in the mysterious computer program, Alex almost jumped with fright at the sound of a voice from behind.

'Oi, mate.'

Reaching down, Alex yanked the memory stick out of the port and spun around to find himself looking up at a fleshy middle-aged face that he'd never seen before. The man, whoever he was, was wearing a heavy leather jacket spotted with raindrops from outside, his buzz-cut greying hair sticking up like the bristles of a paintbrush. He was looking down at Alex with a mixture of curiosity and faint suspicion, particularly in light of his sudden removal of the memory stick.

'Not interrupting somethin', am I?' he asked, speaking in a thick cockney accent that even Alex had to strain to understand. 'You havin' a butchers at the ladies, eh?'

Alex blinked, struggling to bring his mind up to speed with this bizarre turn of events. 'No, nothing like that. I was just looking at… Sorry, what can I do for you?'

'You can take this off me hands.' With that, he reached into his pocket and held out a cell phone to Alex. It was a cheap prepaid burner; the kind of thing available everywhere from supermarkets to convenience stores for £20 or less. 'Consider it a gift.'

Alex frowned. 'From who? You?'

The man's broad mouth split into a nicotine-stained grin. 'No offence, my young friend, but you ain't exactly my type. Know what I mean? Some bird outside asked me to give you this.'

'A woman?' Alex repeated. 'Who was she?'

'Secret admirer, maybe? I dunno, mate. And to be honest, I couldn't give a monkey's toss. But she paid me a tenner for the privilege, so here's your phone.' He nodded to the session timer at the top right of Alex's computer monitor, which had by now counted down to zero. 'Looks like you're out of time.'

Saying nothing more, he turned away and ambled back out of the cafe, returning to his normal life as if nothing had happened. Within a couple of days he'd have forgotten the encounter even took place.

For Alex however, it was about to change his life forever.

–

The room was a hive of activity now as technicians and analysts hurried from terminal to terminal, shouting instructions and requests for more information across the office. Their voices mingled with the click of computer keys and the bleep of phones as work was hastily rerouted to other areas, tasks reprioritized and attention focussed on their new mission. They were in crisis mode now, all of the formidable resources that this room commanded being brought to bear against a single objective.

Yorke surveyed the organized chaos around him, his pulse racing as he pondered whether or not it would be enough to get the job done. As senior department head, their hunt for the mysterious perpetrator trying to use a disavowed Agency identity was his responsibility. Failure would likely have dire consequences for his career.

'Where are we on British security?' he called out. 'Are they moving yet?'

'They're scrambling their field teams now, but it'll take a few minutes to get them moving,' one of his subordinates reported, covering her phone with one hand so she could speak. 'Local police have been informed and are converging on the scene. They'll form a perimeter before security service agents move in.'

All of which would take time to organise, not to mention the fact that it was virtually impossible to lock down even a single block in a densely packed city like London. 'What about our own field agents?'

It was the turn of a balding, slender East Asian man to respond. 'No good, sir. Our nearest ground teams are at the US embassy. It'll take at least twenty minutes for them to be on the scene.'

'Fuck,' Yorke said under his breath. 'Air assets?'

'The Brits won't let us fly drones over their airspace. We're checking with the National Reconnaissance Office to find out if any of our satellites are over the area, but no word yet.'

As if in response to the growing tension in the office, the secure door leading from the corridor outside beeped once as a card was swiped through its electronic reader, then swung open to reveal a man whose appearance briefly halted all conversation.

Most of the technicians working there had only encountered Marcus Cain, the Deputy Director of the CIA, in passing, perhaps seeing him from a distance entering some high-level briefing or leaving the headquarters building flanked by security personnel. He was aloof and enigmatic, almost a mythical force amongst the Agency's rank and file staff. Most of the people in that room had never so much as spoken to him, never mind had to go about their jobs with him standing over them. The fact he was here now only reinforced the gravity of the situation.

Taking a breath to calm himself, Yorke took a step forward to greet him. 'Director Cain, it's an honour to have you here.'

Cain neglected to shake his hand. 'Cut to the facts. What do we know so far?' he asked, his voice as crisp and precise as his tailor-made suit.

'Yes, sir.' Yorke cleared his throat, trying to hide his embarrassment. 'Approximately ten minutes ago we picked up an alert that a disavowed Agency ID had just gone active. We've traced the source to an internet cafe in central London.'

'And what are we doing about it?'

'British security service is vectoring in ground units, plus local police are sealing off the area.'

'Police?' Cain fixed him with a sharp look. 'You mean, beat cops who talk to each other on unencrypted radios? Who just about anyone with a fifty dollar police scanner could overhear?'

Yorke could practically feel himself wilting under the man's intense gaze. Only now did he see the folly of his actions. 'I'm... Sir, I...'

'You're relieved of duty,' Cain said, dismissing him with a single, disdainful look. This done, he raised his voice, addressing the room. 'Everyone listen up. As of now, I'm in charge of this operation. Now, is there anyone in this room who knows what they're doing?'

Reluctantly Santiago raised his hand. 'Me, sir. I think I've got something.'

Cain was by his side within moments, leaving a stunned Yorke to contemplate what might well have been the end of his career. 'Talk to me, son.'

'Just hacked into the cafe's payment system, sir. According to this, the last guy to log in paid for his session by credit card, right before the alert was triggered. Wasn't hard to trace him once we had his card details.' Opening a new window, Santiago brought up a copy of the man's driving license. 'Name's Alex Yates. Used to be a freelance system tester, then he was convicted of computer hacking a few years back. He's been quiet ever since, according to Scotland Yard.' He coughed, suddenly very conscious that one of the most powerful men in the Agency was leaning over his workstation. 'Of course, there's no guarantee this is our guy. Could just be a coincidence.'

Cain glanced at him, his eyes daunting in their intensity. 'If I believed in coincidences, I wouldn't be in this job. Until we know otherwise, we consider young Mr Yates there a high value target. Circulate his details to all workstations and have them get to work. I want to know everything there is to know about him. Politics, education, employment, travel history, the works.'

'On it, sir,' Santiago replied.

Cain nodded, apparently satisfied with his performance for now. 'Find his cell phone number and put a trace on it. And see if you can tie in with any security cameras in the area. London's the most heavily monitored city in Europe, so let's use it. I want this locked down.'

'Yes, sir.' Santiago resisted the urge to reach up and wipe the sweat from his brow. His head was already spinning at the stream of orders he'd just been issued.

Cain was about to turn away, then thought better of it. 'Oh, one more thing. Make sure the Brits send in armed response units. Believe me, they'll need them.'

Santiago said nothing to this, though his gaze lingered on the deputy director a moment longer before he turned around to resume his work.

–

No sooner had his rotund friend departed, leaving Alex alone, than the phone in his hand suddenly started vibrating. Someone was calling, and they were in no mood for waiting around.

Pausing a moment to question the wisdom of taking a call from a phone handed to him in such a clandestine fashion, Alex hit the receive call button.

'Who is—?'

'Don't talk, just listen.' The voice that spoke was female, strong and commanding, with a hint of an accent that he couldn't identify. But such questions no longer mattered. All of those details paled into insignificance after what came next.

'You've been compromised,' she went on. 'Armed response teams are on their way to arrest you. If you want to live to see tomorrow morning, get out of that cafe right now.'

Chapter 7

That was it, right there. The moment when it all went to shit.

My life; my safe and boring and unfulfilling life, had just shattered into a million pieces right in front of my eyes. I was too stupid to recognize it at the time, or maybe I was just too scared to admit it to myself. But like so many things before and after, I really should have seen it coming.

I should have seen it the moment I thought about opening that file.

What is it they say about curiosity and cats?

–

Caught off guard by the sudden intrusion into his world, Alex could barely stammer an answer down the phone. 'W-who the hell are you?'

'Who I am isn't important,' she said, her impatience obvious. 'But what I have to tell you is. The Agency is coming after you. Whatever you've done tonight, it has made you a threat to them. And there is only one way they deal with such threats.'

Alex let out a single breath, almost a grunt, as if he'd been punched in the stomach. He could feel bile rising in his throat, and fought back a growing wave of nausea.

'Bollocks. How could you possibly know this?'

'Because I've been monitoring the police band. An arrest warrant has just gone out over the radio. Local units are being diverted to that cafe as we speak.'

'Now wait a fucking second!' he hissed, his voice rising in pitch despite his best efforts to stay calm. A couple of people looked up from their tables, disturbed by the noise. 'This is ridiculous. Nobody could—'

'Stop talking, Alex,' she commanded.

That stopped him cold. 'How do you know my name?'

'Because clearly you are not as good at covering your tracks as you believe.' Her scorn was impossible to ignore. 'Arran met with you a week ago, and he disappeared not long after. It was no accident. Unless you want to end up like him, I suggest you be somewhere else when the police get there.'

Moving over to the window, Alex peered outside. The street was quiet, with just a few pedestrians moving back and forth. Traffic had calmed down, rush hour having long since passed. All things considered, it looked about as normal and peaceful as any other street in London.

'I don't see anything out there,' he said, wondering if this was some elaborate hoax on her part. 'How do I know this isn't a dose of bullshit and chips?'

'Alex, every second you delay gives them more time to close the net,' she said, forcing calm into her voice. 'For your own sake, get out of there while you still can.'

'And go where, exactly?' he demanded. It wasn't as if he had a private jet standing by to whisk him off to safety. 'Do what?'

Her answer was as blunt as it was chilling. 'Run.'

Before he could reply, he heard something echoing between the buildings outside. A high pitched wail, rising and falling in tone, getting closer. And sure enough, a moment or two later he caught sight of something at the far end of the street. A light, blue and flashing, coming his way.

'Oh fuck. Fuck!' he gasped, backing away from the window in horror. He didn't care who saw him now. 'This isn't a joke, is it? I mean, this is really happening.'

'It is,' she confirmed. 'As soon as the police arrest you, they will hand you over to an Agency retrieval team for interrogation. By the time they're finished with you, you will be begging to tell them more.'

Alex clamped a hand over his mouth, having to fight the urge to throw up. His mind was already conjuring up all kinds of horrific images of interrogation, torture and mutilation.

'I can help you, but only if you listen to me and do exactly as I say.'

'All right,' he said, his voice little more than a desperate whisper. 'What do I do?'

'Leave the cafe and turn left on the street outside. Hurry.'

He needed no further prompting. Ignoring the curious stares of the cafe patrons, he shoved his way through the door and strode outside. Straight away droplets of rain and chill night air assailed him, along with the wail of police sirens rapidly growing closer. His heart was pounding in his chest, the pulse thundering in his ears.

'I'm out,' he said, the phone pressed tight against his ear. 'Where to now?'

'Head west, then take the first side street you can find,' the woman commanded him, her voice chillingly calm despite the intensity of the situation. 'You need to get off the main road fast.'

'Okay.'

'If you have a hat or a hood, put it on. And don't run. You'll only draw attention to yourself,' she advised, as if sensing that he was about to break into a sprint. 'Try to look natural.'

'Easy for you to say,' Alex said under his breath, pulling the hood up over his head.

She ignored that one. 'Do you have a cell phone of your own?'

'Yeah.' Instinctively he reached into his pocket to retrieve it.

'Get rid of it now. They'll use it to track you.'

'But...' He started to protest that the phone was worth a lot of money and that he could simply switch it off, then thought better of it. Now wasn't the time to debate technicalities. 'Fine. Fuck it.'

Passing by a public litter bin, he tossed it in without breaking stride. The wail of sirens were loud and urgent in his ears now. He could see the blue flash of lights reflecting off nearby windows, and did his best not to cringe at the knowledge that the men now hunting him had come screeching to a halt not fifty yards away.

As commanded, he turned left at the first junction into a residential street of three-storey apartment blocks, managing somehow to keep a steady walking pace. His legs felt like jelly, and he was certain that every person he passed was staring at him, yet he forced himself to keep his head down and carry on walking.

He'd always been good at blending in, at passing unnoticed. Just an anonymous young man in a hoodie making his way home. Nothing worth remembering.

'Why are you doing this?' he couldn't help but ask, painfully aware of how exposed he still was. 'Helping me.'

There was a pause, brief but noticeable. 'Not now. You have more important things to worry about.'

Of that he had no doubt. 'I see an alleyway up ahead,' Alex said, spotting a service alley that ran between two buildings. Having lived here for the past year, he knew the area fairly well by now. 'If I remember right, it leads down to a canal... Oh fuck.'

Just like that, his growing hope of escape was dashed as he spotted a pair of police officers heading in his direction, their bright fluorescent jackets standing out like beacons in the dim glow of street lights.

'What is it?'

'Two policemen, heading right towards me.' His pace had slowed noticeably as indecision took hold. 'I won't make it to the alley.'

'Are they running or walking?'

Alex forced himself to look at them, to assess the slow, measured tread of their boots on the cracked pavement. 'Just walking, I think. They're talking to each other.'

'Are their hands on their weapons?'

'Not that I can see.'

'Then they're just a foot patrol walking their regular beat,' she decided. 'Walk past them, carry on talking into the phone and don't pay them any attention.'

'Are you fucking kidding me?' Alex hissed. 'They're not stupid. They'll know something's wrong.'

'They pass hundreds of people just like you every day. They won't stop you unless you give them a reason to, so calm down and keep walking.'

He was committed now anyway, he realized. He couldn't turn around without making it look like he was deliberately avoiding them, and attempting to flee now would only make things worse. One way or another he had to tough it out.

Forcing himself to maintain what he believed to be a casual walking pace, he made his way reluctantly towards the two police officers. Every step was a conscious effort that became harder and harder every time, yet he forced himself to carry on.

As they drew closer, he couldn't help noticing that they were both taller and bigger than him. In his panicky state they seemed to loom like giants before him, powerful and menacing, and watchful for the slightest hint of fear.

'Yeah, I don't know what you were playing at last night, Mike,' Alex said, forcing terse joviality into his voice as he carried on an imaginary conversation with the phone. 'Talk about letting the side down, mate. You were hammered even before the tequila shots started.'

The two officers could plainly hear the sirens from around the corner by now. Alex watched as one of them pointed and said something to his companion, their pace quickening. No doubt they sensed trouble and wanted to investigate for themselves.

They were getting close now, no more than fifteen yards between them, the distance closing fast now that both cops had speeded up. The only relief was that neither of them seemed to have noticed Alex. Their attention was firmly on the noise and commotion coming from around the corner.

'What's that, mate?' Alex said into the phone, almost forgetting the ruse he was trying to maintain. 'Yeah, there's some trouble here by the sounds of things. Probably a couple of pissheads having a punch-up.'

Just ahead, a couple of gangly looking teenagers were standing outside a door leading into the communal stairwell for the apartment block towering above them. One of them had buzzed the intercom and was waiting for a reply, a plastic carrier bag bulging with cans of beer clutched in his hand. His friend spared the two police an unwelcoming glance, perhaps having had run-ins with them in the past.

Ten yards to go. Almost there.

It was then that Alex heard the crackle of a radio. A police radio. And from this distance, despite the static and the distant wail of sirens, he was able to make out the message with terrible clarity.

'All units be advised, suspect on foot near Highfield Avenue. IC1 male, late twenties wearing jeans and dark hooded top. Possibly heading south.'

That was it.

In that instant, Alex knew he'd been discovered. Unable to help himself, he glanced up at the officer whose radio had just betrayed him, saw the dawning realisation in the man's eyes as the pieces came together, saw him reach down for the pepper spray at his belt even as his mouth opened to shout a warning to his colleague.

It was then that something happened. To Alex's left, there was an electronic buzz as the stairwell door was unlocked from one of the flats above. Eager to get in out of the cold and drizzle, the young man with the carrier bag reached out to open it.

Alex reacted on instinct, moving almost before he was aware of what was happening. Rushing forward, he threw his arm out and caught the youth square in the chest, knocking him backward. There was a startled shout as he stumbled and fell in the police officers' path, slowing them down for a few precious moments.

Before his friend had time to react or the police untangled themselves from the makeshift obstacle, Alex had slipped in through the gap and pulled the door shut behind him. There was a faint click as the magnetic lock engaged once more, temporarily sealing him inside.

Desperate and breathing harder as adrenaline caused his heart rate to soar, he glanced around, taking in the empty concrete stairwell that smelled faintly of urine. He might have bought himself reprieve, but it was unlikely to last for long. Already he could hear boots hammering against the door, accompanied by muffled shouts.

'I'm trapped,' he said into the phone, hoping against hope that his mysterious guide might be able to help him. 'The police rumbled me. I had no choice.'

'Where are you?'

'In a stairwell. One of the blocks facing onto the street.'

There was a pause as she considered this new development. 'Is there another exit?'

Alex let out a breath. The only doors on this level led into the residents' flats, and somehow he doubted they'd let him in. 'Not on this floor.'

'Then go up,' she said, speaking with that same controlled, measured voice. 'To the roof. Hurry.'

Alex was too frightened to question or protest. Doing his best to get more air in his lungs, he rushed up the stairs, taking them two at a time. Already the muscles in his legs were burning with the exertion, but he did his best to ignore it, concentrating only on putting more distance between himself and his pursuers.

The buzz of the door below told him the police had made entry. It wouldn't take them long to figure out where he was heading.

His breath coming in painful gasps, he halted as he reached a security door at the very top of the stairwell, its bright yellow sign announcing that it was alarmed and to be used in emergencies only.

'I'm here, but there's an alarm on the door,' he whispered.

'Then you'll have to move fast,' she advised. 'There should be a fire escape on one side of the roof. Find it and use it to get down to the street.'

Alex closed his eyes and took a couple of deep breaths. Easy for her to say.

Wasting no more time, he shoved the door release bar and threw it open, rushing out onto the roof. As he'd expected, it was cluttered with TV aerials, satellite dishes and all kinds of vents and fans whose purpose he didn't understand.

The rain was still falling steadily, having graduated from fine mist to heavy droplets that quickly soaked through his clothes. As the security alarm started wailing behind him, he looked around, desperately searching for the fire escape that would lead him back downstairs.

Sure enough, a retractable ladder was fixed to the edge of the roof opposite. Sprinting over, he shoved the phone into his pocket and bent down to inspect the device, trying to ignore the sickening feeling of vertigo that the sixty-foot drop provoked in him.

The ladder was set into metal runners drilled into the side of the building, and held in place by a simple mechanical latch. One good pull should be enough to release it, sending it all the way down to street level. The climb down wasn't going to be fun, but even for Alex it was better than the alternative.

Reaching out, he grabbed the release handle and pulled.

Nothing happened.

Gritting his teeth, he braced one foot against the wall and pulled again, harder this time, his untested muscles straining with the effort. Still the latch remained stubbornly fixed in place.

'Come on, you bastard!' he yelled, booting it in frustration. 'Why won't you fucking move?'

The gritty rasp of corroded hinges provided its own answer. Years of exposure to wind and rain must have corroded its mechanism, rusting it firmly in place. Freeing it would take more time and strength than he had at his disposal.

'Fuck!'

Breathing hard from his exertions and sweating despite the rain's onslaught, Alex turned away and pulled the phone out of his pocket. The line was still active.

'The ladder won't move,' he said, now struggling to keep the panic from his voice. He was acutely aware that every second he remained up here increased his chances of being caught. 'It's rusted solid. I can't release it.'

He heard a muffled comment on the other end that he was sure was less than complimentary. To her credit, the woman quickly regained her composure.

'Then you have to jump to the next building,' she decided.

'What!'

'Another apartment block backs onto that one,' she explained, her knowledge of his local area disconcertingly accurate. 'The alley that runs between them can't be more than seven or eight feet wide. Jump to the opposite roof, and use their stairwell to get down to the street.'

As she was speaking, Alex crept over to the edge of the roof, surveying the gap between his building and the next. As she had said, the distance between the two apartment blocks wasn't much – probably not even wide enough to drive a car through – but at that moment it looked like a yawning chasm stretching out impossibly far before him. And leaning out, he caught a glimpse of rain-slicked brick walls stretching all the way down to a darkened litter-strewn alleyway far below.

For a moment, he saw an image of himself lying broken and dying in that dark alleyway, surrounded by rusted bins and trash, his body shattered by the crushing impact.

'Fuck that!' Alex hissed, backing away from the terrifying drop that awaited him if his leap of faith failed. 'I'm a sales assistant, not Jason fucking Bourne!'

'Alex, the police will have heard the alarm. They are probably on their way up to the roof as we speak.' She was talking in the same calm yet commanding voice that had brought him this far, but now she was urging him to go one step further. 'I know you're afraid, but if you don't act now, I can do nothing for you. Now trust me and jump!'

'Shit!' Shoving the phone in his pocket once more, Alex backed up several paces, his heart pounding and his breath now coming in shallow, rapid gasps.

Just one jump. One act of courage, one moment of danger, and he would be out of here. His guide, whoever she was, would find him and help him put this right. One day, years from now, he might even be able to look back on this night and laugh about it.

It was a fantasy and he knew it, but it was all he had at that moment.

'Come on, Alex. Just get it done,' he said, trying to psyche himself up, searching for some hidden reserve of courage and determination that he could draw on. 'You can do this.'

One deep breath, and he started forward, running straight for the edge of the roof. The unforgiving brick walls of the opposite building loomed into view, the darkness, the horrific drop, the alleyway below...

It was over almost before it started. Skidding to a stop several feet short of the edge, Alex let out a cry of fear and dismay, and shrank away from the gap.

He couldn't do it, and in some part of his mind he'd known even before he tried it. Whatever courage or madness was needed to make such a leap, he didn't possess it. How could he? This wasn't who he was; this wasn't who he had ever been. He was a keyboard warrior, more used to employing his

44

mind than his body. The prospect of physical injury or death had defeated him.

In any case, he was given little time to contemplate his failure. Before he could reach for his phone again, the door to the roof was thrown open and the two police officers spilled out. They weren't armed, as few police officers in London were, but he did see them carrying riot batons and the distinctive yellow cylinders of pepper spray.

Caught in the open as he was, Alex was spotted by them immediately.

'Police!' the older of the two shouted. 'Get down on the ground now!'

If Alex had any thoughts of resisting, they were quickly dispelled when the second officer moved around behind and shoved him roughly down onto the gravel-coated roof, applying plenty of pressure to make sure he couldn't move. Alex groaned in pain as the sharp gravel cut his exposed skin.

'Alex Yates, I'm arresting you on suspicion of conspiring to commit a terrorist act,' the older of the two officers said as Alex's hands were yanked roughly behind his back. A chill ran through him as a pair of handcuffs snapped over his wrists. 'You do not have to say anything at this time, but it may harm your defence if you do not mention, when questioned, something you later rely on in court.'

Alex took his advice and said nothing, knowing it was futile to respond. He was well and truly in the shit now. The only question was where it was going to end for him.

–

On the other side of the Atlantic in Langley, news of the arrest came through less than a minute later, relayed from British intelligence via the US embassy in London.

'They got him,' Santiago said, relieved that his guesswork seemed to have paid off. 'Apparently Yates tried to make a run for it, but local police cornered him on a rooftop not far from the scene.'

Far from celebrating, however, Cain looked just as tense and unhappy as before. 'Anyone else with him?'

'No, sir. Just Yates, according to the report.'

The older man said nothing for a moment, the muscles in his jaw tightening. 'Where is he now?'

'En route to a local police station.'

'I want him in *our* hands within the hour, no matter what shit the Brits try to give us. Get one of our field teams to that station right away, and make sure they have interrogation experience.'

Santiago hesitated, for a moment tempted to ask what this was all about, but immediately discounting the idea. Such things were far above his pay grade.

'Do we have a problem, son?' Cain asked, fixing him with that withering stare of his.

'No, sir. No problem.'

–

In a darkened shop doorway about fifty yards down the street, Anya watched as Alex was led out to the waiting police car by the two arresting officers, his head down and his shoulders slumped in defeat.

People had drifted out of nearby residential buildings to find the source of the commotion and watch the drama unfold, including a group of drunken young men on their way home after a night out. A couple of them paused to shout jeering remarks at the prisoner as he was helped into the back seat of the car, before turning their attention back to their takeaway meals.

Anya clenched her fists, mastering her temper only with some difficulty. This man, weak and frightened though he might be, was her only link to the information she so desperately needed. Without him, everything she'd done so far would be for nothing.

He was sure to crack quickly under interrogation, and while she hadn't told him anything that could compromise her, she also knew that his eventual confession would eliminate any chance of finding what she needed.

She hadn't come this far to fail now.

Her only saving grace was that the Agency hadn't yet become involved. The British police who had rushed to arrest Alex were certainly acting on their orders, no doubt under the guise of a joint operation against cyber terrorism, but it would take the Agency time to assemble a field team and a suitable place to interrogate him.

If she was going to do something, it would have to be soon.

Chapter 8

I should have made that jump. That's all I could think about in the hours following my arrest. I should have gone for it, taken my chance and for once in my shitty, pointless life shown a bit of courage.

Who knows what might have happened? Maybe I could have saved myself a lot of pain and trouble, or maybe the end result would have been the same. I suppose I'll never know.

They say you regret most of all the things you could have done, but didn't.
Story of my life.

-

This was the end of the line.

This was where it was going to happen.

Alex was sitting bolt upright with his hands cuffed tight behind his back, his wrists throbbing in time to his pulse as the metal dug into his flesh. The wooden chair beneath him was hard and uncomfortable, while the cloth sack over his head submerged him in total darkness, robbing him of all sense of orientation and clinging to his face with every inhalation. Though he wasn't bound to the chair, he dared not stand up, dared not move a muscle in fact.

It had been just under three hours since his feeble attempt to escape via the roof of that apartment block. He knew this because, with little else to do, he had been patiently counting out the seconds and minutes since his capture, measuring the passage of time for no other reason than to keep him from contemplating the fate that awaited him. He'd always been good with numbers, and even better at remembering.

The ride to the police station had lasted sixteen minutes, after which he'd been escorted to a cell and left there for another fifty-two minutes. Fifty-two minutes of sitting there with nothing but four cream-coloured brick walls for company.

No officer had come to charge him or take his statement. No rights had been read, no identification confirmed, no phone calls or legal advice offered. It was as if he'd simply been forgotten about, and for a brief time he had almost convinced himself that that was exactly what had happened.

Perhaps it was all a mistake. Perhaps they had tried and failed to find evidence of wrongdoing and were now debating what to do with him.

Perhaps…

It had been a desperate hope, and finally dashed when the door to his cell was thrown open and a trio of men in civilian clothes moved in, tied a cloth sack over his head and marched him right out of the station. They hadn't said a word despite his attempts to communicate with them, to reason with them, to plead with them.

He'd been bundled into the back of a waiting van, which had departed the police station at a brisk but measured pace. Observing the speed limit, not wanting to get pulled over. There had been at least two men with him in the van, acting like a human vice to keep him pinned in his seat, though again neither of his captors had said a word. Each smelled of cologne and cigarette smoke.

An hour and forty-one minutes of strained silence had thus passed; enough to get well clear of London with almost no traffic on the roads at such an early hour.

The last few minutes of the van ride had taken them down a rough, uneven road, each jolting movement rattling Alex's bones and straining the vehicle's suspension. An unpaved or seldom-used track with no ambient traffic sounds, suggesting a rural location.

Wherever he was, the building in which he now resided was substantial to say the least. The van had driven right inside it, and after disembarking he'd been marched a short distance across a solid concrete floor before being forced down onto the chair. Though he couldn't see, the echoing interior and faint movement of air gave the impression of great space, as if he were in the centre of an empty warehouse or parking garage. The air was cool and damp, and smelled of oil and engine fumes.

Beyond those scraps of knowledge, however, Alex had no idea where he was. It made little difference anyway. Even if he knew the exact address, who could he tell?

He gasped at the metallic clang of a door opening behind him, rusty hinges grating, and felt his heart beat faster as boots clicked towards him across the vast echoing space. They were moving slowly, and apparently circling around from the left, though the acoustics of the room made it difficult to tell for sure.

It was at that moment that Alex caught a scent of something on the air. Something rich and strong and bitter. Coffee.

The footsteps had stopped somewhere in front of him, and no further sounds were heard. Seconds stretched out into minutes as Alex sat there, his back slowly seizing up on the uncomfortable chair, his hands throbbing, his pulse racing. Despite his best efforts to remain calm, he could feel his breath growing faster, the clammy fabric of the hood pressing against him every time he inhaled. It was a terrible sensation to feel so vulnerable, so unaware of one's surroundings. His captor could be holding a knife inches from his face and he wouldn't have a clue.

Finally he could take it no longer. He had to say something, had to break the tension.

'H–hello?' he said, afraid to raise his voice too much.

It certainly wasn't the authoritative challenge of a man seeking to regain control of the situation, but it did get results.

Suddenly the footsteps were coming towards him. Alex tensed, bracing himself for the crushing impact of a fist driven straight into his unprotected face, stomach or any other part of his body that didn't bear thinking about.

To his surprise, however, no such thing happened. Instead he felt a tug at his neck, and a moment later the hood was yanked off, at last permitting him to view his surroundings.

His first impression was one of intense light searing his retinas. A pair of powerful electric lamps were pointed right at him, no doubt intended to blind and disorient him. In his confused state, it took him a few seconds to realize they were headlights, probably belonging to the very van that had brought him here.

His eyes streaming, Alex blinked several times in the harsh electric light as he tried to focus on his surroundings.

The exact dimensions of the room were hard to determine, as he could see little beyond the glare of the powerful headlights. However, the floor provided a little more of a clue as to this room's purpose. Concrete, rough-poured and cracked in places, as if there was no need to finish it properly. A warehouse or storage silo perhaps.

The only other items in view were resting on the ground a few yards away. The first was a simple steel bucket, its frame dented as if it had seen heavy use. It appeared to be filled with some kind of liquid, as he could see it shimmering in the electric lights.

And beside it, laid there as if it were a sacred artefact to be revered, was a sledge hammer. A big, serious-looking thing with a long wooden handle and a flat, uncompromisingly square head that must have weighed five or six pounds all by itself. Alex's heart skipped a beat, and he had to forcibly swallow down the bile that threatened to rise up in his throat.

'You want to know the secret to torturing people? I'll give you a hint – it's not cruelty,' a voice remarked from somewhere close behind. American, smooth and deep, with a hint of a New England accent. Again Alex smelled coffee. 'It's restraint. Precision. Sure, we could break out the hacksaws and start slicing pieces off you, but what's the point in that? It's messy as shit. Chances are you'd pass out from the pain and blood loss before you could tell us anything useful, then we'd have to mess around with adrenaline shots and heart monitors. It's just not worth the effort. No, you'd be amazed what a couple of good strikes with a sledge hammer can do.'

Alex shuddered in horror as he imagined the fragile bones of his hand shattering under the impact of several pounds of solid steel, no doubt wielded with expert precision. Then, suddenly, he heard perhaps the last thing he'd been expecting – laughter. Not sinister or mocking, but genuine amusement at what was apparently a funny joke.

A shadow passed in front of the electric light, and Alex looked up as an unlikely looking figure wandered into view.

He wasn't sure if he'd been expecting a brutish thug dressed in paramilitary gear or some cold, sinister looking G-man in a pristine suit. Either way, the figure now standing before him was about as far from a professional interrogator as he could have imagined.

Dressed in a navy blue polo shirt open at the neck, beige cargo trousers and suede loafers, the man looked like he'd walked right out of some country club lunch meeting. He was even holding a takeaway cup of coffee that steamed in the cool air. His face was clean-shaven and youthful, his short dark hair neatly parted in a Harvard crew cut.

All things considered, he looked an awful lot better than Alex felt at that moment.

'Relax, bro. I was just fucking with you,' he said, taking a sip of coffee as he chortled in amusement. 'Some guys like to go for the Hannibal Lecter approach, really put the shits up people. Others like to go in screaming and swinging fists right off the bat. Me? Not my style. I just tell it like it is, let people make up their own minds.'

Alex frowned, feeling more out of his depth than ever. 'What do you mean?'

His captor wasn't laughing any more, but he was still wearing an amused smirk as he folded his arms and surveyed Alex for several seconds.

'My name's Frank,' he began. 'Yes, I work for the CIA. And yes, that's my real name. I'm from Hartford, Connecticut and I've been with the Agency for seven years. I majored in Political Science at college and my favourite football team are the New York Jets.'

Either this was some bizarre new interrogation technique or Alex was seriously misunderstanding him. 'Why are you telling me this?'

'Because I want us to be honest with each other, Alex. And I want us to get off on the right foot. First impressions count, you know? I don't want you thinking of this relationship as "prisoner and interrogator". It's not like that. Believe it or not, I'm actually here to help you. But you have to help me out first, okay? Can you do that for me, buddy?'

Alex said nothing. He was so taken aback by the man's unusual demeanour that he didn't know quite how to respond. In any case, Frank clearly wasn't one for hanging around.

'So let me break this down. You're deep in the shit, my friend,' he went on. 'Might as well be honest about that. You've been caught trying to use highly sensitive software belonging to the US government, stealing classified information... Hell, we've already got enough on you to put you in a deep dark hole for the rest of your natural life. In fact, the only reason you're not on a flight to Guantanamo Bay right now is because I want to offer you a way out.'

Alex let out an involuntary gasp. 'A way out?'

Frank took another sip of his drink. 'I like you, Alex. You're a smart motherfucker. Straight-A student, top marks at college... sorry, university. Shit, if you were working for the Agency you'd probably be *my* boss by now. Huh?' He let out another laugh, amused by his own joke, then reached into his pocket and held up the memory stick that had apparently brought about this disastrous series of events. 'Tell me, where did you get this, Alex?'

The lies came tumbling out before he could stop them. 'I... I don't even know what's on it—'

The answer was swift and brutal, a backhanded strike against the side of his head that jolted him sideways and caused him to topple right off the chair, landing with bruising force on the unyielding concrete floor. It was all Alex could do to keep from crying out in pain and fear at the sudden and unexpected assault. A second man must have approached him while his attention was on Frank.

Alex was no fighter, and was unused to physical injury. He hadn't been properly hit by anyone since he was a child, and that single blow was far stronger than any of the punches thrown in school-yard fights.

A moment later, his world went dark as a towel was placed over his face, held down hard on either side so that his head was pinned to the floor. A knee driven into his chest with crushing force prevented any movement of his body. With his hands cuffed, he could do nothing to fight his captor off.

He heard the metallic scrape of the bucket being lifted off the floor, followed by Frank's distinctive voice. 'Like I said, the secret is restraint.'

The moment Frank began to empty the bucket onto his head, Alex's heartbeat skyrocketed and panic began to set in. The heavy cloth across his face acted to soak up the water, causing it to seep into his nose and down his throat, inducing an immediate gag reflex.

In desperation he tried to thrash his head from side to side, but his captor's grip was unrelenting and he could manage barely an inch of movement either way. The cloth was held down even harder, forcing his head back, and all the while the steady deluge continued.

Alex bucked and kicked with desperate strength, the cuffs cutting into his wrists, but still he could find no escape. Letting out a cry of panic, his lungs greedily tried to suck in more air only to be met with a renewed influx of water.

Now there was no stopping it. Coughing and screaming into the gag, he thrashed wildly as his body desperately sought oxygen that he knew wouldn't come. His pulse thundered in his ears, adrenaline surging in his veins as the ancient instinct for self-preservation kicked in. But it was all for nothing.

Only then did the realisation hit him – he was going to die. They would just keep on pouring the water into his lungs until it finally overcame him, until his struggles eased and consciousness faded, and there was nothing he could do to stop them.

He was going to die here.

It was at this moment, as darkness began to envelop his mind, that the flow of water suddenly stopped and the cloth was withdrawn. Freed from his captors' remorseless grip, Alex doubled over, coughing and choking violently as his lungs tried to expel the water that had started to fill them.

Looking up through blurred eyes, he saw a second man move into view. This one was far less genial looking than Frank. Shorter, heavier, older and meaner-looking. His shirt sleeves were rolled up to reveal muscular forearms liberally coated with thick dark hair, while the rest of his sizeable torso was covered by a full length leather apron. The kind of thing worn by butchers and slaughterhouse workers.

'I forgot to introduce you to my buddy Larry,' Frank said by way of apology. 'Larry, meet Alex.'

'How you doing, Alex?' Larry replied, nodding acknowledgement. 'I'm looking forward to working on you.'

That made two men at least that he could see. Three of them had escorted him out of the police station earlier, though he had no idea where the third man was. Perhaps he was waiting somewhere in the shadows, getting ready to spring another painful and terrifying surprise just as Larry had, or perhaps he was behind the wheel of the van, preparing to drive his companions out of here once they'd tortured him to death.

Either way, he had no desire to find out.

'No more,' Alex gasped, his voice rasping with the effort. 'No more. Please.'

Frank took another sip of coffee. 'Like I said, you're smart, but you don't strike me as the sort of guy who steals government secrets for fun. What I'm really interested in is the person who gave you this memory stick. So here's my deal. Answer our questions, help us bring a dangerous terrorist to justice and maybe, just maybe, you get to walk away from this and go back to your old life. Considering the level of shit you're in, that's a pretty good deal right there, buddy. Or...' He glanced down at the floor and tapped the steel bucket with his shoe. 'We can carry on like this. Plenty of water out here, and we've got all night.'

The mere thought of going through that again made Alex want to gag. Unable to look at either man, he simply nodded.

He saw a hint of a smile. Compared to some of the men this pair had probably interrogated in their time, Alex must have been a complete walkover.

'Now we're getting somewhere. See, Larry? I told you he'd help us out. He's a smart guy.'

Alex heard a grunt of acknowledgement from Larry, who was probably disappointed he wouldn't get a chance to try another round of waterboarding.

'Okay, Alex. Let's get to it. How did you get the memory stick?'

'It was posted to me.'

'By who?'

Alex swallowed hard, hating what he was about to do. He'd gone to prison before rather than betray his friends, but this was different. He was fighting for his life now. And if he was right, Sinclair was no longer alive to betray.

'Arran Sinclair. A friend of mine.'

'Go on,' Frank prompted, knowing there was a lot more to it than that.

'A week ago he came to me, asked for my help. Some... project he was working on. I refused, then a few days later this letter turned up. When I did some searching, I found out he'd disappeared. I needed to know what was on the memory stick, so I took it to that internet cafe to open it.'

At this, the man in the leather apron glanced at his companion with a raised eyebrow, saying nothing. For his own part, Frank took a long, thoughtful drink before going on. 'Tell me about the burner phone, Alex.'

'I don't know—'

His answer was cut short by a rock-hard fist driven into his exposed stomach. Unable to help himself, Alex doubled over, groaning and gasping for air. Both CIA operatives stood back, watching him in silence until he'd gotten his breath back.

'I sure hope you're not holding out on me, buddy,' Frank warned, his voice betraying an edge of impatience for the first time. 'Otherwise we're all in for a long night, and I'm getting tired.'

'I was only given it tonight,' Alex gasped, spitting acrid-tasting phlegm on the floor. 'Some woman. She paid someone to give it to me.'

The revelation of his mysterious contact's gender prompted a look of interest. 'So you didn't see her in person?'

'No. All I heard was her voice.'

'What did she say to you?'

'She... warned me the police were on their way, told me to leave the cafe if I wanted to live through the night. She said she could help me.'

Frank was getting interested now. 'Describe her voice. Be specific.'

The memory of that conversation was still imprinted on his mind, as it would be for the rest of his life. However long that might be. 'It was deep for a woman; she wasn't young. And she spoke with an accent, maybe Russian. I-I'm not sure.'

Frank thought about it for a few moments. 'Then it seems this is your lucky day, Alex. We're going to take you back to that police station tonight, and in the morning they'll release you without pressing any charges.

Insufficient evidence. You'll go back home, and sooner or later your new friend will contact you again. That's when we'll take her.'

Alex's eyes opened wider. 'She knew the police were on their way to arrest me. She'll know I've been caught. If I try to meet her now she'll—'

Suddenly Larry took a step forward, and Alex felt something jammed against his neck. The harsh clicking sound as the taser discharged was punctuated by Alex's groans of agony as thousands of volts flooded his central nervous system. His body convulsed violently on the floor in a pathetic heap, his muscles jerking and twitching of their own volition.

At last the nightmare ended and he curled into a foetal position, drawing in ragged, shuddering breaths.

'Let me spell this out for you, bro. People like you can and have been made to disappear plenty of times without any problem at all. I could torture you to death out here and all it would take is a few signed forms delivered to my boss to make it all okay,' Frank informed him, his former joviality gone now. 'In fact, the only reason you're still breathing is because you can be useful. That's the only purpose to your life now. If you can't help us, there's no reason to waste any more of my valuable time on you.'

He heard a crisp metallic click, and realized with a kind of detached horror that it was the sound of a round being chambered. Looking up, he saw Larry standing over him, a black automatic gleaming in the harsh electric light.

Frank on the other hand just stood there watching the whole scene unfold with a faint smirk. Alex's life meant nothing to him. He had watched plenty of men die before, and would no doubt see plenty more after today.

Before Alex could answer, the van's headlights suddenly went out, plunging the room into darkness. Alex gasped, wondering what was going on.

'What the—?' he heard Frank say, before his voice was reduced to a strangled, gurgling groan.

'Shit!' the other man shouted, followed by the thundering crack of a gunshot that momentarily illuminated a blur of movement right in front of him. Alex flinched, expecting a round to tear through his flesh at any instant.

But no such thing happened. Instead he saw a shadowy figure leap towards the man in the leather apron, heard a sudden scuffle and a cry of pain. A heavy thump told Alex that a body had just landed on the ground.

A few seconds later, the lights came back on just as suddenly as they had gone out, revealing a scene so shocking that Alex had to blink and look again to believe it.

His two captors were sprawled on the dirty concrete floor, blood pooling around both of their lifeless bodies. Frank was lying on his back, his throat sliced open and his takeaway coffee steaming on the ground nearby, while

Larry's leather apron had been perforated with several well placed knife thrusts that left it glistening crimson in the harsh light.

But even more shocking than this gory spectacle was the assailant who had apparently brought it all about. To Alex's disbelief, a woman was standing between the two dead men, a bloody knife clutched in her left hand.

Tall and athletic, with short blonde hair and striking features, he knew she was a woman he'd seen before. Straight away his mind flashed back to his meeting with Sinclair at Trafalgar Square a week earlier.

Wearing expensive jeans, a black fitted shirt and a stylish brown leather jacket, she was the epitome of effortless sophistication. Her features were strikingly good looking with a foreign air to them, yet there was a hardness about her that made him look a little closer.

Perhaps sensing his restless gaze on her, as attractive women often seemed to do, she glanced his way, and just for a moment their eyes met. Even from the other side of the square, Alex was caught off guard by the pair of icy blue eyes that seemed to bore right through him.

Looking at her now, it was difficult to believe this was the same woman. The fashionable leather jacket and jeans were gone now, replaced by black military fatigues and hiking boots. Her blonde hair was slicked back to keep her eyes clear, her face hard and set with cold, clinical resolve.

And yet it was her without a doubt. Her clothes might have changed, but her eyes hadn't. Neither had what lay behind them. Cold blue and frightening in their intensity, they were focussed now on him as a predator might regard its helpless prey.

She approached him with that deadly blade still clutched in her gloved hand. A splash of her enemies' blood was smeared across her face, the crimson stain highlighting the chilling depths of those merciless eyes.

At any moment he expected that blade to come scything down through the air, cleaving its way through skin, muscle and delicate internal organs.

Yet to his amazement no such thing happened.

'Can you walk?' the woman asked. Confirming what he already knew, her voice was the same one that had tried to guide him to safety back at the cafe.

Such was his shock at her sudden arrival, Alex couldn't even muster a response.

'Can you walk?' she repeated, louder now. 'If you can't, I'll leave you here.'

He blinked, coming back to himself. 'Yes.'

'Good.' Kneeling down beside him, she gripped his wrists and quickly unlocked his cuffs.

Only then did the full impact of what had just happened settle on him. Even as the cuffs fell away from his wrists, Alex stared in horrified fascination at the blood steadily oozing from the severed arteries in Frank's neck.

'Jesus Christ, they're really dead, aren't they?' he said, vaguely aware of how idiotic such a statement must have sounded to her.

She paused only for a moment, surveying the two bodies without emotion. 'More will be coming soon. We have to leave this place. Get up now and be ready to move.'

Without waiting for a reply, she rose to her feet, hurried over to the two dead men, searching through Frank's pockets until she found the memory stick. With the stick safely in her possession, she turned her attention to Larry, snatching up the weapon he'd dropped during the brief confrontation.

Pulling back the slide just far enough to check that a round was chambered and that the firing mechanism wasn't fouled, she glanced at Alex once more.

'Follow me.'

Shell-shocked by everything that had just happened, Alex did the only thing that made any sense given the circumstances. He obeyed.

Chapter 9

Alex's curiosity about where he'd ended up after his long journey from London was answered as he slipped through a huge set of sliding doors into the cool darkness of the world beyond. As far as he could tell, the building was a corrugated iron barn set within a larger farm complex. There were two other structures of similar proportions nearby, their bulk visible only as immense black shapes against the general darkness of the night sky.

He had to admit there was a certain grim logic in the choice of location. Farms by their nature were about as isolated as a place could be in a country like the UK. And with miles of privately owned and unpopulated land all around, there was little chance of passing civilians overhearing something they shouldn't.

'What the fuck is this place?' he asked, keeping his voice low as he followed the woman between the two barns. Unlike him, she moved through the shadows with uncanny speed and grace, her feet barely making a sound on the muddy earth.

'A field interrogation site, set up in a hurry,' she explained. 'If they had had more time to prepare, you would have been harder to get to. It seems they didn't want anyone else to know of this.'

'All this trouble for me? I'm honoured,' Alex said with a nervous laugh, trying to make light of it.

The gesture wasn't reciprocated. Instead she pointed off into the distance, where a stand of trees broke up the night sky. 'I have a car on the other side of those woods. Stay low and follow me.'

'How did you—?'

'Not now,' she cut in, silencing him. 'Stay close and don't talk.'

And that was all she had to say on the matter. Doing his best to follow as she hurried onward, Alex stumbled through undergrowth and over exposed tree roots, swearing more than once as his legs caught on tangled patches of brambles that had burst into life once more with the onset of summer.

Adrenaline and sheer desperation were doing a reasonable job of keeping him going for now, but it wasn't easy to keep up with her, and Alex was suddenly very conscious that this woman was his only remaining lifeline. If he lost her, he might as well turn himself in at the nearest police station.

By the time they emerged on the far side of the small wood, he was sweating and out of breath. Still, they'd made it through the rough terrain more or less unscathed.

The wood was skirted by a narrow, unpaved dirt road probably used by farmers to commute between their fields. Parked in a shallow depression and partially screened by bushes was a black Ford Focus, the conservative little hatchback looking decidedly out of place in such rural surroundings.

His female companion headed straight for the vehicle, and Alex wasted no time following her. He practically collapsed into the passenger seat as soon as the door was unlocked, and was still breathing hard as she fired up the engine and eased the car out of the shallow dip.

Within moments they were on their way, driving at a fair speed despite the rough and winding track. The headlights remained firmly switched off, and though Alex might have questioned the wisdom of driving on a rough farm track at night, he was too exhausted to raise the matter. In any case, he doubted the woman would take kindly to such questions.

He was trembling, he realized as he looked down at his hands. They were shaking almost uncontrollably now, and from more than just the chill night air outside. Over and over he kept seeing his former captors lying on that dirty concrete floor, over and over he replayed the feeling of water rushing into his mouth and nose, drowning him. He felt like he was going to throw up.

'You're experiencing a combat-stress reaction,' the woman said, as if sensing his thoughts. 'The adrenaline in your blood is thinning out, your body is going into shock. Breathe slow and deep, keep your mind focussed. I need you to think clearly now, Alex.'

'Easy for you to say,' he said, wrapping his arms around his chest in an effort to keep warm. The car's heaters were cranked up to full, but the engine hadn't warmed up enough to produce hot air yet. 'How did you find me tonight? At the cafe, I mean. And how do you know my name?'

'Like I said, you're not good at covering your tracks. I was there when you met with Loki a week ago, and I followed you home afterwards. Once I had your address it was easy to learn everything I needed to know about you.'

'Why are you so interested?'

'Loki was working for me, and I guessed you were working for him. I needed to know you could be trusted. But when Loki disappeared three days ago, you were my only lead.'

At last a big piece of the puzzle fell into place. Loki was Sinclair's hacker alias. This woman was the mysterious client who had hired him to hack into the CIA's secure network and steal classified information. She was the one willing to pay a great deal of money to get her hands on it, and she was the reason Sinclair might well be dead. Suddenly Alex's mind was a maelstrom of confused thoughts and possibilities, none of which were good.

She paused a moment to swing the car through a tight bend, bracing herself as it rumbled over a deep pothole. 'Now tell me, why did you try to use the CAM at a public terminal?'

'CAM? I don't understand. What the hell is a CAM?' he asked, trying to sort through his increasingly cluttered and disjointed thoughts.

He heard a faint exhalation of breath, but didn't trust himself to look round. The jolting, swaying movement of the car on the rough road was making him feel nauseous, reminding him of a taxi ride home after a drunken night out.

'A conditional access module. A secure login system for field operatives to access the Agency's servers,' she explained tersely. 'Loki gave you a copy when you met with him a week ago. You've been working on decrypting it for him.'

He most certainly had not. The closest he'd come to discerning the secrets held within the memory stick had been the brief glimpse he'd seen of the source code back at the internet cafe.

Growing tired of his reticence, the woman turned around, glaring right at him. 'Alex, this is no time to hold back. Talk to me! How did the Agency find you?'

And just like that, everything that had happened over the past several hours – the revelation of his friend's disappearance, the arrest, the torture, the interrogation – suddenly came to an explosive climax.

'I don't fucking know!' he shouted, surprising even himself with the violence of his reaction. 'I don't know what you're talking about. I wasn't working to decrypt anything for anyone. I didn't ask to be involved, and I told Arran I wanted no part in this. Whatever you think I am, I'm not. I'm a fucking nobody. I sell TVs for a living, for Christ's sake. I can't answer your questions because I don't know what the hell he was mixed up in.'

Her reaction was as dramatic as it was immediate. Jamming her foot on the brake, she brought the Focus to a shuddering, skidding halt. Alex, having forgotten to put his seatbelt on, was thrown against the dashboard by the sudden deceleration.

'Get out of the car,' she ordered.

'What are you—?'

He was silenced very effectively when she reached into her jacket, pulled out the automatic she'd taken from his dead captors, and levelled it squarely at his forehead.

'Get out of the car,' she repeated, her voice now as cold as her eyes.

One look at her expression was enough to convince him against further protest. Swallowing down the sickening feeling of nausea in his throat, Alex pulled open his door and stepped out into the chill night air. She was right behind, keeping him covered.

'Get down on your knees,' she ordered. 'Put your hands behind your head.'

He felt strangely numb as he lowered himself onto the muddy ground and placed his hands behind his head, hardly able to comprehend how his fortunes had swung so drastically once more. It didn't feel real. So different was tonight from the safe, monotonous predictability of his life that his mind simply couldn't accept what was happening.

Was this how it was going to end? Had he really just been rescued only to be executed by his saviour?

'Look, I didn't mean to shout at you—' he began, desperately groping for the right words.

'Shut up,' she fired back. 'Everything that has happened tonight is of your own making. The moment you tried to run the CAM, it was red-flagged on the Agency's systems. You've destroyed everything Loki and I were working for.'

Alex had no words. No counterargument, no plea for compassion. He understood now the full magnitude of his decision to open that file.

'I didn't know. I... I'm sorry.'

As far as pleas for one's life went, it was woefully inadequate. It certainly wasn't going to undo the damage he had unwittingly caused tonight, but he had never meant those two words more in his entire life.

'So am I,' the woman replied, raising the weapon.

'P-please, don't do it,' he stammered, well aware that he was trembling now in abject fear. The numbness and disbelief had faded away now, and reality had hit him like a brick wall. 'Please. I don't want to die.'

'There's nothing I can do for you. It will be quick.'

Oh Jesus, this was it. He was going to die here on this muddy farm track miles from anywhere, his body found tomorrow or the next day or the day after that. He'd be found with his brains blasted out across the grass.

He saw the police notifying his parents of his murder, saw his mother in tears and his father trying to be strong. He saw the people at his office gossiping about it, trying to figure out what had really happened to him, saw some of them drifting along to his funeral, more because it would get them the day off work than because they really cared for him. He saw it all in the blink of an eye.

I'm going to die wearing a fucking Metallica t-shirt, he thought, as he watched the barrel of the gun glinting in the wan moonlight.

Then, just like that, an idea came to him. An idea born from sheer desperation, and an intuition of why his friend had approached him a week ago.

'Wait!' he cried. 'You said you wanted the CAM decrypted so you could hack into the Agency's servers. That means you want to steal something from them. I can help you.'

That was enough to get her attention, if only briefly. Keeping it, however, would depend on what he said in the next few seconds. He had to make her believe in him.

'Why do you think Arran came to me for help a week ago?' he asked, speaking so quickly he was almost stumbling over the words. 'It's because he knew I was the only one who could do what he needed.'

'You said you were a nobody,' she reminded him. 'A television salesman. What can you possibly do to help me?'

He looked up at her. 'It wasn't always like this. I used to be something, *someone*, very different. I used to do things that mattered, as stupid as that might sound to you. Arran knew what I could do, what I was capable of; that's why he came to me for help. But I turned him away, because I was afraid of what might happen.' Alex swallowed, wondering if this whole mess might have played out differently had he accepted his friend's offer. 'Now I know, and that's something I have to live with. And it seems like after everything that's happened tonight, I've got nothing left to lose. So yes, I can help you. There's nobody better at breaking encryption codes than me; not even Arran himself. I used to hack multinational banking servers for fun. If you're serious about this, if you really want to get into the CIA's systems, then for God's sake don't pull that trigger because I'm the only one left who can get you in.'

She said nothing for several seconds, her gaze searching and intense, looking for any sign of deception. But she didn't pull the trigger. 'Assuming you are telling the truth, what would you need to do this?'

'I need a decent computer setup. Serious hardware that you can't buy from any shop, and somewhere I can work undisturbed.'

'And where would you suggest finding these things?'

A hacking attempt like this wasn't something to be undertaken lightly, and certainly not with the kind of equipment he could buy commercially. Back in the day, it had taken him months to put together the kind of custom-built system he'd needed for such activities. Clearly he didn't have time to build one now, which meant the only option left was to use someone else's.

'I know a man who has everything I need, but...'

'But what?'

Alex swallowed. She wasn't going to like what he had to say next, but it had to come out all the same. 'He's not in this country. He lives in Norway. He used to be part of Valhalla 7.'

'If he was part of the group, then he may have been compromised like the others,' she reasoned. 'What makes you think we can use him?'

Alex shook his head. 'Trust me, there's no way Arran would have approached him this time around.'

'Why?'

Alex gritted his teeth, swallowing down the years of festering anger that still arose whenever he thought of Gregar Landvik. 'Because he's the reason I ended up in jail,' he managed to say. 'It's a long story that you probably don't want to hear. The point is, he was thrown out of the group after that, but there's a good chance he's still active. If we can get to him, I can use his system and break this thing.'

She didn't look convinced. In fact, she still looked all too ready to pull that trigger. No doubt she'd reached the same conclusion he had – his proposal was a long shot at best, with plenty of opportunities to fail.

The only question was how important the potential rewards were to her, how much she was willing to risk.

'If you are lying to me...'

'I'm not. I promise,' he begged, staring right back at her and hoping his eyes betrayed nothing but desperate sincerity. 'I know I fucked things up for you tonight, but I can make this right. I can fix this. Just give me a chance to prove it.'

She said nothing in response, merely kept him covered with the weapon. It was impossible to tell from her expression, but he desperately hoped she was weighing up what he'd said. Surely it had to be worth a try?

He could only pray she felt the same way.

Finally, after what seemed like an eternity, she lowered the gun. Alex released a breath he hadn't even realized he'd been holding.

'Get back in the car,' she instructed, turning away without waiting for him. 'We have a long night ahead of us.'

There it was – a lifeline. It was tenuous and unpredictable, but it was a chance. A chance to fix this, to put right his mistake. A chance to stay alive.

Alex scrambled to his feet even as she fired up the engine once more. Never in his life had he been so relieved to climb into a car.

Chapter 10

I'm not proud of the fact that I was on my knees begging for mercy, but there you have it. No matter how bad you might feel about your life, no matter how hopeless it all seems, when someone's waving a gun in your face you'll say and do just about anything to stay alive. Including making promises you've got no idea if you can keep.

I was clutching at straws, and I knew it. My life was spiralling out of control so fast that I hadn't even had time to realize how bad things were. Only a day earlier I'd been a nobody — just some anonymous sales assistant with a rubbish car, no girlfriend and no prospects. Now I was a wanted criminal, with some very dangerous people hunting me, and an even more dangerous woman by my side.

Talk about a rock and a hard place...

–

Alex couldn't say how long he'd spent in that car with the woman who had saved his life, then very nearly ended it. Another man in his position might have been terrified, wondering whether she might change her mind and kill him anyway, yet strangely no such fear stirred in him. Perhaps he'd exhausted his quota of fear tonight.

And exhaustion was the word that best described his state of mind. After the panic of his capture and the ordeal of his interrogation, the elation of his escape and the sudden terror of his near-execution at the hands of his saviour, it was as if his mind simply couldn't process anything more. The steady hum of the car's engine, the vibration of its movement along the tarmac road and the occasional flash of oncoming headlights had all combined with sheer physical fatigue to induce an almost dreamlike state.

With a kind of absent-minded detachment, Alex watched signposts for Luton, Northampton and then Leicester drift by outside the window. They weren't driving down any of the big motorways that crisscrossed the area, but were instead sticking to smaller country roads. The kind that saw less traffic and therefore had fewer, if any, surveillance cameras.

His companion had said nothing since the resumption of their journey; she just sat there, one hand on the wheel, the other on the weapon resting by her thigh. But there was a tension in the set of her shoulders that belied her lack of movement, an intensity in her beautiful but hard features that spoke of a highly focussed mind never wavering for a moment. Her eyes were constantly checking the rear-view mirror, and he could guess why.

He wasn't sure whether she was his captor or his protector at that moment, yet somehow he felt safer with her than he would have with a dozen armed police officers. Who was this woman? This strange, dangerous, frightening and compelling woman who had come into his life like a force of nature, destroying everything in her path? What kind of life had turned her from a normal, unassuming person like himself into this... machine sitting opposite him?

Sensing his eyes on her, she glanced around. 'You have something to say.'

As far as conversation-starters went, he'd heard better. Clearly she wasn't one for small-talk; as if he needed further confirmation. 'You saved my life tonight, then you almost killed me. I don't even know your name.'

'That's right,' she agreed. 'You don't.'

Alex sighed. 'Well, it's going to be an awkward journey if I don't have *something* to call you.'

She said nothing to this for some time. Whether she was weighing up his words or simply choosing to ignore him, he couldn't tell. But he was smart enough not to press the issue. Trying to cajole the information out of her seemed like a waste of time.

'My name is Anya,' she said at last.

'Is that your real name?'

She looked at him, her eyes glimmering dangerously in the glow of the dashboard lights, but said nothing.

'Fine, forget that one. Where are we going?' he asked. He was aware that his own voice sounded leaden, as if it was an effort to form each syllable.

'As soon as the Agency realize you escaped, they will lock down all airports, railway stations and shipping terminals nationwide. Once they have you contained, they'll use every resource at their disposal to hunt you down. Your name will be on the Most Wanted lists of every major law-enforcement agency worldwide within a matter of hours. We have to get you out before that happens.'

So surreal did that statement sound to a man whose name had never even been mentioned in a local newspaper that Alex actually snorted in amusement. 'And to think, my career advisor said I'd never achieve anything.'

The look on her face made it clear she wasn't impressed by his attempt at humour. 'I'd take this a little more seriously if I were you. We were lucky tonight – we caught them unprepared and off-guard, but they won't make the same mistake again. You are a target now, Alex. Whatever life you once had, it's over. Your friends and family, your home, possessions, bank accounts... they're all gone. The people now hunting you have the resources of the world's most powerful intelligence agency at their disposal, and believe me when I say they'll use them. They will never stop looking for you, no matter how far you run and how well you cover your tracks. Whenever you think you're safe, you're not. Whenever you stay in one place too long, they will find you. And whenever you allow your guard to drop, it will be the last mistake you ever make.'

Alex swallowed hard, staring right at her as if expecting her to erupt into laughter after such a speech. But she didn't. Her eyes remained on the road ahead, her expression one of focussed concentration and, perhaps, a touch of grim acceptance.

'You make it sound like I'm already dead,' he said, hoping she would take that statement for what it was and offer a few consoling words. Some shred of hope that would at least keep him going.

Only then did her eyes meet his. Fleeting, momentary, as if he was worth only an instant of her time. 'You might as well be, unless you learn fast. Learn how to run, to keep moving, to never trust anyone. Survival is what matters now. If you think I am your friend because I saved your life, you're very wrong. I will do what I can to protect you, until you get what I need. After that, you're on your own.'

And there it was. Never had Alex been brought back down to reality with such crushing, absolute force. She was no more his saviour than he was hers. He was a tool to be used until it had served its purpose. After that, why should she care?

'Why did you rescue me?' he asked, almost resentful now.

Anya was silent for a time, her eyes never leaving the road. He began to wonder if she was ignoring his question.

'I believed you could help,' she finally said. 'For your sake, I hope I wasn't wrong.'

—

Langley, Virginia

It was by now early evening in Virginia, the sun drifting down through a warm, hazy sky and glistening off the waters of the Potomac. The day shift at Langley were mostly heading home for the night, finishing up after a long day while their night-shift comrades took over their stations.

Marcus Cain however had no intention of leaving. He was holed up in his expansive office on the top floor of the New Headquarters Building, staring absently out the windows without really seeing anything. His restless thoughts were turned inward, pondering events three thousand miles away in London, and what they meant for him.

A disavowed Agency ID had started all of this; an identity belonging to a woman Cain had once known all too well. A woman so well acquainted with the Agency's inner workings, power struggles and dark secrets that she now represented a threat to its very foundations.

Anya.

Two years ago he'd arranged for her to escape the Russian prison she'd been languishing in, believing he could manipulate her into doing what she did best – killing the men he deemed to be enemies. Anya, always the faithful soldier, had once again exceeded his expectations and cut a bloody path through those who posed a threat to him.

But now the game had changed. Now she was coming after him. How and when it would happen, he didn't know. All he knew was that sooner or later she would make her move, and it seemed it had started today.

Whatever involvement the young man called Alex Yates might have in this, Cain was quite certain that Anya was behind it. And he intended to learn everything Yates had to say about it.

Absently he reached for the glass of malt whisky on his desk, holding it up to the light of the setting sun. Glenlivet, thirty years old. Not easy to come by these days. The single bottle he kept in his office was worth nearly $700. At the rate he'd been getting through it lately, he didn't imagine his investment would last much longer.

For a moment he caught himself wondering how many nights he'd stayed late in this gilded cage, the bottle his only companion. How many nights had he sat in this chair, endlessly replaying the decisions, the mistakes, the compromises and the betrayals that had led Anya and himself down this path? How had it come to this?

They had been friends once. More than friends, in fact. Much more.

Almost from the first moment he'd met her two decades earlier, he had sensed something special in the wild, beautiful, fearless young woman. He'd felt a bond, a kinship that he'd never experienced with anyone else on this earth before or since. With her, there had been no questions, no doubts, no fear. He had felt like he could do anything.

The two of them could have achieved incredible things together, could have defeated any enemy and overcome any obstacle, yet here they now were. Bitter enemies, locked in a battle that only one of them could emerge from.

The only question was who would prevail.

His dark thoughts were interrupted as his cell phone started ringing. His private cell phone whose number was known only to a select few. In this case Tom Holloway, the divisional director of all Agency resources in the United Kingdom. The man Cain had personally charged with organizing Yates's clandestine interrogation.

Leaving the whisky, Cain hit the button to receive the call.

'What do you have, Tom?'

There was a pause. The uncomfortable silence of a man preparing to deliver bad news. 'Sir, I'm afraid we have a problem.'

Cain's jaw tightened. 'What kind of problem?'

'The field team we sent to interrogate Yates...' Holloway sighed. 'They didn't report in, sir. We sent in additional field teams, and...'

'Go on.'

'They're dead, sir. All of them. And there's no sign of the prisoner.'

Letting out a breath, Cain closed his eyes, mastering his temper with difficulty. Anya it seemed had made her next move with typical ruthless precision, and now they'd lost their only lead.

'I thought I told you to secure the prisoner for interrogation, Mr Holloway. I was very specific about that,' he said, his voice dangerously cold.

'With respect, you also specified that it had to be done discreetly, sir,' Holloway reminded him. 'A small team, no witnesses, no records.'

Reaching out, Cain picked up his glass of whisky, watching as the sun glimmered through its amber-coloured contents, then tipped it back and swallowed a generous mouthful. He had made a mistake today, and he knew it. He'd underestimated Yates's value, had entrusted an important task to men who were clearly not worthy of it. And as a result he'd allowed Anya to regain the initiative.

It was a mistake he couldn't afford to make again.

'We're putting together a team now to hunt for Yates,' Holloway said, as if such an effort had any chance of success. 'We'll find him, sir.'

Cain let out a breath as the whisky lit a fire in his stomach, his anger abating slightly as his mind rapidly assessed the situation. This might have been a setback, but it was one that presented its own advantages.

By risking so much to recover Yates, Anya had tipped her hand to him. Yates was important to her, which meant she couldn't afford to lose him. He was a weakness that Cain might just be able to exploit.

But first he needed someone he could rely on. Someone to take charge of the situation. Someone who knew what Anya was capable of, and how to beat her.

'Don't trouble yourself, Holloway,' he said, pouring himself another glass. 'I'm sending someone to help you.'

Part II

Execution

In 1988, graduate student Robert T. Morris, Jr. of Cornell University launches a worm on the government's ARPANET system. The worm spreads to 6,000 networked computers, clogging government and university systems. Morris is dismissed from Cornell, sentenced to three years probation, and fined $10,000.

Chapter 11

I dream.

The same dream I've had many times before. A lifetime of memories to pick from, and yet my subconscious chooses to relive this one particular moment again and again.

I'm ten years old. It's a Saturday afternoon in April. It's been raining all morning, as it often does at this time of year, leaving me and all the other kids stranded in homes full of washing machines and shopping bags and DIY projects that'll never get finished. But finally around lunchtime the rain eased up, and now the sun's shining through gaps in the cloud.

That's good enough for me. I'm out the door before my father can set a curfew or my mother can give me errands to run. I'm free as only a 10-year-old boy without a care in the world can be, and I'm on my way to the park to see who fancies a game of football. Nobody bothers calling each other to organize such things; we all just instinctively head there like geese migrating south in winter. We can't explain it because we don't need to. Everyone just knows.

Sure enough, one of my friends is there already. Binyamin, or 'Ben' as he prefers people to call him. His parents are from Pakistan. I know, because he once showed me Pakistan on the globe at school. The old one where some of the countries have names that are different from today.

I like Ben. He's smart, he can draw better than anyone I know, and he always seems to know the right thing to say to make people laugh. But there's something else about him; a kind of sadness that I don't understand. But I can feel it beneath the surface, like a stone at the bottom of a pond. I asked him once why his parents left Pakistan to come to Britain, and I think the sadness came up to the surface then. He said bad things happened there, and they didn't like to talk about it. So I never did.

But Ben isn't alone at the park. There are three others boys around him, closing around in a circle with him in the centre, trapping him. I know them well enough, especially the biggest of the three.

Richard Gilmore.

Every year, every class had to have a bad apple. It was inevitable. Some kid that started out a little angrier, a little more needy and domineering than the rest. Just a minor difference, a tiny divergence that got bigger and bigger as time passed. And Richard Gilmore was our bad apple.

He'd always disliked Ben. I can't really say how or why it started. Maybe it was because Ben's dark skin and hair marked him out as different, or maybe because he *got attention by making people laugh and warm to him, whereas Richard had to do it through force and fear. But whatever the reason, that dislike had gradually turned into real hatred over the years, and lately he'd added a new word to the mix – Paki.*

The very word sounded dirty and unpleasant, conjuring up all kinds of images of strange men glowering at you in dimly lit shops; the kind that could never be trusted, that your parents warned you never to speak to but wouldn't say why.

He's using it now, hurling it at Ben while his friends look on and laugh, enjoying the show. But Ben is standing his ground, refusing to rise to it, refusing to let Richard provoke him.

Richard senses it too, and it doesn't take long for the verbal assault to turn physical as he shoves Ben backward, closing the gap before the smaller boy can regain his balance. He shoves him again, sending him staggering into one of his friends who quickly pushes him back toward Richard, wiping his hands on his jeans as if they've been tainted somehow.

It's at this moment that Ben spots me. He doesn't say anything, doesn't call to me or beckon me over. But I can see the look in his eyes as plain as day. Hope, relief, gratitude at seeing one of his friends. Someone who will come to his aid, who will wade into the fray without fear or hesitation, who will help him teach Richard Gilmore a lesson he won't forget.

I'd love to say that's exactly what happens, but it doesn't.

What happens is that I stop, turn slowly around and walk away even as Richard throws the first punch and his friends cheer him on. Ben, outnumbered and frightened, stands his ground and refuses to go down, at least until he can't stand any longer. He takes a good kicking that day – the first of many. And I walk away without a scratch.

I don't even have the good grace to feel guilt or remorse. All I feel is relief.

Relief that it isn't happening to me.

Relief that I'm safe.

–

Alex awoke with a start, his breath coming in gasps, his eyes streaming in the harsh light shining right at him. He made to sit up straight, but suddenly something jerked him backward, forcing him into his seat.

In a moment of wild panic, he was seized by the terrifying notion that he'd never escaped from the farm the night before, that everything that had happened over the past several hours was nothing but a feverish dream conjured up by his tortured, desperate mind as his captors went to work with that sledgehammer.

'Calm down,' a female voice said, and he felt a hand on his arm. Warm, firm and somehow reassuring. 'You're awake, Alex.'

Closing his eyes for a moment, Alex exhaled and drew in a deep breath, trying to calm his frantic mind that had jolted awake so suddenly.

Strangely, he could no longer hear the sound of the car's engine, nor feel its movement. All he could hear was the distant sound of waves crashing against a shore and the occasional screech of a seagull overhead.

Opening his eyes, he looked around to find Anya sitting in the driver's seat, silhouetted against a backdrop of scattered cloud and open sea. She had changed clothes at some point while he'd been asleep, discarding the military-patterned assault gear in favour of jeans, a dark blue jumper and a casual jacket. With her hair neatly combed and her gaze as alert as ever, she gave little outward sign that she'd been driving all night long.

'You were talking in your sleep,' she remarked, a hint of curiosity showing in her icy blue eyes. 'Bad dreams?'

'My whole life is a bad dream at the moment,' he evaded, as he surveyed their surroundings.

They were parked at the edge of a wide harbour area, around which were moored vessels of all kinds; from small yachts and pleasure craft up to large commercial fishing trawlers, all bobbing on the undulating waves stirred up by a fair breeze. The sun was just rising above the horizon, its blinding rays reflecting off the whitecaps and making his eyes water.

The place was clearly still in use, yet the harbour itself appeared quite neglected. Grass and bushes grew uncontrolled along the boundary of the property, weeds trailed over rusted winches and cranes once used for lowering boats into the water, while many of the giant stone blocks that formed the harbour wall had begun to give way under the relentless assault of time and tide.

'Where are we?' Alex asked, rubbing the sleep out of his eyes. He was hungry and thirsty, his tongue felt like a carpet stuck to the roof of his mouth, and he was increasingly aware of the need to urinate.

'An estuary on the east coast of Scotland,' she replied, either unwilling or unable to elaborate. 'Come on, follow me.'

Without waiting for him, she pushed open her door and stepped outside, tucking the gun down the back of her jeans. With little option, Alex followed a moment later.

Whatever vestiges of sleep still clung to him were quickly whipped away by the cool fresh breeze that blew across the exposed harbour area, carrying with it the distinctive tang of salt and seaweed. Clad only in a thin t-shirt and a hoodie that was still damp from the soaking last night, Alex suppressed a shiver as the chill breeze seemed to penetrate to his core. He might have been enjoying the sultry warmth of spring in London a few days ago, but this was like a different world.

Wrapping his arms around his chest, he followed Anya as she strode along the harbour wall, her keen eyes scanning the rows of docked craft.

He had to admit there was a certain logic to her plan. If the airports, railway stations and ferry terminals were indeed on the lookout for him, it made sense to use a private boat to make their escape. Then again, the last time he'd been out on the open sea was a ferry trip to the Isle of Wight as a teenager, and he'd spent half the journey throwing his guts up.

Up ahead, Anya came to a halt, apparently having found what she was looking for. Straight away Alex's heart sank when he saw the object of her interest.

He'd been hoping for a high-powered luxury yacht to ferry him to safety. Instead he found himself looking down on an old, rusted and neglected fishing trawler, perhaps thirty-five feet in length, its deck cluttered with everything from old car tyres to spare planking and empty pots and pans. The paint on its high prow was peeling to such an extent that it was difficult to tell what colour the vessel had originally been.

The wheelhouse, resembling a squat garden shed, was positioned at the stern, with a large hatch in the centre of the deck leading down to what Alex presumed was the cargo hold.

'Wow, what a beast,' he remarked sarcastically. 'Yours?'

She glanced at him. 'Not exactly.'

With that, she leapt down from the quayside and landed nimbly on the deck, heading straight for the wheelhouse. The door was secured with nothing more sophisticated than a small padlock, which she made short work of with a few good strikes from the butt of the handgun.

'Jump down, Alex,' she called, beckoning him to join her. 'I need your help.'

Alex looked around. There were a few houses overlooking the harbour – mostly newer villas that had probably been sold at inflated prices on account on the sea views they commanded – but at such an early hour there were no obvious signs of activity. However, that didn't mean nobody was watching.

'The longer you stand there, the more suspicious you look,' Anya prompted, sensing his hesitation.

'Fuck it,' Alex sighed, resigning himself to the inevitable.

Waiting until the boat's rocking motion carried it as close to the harbour wall as possible, he took a deep breath and leapt down, landing harder than he'd intended on the unyielding deck. Ignoring the twinge of pain in his knees, he forced himself up and limped over to the wheelhouse.

The inside was little better than the deck area, the old-fashioned engine console cluttered with yellowed newspapers, tobacco tins, empty bottles, paintbrushes and a hundred other bits of assorted junk that Alex had no interest in examining further. The air smelled of damp and dust and wood varnish.

Beyond the grimy windows, the deck sloped upwards to what looked like a ridiculously high bow. There were no indicator lights on any of the machines, no power of any kind, for that matter. More than likely the vessel was semi-derelict, and would sit idle at its mooring until the hull planking finally gave way and it sank.

'The engine start switch is here,' Anya explained, pointing to simple red knob on the console. 'When I call out to you, turn it clockwise and hold it down for at least five seconds. Understand?'

'There must be a dozen boats here that are less likely to sink than this heap of shit,' he felt compelled to point out. 'If we really have to steal *something*, why not one of them?'

'Because this boat has not been used in a long time,' she explained, speaking with the long-suffering patience of a school teacher dealing with a dim student. 'It will be days or weeks before the owner reports it stolen. Now, be ready.'

Saying nothing further, she opened the hatch in the floor leading to what he assumed was the engine room, and clambered down. It was too dark for him to see what she was up to down there, but he heard several metallic clangs echoing from the depths.

'The hull is still sound, and there's some power left in the batteries,' she called out. 'Turn the switch!'

'Aye aye, captain,' he mumbled, turning the red knob.

Sure enough, an ancient starter motor turned over down below, sluggish and laboured at first but gradually gaining traction. The main engine coughed once, then twice, seemed to falter for a few moments, and then finally came to life with a rattling, gear-grating roar. It was rough and unrefined, and had no doubt seen far better days, but at least it sounded willing to go one more round.

Anya was back up in the wheelhouse within moments, her hands smeared with grease and dirt. Moving him aside, she took over at the wheel and quickly scanned the few gauges on the console, pushing a loose strand of blonde hair back from her face as she did so.

'There should be enough fuel to make it.' Satisfied that things were running as they should, she nodded to Alex. 'Go outside and cast off the mooring lines. Quickly.'

And so it was back outside into the fitful breeze and chill morning air as he hurried across the deck, struggling to untie the heavy lines that kept the trawler moored in place. It was no easy task. The ropes were swollen with moisture and encrusted with salt, and his hands were more accustomed to dancing across a keyboard than heavy manual work like this. Still, after a lot of grunting and swearing, the first line slipped free. The second came more easily, partly because it wasn't secured as tightly and partly because he was starting to get the hang of the awkward procedure.

As soon as the vessel was free, his companion wasted no time throttling up the engine. The old boat shuddered with increased power and grey smoke vented from the small funnel atop the wheelhouse, but sure enough they began to make headway through the choppy waters.

As the harbour walls slipped past and the prow swung out towards the main channel, a thoroughly chilled Alex hurried back into the wheelhouse and closed the door behind him, grateful to be out of the wind.

Anya was at the wheel, her eyes forward as she steered them through the harbour entrance into the open channel beyond. As she'd said, this was an open estuary of some kind, with the opposite shore visible about a mile distant; mostly trees and farmland interspersed with small coastal villages.

Ahead of them, a pair of massive road and railway bridges spanned the widening channel leading out to sea, and straight away Alex recognized the distinctive red cantilever structure of the Forth Rail Bridge. Now well over a century old, it was still the only rail link across the estuary, carrying commuters to and from the capital city, Edinburgh.

At least he knew where he was. The question now was where he was headed.

'So what's the plan, captain?' he asked, trying to ignore the queasy feeling in his stomach elicited by the trawler's pitching and rocking in the choppy waters.

'We head east, across the North Sea to Norway. A fishing trawler like this should not attract attention. After we make land, we find a car and get you to your friend as fast as possible.' She glanced at him, noticing for the first time that he was shivering. 'There should be a sleeping berth forward. Go and see if there are any spare clothes. And check for tinned food.'

Having not eaten since the previous evening, Alex would normally have been famished by now. However, food was the last thing on his mind at that moment, as another wave buffeted them. It was little more than a minor swell, yet for him the deck seemed to be pitching and rolling dangerously beneath his feet.

'You don't look well,' she said, observing his pale complexion. 'Are you all right?'

Not wishing to give her another reason to berate him, he waved her concern off. 'I'm fine. Don't worry about me.'

–

An hour later, Alex clung to the guard rail just aft of the wheelhouse, doubled over as his stomach constricted in another painful, violent heave. After ten minutes of near-constant vomiting, he could have sworn his stomach would be empty by now, but apparently not, as a thin stream of mucus and undigested food landed in the churning waters below.

Apparently sea sickness was something that didn't abate with age.

Another gust of wind whipped across the deck, chilling him and carrying salty spray that stung his eyes. He'd managed to find a ratty-looking woollen jumper and a waterproof jacket that was too big for him in the cramped accommodation area in the bow, and Anya had insisted he wear the lot.

Aside from keeping him warm, it would also make him at least look the part of a deck hand on casual inspection.

Not that he imagined there were many eyes on him at that moment. Since leaving the wide mouth of the Forth Estuary they had steered a course due east, the rolling fields and small coastal towns gradually fading into the hazy distance. Ahead lay nothing but sombre grey sea.

Spitting acrid-tasting phlegm into the churning waters below, he wiped his mouth and stumbled back into the wheelhouse. Being indoors made his seasickness worse, but at least it was relatively warm in there.

Anya was where he'd left her, having tied the wheel in place to maintain their heading, while she attacked the can of tinned peaches she'd been able to pilfer from the trawler's meagre galley down below.

She glanced up as he entered, her expression almost achieving sympathy. 'How are you feeling?'

'How do you think?' he retorted, leaning against the wall with a weary sigh. 'I suppose this kind of thing never troubles *you*.'

Saying nothing, she handed him a steaming mug of tea. Served in a dented and stained tin cup, and with no milk or sugar, it was about as unappealing a beverage as he could have wished for at that moment. He shook his head, waving it away.

'You need fluids,' she persisted. 'The sickness will dehydrate you.'

'I suppose a bottle of Carlsberg and a smoke is too much to ask for?' he asked, though he was unable to summon up the wry smile he'd hoped for.

'Cigarettes are bad for you.'

'Yeah? You know what else is bad for me? Waterboarding, and tasers, and fists. I've had plenty of *them* over the past couple of days. Where's your health warning about that?'

When Anya didn't respond, he reluctantly accepted the mug of tea and took a sip, more to appease her than out of a genuine desire to drink.

'I need to know a few things from you, Alex,' she said, setting the tin of fruit aside. 'Answer my questions honestly and everything will be fine.'

Alex glanced up from his mug of steaming brown liquid that more or less passed for tea. 'And if I don't?'

'I'll know,' she promised him. There was no need to say anything beyond that – her actions last night had demonstrated her ability to kill without remorse.

'Fair enough,' he conceded. 'Ask away.'

'How did you come to know Loki?'

'Through university,' he explained, taking another tentative sip. It settled on his stomach and stayed there, which he took to be a good sign. 'We were staying in the same halls of residence, got chatting over a few beers...' He shrugged. 'You know how it is.'

The look in her eyes suggested otherwise. Somehow he couldn't picture her as a free-spirited teenage student.

'What happened after that?' she prompted. 'You worked together, yes?'

He nodded slowly. 'We formed our own group called Valhalla. Myself, Arran and another guy called Gregar Landvik. We were the founders. Over time we attracted other people like us, and we started working together on bigger projects.'

'For what? Money?'

He shook his head. 'It wasn't like that. We were a white-hat group, at least to begin with.'

At this, her blonde brows drew together in a frown. 'White hat?'

For perhaps the first time, Alex felt as if he had her at a disadvantage. It felt strangely reassuring to know there were some areas in this world where his knowledge was superior.

'Good guys,' he explained. 'People who hack for the right reasons.'

This prompted a look of what might have been called amusement. 'There is a right reason to do such things?'

That was an interesting statement coming from someone who had killed at least two men in the past twenty-four hours, he thought. 'Look, people do this for all kinds of reasons – some good, some bad. Whatever your reason, there's a hat colour to describe it. White hats break into systems to show people their weaknesses. They help them protect themselves from real criminals. Blue hats are employed by companies to test the strength of their security. We actually dabbled in that for a while ourselves. Black hats are the ones out to cause serious damage, either for profit or just for shits and giggles. They're the ones who make the headlines, the ones who crash stock markets or leak government secrets.'

Anya nodded thoughtfully, mulling over everything she'd heard. However, she hadn't missed his earlier remark. 'You said you were a… "white-hat" group to begin with. What changed?'

Alex's face darkened. 'We had a disagreement – Arran, Gregar and I. Each of us wanted to take the group in a different direction. I wanted us to go legitimate, hire ourselves out to test system security for big companies. Gregar was always chasing the easy money. He wanted us to be like mercenaries, stealing secrets for cash.'

'And Arran?' she prompted.

Alex took another sip of tea. 'Well, there's another kind of hat. You don't see them very often, but there are hackers who think they're serving a higher purpose. Activists – exposing secrets, freeing the truth and all that. We call them grey hats. Arran wanted to go on some kind of crusade against the Big Bad. Dodgy companies, corrupt politicians, shadow governments. He believed we could make a real difference, expose all those dirty secrets to the world. And for a while he even made me believe it too.' He sighed, thinking about the disastrous hacking attempt that had proven to be a bridge too far for him. 'For a while.'

'What happened?' She seemed genuinely interested now, perhaps having found something in his tale that she could relate to.

'No,' he said at length. 'No. That's something I'd rather not go into.'

He looked at her, expecting her to press him on the matter. He wouldn't have blamed her. He supposed she could have forced him to tell her everything, could have threatened him or cajoled him into it. And yet, to his surprise, she seemed to accept his refusal, as if they were two normal people having a casual conversation.

'Tell me something,' he said, deciding to indulge his own curiosity. There was something about the chain of events leading up to their present situation that he still didn't understand. 'How the hell did you find Arran? Or did he find you?'

Anya looked at him for a long moment, saying nothing as the boat pitched and rocked around them.

'Come on, I've practically bared my soul to you,' Alex reminded her. 'Would it kill you to give me just a little back?'

Reaching up, the woman sighed and ran a hand through her short blonde hair, leaving a few locks sticking up. 'He was recommended to me by a senior officer in the Norwegian intelligence service,' she said at last. 'A man I've known for twenty years and trust completely. He assured me that Arran had been vetted by him personally.'

Alex frowned. This was starting to sound oddly familiar. 'What was his name?'

'Halvorsen,' she said, her tone guarded.

And just like that, the penny dropped. 'You mean *Kristian*? Kristian Halvorsen?'

Anya stared at him, her eyes reflecting her surprise. 'You know him.'

'Of course I know him.'

'How?'

'It was back when we tried our hands at being blue hats. Kristian was the CEO of some company based in Norway... paper merchants or some shit like that. He hired us to test the security of his corporate network.'

Even now he could recall the ease with which he had broken through the seemingly complex security system, and the shock on Halvorsen's face as he remarked that he would have to get his technical people to look into it.

'Kristian is not a paper merchant,' Anya assured him. 'He's a case officer.'

'You're having a laugh, right? I mean, he's about the most boring guy I've...' Alex trailed off, realizing at last the trap he'd fallen into. Kristian hadn't been testing the company security system that day; he'd been testing Alex and Arran, vetting them for future work. And Alex, in his arrogance, had fallen for it.

'Oh, shit,' he said quietly.

'He would not be a very good spy if he advertised his profession,' Anya observed. 'In any case, he recommended Loki to me nearly a year ago, said he was a skilled computer expert who could back me up with no questions asked. He was right in that respect. Loki has been useful and proven his worth to me, so he was my choice to break into the Agency's system.' She let out a faint sigh; a modest but telling expression of regret. 'Maybe I asked too much of him.'

'Do you think he's still alive?' Alex asked, not sure if he wanted to know the answer or not. 'I mean, they wouldn't just kill him without getting information from him, right?'

He saw a shadow pass over her then, and her eyes took on a faraway look. It was the look of one who had long ago learned harsh lessons that Alex could scarcely imagine.

'The Agency would have no problems doing both,' she said at length, then turned her eyes on him once more. The look in them was almost sympathetic. 'I wouldn't hold out much hope for your friend.'

Alex let out a breath and bowed his head, feeling like he'd just been punched in the guts. He'd always known that the chances of seeing Arran again were slim at best, but he'd clung onto the notion anyway, refusing to give up on his friend. To hear the harsh reality laid out in such stark and uncompromising terms was almost more than he could take.

'And what about me? Am I going to end up like him too?' Alex asked, deciding he might as well get all the bad news out of the way at once. 'No matter how this ends, I'll be a wanted man for the rest of my life. What the hell am I supposed to do?'

'Your situation won't improve until we find the information I need.'

'Really,' he said, picking up on her vague and evasive answer. 'What exactly is this "information" that's so important to you, anyway? Must be something pretty serious, considering the CIA are ready to kill anyone who even gets near it.'

At this, Anya merely shook her head. If it were possible, he could have sworn she looked uncomfortable. 'You're in enough danger already. It's better that you don't know any more.'

'What, you think I could be any deeper in the shit than I am already?' Alex scoffed, almost laughing with grim humour at her attempts to protect him. 'Arran and the rest of Valhalla 7 could be dead already because of this. My *life* might depend on this fucking thing. I at least have a right to know what it's all about.'

Whatever brief softening of her demeanour he'd experienced during their earlier conversation was well and truly gone. Now the walls were back up, the defences at the ready.

'You have a right to know what I tell you; nothing more,' she said, her tone dangerously cold. 'You are alive because I chose to spare your life. Your only task is to do what I tell you to do, so don't think for one moment that you can demand anything from me. Do we understand each other?'

Alex said nothing for several seconds, startled by the change that had come over her.

'We do,' he said at last.

The brief confrontation over, they lapsed into uncomfortable silence, each preoccupied with their own thoughts. Alex in particular was deeply unsettled by his companion. He might have understood her instructions, but the will behind them was a complete mystery to him.

Chapter 12

Olivia Mitchell groaned, her mind stirred from the depths of sleep by the harsh buzz of her cell phone. She blinked a few times, eyes adjusting to the weak daylight filtering in through the drawn curtains, then glanced at the alarm clock on her bedside table – 06:32.

'Christ,' she said, her voice husky and her throat dry. Having served more than a decade in the US Army before her posting here, she was no stranger to late shifts and early starts, but this was the first day off she'd had in nearly two weeks. She'd been hoping not to regain consciousness before 10 a.m.

Whoever was calling, however, had other ideas.

The phone carried on ringing and vibrating, moving an inch or so across the hard table surface with each surge. With her mind still fogged by sleep and the pounding ache of a hangover, she reached over and snatched it up.

'Yeah?' she mumbled, eyes still closed against the sunlight filtering in through the half-drawn curtains. She arched her back, feeling the vertebrae crack satisfyingly as they realigned themselves.

The voice that addressed her was male, focussed and uncharacteristically serious. Vincent Argento, a young but very ambitious officer with the CIA's Security Protective Service, whom Mitchell had been sent here to mentor. One old has-been whose career was on the slide grooming one of the Agency's next up-and-coming stars.

That wasn't exactly how they'd sold it to her, but that's what it amounted to. In any case, she hadn't been in much of a negotiating position when they'd offered her the job.

'Olivia, it's Vince,' he began. 'Don't hang up.'

'Give me a reason not to,' she replied sourly, dragging herself up to a sitting position and running a hand through her dishevelled hair. It felt tangled and greasy. 'Unless the president's been murdered or we've gone to war overnight, it's officially not my problem.'

She reached for the tab of Alka-Seltzer by her bed and dropped two tablets into a glass of water, watching as the effervescent solution went to work. The bottle of wine she'd polished off last night was still standing on the sideboard on the far side of the room, the sour aroma of fermented grapes drifting across to her.

'We've got a Tempest Red.'

Mitchell stopped, the hangover and the fizzing glass temporarily forgotten. Those two words were more than enough to get her attention.

Tempest Red was a coded message; one of many used by Agency personnel when talking on unsecured phone lines. *Tempest* was the code word for CIA field operatives, while in broad terms *red* meant 'murdered, killed or otherwise taken down'.

'Go on,' she prompted, sitting up a little straighter.

'One of our field teams was sent on a high-priority recovery op late last night,' Argento explained. 'They didn't report in as scheduled. You can guess the rest.'

Indeed she could. What she couldn't yet comprehend was how three highly trained field operatives could have been taken down, particularly in a friendly country like the UK. Was it some kind of Al-Qaeda hit, or even the IRA taking a pop at them? Whatever, she knew she wasn't going to get answers on an open line like this.

'Okay,' she acknowledged, reaching for the glass of Alka-Seltzer and forcing herself to swallow a mouthful. 'What do you need from me?'

'It pains me to say this, but we could use your help down here,' Argento admitted. 'We need everyone with field experience running the scene.'

All thoughts of sleep were forgotten – Mitchell's mind was firmly in work mode now, hangover notwithstanding. She might not have been part of the Langley club, but even she recognized how critical the deaths of Agency field operatives were.

'All right, I'm on my way.' She closed down the phone without waiting for Argento's response. She would get the location of the crime scene and other details from her superiors, who were almost certainly all over this by now.

'Rise and fucking shine, campers,' she mumbled, downing the remainder of the Alka-Seltzer and throwing the bed covers aside before making her way to her dormitory's cramped shower room.

As she stripped off and waited for the water to heat up, she surveyed her reflection in the mirror with a critical eye. Mitchell was a couple of years shy of forty, and although she was still in good shape as far as it went, a combination of late nights, early mornings and liberal doses of alcohol were taking their toll. Her eyes were outlined by dark rings of fatigue, her face drawn and pale, her mouth, eyes and forehead marked by faint worry lines that hadn't been there a few years ago.

On second thoughts, she reached out and turned the temperature control all the way to minimum. Taking a deep breath, she forced herself beneath the frigid jet of water, letting out a pained gasp as it stung her skin and chilled her all the way to the core. Still, it did the trick. Whatever remaining fog still lingered over her mind, it was well and truly gone now.

Murder before breakfast, she thought, as the water sluiced down around her. What a hell of a start to her day.

Chapter 13

In the end it took Mitchell nearly two hours to find the small, isolated farm compound where the three operatives had been killed. Despite having a top-of-the-line GPS stuck to her windshield, she had twice gotten lost on the winding no-name country roads, much to her frustration.

One thing she would never understand about the UK was the ridiculous road system, which seemed to have been dreamed up by some lunatic a thousand years earlier and had remained unchanged ever since. She supposed the rolling fields and hedges interspersed with small stretches of woodland must have made for pleasant Sunday driving, but it was a nightmare for anyone trying to get somewhere in a hurry.

Her mood wasn't helped by the pounding headache that still plagued her, though she did her best to push it aside as she pulled her car to a stop outside the barn that seemed to be the centre of activity.

Security teams had already established a discreet but airtight perimeter around the entire area, sealing off every road in or out, and posting operatives on vantage points overlooking the surrounding farmland. Nobody would get near this place without them knowing.

There were no British police or security forces present. They knew that an incident had occurred here last night, just as they knew about most Agency activities in the UK, but the parties usually operated on a 'don't ask, don't tell' principle. They didn't ask what went on in places like this, just as the US government didn't ask what the Brits did at similar sites in North America.

It was a mutually beneficial arrangement that neatly skirted the uncomfortable issue of both countries sanctioning the kidnapping and torture of their own citizens.

She had barely killed the engine when a young man in civilian clothes emerged from the barn and approached her car with the long, purposeful strides of someone used to having things happen his way. Vincent Argento, her junior comrade in the Agency's criminal investigation team, looked every inch the Italian-American poster boy. Tall, lean and good-looking, with jet black hair and olive-coloured skin, he walked with the confidence that only handsome young men in their prime seemed to possess.

'Christ, you stop for breakfast on the way?' he asked as Mitchell emerged blinking into the bright sunlight. In stark contrast to her dark mood the weather was annoyingly good – a rare enough thing in England.

Mitchell gave him a harsh look. 'Remarks like that won't get you in my good graces.' She glanced towards the barn, guessing the bodies were inside. 'Tell me what you've got.'

He led her towards the cavernous structure, giving her a brief overview as they walked. 'Three men – one in the truck, the other two on the ground nearby. All experienced operatives and all armed, killed at close range with the same bladed weapon, most likely a field knife. No sign of their killers, or the man they were sent to recover.'

Mitchell frowned. Anyone who could take out three armed Agency field operatives at close quarters was clearly not to be fucked with. A team working in close cooperation might have accomplished such a task, but why use knives? Knives were messy and unreliable – certainly not an efficient means of killing people.

Entering the darkened space within, they were just in time to watch one of the victims being loaded into a black plastic body bag. His throat had been cut to such an extent that the windpipe had been completely severed, leaving behind a yawning gap of torn and bloody flesh. Mitchell said nothing to this.

Argento glanced at her, guessing her thoughts. 'Not a pretty sight, huh?'

'Never is,' she remarked quietly, forcing her mind back into analytical mode. 'Tell me about their target.'

Argento handed her a small dossier that had been prepared on the subject. 'Alex Yates, twenty-eight years old. He's a sales assistant based in London.'

Mitchell surveyed the file briefly. The picture on the front cover, likely lifted from Yates's passport, depicted a distinctly average-looking young man in his mid twenties. Even features, scruffy light brown hair, pale complexion with a hint of stubble, and eyes that were somewhere between blue and grey in colour.

'Why's the Agency so interested in him?'

Argento flashed a brief smile. 'Young Alex there used to be quite the cyber hell-raiser. Ran a software security outfit by day while hacking secure networks by night. Then he got caught by the Brits trying to hack a government database, did a couple of years inside before being paroled. Seems he's back to his winning ways, because last night our cyber-crime unit detected him trying to hack into the Agency's network. Local police arrested him without much trouble, and we sent a field team to bring him in. We know they made it as far as the police station where he was being held, but after that, they went dark.' He gestured around them. 'You can guess the rest.'

'This one was off the books,' Mitchell surmised, thinking about the long winding roads that had brought her here. The nearest village had to be a good two or three miles distant. 'They didn't want any tape recorders or witnesses.'

Argento arched a dark brow. 'That's against protocol.'

'Depends whose protocol they were following.'

In reality this kind of thing went on more often than anyone was willing to admit. Mitchell herself had taken part in more than a few 'field interrogations' as an Army CID officer, either due to time constraints or because the subject matter was sensitive enough to warrant it. If these three men had brought Yates here to interrogate him as some kind of black operation, she was willing to bet they had done it on some higher authority.

Argento said nothing to that, and Mitchell didn't follow it up. Such things were mere supposition at this stage; what she needed were hard facts and an understanding of what exactly had happened out here.

'So they bring Yates out here and strap him to a chair so they can start their interrogation,' she said, indicating the wooden chair standing in the centre of the concrete expanse, which she was quite certain hadn't been placed there by chance. 'Before they can finish, they're hit by an unknown number of assailants who take out all three men, free Yates and evac him.'

The younger man nodded. 'That fits with what we've found. Their trail leads outside, cuts through a small wood to a dirt track about half a mile from here. Seems they had a car waiting.'

'Any idea of the make and model?'

'Hard to tell, but the wheel spacing's too small to be an SUV. Probably a hatchback of some kind. Tyre marks suggest a front-wheel drive.'

Mitchell pursed her lips, considering what he'd said. Such a vehicle was hardly ideal for the bumpy, uneven roads in this part of the world. Then again, a knife was far from a perfect weapon to take down three armed men either.

'I want to see the bodies.'

With Argento close behind, Mitchell made her way over to the line of body bags, helped herself to a pair of surgical gloves from a box placed there by the forensics teams, then unzipped the first bag and bent close to examine the occupant. The sight of blood and death didn't frighten her; she'd seen more than enough of both in her life to have become numbed to it. The only thing that concerned her was the manner of death.

There were three stab wounds that she could identify. The first two were in the upper abdomen, angled upwards to pierce the lungs without the danger of fouling the blade between two ribs. Either stab wound would probably have proven fatal as air from the torn lung filled the chest cavity, slowly suffocating the victim.

However, it was the third wound that had dealt the finishing blow. On the left side, just below the armpit. A single deep thrust, angled perfectly to slide between two ribs and straight into the heart, probably severing both the left and right ventricles and causing catastrophic damage to the cluster of vital arteries near the top.

This was no frenzied knife attack by a desperate killer, but a series of precise, almost surgical strikes calculated to cause maximum damage with the fewest number of thrusts. Not many people were that handy with a blade.

'I can't understand the MO here,' Argento went on. 'The killings themselves look like the work of a serial killer – all up-close and bloody – but an extraction like this had to be done by a pro. It's like they're trying to misdirect us.'

Mitchell wasn't so sure. Most killings were a matter of necessity rather than desire, and somehow she couldn't imagine a serial killer choosing to target a group of armed men. No, there was a more fundamental explanation for this.

'Or they were forced to improvise,' she suggested, the disparate pieces of information slowly coalescing into a more rational chain of events in her mind. 'When Yates was lifted, they tracked him out here in whatever vehicle they had available, and took down the Agency field team protecting him. They used a knife because they didn't have time to get their hands on a better weapon. Then they high-tailed it out of here in the same car.'

'If they did all this as a scratch operation, I'd hate to think what they could do if they were properly prepared,' Argento mused.

Mitchell preferred not to dwell too long on that.

'I want to take a look at the tracks,' she decided instead.

Pausing only a moment, Argento led her outside.

It wasn't hard to pick up the trail, especially for Mitchell. She'd done her share of tracking in the military, and one set of prints in particular was easy to pick out.

'Nike trainers,' she said, indicating the distinctive brand symbol that had been imprinted into the soft ground at regular intervals. The steps were awkward, the trail winding, and in one or two places she noticed a disturbance in the undergrowth where someone had blundered right through it. 'That'll be Yates.'

'You noticed, huh?' Argento remarked with a smirk.

'Even *you* could follow these tracks,' she countered without looking up.

The other trail however couldn't have been more different.

'His friend's a whole other story. They had a real serious ghost-walk going on,' Mitchell carried on, creeping forward with her eyes firmly fixed on the ground.

In her mind she could already imagine Yates stumbling through the darkened woods, trying to keep up with a far more confident and capable accomplice.

'Weight distributed to the outside of the feet, even pressure with each footfall, minimal ground disturbance...' She paused a moment, struck by a sudden realisation. 'Whoever she is, I bet she's had military training.'

Argento glanced at her. He hadn't missed the gender she had assigned to Yates's mysterious rescuer. 'And you know it's a woman, how?'

'Because I know what to look for. Shorter stride length, smaller boot size, lower weight.' She nodded to herself, her conviction growing by the second. 'Our killer is a woman.'

Chapter 14

Darkness had fallen by the time Alex and Anya sighted the faint lights of land in the distance. Aside from several more bouts of nausea on Alex's part, the voyage across the North Sea had been largely uneventful, their only sighting of another vessel being the gas flare of an oil rig on the northern horizon.

They continued on for another ten minutes or so before Anya finally killed the engines and allowed the vessel to drift to a halt. A small fishing trawler like this was unlikely to attract much attention, but even so, she was unwilling to risk a closer approach.

'So what now?' Alex asked, surprised by how quiet it was without the constant rumble of the engines down below. All he could hear was the lapping of the waves against the hull, and the occasional creak and groan as the vessel's timbers flexed with the movement.

'Wait here,' Anya instructed, clambering down the hatch to the vessel's lower deck.

It was several minutes before she returned, during which Alex began to perceive a gradual change in the trawler's motion. It wasn't easy to pin down at first, but he was left with the impression that the vessel wasn't riding the swell in quite the same way as it had earlier.

He glanced down as Anya emerged from the bowels of the small ship, then pointed to a large plastic container fixed to the deck outside. 'I'll need your help with that,' she explained calmly. 'I don't want it to be caught in the rigging as we go down.'

Alex blinked, taken aback by her remark. 'Wait. What?'

The woman let out a faint breath; a small but noticeable show of impatience. 'The boat is sinking, Alex. I just opened the water intakes. There's nowhere to dock around here, and it will attract too much attention if we beach it. We'll paddle ashore in the life raft. Now, come on.'

Without waiting for an answer, she opened the door and strode out onto the deck. Alex followed a few moments later, pulling his oversized coat a little tighter against the chill night air. The deck was listing noticeably beneath his feet now.

Opening the container fixed to the deck, Anya hauled out a bulky inflatable life raft. Alex moved forward to help, and together they carried it over to the vessel's starboard side. It was surprisingly heavy, requiring both of them to manhandle it over the gunwale.

Grasping the inflation toggle, she gave him a single nod, indicating that he should let go. As the survival raft tumbled into the water, there was a loud hiss as the compressed gas cylinder inside went to work, causing the roughly octagonal lifeboat to unfold and inflate in a matter of seconds. Much to Alex's relief, there were no obvious defects; it appeared the raft was in far better condition than its parent vessel.

A long, painful groan from the trawler's wooden frame reminded him it was sinking beneath them, the heavy engines and fuel tanks causing the bow to slowly rise up as the stern settled lower in the water.

'You first,' Anya said, holding a single line to keep the raft from floating away.

Gingerly Alex clambered over the gunwale and looked down, very much aware of the dark undulating waters all around. He could swim to a reasonable standard, but in freezing water and burdened with a heavy sweater and overcoat that would inevitably pull him down, he didn't fancy his chances if he missed the raft.

In any case, he was spared the difficulty of having to make the leap over the side, as a single hard push between his shoulder blades sent him tumbling through the air. He let out a startled cry as he fell, convinced he was about to land in the sea. Fortunately for him, the trawler's gradually sinking stern had reduced its height above sea level to mere feet. Landing more or less in the centre of the life raft, he bounced once on the flexible surface before coming to rest.

He looked up, about to voice his anger at Anya's decision to push him over the side, only to see the woman leap down beside him. She landed with graceful ease, twisted around before she'd even come to a stop, and unfixed a collapsible paddle from the side of the raft.

'You could have warned me,' Alex remarked with sour grace.

'Yes. I could have,' she acknowledged. 'Now help me paddle. We don't want to be dragged down with the trawler.'

Already water was sluicing in through the stern deck scuppers, forcing the bow higher into the air. The complex masts and rigging overhead could easily come down on them as the vessel sank, dragging them down with it. Seizing a spare paddle, Alex attacked the water below in an effort to propel them away. Their efforts were oddly unbalanced, with Alex creating more spray than momentum, but after a minute or so they had put enough distance between themselves and the stricken vessel to halt for a moment and watch it sink.

There was nothing very dramatic about it; no great crashing of gear coming loose inside, no frothing sea or cracking timbers. The stern dipped below the surface, water rushing in through the open hatch to the engine room below, and the trawler quietly slipped away, heeling over to starboard as it vanished beneath the waves.

And just like that, they were alone. Two people in a rubber life raft, with hundreds of miles of open sea behind them and the darkened coast of Norway an unknown distance ahead. As a chill breeze sighed in from the north, Alex caught himself hoping it wasn't too far. He was tired after paddling just fifty yards from the sinking trawler.

'There's a swell building up,' Anya said, gauging the raft's movements. 'We should get ashore before it gets any worse.'

Alex wasn't about to argue. Seizing his paddle again, he was about to resume his efforts when a thought suddenly crossed his mind. Despite everything, despite the ordeal he'd been through and the unknown dangers that lay ahead, he couldn't help but chuckle in amusement.

'You know, I might be up shit creek,' he said, then held up his paddle. 'But at least I've got a paddle this time.'

His remark was met with stony silence.

'You don't go in for humour much, do you?'

Somehow he couldn't imagine her stretched out on the couch with a tub of ice cream and Comedy Central on the TV. Then again it was hard to imagine what, if anything, a woman like Anya did when she wasn't stealing top secret files, killing people and commandeering fishing trawlers.

Without looking at him, she dipped her paddle in the water and began pulling with slow, deliberate strokes. 'I suppose it depends on what you consider humour.'

There wasn't much Alex could say to that. Together the two of them resumed their advance towards the shore. It was slow going; the raft was designed with stability rather than speed in mind, and their efforts weren't helped by Alex's lack of experience. Still, even he seemed to get the hang of it after a while, encouraged by a few terse words of advice from Anya, and before too long he spotted a rocky coastline up ahead.

Their paddling, plus the incoming tide, carried them into a relatively sheltered bay between two spurs of tree-covered land. Alex's arms were aching when at last he felt the raft grate against solid ground.

Gratefully throwing down his paddle, he clambered over the edge and onto a narrow pebble-covered beach. Up ahead, thick stands of spruce and pine trees crowded close to the shore, their thick coverage blocking out the night sky above.

A loud hissing and bubbling sound from the waterline told him that Anya had put her knife to work on the life raft, slashing its rubber hull and allowing it to sink from view. A few heavy stones laid on top were enough to finish the job.

Alex however cared little as he let out a relieved breath and sank to his knees, exhausted, seasick and thoroughly grateful to be back on dry land. He felt as if he could curl up right there on that beach and happily fall asleep.

'Get up,' Anya said, tapping his shoulder none too gently. 'We have to move inland. If I'm right, the nearest town should be about twelve miles from here.'

Alex glared at her. 'For fuck sake, don't you ever stop?'

'The people hunting you won't. We can't afford to either. Now get up.'

Alex closed his eyes and forced calm into his mind, reminding himself that he owed his life to this woman. Still, that didn't stop him from wanting to punch her lights out at that moment.

Without a word, he struggled to his feet and began a weary trudge up the beach.

Chapter 15

With darkness falling, work at the farm crime-scene was winding down. Mitchell was busy typing out her initial report when the sound of a car pulling to a halt outside drew her thoughts back to the present. Turning towards the barn entrance, she saw a man climb out of a black BMW and head straight towards them.

One look at him was enough to tell he was a serious customer. Early forties, muscular build, short dark hair and with the kind of tanned, chiselled, weather-beaten face of a man used to spending time outdoors.

He was dressed in a dark business suit with an open shirt collar – the kind of outfit that was endemic back at Langley – but the veneer of corporate formality did little to disguise his dominant, almost aggressive posture as he approached. A field operative to be sure, possibly from a military background judging by his faint but noticeable swagger. Nobody swaggered quite like a soldier, as she had long ago learned.

The question was, what was he doing here?

'Who's the officer in charge here?' he asked, forgoing any kind of greeting.

'That would be me,' Mitchell replied, meeting his piercing gaze evenly. Any show of weakness or hesitation at a critical moment like this would put her at an immediate disadvantage. 'Olivia Mitchell, Security Protection Service. And you are?'

'The name's Hawkins,' he replied. 'Don't take this the wrong way, Mitchell, but it seems like I'm your replacement.'

He handed over a single folded sheet of paper, which Mitchell was quick to read. Sure enough, it was a set of orders direct from Langley, informing her in no uncertain terms that Case Officer Jason Hawkins was taking over the investigation, effective immediately. Full cooperation was to be extended to him at all times and, bizarrely, there was a caveat stating that no official records of the investigation were to be submitted without his express consent.

'Well, you've got my attention,' she conceded. Faced with such a jurisdictional sledgehammer, there was little else that Mitchell could say.

'Good. Now I need your cooperation.'

'I'm listening,' she prompted.

'First up, I need everything you have on this crime scene. Every piece of evidence, every photograph, fingerprint dusting, forensics report and observation. I read the initial reports on the flight over, but every detail counts. Second, everything that happens with this investigation comes through me first. Every report, email and phone call. That applies to you and the rest of your team. Clear?'

Mitchell folded her arms, not sure whether to feel impressed or intimidated by his curt, no-nonsense demeanour. One thing was for sure; the man didn't fuck around.

'You've made it that way.'

A flicker of a smile showed on Hawkins's lean, weathered face. 'You're pissed at me, right, Mitchell?'

Mitchell blinked, taken aback by his candour. 'I didn't say that.'

'You didn't have to,' he assured her. 'Hell, I'd be pissed if some asshole from Langley waltzed in acting like he owned the place and took over my investigation without a word of explanation.'

'You're very honest about yourself.' She didn't dispute his assertion.

He shrugged, knowing it wasn't entirely meant as a compliment. 'Let me tell you something. I flew three and a half thousand miles in the middle of the night to be here, because I'm one of those people the Agency keeps on standby just for situations like this. You don't hear about guys like me most of the time because it's our job not to be heard about. It's our job not to be seen or talked about. We fix problems and we do it quickly and quietly because that's what we're paid to do, and believe me, right now we've got a real big problem that needs fixing. What I'm asking from you right now is to be straight with me, and to trust that what I'm doing is in the best interests of all of us. You do that and I'll be straight with you. Fair enough?'

It was tough to argue with that assessment. 'Fair enough.'

He nodded. 'Good. Now, I'd be obliged if you'd gather your team together. I've got a few things I'd like to show them.'

'You said you were here to solve problems,' she remarked. 'What exactly are we up against?'

Hawkins looked at her for a long moment. 'Someone that'll make you glad I'm around.'

Mitchell wasn't entirely sure there was anyone who could make her glad to have this guy around. Still, she decided to keep such thoughts to herself for now. If Hawkins knew something that could aid their investigation, she had little choice but to play along.

It took less than a minute to call together the small field team charged with policing the site, half a dozen men and women congregated around the rough wooden table in the centre of the barn.

'Okay, listen up,' Hawkins began, wasting no time on pleasantries. 'First up, my name's Hawkins and I'm taking over this investigation, effective immediately. Agent Mitchell will brief you more fully on this, but for now consider this your heads-up. Second, this is no longer a murder investigation. The details of this crime scene are locked down, on my authority. What we're looking at here is a manhunt, plain and simple.'

Mitchell frowned, far from happy at the sudden change in emphasis. Much as she wanted to see those responsible for the deaths of three field agents answer for what they'd done, Hawkins made it sound like they were to be hunted down and executed like wild animals.

She caught Argento's eye, sensed he was harbouring similar thoughts and that no comment was necessary. They would talk privately once the briefing was over.

'We have two targets for this op.' First, Hawkins laid a printed photograph of Alex Yates on the table before him. 'The first is this man – Alex Yates. You already know as much about him as I do at this point, which isn't a whole lot. He's a civilian with no known training in escape and evasion, so he should be considered a soft target. However, he may still have information that's valuable to us, so his arrest and recovery is high priority.'

He paused, as if momentarily undecided about what to say next. Mitchell could tell that he was weighing something up in his mind, perhaps judging how much to reveal to them. And then, just like that, he laid a second photo next to the one of Yates.

Curious, Mitchell leaned in closer to get a better look.

The image was clearly some kind of official ID photo; a head-and-shoulders mug-shot of the subject looking straight at the camera. In this case, it depicted a woman, probably in her mid-thirties, with short blonde hair, tanned skin and the kind of definite, finely chiselled features that came from living a life that was both active and difficult.

There was a vaguely foreign look in the shape and arrangement of the face, perhaps suggesting Scandinavian heritage. Wherever she was from, even Mitchell could tell that she was an attractive woman, with the kind of natural beauty that needed no make-up to enhance.

But it was the eyes that really caught her attention. Cold and blue, there was a piercing intensity to them that was obvious even in a photograph. It was the kind of look that Mitchell had seen before in the eyes of soldiers returning from the frontline; soldiers who had seen things that no human being ever should. With a chill of recognition, she realized it was the same look she'd seen in the man now delivering the briefing.

'We have strong reason to believe that our second target is this woman. Her identity is classified, but she travels under any one of a dozen aliases that we know of, plus God knows how many we don't.' Glancing up from the photo, he surveyed each of the field operatives gathered around the table. 'I cannot emphasize enough how dangerous this woman is. She's highly trained, highly motivated and absolutely without anything approaching mercy or compassion. She's wanted for a string of attacks against US citizens, both military and government, and we believe she may be using Yates to help plan another strike. It is imperative that we take her down before she has a chance to reach this goal.'

'Excuse me, sir,' Argento piped up. 'You're saying one woman did all this? Killed three armed field operatives with just a knife?'

'It's what she was trained to do.'

'Trained by whom?' Mitchell asked, though she had a feeling she knew the answer.

'By us, of course,' he replied, staring right at her. 'She used to be an Agency operative. The kind we sent in to... solve problems.' His choice of words wasn't lost on her. 'And believe me, she was very good at what she did. Maybe a little too good. The thing is, it takes a certain kind of person to do work like that.'

'You mean psychopathic killers,' Argento interrupted.

'That's not quite how I'd put it.' Hawkins's voice was calm and even, but the look in his eyes told a different story. 'But whatever issues she had, the job brought out the worst in her. She became paranoid, delusional, violent... Then five years ago she snapped, killed most of the men in her unit and disappeared. We've been hunting her ever since.'

'You've been after her for five years?' Mitchell asked, amazed that one person could evade the formidable resources of the gency for so long.

'She's been trained to blend in and disappear, plus she knows how we operate. She knows the Agency's weaknesses and how to exploit them,' Hawkins explained, glancing down at the photo again. 'Fortunately for us, the door swings both ways. We created her, and with your help we're going to destroy her. She took a hell of a risk coming here to recover Yates, which means he's something she can't afford to lose. He's the key to bringing her down.'

Argento looked dubious. 'Great. So how do we find him?'

'By thinking as she does.' Hawkins folded his muscular arms. 'This country has the highest number of CCTV cameras per head of population in the Western world, so you can bet she doesn't come here too often. If it were me, I'd want to get the fuck out of Dodge as quickly as possible, which means she'll try to get Yates out of the country.'

The nature of the UK as an island with no land borders made their task a little easier in this regard. It wasn't as if she and Yates could simply cut a hole in some fence and disappear.

'Yates's passport has been red flagged,' Argento pointed out. 'All airports, rail links and ferry terminals have been sent copies of his picture. If he tries to leave the UK, we'll know about it.'

Mitchell shook her head, saying nothing. If this woman was as smart and resourceful as Hawkins seemed to believe, she would never attempt anything so obvious.

'There are other ways out,' Hawkins remarked.

'Private aircraft?' another man suggested. 'There are plenty of small strips around here. A Cessna could make it across the Channel easily enough.'

At this, Hawkins shook his head. 'Too easy to track. Any plane that takes off in UK airspace would be followed by radar. No matter where it landed, someone would be waiting for it.'

If air and land weren't possible, that left only one viable escape route in Mitchell's mind. 'So they took a boat,' she concluded. 'Something sturdy enough to get them across the Channel, but small enough to escape detection.'

A look of grudging respect showed on Hawkins's face. 'Not bad. Check in with the coastguard, look for any reports of missing boats in the last twenty-four hours. Get on it.'

One of the field agents was already reaching for his cell phone.

'Everyone else, pack it up here,' Hawkins went on. 'If we get the call, we'll need to move quickly.'

As the rest of the field team began packing away their gear, Argento moved a little closer to Mitchell. 'You believe that bullshit he just served up?' he asked, nodding towards Hawkins.

The man was already on his phone, making sure he was out of earshot of the others. Mitchell was willing to bet he was reporting in to his mysterious sponsor.

'I don't know,' she admitted. A lot of things about this operation left a sour taste in her mouth, but like the rest of them she was under orders to cooperate to the fullest extent. 'Whether he's telling the truth or not, he knows a whole lot more than he's saying.'

'No shit.' He sighed and shook his head. 'Black operations, secret interrogations, murders, rogue agents... Sorry about the cliché, but I've got a fucking bad feeling about all this.'

Mitchell said nothing to that, preferring to keep her thoughts to herself for now. However, that didn't mean she disagreed with her colleague's assessment.

'You know, I could run our mystery woman's picture through the facial-recognition database,' Argento suggested. 'Might turn up a lead.'

Mitchell shook her head. Though their clearance as special investigators within the Agency theoretically gave them access to its entire personnel roster, both were savvy enough to know that there were levels of clearance over and above whatever they might have been granted. In any case, such searches were always logged within the system, and the last thing they needed was such clandestine activity making its way back to Hawkins.

'Leave it for now,' she said quietly. 'Let's wait until we know more.'

'Fair enough.' He gave her a sidelong glance. 'Bet you wish you'd stayed in bed today, huh?'

Mitchell gave him a look that was enough to wipe the wry smile from his lips. 'You have no idea.'

Chapter 16

If Alex had been tired when he trudged up the beach away from the shore-line, an hour later he was dying on his feet, as he struggled to follow Anya through the dense pine and spruce forest that blanketed the area inland.

As always, the woman moved with the speed and grace of a natural predator stalking its prey, making no allowances for the fact that her companion was neither physically fit nor experienced at travelling through woodland at night. She would entertain no thought of stopping or resting, and as a result whatever reserves of strength that remained to Alex were rapidly dwindling. It was all he could do just to keep up with her.

They were traversing a steep ridge that ran in a generally north-west direction. Below, perhaps fifty yards downhill on their left, lay a narrow paved road that paralleled their course. They had stumbled upon it shortly after leaving the beach, and despite Alex's protests that they would make much quicker progress on tarmac than cluttered woodland, Anya had walked right across and into the steep wooded slopes beyond.

The only time she had ventured close to the road again had been to study a sign, confirming they were roughly where she expected to be.

'Do you *ever* get tired?' Alex asked, sweating and out of breath, and more than a little irked by her seemingly limitless reserves of fitness. She was at least ten years his senior, yet he felt like an old man at that moment.

If she'd sensed that he was hinting to slow down, she gave no sign of it. 'Endurance was part of my training. So was learning to stay quiet.'

It was his turn to ignore the hint. 'So what are you? Some kind of super soldier?'

He heard a faint snort of amusement. 'Not exactly.'

'Come on,' he persisted. 'You know my life story by now, but I know sweet FA about you.'

'There isn't much to tell.'

'Well, that's bollocks for a start,' Alex countered. 'You do things with a knife that make Rambo look like a pacifist, you hire people to steal top-secret files from the CIA, and you seem to know everything there is to know about staying alive when the whole world wants you dead. I'm guessing this sort of thing isn't a weekend hobby for you. So how did you get caught up in all of this?'

'Do you always talk so much, Alex?' she asked tersely.

'I don't know. Are you always so evasive, *Anya*?' he fired back.

He heard a faint sigh of exasperation. 'The less you know about me, the better.'

'For who?'

'For both of us. If you're captured again, it will only make things worse for you.'

Alex sighed and looked up at the sky. Through the dense canopy overhead, he was able to make out a faint speckling of stars. 'That's really comforting, thanks.'

Suddenly Anya stopped in her tracks, her head cocked to one side as she listened intently. 'Down!' she hissed.

Alex dropped to the damp, cold ground beside her. He too strained to listen, but could detect nothing out of the ordinary. Just the creaking and groaning of the spruce trees swaying in the night breeze, and the faint roar of a river down the slope to his right.

Moments later, though, a pair of headlight beams cruised by on the road below, the low hum of a vehicle engine carrying towards them. Anya kept her eyes on it the whole time, her hand on the automatic inside her jacket as she watched for any sign that it was anything other than a random civilian on his way home after a late night.

To her relief, the car carried on its way, neither stopping nor slowing, and her grip on the weapon relaxed.

Alex too was watching the car, though from an entirely different perspective. Crouched on the forest floor with cold and damp seeping into his legs, his mind was tormented by thoughts of comfortable leather seats, heaters turned up to maximum and perhaps even thermos mugs of coffee.

'Remind me again why we don't just flag down a lift?' he asked as Anya rose to her feet and resumed her march. 'Is this some kind of punishment, like you're still pissed off with me because I messed things up?'

'I have no interest in making you suffer,' she assured him without turning around. 'And to answer your question, this is not a tourist area – two foreigners trying to hitchhike in the middle of the night will attract attention. And attention is the one thing we don't want.'

'So what are we supposed to do? Keep walking until we reach the fucking North Pole?'

'If I'm right, the town of Egersund is only three or four miles from here,' she explained with terse patience. 'We'll wait until dawn, then I will go into town and try to find us a car. Things will be easier after that.'

'For you, maybe,' he complained with bitter resentment. 'I'll be freezing my arse off in some godforsaken forest while you're scoffing down eggs and bacon.'

Stopping abruptly, she whirled around and took a step towards him. Instinctively he backed off a pace, alarmed by her sudden change in demeanour. 'You whine like a mule, Alex,' she said with cold, repressed anger. 'If walking through the woods at night is the hardest thing you've had to do in your life, you should be very grateful for that. Now shut up and follow me.'

As she turned away and resumed her walk, he stomped right past her, determined to take the lead. It was nothing more than petty resentment driving him on now, but he didn't care. He was frustrated, as much with himself as with her, and it was blinding him to everything else.

'I said follow, not run away,' he heard her warning. 'The ground is uneven here.'

'Fuck off!' Alex fired back over his shoulder, beyond caring now. 'You're right – I haven't lived your life. I sell TVs for a living. I don't murder people or jump between buildings or do any of that spy-game bullshit. I'm not like you. I'm normal! And you know what? That's a good thing. Anything's better than being... like *you*.'

What happened next was as sudden as it was inevitable. Ducking down to avoid an overhanging branch, he failed to notice the patch of rocky scree ahead, didn't veer left to avoid it like he should have done. Only when his foot slid out from under him did he snap back to awareness, but by then it was too late.

Caught off balance, he slipped, pitched sideways and tumbled down the steep slope with a startled cry. There was nothing he could do to control his descent. Sharp rocks and barbed bushes tore at his clothes, while heavy impacts hammered his body with bruising force.

Then suddenly the gnarled, twisted trunk of a pine tree rushed up to meet him. Alex let out a scream of pain as he hit hard, the collision feeling as if it had crushed his ribcage.

Winded and stunned by the impact, he could only flail desperately at the trunk as he slid backward and tumbled down the last section of slope. Then something strange happened. The muddy, rock-strewn ground beneath him vanished, replaced by nothing at all. He was weightless, as if suspended in mid-air, his sense of orientation replaced by an odd feeling of confusion.

It lasted only a second or so, before he tumbled right into the fast-flowing river at the base of the slope.

The freezing water closed about his head in an instant of foam and confusion. All at once a million tiny pinpricks of ice drove themselves into every inch of his body, the sudden shock and agony of it unbearable.

Instinctively his body recoiled against it, he opened his mouth to scream in pain and alarm, and instead inhaled a lungful of river water. Fighting with the wild strength of a dying man, he clawed his way upward and broke the surface, coughing and spluttering and trying desperately to draw air into his lungs.

He went under again before he could get much air down. The flow of the current seemed to be rolling and spinning him around, turning him head over heels so that he was no longer even certain which way was up.

When he eventually broke the surface again, he was feeling light-headed and dizzy. His limbs felt like lumps of lead and he was rapidly losing the feeling in his extremities, but in some part of his mind he realized he had to get to the shore. The river's current was carrying him downstream, but it was also trying to pull him out into the main channel. If that happened, he knew that he'd quickly succumb to hypothermia.

He looked around, trying to get his bearings in the darkness. The left bank of the river which he'd just tumbled down was too steep for him to climb. It seemed as if the watercourse was hemmed in by the ridge above, and had carved a deep channel against the stubborn landmass barring its path. That was probably why he'd fallen in, instead of coming to rest at the foot of the ridge.

The grade on the other bank however looked much easier, with the rocky shore giving way to grass and low bushes stretching for some distance, probably part of an ancient flood plain. If he was to get out, it would have to be that way.

Summoning up what strength remained to him, he began to kick for the shore. The river was resisting him, and no matter how hard he kicked, it seemed to make little difference. Still, gradually the shore began to creep closer, even as his stamina began to fail him. He was so cold. If only he could rest for a moment…

No! He had to keep going. He wouldn't give up without a fight; not now.

Kicking with renewed effort, he clawed his way towards the shore with the last of his strength, every precious effort bringing him inches closer to his goal. And after what seemed like an eternity, he finally felt solid ground under his feet.

Half-frozen and exhausted by his effort, he crawled up the small rocky beach until he was clear of the water, then collapsed face-down on the ground. Instinctively he curled into a ball, trying to generate a little warmth that would help revive him.

It was a bad move. The effort of kicking and swimming, as draining as it had been on his stamina, had also kept his core body temperature up. Now that he'd stopped moving, the creeping cold began to seep in.

He knew he had to get up, knew that if he stayed here he'd go down with hypothermia in mere minutes. With great effort, he managed to rise to his knees, then get one foot under him and force himself to stand.

He wasn't thinking clearly as he stumbled through the long grass and tangled bushes away from the river, heedless of the branches and thorns that tore at his clothes. He barely felt it now.

He couldn't see much. There was only a thin sliver of moon overhead to light the way, and his vision seemed to be growing dim as if his eyes were giving up.

In the back of his clouded mind he was aware of something. A sound. A voice, faint and indistinct. Yet it was familiar somehow. He felt like it was calling out his name.

Then a sudden thought leapt into his head. Anya! Where was she? Was she looking for him, trying to help him, or had she just carried on her way and dismissed him as more trouble than he was worth?

With some effort, he drew a deep breath that made his bruised ribs ache. 'Anya!' he yelled out, hearing his own voice echo back to him from the steep slope nearby. 'Anya! I'm down here...'

His foot caught on something unseen and he landed in a bruised, exhausted heap, too weary to rise again, too weary to feel the pain in his chest. His last conscious act was to roll over onto his back, finding himself confronted with the vast darkened sky overhead. There were stars up there, millions of tiny points of light shimmering cold and hard in the darkness, and somehow it gave him comfort to know he was going to die with such a view laid out before him.

He should have been afraid, knowing that this could very well be his last sight. But he wasn't. He felt strangely light and free, as if none of it really mattered. His last thought as his vision blurred and his consciousness began to fade was that, on the whole, he was disappointed with how his life had panned out. Most of all he was disappointed in himself.

Then his eyes fell shut and he knew no more.

Chapter 17

'We've got something!' Argento said, striding into the centre of the barn with his cell phone in hand. 'Scottish police just reported a fishing trawler stolen from its mooring this morning.'

Hawkins, in the midst of a cup of coffee, was on it in an instant. 'Where?'

'A small village on the east coast, near Edinburgh. And get this – they found a rental car abandoned nearby. A late model Ford Focus.'

Mitchell too was quick to see the importance of the discovery. 'Have they run a trace on the rental company?'

'Way ahead of you.' Grinning, Argento held up his phone. Displayed across the screen was a scanned image of the driver's license used to hire out the Focus. The driver in question was the spitting image of the woman Hawkins had shown them.

Abandoning his coffee, Hawkins rose to his feet. 'If she hauled ass four hundred miles north, I'll bet she wasn't planning on a cross-Channel trip. Anyway, there aren't many places she could put ashore in France without being seen.'

Argento could see his reasoning. 'So that leaves Denmark, Germany or—'

'Norway,' Mitchell finished for him. She had to admit, the idea wasn't entirely without merit. With a large coastal area and low population density, and an easy trip across the North Sea, Norway was a logical place to retreat to.

Hawkins jabbed a finger at Argento. 'Contact Langley and have them plot the shortest route from Edinburgh to the Norwegian mainland, then concentrate all available surveillance assets on that area – satellite, drones, whatever. Look for any vessel matching the one stolen in Scotland. And tell them to have an aircraft standing by for us at Menwith Hill. Everyone else, get ready to move! We're heading north.'

As the rest of the field team loaded their remaining gear into the vehicles on standby, Mitchell approached the officer who had so abruptly assumed command of the operation. Hawkins was about to make a call on his cell phone, no doubt to report in on his findings, but paused for a moment to regard her.

'Something I can help you with, Mitchell?'

'I'd like a word.' Her voice was calm enough, but the look in her eyes was quite different. 'Now.'

'You're in my good graces right now,' he said, though it sounded like more of a threat than a compliment. 'Be a shame to ruin that.'

'I'm not here to make friends.'

His smile was one of amusement and, she thought, faint mockery. Slipping his cell phone in his pocket, he folded his arms and looked at her for a long moment. 'Okay, you have thirty seconds. Talk.'

That was more than she needed. 'Let's be clear about one thing – just because I'm cooperating with you, doesn't mean we have the same agenda. I'm here to make sure that whoever killed three of our men last night is brought to justice.'

Hawkins raised an eyebrow. 'And that's different from me, how?'

'Because I'm not out to settle old scores, or become an executioner. This woman you threw into the mix earlier; the one with no name… She might be everything you say she is, or she might not. Either way, she deserves a chance to tell her side of the story. So does Yates. So I'll help you catch them and bring them in, but we bring them in alive.'

Hawkins regarded her in thoughtful silence, as if trying to get the measure of her. 'People have tried to capture her alive before. Didn't work out too well.'

'That was then, this is now. And my point still stands. I'm a cop, not an assassin. We clear on that?'

The smile was back. It was the smile of a man who knew a hell of a lot more about what they were up against than she did. A man who knew she was going to fail.

'Crystal.'

Saying nothing more, Mitchell turned and walked away, her back straight and her chin up. She could feel Hawkins's eyes on her the whole time.

Chapter 18

Vaguely Alex became aware of a voice. A woman's voice calling out to him, saying something he couldn't quite make out. Curious, he began to rouse from the darkness that seemed to be swallowing him up.

'What?' he mumbled, forcing his eyes open with great effort.

Straight away he found himself staring into the face of a woman. A woman with short blonde hair and intense, haunting blue eyes. A woman who was hard, cold, beautiful and terrible all at once.

Anya.

He watched as her right hand was drawn back, and frowned for a moment in confusion as it swung down towards him.

The sudden impact as her open hand collided with his cheek sent shockwaves of pain reverberating through his head. The effect was akin to being doused with cold water in the midst of deep sleep, and he let out a gasp as his eyes snapped wide open.

'What the fu—?' he began.

'Quiet!' she hissed. 'You fell down the slope and into the river. Are you hurt?'

'How did you find me?'

'*Are you hurt?*' she repeated, shaking him.

He thought for a moment, trying to collect his wits. The slap had temporarily jolted his brain back into action, but his body felt heavy and numb. Still, even in this condition he could feel the waves of pain radiating outward from his ribcage.

'My chest,' he said, sounding unsure. 'I think I hit a tree.'

She nodded, her expression grave. 'You may have cracked a rib. Your breathing seems unaffected so I don't think you punctured a lung. I'll look at it properly later, but first we have to get you out of here before you freeze to death.'

'What about… a fire?' he asked, having to focus hard on each word.

Anya shook her head. 'There's no deadfall nearby, and no time to strip tree branches. You have five or ten minutes at most before hypothermia sets in.'

Leaning forward, she unzipped the heavy waterlogged jacket he was wearing and pulled it off, though she left the woollen sweater in place. Even wet, it would still retain some body heat. This done, she took off her own jacket and helped him into it. It was a little small for him, but it was warm and dry, and straight away he began to feel the difference.

'This will help, for now at least,' she said. 'Can you walk?'

'I... I think so.'

'Good. Hold on to me.'

Placing his arm around her neck, she pushed herself up off the ground with some difficulty, having to support most of his weight as well. With awkward, unsteady steps, they started forward through the long grass.

'I can't make it across that river again,' Alex gasped, knowing how close he'd come to drowning last time. Attempting to swim it again would be suicidal, though if his mind had been in better order he might have questioned how Anya had made it to him without getting wet herself.

'No need,' she assured him. 'There is a crossing point nearby; that's how I got to you. The slope on the other side looks like an easy climb.'

'Easy... for you to say,' he said, managing a weak laugh. The physical exertion of walking combined with the warm and dry jacket around his torso was helping to generate a little body heat, but it was a temporary reprieve at most.

Sure enough, a couple of minutes of unsteady walking, with Anya doing most of the work, brought them to the edge of the river, where a bridge of sorts crossed the narrow waterway. Little more than several felled tree trunks lashed together, it looked unstable and slippery, but it was an awful lot better than the other option.

'Hold on to me,' Anya said, helping him across. The logs creaked and sagged visibly beneath their weight, the swirling water beneath seemingly eager to engulf them, but nonetheless the improvised bridge held firm.

Once across, they started up the far bank. As she'd described, the terrain here was much easier than upstream, and there was even a rough path winding its way through the trees. It seemed this area was used from time to time, perhaps by hikers.

'I'm sorry, Anya,' Alex mumbled as they trudged step by step up the hill. His chest was tightening, making it hard to draw breath. 'For... taking it out... on you. I was being an arsehole earlier. You didn't... deserve it.'

The woman said nothing right away, and he couldn't see the expression on her face.

'I pushed you too hard,' she finally admitted. It was as close to an apology as he was likely to get.

Despite himself, Alex couldn't help laughing in amusement at the exchange. 'Well, this is... a beautiful moment. Brings a tear to my eye.'

'Just concentrate on getting over this ridge.'

Alex couldn't rightly say how long it took them to ascend that slope, since all concept of time quickly became irrelevant to him. All he could focus on was putting one leaden foot in front of the other, forcing his lungs to draw breath that never quite seemed to be enough to satisfy his body's craving for oxygen.

In reality the path they were following was probably an easy five-minute walk for anyone of moderate fitness, but in his battered and exhausted condition it felt like trying to scale Mount Everest. Every step became harder than the one before. Twice he stumbled, and twice Anya saved him from falling, her quiet but commanding voice urging him to keep going.

He was gasping for breath by the time they finally crested the ridge, with spots of light dancing across his eyes and the world swaying uncontrollably around him.

'The road is close,' Anya said, trying to urge him forward, to make one last effort. 'You can rest when we get there.'

Alex tried to take a step forward, but the lights in his eyes suddenly coalesced into a lightning flash that sent him stumbling forward, his legs giving way beneath him. There was no thought of getting up this time, no matter how much encouragement Anya might give him. He was done.

'No more,' he gasped, shaking his head. 'No more.'

Anya looked down at the bruised and bedraggled young man, knowing he was almost out of time. He had given everything he had left just to get up the ridge, but his body could carry him no further. Already it was beginning to shut down as cold and exhaustion gained the upper hand.

For a moment she just sat there, kneeling by his side as she weighed up what to do next. The logical course of action was to leave him here to succumb to hypothermia, cut her losses and make good her escape. She was confident she could vanish back into anonymity just as she had done before.

It was a cold and clinical choice, but then it wouldn't be the first such decision she'd been forced to make. Survival often required both ruthless thoughts and actions.

And yet, looking at him now, she realized that he was in this position largely because of her. He had inherited the memory stick she'd given to Sinclair, through little more than bad luck. But she had started the process that had destroyed his life.

His life, and his death, was her responsibility now.

The distant sound of an approaching vehicle on the road finally decided her. She drew the automatic from her jeans and quickly checked it. It was a Heckler & Koch USP .45; a big, powerful, German-made weapon that was popular with both the Agency and special forces units worldwide. The grip was a little too big for her hands, but it was a reliable, accurate weapon that could put down any unarmoured target within thirty yards.

Pulling back the side far enough to check that a round was in the breech, she pushed it down the back of her jeans to hide it from view, then leaned in close to Alex.

'Stay here, Alex,' she whispered. 'I'll come back for you.'

He would have to take his chances for now. Either she would return to him in time to save his life, or he would succumb to hypothermia and die right here. For now, there was nothing she could do about it.

Leaving him, she turned and sprinted the short distance down the slope to the nearby road, backing up against the solid trunk of a spruce tree. The car was getting closer now, she could see the glow of the headlights flitting between the trees to illuminate the tarmac road nearby. The engine note was too high to be a truck or heavy-goods vehicle; she guessed it to be a mid-sized family car, which was both good and bad news. Such a vehicle would be less obtrusive, but then it might well contain an entire family; all of whom would have to be dealt with. Even she would struggle to control three or four people while she retrieved Alex from the nearby woods.

Still, there were some things in life that simply couldn't be planned for. It was the ability to improvise and overcome such problems that made the difference.

The car was almost on her now, driving at a steady forty or fifty miles per hour judging by the low revs. The driver was cruising, unhurried, perhaps weary after a long night behind the wheel. They wouldn't be expecting what happened next.

Taking a breath, Anya pushed herself away from the tree and staggered out onto the road, waving her arms frantically and doing her best to look terrified.

'Help! Help me!' she cried.

Straight away she heard the squeal of brakes and the crunch of tyres skidding on tarmac, and suddenly the headlights dipped as the vehicle's momentum carried it onward. She was standing more or less in the centre of the narrow road, so unless he felt like running her over, the driver was left with little choice but to stop.

At least she knew the car was fitted with good brakes, she thought, as it skidded to a halt maybe twenty feet away. Straight away she was moving, closing the distance between her and the car before the driver had a chance to recover his wits.

She was counting on surprise and perhaps a misplaced sense of chivalry to aid her. From the driver's point of view, Anya was a woman in distress, alone on a dark road in the middle of the night. She might have been the victim of a sexual attack, a car-jacking, or even a simple traffic accident further down the road. Either way, he was unlikely to perceive her as a threat. Not yet, at least.

As she approached, she recognized the car as a Volvo S40; a solid if unspectacular family saloon manufactured in neighbouring Sweden. She heard the buzz of an electric window coming down, followed immediately by a gruff Norwegian voice.

'What the hell are you doing?' the driver demanded in Norwegian. 'I almost knocked you—'

He stopped mid sentence as Anya drew the USP and levelled it at him. Approaching the window, she peered inside to get a look at the driver.

The face staring back at her was old, easily in his eighties, deeply tanned and lined like old leather. His silvery white hair, combed straight back, was matched by a neatly trimmed moustache of similar colour. To Anya's surprise, there was little fear in his expression, just a moment of alarm at the sight of the weapon, followed by a kind of weary acceptance of what was clearly going to be a difficult night.

'First time I've been held at gunpoint by a woman. Are you going to kill me?' he asked, his voice flat and completely calm. Then again, she supposed if she lived to be as old as him, death would hold little fear.

'I just need your car. My friend is hurt,' she said, speaking in Swedish since she was far more fluent in it. Anya had never had much reason to learn Norwegian, but fortunately the two Scandinavian languages were similar enough to be mutually understandable.

'I could drive you to a hospital.'

She shook her head. People asked questions in hospitals. 'Get out, slowly.'

This prompted a wry smile. 'Young lady, I'm eighty-three years old. Slow is the best I can hope for these days.'

Anya might have smiled too if her situation had been less serious. It had been a long time since anyone had referred to her as 'young lady'.

With surprising dignity, given the duress he was under, he unbuckled his seatbelt, eased himself out of the car and backed off a couple of paces. Despite his age, he was still a big man, easily standing six feet tall and with the broad shoulders of a man accustomed to physical activity. Only an expanding midriff betrayed his advanced years.

Anya kept him covered the whole time, more out of professional habit than because she expected him to try anything. He was old enough and wise enough to know better, and he certainly wasn't going to die over a car that was insured anyway.

Moving forward, she quickly patted him down, making sure he didn't have a cell phone or weapon on him. The last thing she needed was for him to call the police the moment she left the scene. As expected, he made no effort to resist.

Satisfied he posed no immediate threat, she removed the keys from the car's ignition, hit the remote fob to lock the doors, then slipped them into her pocket.

'What's your name?' she asked.

'Jostein.'

'Jostein, I want you to turn around and go back the way you came. Don't look back or try to return to your car. I don't want to shoot you, but I will if you disobey. Do you understand?'

The old man glanced back down the empty road. 'You know I will report this to the police as soon as I can.'

Anya nodded. 'I'm sorry I had to do this. Now go.'

Sensing she wasn't going to relent, Jostein turned and began to walk away at a measured, unhurried pace. However, he stopped after a few yards and glanced at her.

'I hope your friend is all right.'

With that, he turned away and resumed his walk. Anya waited until he was about thirty yards down the road before shoving the USP down the back of her jeans and sprinting into the woods, leaping over tangled brush and gnarled roots just waiting to trip her. Every second she left her companion alone increased his chances of death by exposure.

Alex was lying exactly where she had left him, his eyes closed and his face deathly pale. His soaking hair was plastered to his head. His body was a limp weight in her arms when she tried to lift him.

'I'm here, Alex. I came back for you,' Anya said, trying to rouse him. 'There is a car waiting for us on the road.'

There was no response. The young man didn't stir. Anya felt an unfamiliar knot of fear tighten in her stomach at the realisation that she might be too late. Danger to herself was of little concern, yet she felt a sense of guilt and responsibility towards this man.

Forcing those thoughts aside, she tilted her head down so that her face was just inches from his. And for an anxious second or two she waited.

There! Her heart leapt as she felt the momentary warmth of his breath on her cheek. It was faint and shallow, but nonetheless real. He was alive, but he wouldn't stay that way for long if she didn't get some warmth into him. And there was no way he could reach the car under his own power.

There was only one course of action. Summoning up what reserves of energy she had left, Anya took a couple of deep breaths to get more oxygen into her bloodstream, then hooked her arms beneath Alex's unconscious body and, muscles straining with the effort, heaved him up from the ground.

Anya was no stranger to physical exertion, and still exercised regularly to keep herself as strong and fit as possible. But all the training in the world couldn't give her the muscle mass and brute strength of a man. That fact weighed heavily on her mind as she struggled through the dense forest, doing her best to sidestep the obstacles she had leapt over with such ease mere seconds earlier.

Alex was a leaden weight in her arms, his size and shape making him difficult to balance, and threatening to overcome her more than once. Ignoring the burning ache in her muscles, Anya forced herself down the slope step by step, concentrating on nothing but raising and planting her feet firmly in the soft ground.

A lifetime ago, when she'd still been a young woman undergoing the rigorous training needed to prepare her for the career she'd chosen, she had taken part in more forced marches than she cared to count. Weighed down by heavy equipment and forced to slog through wind and rain for hours at a time, her only defence had been to retreat into her own mind, shutting out the pain and the cold and the discomfort and focussing only on what was absolutely essential.

In her mind, she repeated the mantra that had been drilled into her again and again during training, the words that had kept her going during her darkest hours.

I will endure when all others fail. I will stand when all others retreat. Weakness will not be in my heart. Fear will not be in my creed. I will show no mercy. I will never hesitate. I will never surrender.

It had worked for her then, and it still worked now.

I will endure when all others fail.

Plodding steadily onward, she let out a sigh of relief as the road finally came into view. Mercifully the car was still there as well, Jostein having kept his promise not to return for it.

'Almost... there, Alex,' Anya said through gritted teeth, as she staggered the last few yards across the paved road and practically collapsed with her unconscious companion beside the passenger door.

Alex let out a pained grunt as he hit the ground, but otherwise didn't stir. At least she knew he was still alive.

A quick fumble with the key fob was enough to disable the central locking. Breathing hard, she hauled the door open and with a last great effort heaved Alex into the passenger seat and slammed the door shut.

Freed from the heavy burden of his unconscious body, Anya felt like she was floating on air as she rounded the car, slipped into the driver's seat and started it up. The engine rumbled back into life, and she cranked the heaters up to maximum before throwing the Volvo into gear and accelerating away from the scene.

The car's climate-control system was nothing if not efficient, and within seconds the temperature in the enclosed space had risen to a sweltering twenty degrees. Already warm from her exertions, Anya was soon sweating as hot air blasted her face and body. She reached out and angled the air vents towards Alex, knowing he needed it far more than she did

Anya wasn't driving with any particular destination in mind yet. Her main concern was putting as much distance between herself and Jostein as possible, which was just as well because she saw no forks or junctions in the road as it wound between rocky escarpments and dense evergreen forests. Occasionally she caught glimpses of the moonlit sea far off to the west. For now however she was interested only in putting as much distance between herself and the site of the car theft as possible.

Her actions would certainly result in follow-up by local police, though she wasn't particularly concerned about that. She had made a career out of evading the best intelligence services in the world for the past two decades, and even with Yates to worry about she was confident she could give the Norwegian police the slip.

Of greater concern was the prospect of the Agency making the connection between the car theft and the stolen trawler, and redirecting all their resources here. This was exactly the scenario she hoped to avoid. If it happened, everything she had gained by fleeing the UK would be undone.

Still, she had Yates, and with him a chance to find the answers she so desperately needed. It was a risk, but she had faced and overcome many such risks in her life, and she hadn't come this far to give up now. Her only option was to press forward.

A low moaning from the passenger seat directed her thoughts back to more immediate matters, as Alex began to show signs of regaining consciousness. It seemed the threat of death by hypothermia was abating, but nonetheless she wanted to check him over properly. If he died from exposure or the injuries he'd sustained in the fall, all of this was for nothing.

Spotting a turn-off into a narrow forest track up ahead, she swung the wheel left, taking the car off the main road. The vehicle bumped and wallowed through dips and potholes before coming to a halt about thirty yards from the main road. As soon as they'd stopped, Anya switched off the headlights but left the engine running.

With hot air continuing to pump from the heating system, Anya switched on the internal light and twisted around in her seat to examine her patient. He was a sorry-looking sight – wet, bedraggled, bruised and smeared with mud and dead leaves that had stuck to him while lying on the forest floor. Still, she thought she saw a hint of colour returning to his face.

Even if his clothes were still damp, the warmth would be seeping through to the skin beneath, helping to raise his core temperature above the critical level needed to maintain his vital functions. At least he didn't look as deathly pale as before.

His breathing was shallow and laboured, reminding her of the injury he'd sustained during his fall down the hill. Reaching out, she unzipped his jacket and pulled up the thick jumper beneath.

As she'd feared, the skin down one side of his chest was badly discoloured, with patches of haemorrhaging clearly visible. The blunt-force trauma of a high-speed impact with a tree trunk was more than sufficient to snap ribs and propel the jagged ends into the delicate internal organs they were supposed to protect. If he was bleeding internally, then he was in serious trouble and there was little she could do for him.

Gently she reached out and touched around the injury, starting with the base of his chest and slowly working her way up, feeling the protrusion of each rib bone as she went. There were no obvious breaks or fractures that she could detect, but her examination certainly prompted a reaction from the patient.

His eyes fluttered once, opened a crack and seemed to falter, then finally flew open as his consciousness returned and the first wave of pain hit him.

'Ow, Jesus Christ!' he groaned, clutching his chest and blindly pushing her away as his mind struggled to reassert itself. 'What the hell are you doing?'

'Trying to find out if you've broken any ribs,' Anya explained, sounding more patient and understanding than she felt at that moment.

He pulled the jumper back in place, covering his chest. 'And?'

She shrugged. 'You will live, I think. How does it feel?'

'Like Mike Tyson's been wailing on it for fifteen rounds. 'He tried to sit up straighter in his seat, but immediately thought better of it. 'Remind me not to go picking fights with pine trees any time soon.'

She would rather he remembered to stay close to her and watch where he stepped, but decided now wasn't the time for such rebukes.

'You should recover in a few days,' she said instead, thinking it would raise his spirits.

'Assuming I live that long,' Alex remarked with sour grace. He glanced around, taking in the interior of the Volvo. 'By the way, where did this car come from?'

'It's not important now,' she said, seeing little point in telling him that car-jacking had been added to the list of crimes he'd become embroiled in. Instead she decided to focus on their objective. 'What matters is getting you to a computer so you can finish what Loki started. Tell me what you need to make this happen.'

'I need you to head east,' he said simply. 'To Drammen, near Oslo.'

'And what will we find there?'

She could have sworn she saw a faint, knowing smile. 'A man who knows about these things.'

That wasn't making her any happier. 'Do you trust him?'

'I don't trust anyone, including you,' he said truthfully. 'But we need his help, and his computers. Well, mostly his computers.'

'And if you find this man, then you can break the Agency's firewall?' She needed to know for certain that he wasn't stalling for time or trying to mislead her. If so, she wouldn't hesitate to dump him here and let him take his chances.

'If it's possible, I'll find a way.'

Anya said nothing further. In matters like this, she had little choice but to defer to his experience. Drammen it was, then.

The only problem was that Drammen was easily a six-hour drive away, and she hadn't slept in over two days – a fact that her body had been reminding her of with increasing urgency of late. She was no stranger to fatigue and sleep deprivation, but even she couldn't keep going forever. Sighing, she put the car into reverse and backed up onto the main road.

Stealing a glance at Alex, she noticed that his eyes were already starting to close. The combination of exhaustion and the sudden warmth of the car was threatening to overwhelm him.

'I need you to stay awake, Alex,' she warned.

'Come on, mate,' the young man groaned. 'If you need a navigator, trust me, I'm not your man.'

'Hypothermia is still a risk. I need you to stay awake, at least until your core temperature is up.' She didn't look at him as she swung the wheel over, threw the engine into first gear and accelerated away. In truth, she could use something to focus her attention on besides the sleep-inducing monotony of a dark and winding road. 'Talk to me.'

'About what?'

'Anything.' She paused a moment, struck by how difficult she found it to think of a conversation starter. She'd never had much interest in making small talk, and that situation hadn't been helped by four years spent in solitary confinement in a Russian jail. 'Tell me your favourite movie.'

At this, Alex laughed in amusement, though it ended in a painful wince as his bruised ribs reminded him of the fall he'd taken earlier. 'Are we really having this conversation?'

'Come on. Tell me,' she pressed him. She wasn't really interested, but if it kept him awake then it was good enough.

Alex was silent for the next few seconds. Clearly he was giving it more thought than the situation really warranted. 'Well, *Flash Gordon* is up there for sure, but I'd have to say *Big Trouble in Little China*,' he decided at last. 'That's the best film ever.'

'Why?' she asked, feigning interest. 'Tell me about it.'

'Well, it's about a truck driver who stumbles into the middle of a gang war in Chinatown. I like it because it's not what it appears to be. Most people assume he's the main character because the story's told from his point of view. But he's not. He's just the sidekick. It's his mate who does all the work and the fighting, and who gets the girl at the end...'

Anya said nothing to this, content to let him talk now that he seemed to be on a roll. Pushing a lock of blonde hair back from her face and doing her best to focus on the darkened road ahead, she settled down for a long night behind the wheel.

Chapter 19

Although technically classed as a Royal Air Force base, RAF Menwith Hill was British in name only. In reality the sprawling facility was America's biggest electronic surveillance hub in Western Europe. A key element of the ECHELON global monitoring system, its distinctive white radomes worked ceaselessly to intercept electronic signals of all kinds, from emails to telephone calls and coded radio messages.

Operations there had started during the dark days of the Cold War, when the Soviet Union had been the main enemy of the West, but these days the remit was much broader. The enemies of the twenty-first century didn't sit behind neatly defined borders, didn't possess armies and navies and air forces that could be tracked. They existed everywhere and nowhere, making places like Menwith Hill more vital than ever.

The base was home to nearly 2,000 signals technicians, with contingents from the US Air Force, the National Security Agency and, of course, the CIA. Mitchell had been based here for the past six months, and although the damp and windy climate on the Yorkshire moors was a far cry from the Arizona sun she'd grown up in, it had become a home of sorts. At least, it was about as close a thing to home as she needed right now.

Home however was the last thing on her mind as she filed into the small briefing room along with several other field agents who had been with her at the murder site. It was just past 6 a.m. and nobody was feeling very enthusiastic. Beside her, Argento ran a hand through his short dark hair, stifling a yawn as he gulped down some coffee.

As Mitchell had expected, Hawkins was there waiting for them, looking just as slick and composed as he had the previous day. She wondered if he even needed sleep.

'Okay, we're short on time so I'll make this quick,' he began. 'For the past few hours our air assets have been combing the Norwegian coast looking for signs of the missing trawler. Initially they turned up Jack shit – no vessels matching the description anywhere in the area. It wasn't until the sun came up that one of our drones spotted an oil slick a couple of hundred yards offshore, near the town of Egersund.'

Hitting a couple of keys on the laptop in front of him, he brought up a satellite image of what looked like a remote stretch of rocky, jagged coastline fringed by dense forest. Sure enough, a slick was visible in the choppy waters offshore.

'Satellite radar imaging confirmed the wreck of a fishing boat lying in shallow water nearby, matching the one stolen in Scotland. Looks like they scuttled it and made their way ashore in a small boat or life raft.'

Mitchell glanced at Argento, sharing a look of surprise at this revelation. Whatever she might have thought of him, Hawkins was ruthlessly efficient when it came to pursuing his goal. He also must have wielded some serious clout within the Agency to have such high-value assets tasked to this operation. Another sign – if it were needed – that this was far more than just a hunt for a murder suspect.

'It seems things didn't go according to plan, though,' he carried on. 'Local police just filed a report from a Norwegian citizen that his car was hijacked at gunpoint on the road south of Egersund during the night. The perp was described as a tall blonde woman in her forties, who claimed she had an injured friend she was trying to help.'

Mitchell sat back in her chair, amazed by this sudden turn of events. Yesterday Alex Yates and his mysterious companion had been a dead end, any clues to their whereabouts and intentions rapidly drying up. Now they not only had a location, but a possible insight into the man's state of health.

'So if we're assuming Yates was hurt as they made their way ashore, what about local doctors and hospitals?' Argento suggested. It was an obvious enough idea, but their line of work was all about covering the bases.

Hawkins shook his head. 'Unless her IQ's taken a dip lately, there's no way she'd risk exposing herself or Yates by taking him to a hospital. And it's not like there are many backstreet doctors in Norway she could look up.'

'So what's our play?' Mitchell asked. It seemed obvious that Hawkins hadn't called them in here just to bring them up to speed on current events.

Hawkins regarded her with a cool, assessing gaze. 'We're going over there,' he said simply. 'We've flagged all our assets in-country to be on the lookout for her, but we need a team on standby to take her down. I picked the six of you because you're the most experienced field agents available, so I'd appreciate it if you didn't prove me wrong. Now, our comrades back at Langley have already prepped a diplomatic flight to Oslo, which leaves in –' He glanced at his watch '– just under thirty minutes. If you're not ready by then, you're not going. Questions?'

'Have we told the Norwegians anything about this?' Argento asked.

'Any serious questions?'

'They're an asset we could use,' the younger operative pointed out, though he looked daunted by Hawkins's withering gaze. 'Better to have them on side than against us.'

'Unless she has sources inside their government or police service, or the fact we'd have to admit that one of our own operatives has gone rogue and is on the loose in their country.' Hawkins shook his head. 'No, we take care of our own problems. We go in as a small, flexible, secure team, we get the job done and we come home the same way.' He looked around the room. 'Any other questions?'

Nothing further was said.

'Good. Now grab your gear and get ready.'

Part III

Termination

In 1996, the U.S. General Accounting Office reported that hackers attempted to break into Defense Department computer files some 250,000 times in 1995 alone. About 65 per cent of the attempts were successful, according to the report.

Chapter 20

Drammen, Norway

Alex awoke to the sound of birds singing. He couldn't remember when he'd drifted off last night; only that the monotony of the darkened road and the gentle hum of the engine had gradually overcome the pain of his injuries and the clammy dampness of his clothes. Opening his eyes a crack, he peered around, trying to make sense of his surroundings.

It was morning, and their car was parked in a grassy clearing overlooking a small lake, its still waters reflecting a pristine blue sky unmarked by even a wisp of cloud. Tiny insects flitted back and forth, briefly glowing iridescent as they passed through the bright shafts of sunlight that filtered down through heavy tree cover.

Such was the peace and tranquillity of the scene which confronted Alex in those first few moments that he just sat there staring, mesmerized by the simple, unspoiled beauty of it. In a place like this, he almost thought he could forget the dark turn his life had taken over the past few days.

Remembering his female companion, he twisted around in his seat to look for her, stifling a groan of pain as his injured ribs protested. He was suddenly very conscious of his tumble down that hillside the night before. After lying motionless for several hours, his muscles had seized up and the various cuts and bruises were making themselves felt.

Still, he managed to turn enough to look at her. Anya was still behind the wheel, though it was clear she'd done enough driving for one night. She was leaning back in the seat with her head resting against the window, her eyes closed, her breathing slow and regular.

Alex was almost taken aback by the realisation she was asleep. He'd never seen her sleeping before, and after spending the past couple of days with her, he'd begun to question whether she ever needed rest. It gave him a faint sense of reassurance that she was human after all.

And yet looking now at the formidable, intimidating woman who had turned his life upside down, he found himself strangely intrigued. This was the first time he'd had the opportunity to really look at her, and he couldn't help but take advantage of it.

In terms of structure and appearance, her face bore all the hallmarks of classical feminine beauty mingled with a slightly foreign look that he couldn't quite identify. A firm, well-defined jawline, full lips slightly parted to reveal a row of white teeth, high cheekbones and a small, straight nose. A few locks of short blonde hair had fallen across her eyes, and Alex felt an odd urge to reach out and move them aside. Only a faint pattern of lines around her mouth and eyes gave some hint as to her true age, though even that was hard to guess.

None of this was new to him of course. He'd recognized that Anya was an attractive woman the very first time they'd met, even if she was a little old and frightening for his tastes, but it was different now. With her iron will and dangerous, calculating mind now temporarily at ease, and the first rays of the dawn light playing across her face, Alex was taken aback by how beautiful and peaceful she looked.

But there was something else about her that had caught his attention. Pushed down the front of her trousers and partially hidden by the black jumper she wore, Alex spotted the distinctive metallic gleam of the automatic she'd been carrying since their escape from the farm.

It was right there, and despite the logical part of his mind cautioning him to leave the weapon well alone, he couldn't take his eyes off it. Another part of his brain was harbouring altogether different thoughts that had nothing whatsoever to do with caution or logic.

Whether she was a saviour, a protector or a kidnapper was a matter of perspective at this point, but the fact remained that she possessed their one and only weapon. Therefore she made all the decisions, held all the cards and was free to withhold any information she chose. And whether he agreed with her or not, he had little choice but to obey her instructions. This might well be his only opportunity to change that balance.

If he was armed, he could force her to reveal what exactly they were caught up in, what secrets she was so desperate to recover, and why the CIA wanted her dead.

Almost without realizing, he found himself reaching out for the gun, his hand moving inch by inch towards it. Just one swift movement, and he would feel his fingers close around the butt. He imagined himself yanking the weapon free and turning it on her while she was still groggy from sleep, then forcing her to confess everything she knew.

'If I were you, I'd think very carefully about what I was about to do,' a female voice warned him. 'And who I was about to do it to.'

Alex jerked his hand back as Anya's lashes parted, revealing those icy blue eyes that had so caught his attention the first time he'd encountered her. They were clear and focussed, betraying no hint of tiredness, and staring right at him.

'Don't flatter yourself,' he said, hoping to hide his embarrassment with a scathing put-down. 'You're not my type. I was just checking if you were awake.'

'You should always assume I'm awake,' Anya said, sitting up and stretching. Alex heard the muted pop as stiff joints and muscles eased up.

'Do you ever sleep?'

She glanced at him. 'When I can. Otherwise, I rest and keep watch.'

He decided to let that one pass. Whatever experiences and hardships had moulded her into the woman she was today, they were far beyond his own understanding.

'So where are we?' he asked instead. 'I assume you didn't stop to admire the view.'

Anya ran a hand through her hair. 'We are a mile or two west of Drammen. I thought it best to wait until dawn before we make contact with your... "friend".'

The disdain in her voice was obvious.

'Probably a good call,' he allowed. 'We shouldn't make contact until after nine.'

'Why?'

'That's when his parents go out to work,' he explained. 'I've got an idea, but I'll need you to play along.'

Before she could respond to that, Alex opened his door and stepped out into the cool morning air. He had some other business to attend to first.

Chapter 21

'No point in running, my friend,' Gregar Landvik said through his radio headset, as he levelled his weapon at a distant target. The unfortunate soldier believed himself hidden behind cover, but hadn't counted on Landvik's outflanking move. 'I can see you.'

A single burst of fire was enough to end it, scoring him a long-range kill that added another fifty points to his onscreen tally. He was only a hundred points away from top of the leader board in what was proving to be a fiercely contested online battle.

'Better luck next time, noob,' he taunted, moving off in search of another target.

'Fuck you, Plisken!' the opposing player retorted, using Landvik's Xbox username.

Landvik laughed at the reaction he had provoked. In games like this, making other players lose their cool was almost as important as gaining the top score.

'Only in your dreams, my friend.'

However, his game was rudely interrupted by a sudden banging at the front door. Landvik ignored it, struggling to stay focussed on the game as he sprayed a burst of automatic fire at a player who was wildly evading and returning fire.

More than likely it was some lost delivery man. The houses out here were pretty remote and often lay at the end of long winding driveways that proved a nightmare for postal workers and delivery trucks. The rural location was also a pain in the ass for him since decent internet connections were as rare as rocking-horse shit in this part of the world, but the alternative was to move out, find a permanent job and buy his own place.

And that didn't bear thinking about.

'Got you!' Landvik smiled in satisfaction as another fifty points were added to his tally. The knocking at the front door continued, loud and urgent.

'Go away! I'm busy!' the young man yelled, trying to focus on his game.

Much to his irritation, however, that only seemed to encourage whoever was out there to hammer on the door even harder.

The distraction was starting to impact his concentration. His next burst of gunfire missed his target, and the opposing player responded with a shotgun blast at point-blank range that put him down for good.

'God damn it!' he snapped. Exiting the game, he tossed the controller onto a nearby beanbag and hauled his considerable bulk out of his favourite gaming chair. He'd already learned the value of restraint after breaking two previous controller units against the hardwood floor in frustration.

'All right! I'm coming.' Barefoot, he padded through the expensive, minimally furnished hallway towards the front door. It was supposed to be sleek and modern, but it looked like a pretentious art gallery instead of a house. Landvik didn't care too much, though. As long as the decorators left his room alone, they could do what they wanted with the rest of the house.

The banging had at last eased up. Mindful that the door was still barred and locked, Landvik leaned in close and surveyed the scene outside through the spy hole. Straight away his anger vanished, replaced by uncomprehending surprise.

'What the fuck?'

All thoughts of caution now abandoned, he undid the security latch, unlocked the door and swung it open to reveal a young man of slender build, light brown hair and the kind of pale, even-featured, nondescript face that could only belong to an Englishman.

Unshaven, cut and bruised, and dressed in tattered clothing that looked like it had been stolen from a penniless fisherman, Alex gave the appearance of a man who had been sleeping rough for the past couple of days.

'Alex, what are you—?'

He never got a chance to finish. Alex's fist leapt out, striking him square in the nose and jerking his head back with the force of the impact. Shocked by the sudden and unprovoked attack, he stumbled backwards, bumping into the wall behind and falling to his knees.

'Ow! What was that for?' he asked, clutching his nose. He could already feel the wetness of blood on his hands.

'Two years, Gregar!' Alex shouted, taking a step towards him with his fists clenched, eyes alight with long-building rage. 'Two years I spent in prison because of you, you stupid fat bastard! I lost everything because of you. Everything!'

'That's not true,' Landvik protested, looking up at him fearfully. No doubt he sensed – correctly – that he was about to get a real kicking instead of just a bloodied nose. 'I'd never betray anyone in the group. You know that—'

'Shut the fuck up!' Alex snarled, trembling visibly as he tried to hold his anger back. 'I'm not interested in your bullshit excuses, Gregar. You should think yourself lucky. The only reason I never came here to kick the shit out of you before was because they took my passport away.'

This wasn't the Alex Yates he used to know. The laid-back, easy-going young man who would agree to just about anything was gone now. Landvik had no idea who this person was. He knew only that he was afraid of him.

122

'Alex, if it's money you want, I can—' He was cut off when Alex drew back his fist to strike him again, prompting him to curl up in an effort to protect himself. 'No! Don't, please!'

'Money,' Alex repeated, his tone laced with disgust. 'That's what it always came down to with you, isn't it? Fucking money.' He shook his head. 'No, this isn't about money, you prick.'

Landvik could feel his heart pounding. If Alex didn't want money, then why was he here? Had he really travelled all the way here just to take violent revenge for his imprisonment?

Before Landvik could bring himself to ask, another figure suddenly appeared in the doorway, having backed up against the wall without him noticing. It was a woman, tall and blonde-haired, with eyes that flashed dangerously and seemed to see right through him. Moving with the confidence that made it plain resistance would be extremely unwise, she strode into the hallway and turned around.

'Explanations can wait,' she said, her voice unnervingly calm and controlled next to Alex's simmering anger. 'For now, we need your cooperation.'

'W-who the hell are you?' Landvik stammered, caught off guard by her forceful entry.

'That's Anya,' Alex explained, pulling the door closed behind him. 'She's here to make sure you don't fuck me over like you did last time.'

'I told you, I didn't—'

'Anya, if this fat prick opens his mouth except to answer a direct question, shoot out his kneecaps,' Alex ordered. 'Or anything else that takes your fancy.'

Without hesitation, the woman reached into her jeans and withdrew a bulky automatic pistol, calmly levelling it at his groin.

'No! Don't!' Landvik pleaded, his mind already conjuring up horrific images of what would happen if she pulled the trigger.

'So you're going to do what I say?' Alex prompted.

'Of course!' Landvik promised. 'Whatever you want. Just tell me and it's yours.'

Even as he was speaking, Anya was making her way from room to room, quickly searching the house. Searching for what, Landvik couldn't say for sure, though he suspected she was checking that he was the only occupant. That thought did little to assuage the growing feeling of terror that was creeping up inside him.

He blinked and shook his head, trying to process this bizarre chain of events. 'What are you looking for?'

She said nothing until she'd completed her sweep. Returning with the weapon in hand, her eyes were focussed on him. 'Are you expecting anyone else today?'

'W-what?'

'Answer the question, boy,' she snapped. 'And do not think to lie to me. If you do, I will know about it, and I will make you wish you hadn't.'

He swallowed. 'No. There's no one. My parents are out at work, they never come home before six.'

She surveyed their opulent surroundings, quickly assessing the place. Maintaining a property like this would be no easy task for a busy working couple, and she doubted their son did much to help. 'What about cleaners, gardeners, maintenance people? Think hard.'

He shook his head. 'There's nobody. Not today, at least.'

Those pale blue eyes seemed to bore right into him as she assessed the validity of his words. The seconds seemed to stretch out into hours as he wilted under that remorseless stare. Nonetheless, she finally nodded to herself and released him, apparently deciding he was telling the truth. Leaving them, she hurried off to make a quick survey of the house.

'Lucky you decided to be honest for once in your life,' Alex remarked. 'Because I need your help.'

'Help with what?'

'First I need your computer. I assume you've still got a decent setup here?'

Landvik might have laughed if the situation had been less terrifying. Of course he had a decent computer setup. Out here in the middle of nowhere with nothing but time on his hands, particularly during the long dark winters, he'd immersed himself in the online world to escape the real one. As a result, he made sure he stayed up to date with the latest hardware.

'The best, hardware and software,' he remarked with a touch of pride. 'Just like the old days.'

He and Alex had been as thick as thieves during their time as students, testing their hacking skills against the university's secure network before moving on to bigger challenges. He still dabbled in it occasionally, though mostly for fun these days. Like the online gaming, it was a way of passing the time.

'Good. Then you will not mind if we use it,' Anya said, striding back along the corridor towards them.

Landvik hesitated, taken aback by the sight of her. Even if she was a decade older than him, she was nonetheless a tall, athletic, strikingly attractive woman, who moved with a confidence and purpose that was both arousing and intimidating.

'Use it for what, exactly?' Whoever this woman was, no way was he giving away anything to her. She could be police for all he knew.

He almost jumped when he felt Alex's hand rest on his shoulder. Turning to look at his former friend, he was surprised by the determination and purpose in Alex's eyes.

'Get yourself cleaned up, Gregar,' he advised. 'We've got work to do.'

Chapter 22

Half an hour later, and Alex was seated in front of Landvik's formidable computer system, his fingers dancing across the keyboard as he scrawled through the complex encryption program now running from Anya's memory stick.

He'd been right about Landvik's system. The hardware amassed in this room made the average hacker's setup look like a child's playroom by comparison. Then again, Landvik's father was a successful businessman who spoiled his only son rotten, and had no doubt bankrolled the entire thing without really understanding what he was funding. Even at university he seemed to possess nearly unlimited funds, while his fellow students lived on instant noodles and almost-expired milk.

Before starting it up, Alex had taken the precaution of disabling the system's internet access, and had even physically disconnected the network cables as an added safeguard, ensuring there was no way the program could send out its digital cry for help again. No way would he trust it with internet access until he was certain he had it under control.

And he knew he could master it. No matter how clever or complex it might be, sooner or later he'd crack it and bend it to his will. He might not know anything about survival or navigation or any of the hundred other skills that Anya apparently possessed, but when it came to computers he was unmatched.

Pausing a moment in his work, Alex tore into the tuna and cheese sandwich sitting on the desk in front of him, washing it down with a can of Red Bull. He hadn't eaten anything approaching a decent meal in nearly twenty-four hours, and had determined to put that right as soon as he set foot in Landvik's house. What the hell – Landvik himself had food to spare by the looks of him.

Despite everything, he caught himself smiling as he tossed the empty can into a nearby waste bin. Marcel Proust might have found his childhood rushing back to him with the simple taste of Madeleine cake, but for Alex the combination of sugar, taurine and God only knew what other chemicals went into the energy drink was enough to evoke the world he'd once been part of.

A world of late nights and tight deadlines, of challenges and accomplishments, of camaraderie and friendship. A world where he'd finally felt part of something bigger than himself, something he cared about.

The sound of footsteps in the corridor outside interrupted his thoughts, and he turned around just as Anya walked into the room.

She approached his workstation and leaned over to inspect his progress, though it was clear from the look in her eyes that the raw computer code filling most of the screen meant little to her.

'Interesting stuff, eh?' he prompted.

'How do you make sense of all this?' She was still staring at it as if mesmerized.

Alex shrugged. 'It's a language like any other. Once you understand the key words, it all starts to come together.'

The woman glanced away from the screen, turning her attention to him. 'I'll take your word for that. What's your progress so far?'

'Well, I found the subprogram that got me in so much trouble at the internet cafe,' he explained. 'Took me a while to find it because it's pretty well hidden, but basically it acts like a homing beacon every time you start it up – fires off a little burst of data to an encrypted IP address. It was a tricky little bastard to remove without making the whole thing fall apart, but I managed to snip it off.'

'That sounds promising,' Anya remarked, though her tone was guarded. She sensed a 'but' in there somewhere.

'It is, but that's the easy part,' he confirmed. 'The hard part will be fooling the CIA's system into thinking this is still an active identity. If we tried to log in with it right now, it would probably trigger their security protocols, and we'd have half the US military on our doorstep before I could finish my sandwich.'

Anya nodded. No doubt she was well aware of this problem. 'So how will you get around this?'

'No idea.' Alex flashed a grin at her. 'But don't worry, I've never come up against a system I couldn't break. Right now I'm picking the code apart line by line. It's tedious but it gets results. Once I understand how the thing works, I'll crack it.'

Anya said nothing. No doubt she harboured her own thoughts on his chances of success.

'By the way, where's Gregar?' Alex felt compelled to ask. He might have been a traitor and a dickhead, but he didn't deserve the kind of tender mercy that Anya seemed to have no qualms about dishing out.

As if guessing his thoughts, she gave him a disapproving look. 'In the bathroom, cleaning himself up. I secured the door, so he can't leave. Apparently his nose is bleeding again.' He saw a trace of an amused smile. 'He thinks he might be a haemophiliac.'

'He's a twat,' Alex informed her. 'There's no cure for that.'

She said nothing to this, though neither did she dispute his damning assessment. Instead she nodded to his right hand. The knuckles were bruised and swollen. 'How is your hand?'

Alex flexed and clenched the fingers. 'Hurts like a bastard, actually,' he admitted ruefully. 'I don't think I'm built for this whole fighting thing.'

'You're quite an actor, Alex,' she remarked, thinking about his earlier confrontation with his former friend.

He snorted. 'Who was acting? He deserved everything he got. The only reason I didn't kick the shit out of him is because I might need his help with this.'

Alex hardly considered himself a violent man, but in Landvik's case his assault had been well justified. The man's jealousy and greed had cost him two years of his life, his freedom and his future. A bloodied nose was scant recompense for such betrayal.

'What happened between you?' Anya asked.

'It's an epic saga,' he replied with false grandeur. 'One day they'll write operas about it.'

She fixed him with the look of mild disapproval she reserved for when his attempts at levity weren't appreciated, which was often. 'I'm serious, Alex. You wouldn't tell me before, and I can understand if it was difficult. But I need to know now.'

Alex sighed. She was right, of course. With Landvik now under the same roof as them, it was only natural she'd want to know what kind of man he was.

'I told you before that the three of us had different ideas about what Valhalla should be used for,' he said finally. 'Gregar wanted us to go underground and chase the easy money – hackers for hire, or some bollocks like that. Arran and I both argued against it, told him it wasn't why we'd gotten involved in this. He fought back, tried to get the others in the group to side with him, and we ended up expelling him. It was harsh, but we couldn't think of any other way to deal with him. But he wasn't finished with us.'

Alex had paused in his work, thinking over the final bitter act of revenge that had virtually destroyed his life. 'A month or so later, I was trying to crack the encryption on a government firewall for Arran. We were working to prove they were spying on British citizens, and my hack was a vital part of the project. Then, all of a sudden, armed police come storming into my house while I'm right in the middle of it. Someone had tipped them off about what I was doing; someone with detailed knowledge of how and when I'd break the firewall.'

He laughed then. Not an amused laugh, but the laugh of a man replaying the punchline of a cruel joke. 'I should have known he wouldn't just let it go. We'd hurt his pride, humiliated him. And he got back at us the only way he knew how. Well, he got his revenge all right. I did a two-year stretch inside, Valhalla was no more, and everything we'd worked for was gone.' He glanced at Anya. 'Probably doesn't mean much to you, but there it is.'

'Why did you do it?' she asked. 'You seem like a smart man. You must have suspected you would be caught sooner or later. Why take the risk when you could have made an honest living?'

'What? Are you here to give me a lecture on the evils of breaking the law?' he asked, making no effort to hide the mockery in his tone. His admission of past mistakes had stirred up pride and anger, and he was in no mood for a sermon from someone who killed people with her bare hands.

'I only want to understand.'

'No you don't,' he retorted. 'You just want something else you can use against me in case I get out of line. That's what you do, isn't it? Find a weakness in people, use it against them?'

Those eyes were focussed on him again, cold and clear and dangerous. 'Alex, I—'

'It's because it was the only thing I was ever good at, okay?' he snapped, blurting it out before he could stop himself. 'That what you want to hear?'

He paused then, taken aback by the anger and resentment that had suddenly welled up inside him. Even he hadn't expected to say it, to finally make that admission and face up to the truth about himself. And yet, now that he'd said it, he didn't regret it. If anything, he wanted to give her more, to finally let out everything he'd been holding inside for so long.

'Guess what? I'm not pretty and I can't sing. I wasn't in the football team at school and my chat-up lines suck. In fact, generally I'm pretty shit at most things. But not this. *This* is something I'm good at.' He gestured to the computer hardware all around him. 'It's illegal and dangerous and probably stupid, but it's all I had. And it made me feel good to know I could do things that other people couldn't. That's what you want to hear, isn't it? Well, I admit it. I did this because it made me feel better about being me. I did it because I wanted to belong to... *something*, I wanted to be with people who understood me and respected me for what I could do.' He sighed and shook his head. 'But don't worry – I don't expect someone like *you* to get it.'

He might have expected casual dismissal or even a scathing reprimand from a woman who had clearly put her life on the line more times than she could count, who had seen and done things he could scarcely imagine. Strangely, however, Anya seemed almost taken aback, as if his outburst had struck a chord with her.

'You're wrong about that,' she said, her voice uncharacteristically soft and quiet. 'I do understand. And if it means anything, I wasn't looking for weaknesses.'

Alex let out a breath, realizing to his embarrassment that he'd gone too far. Simple curiosity didn't warrant such an outburst, and considering her behaviour so far he was more than a little surprised she hadn't threatened to kill him for it.

'Take it you've found enough weaknesses already, eh?' he remarked, hoping she would take it as a gesture of reconciliation. Instead however she opted to keep her thoughts to herself.

'Anyway, now you know my dirty little secrets,' he said, turning his eyes back to the monitor in front of him. 'Shame I don't know yours.'

She said nothing to this. Instead she did a slow circuit of the dimly lit room, eyeing the unmade bed, the posters of video-game characters on the walls – most of which were female and scantily dressed – and the rubbish scattered around the overflowing waste-paper bin. There were a lot of used tissues in there, and Landvik didn't look like he had a cold.

'Most people would take that as a hint to give something back,' Alex prompted. 'Maybe tell me something about yourself that I don't know – like *anything*?'

'What would you like to know?' Anya asked without meeting his gaze.

'We could start with how you're involved with the CIA.'

She sighed faintly, as if she had been asked that question many times before and was weary of giving the same answer. 'I used to work for them.'

'Hardly earth-shattering news, but fair enough,' he conceded. 'How did that come about? You sound about as American as I do.'

She gave him a look that he'd come to recognize when he said something that was plainly idiotic. 'They employ people from many countries, Alex. Even yours.' She let that one hang for a moment or two before going on. 'In my case, they recruited me after I defected from the Soviet Union.'

Alex stared at her, his work temporarily forgotten. This was the first time she'd revealed anything substantial about herself, and he was intrigued by this strange, enigmatic woman who had been his sole companion for the past couple of days.

'You're Russian?'

She gave him what he could only describe as The Look. The kind of look his friend Danny, a Glaswegian native, had once given an Australian bartender who'd mistakenly called him English. 'Lithuanian,' she corrected him.

If Danny was anything to go by, it would be very unwise to question that one further. 'So what did they want with you?'

The look in her eyes was difficult to read, but for some reason he was reminded of himself when he'd been talking about Landvik's betrayal. 'We each have our talents, Alex. Mine didn't start with killing people. That only came later.'

'So you were some kind of... super-spy?'

She shook her head. 'A soldier. That's what I believed, at least. A warrior, fighting for a noble cause. And I was very good at what I did.'

Alex rubbed his jaw, feeling the bristles of a couple of days' growth. 'So how come you're working against them now?'

For a moment he saw the muscles in her shoulders tighten beneath the skin, saw her head lower and her hands curl into fists.

'Because I was wrong,' she said, her voice strained and tense. 'I wasn't a soldier. I wasn't fighting for a noble cause, and I wasn't serving worthy masters. I was exactly what they needed me to be. But by the time I realized how wrong I was, it was too late. Now I'm an outcast, a dirty secret to be covered up. They want me gone so they can pretend I never existed.' She looked at him then, her eyes shining in the dim light. The look of grief and betrayal and barely suppressed rage in them was enough to make the breath catch in his throat. 'Well, I won't go quietly.'

And just like that, she blinked and the emotions vanished. She was herself again. Cold and detached and controlled.

Alex let out a breath he hadn't realized he'd been holding. He had no idea what to make of what he'd just heard. She had opened up to him more than at any point since they'd met, yet he felt like he had more questions about her than ever before.

'I'm sorry,' he mumbled, looking away. 'It's none of my business.'

Anya let out a breath, the taut muscles relaxing a little as she forced calm into her body once more. 'I'll leave you to your work,' she decided. 'Call out if you need anything.'

Saying nothing further, she turned and left the room.

—

The big open-plan living room down the corridor was just as expensive and tastefully furnished as the rest of the house, with high-quality furniture and a kitchen that looked as if it had just come out of a showroom. The room's floor-to-ceiling windows had been designed to showcase the impressive views out over the lake and rolling woodland beyond. A set of sliding doors led out onto a tiled balcony, probably for dining and socializing during the summer months.

Making her way outside, Anya gripped the steel railings that encircled the balcony, closed her eyes and bowed her head. She could hear the gentle lapping of water at the lake shore below, the chirp of birdsong and the rustle of tree branches nearby. A faint breeze sighed past, stirring a few locks of hair and raising goosebumps on her exposed skin.

She exhaled, listening to the sound of her own breathing.

Normally she would have found such an idyllic location very much to her liking, but not today. Today her thoughts were turned inward.

Her career had often required her to take emotion out of the equation, to shut it down and lock it away in some dark corner of her mind, so she could focus clearly on the tasks at hand. It was this ability to be clinical and decisive that had saved her life more times than she could count.

And yet her conversation with Alex had stirred up long-buried feelings that she was having trouble locking away again. Feelings that threatened to overwhelm the barrier of cold detachment she had erected. Even now, the depth of her betrayal staggered her, enraged her, tortured her.

It was a betrayal all the more difficult to bear because of the man at the heart of it all. A man she had put her faith in. A man she had once believed could do great things. A man she had risked and sacrificed everything for.

A man named Cain.

Anya, once the loyal soldier, so easily manipulated and deceived by men who had made careers out of lying. Just another pawn to be used and sacrificed when she'd served her purpose. Now she was a ghost, a sad relic of another age lingering on in this world. Sooner or later her time would be over, but not yet.

Not yet. She still had one more battle to fight.

This had started with Cain, and it would end with him.

She would make sure of it.

–

The bathroom down the hall from Landvik's office was just as pristine and sterile as the rest of the house. Spotless white tiles, an ultramodern shower unit and a sink cut from a single block of marble. Even the picture hanging on the wall by the door was some piece of modern-art nonsense that his parents had bought simply because they could.

The small ventilation window above the toilet was hinged and locked so that it only opened a few inches. Even if the mechanism could be broken, the frame was scarcely big enough for a small child to clamber through, never mind a man of Landvik's size.

Neither could he open the door, which Anya had barred from the other side when she led him in here. He was trapped here, imprisoned until she decided to let him out.

Throwing the bloodied wad of tissue in the toilet, the young man let out a sigh and looked up at his reflection in the mirror. It wasn't a heartening sight. His nose was swollen and red, his unshaven face marked by splashes of dried blood, his eyes glassy and unfocussed.

But in truth, the superficial injury meant little to him. A bloodied nose would heal up soon enough, and it wasn't as if he was well known for his dashing good looks anyway.

What concerned him now was Alex, and more importantly the woman he'd apparently taken to associating with. What the hell had his former friend become involved in? And who had he become involved with?

Landvik himself had crossed the line of legality plenty of times during his online forays, and had dealt with a few unsavoury characters as a result. But always from behind the safe, controlled anonymity that his digital identity afforded him. Never up-close and personal like this, and certainly not with people like Anya.

She was a killer if ever he'd seen one. Cold, clinical, unflinching. Less of a criminal and more of an assassin.

Alex had barked orders at her earlier as if she was his to command, yet even Landvik could sense from her body language that she took instructions from no one. Had it been a ruse? Was she in fact the one in control of this situation?

If so, that didn't bode well for him. He'd seen her face and could identify her with ease if it came to it. If she was as ruthless as she appeared, she'd have no qualms about executing him once she had whatever she needed here. The thought was almost enough to make him throw up in that expensive marble sink.

'Get a hold of yourself, shithead,' he whispered at his reflection. 'Think.'

Splashing water on his face with trembling hands, he took a deep breath, forcing some semblance of calm into his mind. One way or another he had to figure a way out of this situation, and fast. That meant getting the hell out of this bathroom and finding a way to call for help without being noticed.

And since any attempt to force his way out would be suicidal, the only option was to get them to release them. That meant earning their trust. Well, perhaps not Anya's – he doubted she trusted anyone – but at least Alex's. Alex was his friend, or had been.

That was his way out.

Chapter 23

'Fuck!' Alex growled, hurling his second empty can of Red Bull into the corner of the room without even bothering to aim at the waste basket. A combination of frustration, growing impatience and high doses of caffeine was making him jittery and filled with energy he couldn't expel.

The fact that he'd hit a brick wall hadn't helped matters either.

His patient dissection of the encryption program had uncovered a possible loophole that he could exploit; a means of bypassing the security lockdown that had been tagged against Anya's identity. The problem however was turning theory into practice. The encryption scheme was unlike any he'd ever seen before, and was proving stubbornly resistant to his attempts at breaking in.

Time was marching on, and he was increasingly aware that he needed to make the breakthrough now, before Landvik's parents returned home. It was a stupid fucking problem to have when the man was pushing thirty, but it was there all the same.

'Alex.'

'What?' he snapped, turning to face the doorway. Anya was standing at the threshold, and beside her, much to his dismay, was Landvik.

'He insisted on speaking with you,' Anya said by way of explanation.

'What do you want, Gregar?' Alex demanded, eyeing him in much the same way he might have regarded a dog turd stuck to his shoe.

'To help you,' the Norwegian replied, looking surprisingly contrite now. 'And... to apologise.'

Alex's eyes narrowed. 'For what?'

'For what happened to you. For all the shit you've been through.' He swallowed, searching for the right words. 'I didn't do it, Alex. I know you don't believe that, but it's the truth. For a while, I wished I had thought of it. I was so pissed at you and Arran for shutting me out, and I wanted to get back at you. But I'd never take it that far. We're friends, Alex. Or... we *were* friends once. No matter how angry I was with you, I wouldn't turn you in to the police.'

Alex had to admit, even he was taken aback by the sincerity in Gregar's voice. Perhaps he was a better actor than Alex had given him credit for.

'That's just beautiful, mate,' he said, his tone laced with sarcasm. 'But apart from the fact it's in your interests to keep me sweet when your life's at stake, what reason do I have to believe you?'

And then something happened that Alex had never expected. Anya spoke up on Landvik's behalf.

'Because he is telling the truth,' she said.

Alex looked at her as if she were mad, which she quite possibly was if she believed Landvik was being straight with them. 'Come again?'

'He is not lying to you, Alex,' the woman said calmly. 'I can't vouch for his character, but what he has said is the truth.'

'How can you know that?'

'Because I've dealt with enough liars in my life to know the difference.'

Alex frowned. There was more to that statement than she was telling him – he was certain of it – but now wasn't the time to try to unravel her life story. Anyway, he'd spent enough time already banging his head against a brick wall today.

'You're serious about this, aren't you?' When she didn't respond, Alex turned his eyes on Landvik. 'So if it wasn't you, who did it?'

The big man made a helpless gesture. 'I don't know, Alex. All I can tell you is that it wasn't me.'

Alex let out a breath, slumping back in his chair. Unconsciously he glanced down at his hand, the knuckles bruised and red from where he'd struck his former friend earlier. Venting his anger without even questioning what he was doing.

Was it really possible? Had he been wrong all this time?

'Say I believe you, and I'm not sure I do...' he said at last, his voice quiet and subdued. After so long, he wasn't ready to admit it to himself yet, and certainly not to Landvik. 'Where do we go from here?'

'Well, it seems like you could use some help,' Landvik observed with typical dry humour. 'I know this system a lot better than you. At least I can stop you fucking things up worse than they are already.'

'I kind of doubt that.'

'If you think he can help, then say so now,' Anya prompted. 'Otherwise he's going back where he came from.'

'He knows I can help,' Landvik chipped in, his eyes on Alex the whole time. 'He just doesn't want to admit it.'

Alex glanced up at Anya, then back to his former friend. 'If you try to fuck us over, believe me when I say it'll end badly for you. And I'm not talking about a broken nose here. Are you sure this is what you want?'

He nodded. 'If it gets the two of you out of my house a little sooner, I'm in.'

Alex sighed, threw up his hands and turned back to the computer terminal. 'Fine. Pull up a chair. Let's just hope you're better at coding than I remember.'

Chapter 24

US Embassy, Oslo

The United States embassy building in which Mitchell now found herself was about as nondescript as they come – a big, monolithic glass block that seemed to have been dropped without warning on the centre of Oslo. Aside from the diplomatic seal on the lobby floor and the scattering of armed security guards, there was little to distinguish it from any of the dozens of other midrise office blocks in the area.

Still, it was infinitely better than a similar compound in Afghanistan, which had reminded her of a Lego castle surrounded by more fortifications than the average WWII bunker. And at least the coffee was good here, she thought, as she took a sip freshly poured from an urn in one corner of the room.

She and the rest of the team led by Hawkins had requisitioned a large open-plan office area on the top floor from which to continue their search for Yates, much to the chagrin of the diplomatic staff working there. However, a few terse orders from Hawkins had been enough to get them moving.

The man was nothing if not driven.

She could see him from where she stood. Unsurprisingly, he was on the phone to someone while the rest of the team worked to tie in with local police and follow up possible leads. He seemed to spend much of his time on the phone, though who he was talking to was a mystery.

One thing was certain – they were higher in the food chain than he was. She could tell from the tension in his shoulders, the set of his jaw, the look in his eyes, that he was intimidated by whoever he was conversing with. That certainly gave her pause for thought. Whoever could intimidate a man like Hawkins must have been powerful indeed.

'Penny for your thoughts,' a voice beside her prompted.

She glanced around at Argento, who had approached while she was preoccupied with Hawkins. 'Same questions, no answers. Who are we really chasing, and why?'

She saw a wry smile. 'I can name one person in this room who isn't going to give us any answers.'

Mitchell took a sip of coffee. 'I hear you.'

'So what do we do?'

There wasn't much they could do at this point. They were no closer to catching Yates than Hawkins himself, and that situation didn't seem likely to change any time soon.

'We wait,' she decided. As unpalatable as it might have been, it was their only option until they caught a break. 'But when the time comes, we bring Yates and the woman in alive. Agreed?'

Argento didn't respond. He didn't need to.

–

'I'm telling you, the best way in is through their server grid,' Landvik persisted, his voice rising in volume as frustration threatened to get the better of him. 'Just like we used to do it in the old days. We upset the load balancers to trigger a switchover, then—'

'Wait for them to trace the source of the overload and shut us down,' Alex interrupted him. 'Come on, Gregar. We're not hacking the payroll system of a local supermarket here. That shit was getting old when we were just starting out.'

His friend chewed his lip. 'What about a port scanner?'

Alex shook his head. 'They'd be ready for it. Any unusual activity would be flagged within seconds.'

The two men had been collaborating for the past thirty minutes, composing and discarding a dozen possible ideas and strategies without making any real breakthrough.

Alex kept coming up against the same problem that had dogged him since the beginning. The only way they could get in was to find a way to make use of Anya's conditional access module, but so far it had defeated their best attempts to subvert and overcome the lockdown that had been placed on it.

'The only way to get past the firewall is with the CAM,' he decided. 'The answer's in here somewhere. We just need to find it.'

'How?' Landvik asked. 'You can't log into a system with a compromised ID. And since we don't have any valid ones to replace it with, it's a waste of time.'

Alex closed his eyes for a moment, rubbing the bridge of his nose as fatigue, pain from his injured ribs and a growing headache pressed down on him like a physical weight. He felt like shit, plain and simple, and his failure to deliver on his promise to Anya wasn't helping his mood.

'I need a smoke,' he decided. Nicotine – and often something a little stronger – always used to help him sort through complex problems like this.

Landvik shook his head. 'Not in here. If my dad smells smoke in the house, he will literally take his rifle and hunt us both down.'

Just my luck, Alex thought with grim humour. It wasn't bad enough that the CIA wanted him dead; now he'd have to contend with a mad Norwegian with a cleanliness fetish.

'I'm sorry, Alex,' his friend went on, his voice quieter now. 'We gave it a good shot, but I don't think we can win this one.'

'This isn't school sports day, man. They don't give marks for effort.'

'So what? We've had failures before. You pick yourself up and move on. Why is this one so important?'

Unable to help himself, Alex slammed his fist down on the table, sending a shiver of pain up his arm. 'Because I don't want to end up like Arran,' he snapped.

At this, Landvik frowned. 'What do you mean? What happened to Arran?'

Alex winced, wishing he'd never spoken. 'Forget it. You'll live longer.'

'Fuck that. We might have had our differences, but Arran was still a friend. If something happened to him, I want to know right now.'

Sighing, Alex leaned back in his chair. 'A week ago he contacted me, offered me a job. I refused, so he took it on himself. Then he disappeared.' He glanced at Landvik. 'You figure it out.'

Landvik's eyes were wide as he turned slowly to look out the window, seeing nothing. Whatever else he might have been, he obviously still considered Arran a friend. 'Fuck.'

'Yeah, that more or less sums it up,' Alex agreed. 'And unless I make it further than Arran did, I'm next. Maybe now you understand why this is so important.'

Landvik shook his head. 'What about this Anya you've brought with you? Where the hell did you find her?'

Alex almost laughed at the irony. 'I didn't. She found me.'

'Then maybe it's time she lost you.'

Alex looked up at him. 'What are you saying?'

'Come on, Alex. You're stupid, but not that stupid. Do you really think she would keep us around if we were of no use to her?' Landvik asked, staring him hard in the eye. 'Or that she'll let us go now we know what she looks like?'

Alex couldn't help wondering about that. 'She saved my life twice in as many days.'

'Why? Because you promised you could deliver?' He eyed Alex shrewdly. 'What do you think she'll do when she finds out you were bullshitting?'

'I wasn't bullshitting!' Alex hissed, trying to keep his voice down. 'I meant what I said.'

'But that doesn't change the fact you can't deliver. One way or another, failure is failure, and that's all she'll see.'

Just for a moment, Alex felt completely torn. Torn between a possibly misplaced sense of loyalty to Anya and what she'd done for him so far, and

Landvik's very pragmatic assessment of his situation. Was he right? Was Anya merely stringing him along until he'd served his purpose? Should he try to cut and run now while he had the chance? If so, could he really spend the rest of his life looking over his shoulder, wondering if this was the day she finally caught up with him?

Sensing that his friend was wavering, Landvik leaned in closer, his voice low and urgent as he tried to strike the killer blow. 'Maybe you should think about a different option.'

'What option?' Anya asked from the doorway, cutting short their conversation before Alex had time to consider his reply.

Landvik, to his credit, reacted immediately to her unannounced arrival and swung around to face her.

'Another way into the system. We're beating our heads against a brick wall with this.' He threw up his hands in a gesture of helplessness. 'The encryption scheme is too strong to break. We can't use the compromised ID you've given us, and there's no way to create a new one.'

Anya said nothing to this. She had wisely stayed out of their discussions and arguments so far – a silent and brooding presence occasionally taking a break from patrolling the house to watch their petty bickering.

She looked directly at Alex, ignoring his companion. In matters such as this, she trusted only his opinion. 'Is he right, Alex?'

He didn't respond. He didn't know what to tell her.

'Alex, I want you to be honest with me,' she pressed, her tone harder and more commanding now. 'Can this be done, or are we wasting our time?'

Alex's head was pounding as the physical and mental toll of the past couple of days seemed to pile in against him. Images of the two dead men at the farm mingled together inside his mind with the moment of realisation that he was a hunted man, the failed escape bid across the rooftops, and the awful feeling of water being poured down his throat. And everywhere, drowning out everything else, he saw line after line of computer code descending on his mind like a net, trapping him, smothering him, drowning him.

All because he'd been stupid enough to use that memory stick.

And then, just like that, it came to him.

'Oh my God,' he gasped, snapping back to awareness.

'What?'

Alex could have slapped himself. Like most complex problems, the maddeningly simple solution had been staring him in the face all along. Straight away he turned around and went to work, attacking the computer code he'd been so carefully picking apart all morning.

'I don't believe it. All this time I've been looking for a way into their system without being detected, a way to use this module you gave me without it giving us away,' he said, his voice working almost as fast as his fingertips on the keyboard. 'But I was wrong. The only way in is to *let* it give us away.'

The woman was frowning now. She might not have known much about software engineering, but as a soldier she understood that giving one's enemy exactly what they wanted was a quick way to lose a battle. 'How will that help?'

'The minute the CAM goes live, it sends out a ping. A little burst of data telling the Agency it's online and being used. Their automatic response is to run a trace programme to find the source of the ping, basically following it back to its source. That's how they found me in London.'

'I know all this,' she reminded him. 'Tell me how you can use it.'

'Don't you get it? That trace programme is our way in. To run it, they have to make a connection with this computer. The second they do that, we've got them.'

Finally the penny dropped for Landvik. 'You're talking about using a stalker. You clever little shit.'

Anticipating Anya's question, Alex decided to offer an explanation. 'A stalker is a special program we normally use to hack corporate networks. It's not exactly designed for this, but if it does its job, it'll hijack their connection and give us a back door through their firewall. Kind of like a trace in reverse.'

'Their system won't know anything's wrong, because the trace was activated at their end,' Landvik carried on. 'Once we're inside, we'll have the run of the entire network. Fucking genius.'

Anya however was less interested in massaging egos. 'Will it work?'

'Well, that depends on your point of view,' Alex said, without taking his eyes off the screen. 'The stalker will get us inside. The problem is that I'll have to find and shut down the alert before they break into our own system. Gregar's firewalls should buy us the time we need, but there are no guarantees. It's a calculated risk.' At this, he paused a moment and turned to look at her. 'It's up to you, Anya. Do you want to go for it?'

Anya said nothing for several seconds. For perhaps the first time, she looked genuinely undecided about what to do, and he could understand why. He was asking her to trust him, to put her faith in him and know he wouldn't let her down. It was a big ask.

Taking a breath, she nodded, the decision made. 'Do it.'

That was all he needed. 'All right. Gregar, get ready with the stalker. The second the trace hits us, send it.'

'On it.'

Reaching down, Alex picked up the network cables he had disconnected earlier to prevent the system going online, took a moment to send a silent prayer to whatever deities might govern the world of computers, and plugged them in.

Within seconds, the tool Landvik was using to measure the flow of data to and from his machine noted the sudden jump in usage. 'I see it. The ping just went out.'

'Get ready,' Alex said quietly, clenching and unclenching his fists as he prepared to spring into action, like a sprinter waiting for the starting gun.

Then, sure enough, it came.

'That's it!' Landvik cried. 'Their trace is active. It's at our firewall.' A single mouse click was enough to unleash his counter attack. 'Stalker's away.'

'How long will it take?' Anya asked.

Her answer came before Alex could even articulate a reply, which was just as well because he needed every ounce of concentration now. A single chime sounded, followed by a pop-up message informing him that the program had succeeded in establishing a connection.

And that was it. In a moment or two, they were inside.

'Yes!' Alex cried, punching the air. 'Get in, son!'

'We're in,' Landvik gasped, hardly believing it had worked.

For a few seconds Alex just sat there, mesmerized by the sheer scale of his accomplishment. He had done what no spy or intelligence agency had ever managed. Sitting here in an untidy bedroom in the middle of nowhere, he now had full and unlimited access to one of the most secure and secretive organisations on the planet.

But first he had to cover his tracks.

'Right, let's disable this trace before they find us,' he said, mindful that the CIA's best cracking tools were at this very moment working to break through Landvik's own firewall to discover their location. He was packing some of the best triple-layered security available, but even this wouldn't hold off a determined attack forever.

With the determination born from urgency, he went to work. There was no web page or graphical interface of any kind to work with now; just row after row of files and directories. He had bypassed all of the usual tools and browsers that he assumed CIA employees used to navigate their own system, instead delving right into the hidden file structure beneath it all.

'They're through the first layer,' Landvik warned, monitoring his system security with a look of growing alarm. 'Damn, they're fast. The second one's about to go.'

For the next thirty seconds, Alex's fingers danced over the keyboard as he trawled through level after level of files and databases, searching for the core of the vast system, the central point from which everything else branched out. It might have belonged to the world's premier intelligence agency, but it was a system like any other, and he'd trawled through so many just like it that he felt almost as if he were navigating by instinct.

'Second layer's gone,' his friend said. 'Shit, they're at the last line. We're down to seconds, Alex.'

But Alex wasn't listening any more; all his attention was focussed on the task at hand. That was all that mattered now. Bringing up the massive database of user identities, he hurriedly scrawled through, searching for the one allocated to Anya.

A bead of sweat trickled down his temple, but he paid it no heed as his eyes flitted from line to line, his brain surging ahead.

'It's about to go!'

There! He had it. Highlighting the alert-flagged ID, he delved straight into its database entry and with a single mouse-click disabled the alert.

'Did it work?' he asked, his muscles tight, his heart pounding.

Several tense, anxious seconds passed while Landvik consulted his screen. 'I... I think so. All activity in the firewall has stopped.' He looked at his friend, a slow smile growing on his face. 'I think we did it.'

Letting out a breath, Alex slumped back in his chair, mentally and physically drained.

'So what happens now?' Anya asked.

Alex nodded slowly, wiping the sweat from his brow. 'We're in. No user ID, no restrictions, nothing. We can access anything, anywhere on their network now.' He glanced up at her, weary but proud. 'The only question now is what you want to look for.'

Anya exhaled, and for a moment her mask of self-control slipped aside. Alex saw elation and relief, and something else. Trepidation. She was afraid of what she was going to find.

'One file,' she said, leaning in close. 'The name is D1189.'

'Doesn't exactly roll off the tongue,' Landvik observed, as Alex inputted the details and turned his search engine loose on the vast network.

'It is just a reference number,' she explained, her attention focussed on the screen. 'The file was created in November 1989.'

'What does the D stand for?' Alex couldn't help asking.

With his back to her, he could feel rather than see her eyes on him. 'Deniable.'

Alex paused for a moment, then went back to work.

'I need a smoke,' Landvik decided. 'Call out if you need me.'

Neither Anya nor Alex looked up, which Landvik took as tacit acknowledgement of his intentions. Saying nothing more, the young man backed out of the room and left them to it.

'It's about you, isn't it?' Alex said, once his friend's footsteps had disappeared down the corridor. 'This file you're looking for. It's yours. What are you expecting to find?'

'Just concentrate on your work,' Anya advised him, the tension in her voice unmistakable.

Alex knew better than to argue.

–

In the open-plan living room nearby, Landvik was pacing back and forth as he pondered what to do next. The stunning views that the room's full-length windows commanded over the nearby lake and woodland beyond were lost on him. All his thoughts were now focussed on finding a way out of this situation.

He may have been willing to give Alex the benefit of the doubt, but the woman was another matter entirely. He'd seen the look in her eyes, the way she carried herself, the constant wariness. She was a stone-cold killer, as sure as day.

He had to do something now, before it was too late. For all he knew, he might end up as a hostage once Anya had gotten what she wanted here, or a 'suicide'.

His mind was racing, desperately considering his options. All the doors and windows in the house were locked. Anya had confiscated all cell phones and disabled the landlines, making it impossible for him to escape or call for help even if he'd harboured such thoughts.

He could try to take her down first. His father kept a hunting rifle and a supply of ammunition in a cupboard under the stairs. But a heavy rifle wasn't much of a weapon for fighting in a confined space like this, and with only a couple of half-hearted shooting lessons under his belt, he was barely competent in its use.

Even if he was somehow able to retrieve it from its storage cabinet and load it without attracting her attention, he doubted a fat computer hacker with an old bolt-action rifle would present much of a threat to someone like her. No, confrontation was out of the question.

Another option was to summon help. Anya might have taken his phones, but there was another way to make contact with the outside world. His father, keen to protect the house he'd invested so much money in, had made sure the place was fitted with a top-of-the-line security system. Motion sensors, concealed video-entry system, and most importantly for him, a silent alarm.

There were hidden triggers in every room, meaning they were always within easy reach in the event an intruder made it inside. One press of the button would put trigger an automated phone call to the security company managing the system, who would in turn contact the police.

The drawbacks to this were obvious however. The moment Anya saw police cars approaching, she'd know what he had done. She might take him hostage, or panic and kill him. Either way, he had no desire to be caught in the crossfire.

In his mind, the best option was simply to get the hell out of here.

But he certainly wouldn't make it far on foot, even if he could find a way out. He was a good sixty pounds overweight, and he hadn't done anything approaching strenuous exercise in nearly a decade. Someone like her could run him down before he'd made it a hundred yards.

If he was going to do this, he needed a vehicle.

His father's weekend car, a Mitsubishi Outlander, was safely parked in the house's integrated garage. Anya had made sure to take the keys, but she had missed the spare set hidden away in a metal tin in one of the kitchen drawers. With so many possible exits and escape routes to secure, he could only assume that she had simply overlooked it.

That was his play.

Almost before he was aware of it, he was heading towards the kitchen area. If he could get to the vehicle and force open the garage doors, he'd be out of here in under a minute. He felt bad for leaving Alex behind, but what else could he do? Playing hero was a quick way to get killed.

The sound of soft footsteps in the hallway alerted him that Anya was on her way, probably to check on him. Cursing the bad timing, he abruptly turned around and recrossed the room, heading for the balcony that lay beyond the living-room windows.

His only thought was to get outside, away from her.

'Are you all right?' he heard her ask.

'Fine,' he lied without turning around. He was moving towards the glass door leading outside. 'Just going onto the balcony for a smoke. My dad won't let me do it in here.'

He was just reaching for the handle when she called out to him again.

'Gregar?'

He closed his eyes as his stomach knotted with panic. What did she want? Had she guessed his intentions? Forcing himself to stay calm despite his wildly beating heart, he slowly turned to face her, wondering if he'd find himself staring down the barrel of a weapon.

Instead he saw Anya standing by the kitchen counter. She was holding out the lighter and packet of cigarettes that he'd left lying there.

'You will probably need these,' she said.

Gregar let out a nervous laugh. 'Good point. My mind's been all over the place today,' he said, which was certainly true.

Quickly crossing the room, he reached across the counter and took the packet, hoping she couldn't see the tremor in his hand as he reached beneath the counter and hit the silent alarm trigger. However, she tightened her grip on the packet as he tried to take it, her eyes locked with his.

He froze, his body tensing up. He could almost feel the beads of sweat forming on his forehead.

'You should try to cut down,' she advised, glancing down at the cigarettes. 'These are bad for you.'

Such was his relief, it was all he could do to keep from bursting into nervous laughter.

'Yes. But they keep the weight off.' He managed to flash a wry grin.

She didn't laugh. Instead she eyed him a moment longer, leaving him with the impression she knew exactly what he was thinking, before finally releasing her grip on the packet.

'The doors are locked. You smoke in here, or not at all,' she instructed, turning away to go back to the bedroom.

–

'We've got them!' Argento said, having just taken a call from the National Security Agency monitoring station back at Menwith Hill. 'NSA just intercepted a call from a Norwegian security company to local police. One of their clients near the town of Drammen just hit their silent intruder alarm.'

Hawkins immediately looked up from his computer. 'Give me a reason to get excited about that.'

'The house is fitted with a video entry system that logs all new arrivals. We were able to intercept the image the security company forwarded on to the police.'

Saying nothing more, he spun his laptop around, allowing Hawkins to view the slightly grainy black-and-white image that had been sent through. Sure enough, it showed a young man and a woman standing at the front door.

Their features were unmistakable. It was Yates and Anya.

'You got a location?'

'Drammen, about thirty miles south-west of here. By the sounds of things, local police have requested an armed response unit.'

Hawkins practically jumped out of his seat. 'Call NSA and have them put a false alarm call through to Norwegian police, and have them vector in any drone or satellite assets we have to that location. I want our chopper fuelled and ready to lift off in three minutes. Everyone else on me. Move!'

Chapter 25

A ping from the main terminal announced that the search engine had found a result. Swinging his chair back around, Alex stared at the screen.

'Yes!' he cried, clapping his hands in excitement as he surveyed the results of three hours of solid work on screen before him. 'We're in business.'

Just as she'd said, the search had returned a single file, buried deep within a hidden directory set apart from the main file structure. It would have been invisible to anyone using the system with standard access, but Alex's unrestricted access allowed him to see what others couldn't.

Anya was by his side within moments, leaning forward to survey the screen. 'What happens now?'

'Now we download this bastard,' Alex said, as he carefully highlighted the file and hit download.

Download in progress...

Whatever the file was, it was big. According to the on-screen status bar, it was going to take several minutes to download in its entirety.

The woman glanced at him with a raised eyebrow, but didn't pass comment. 'How long will this take?'

'Well, it's pretty big, and the connection here isn't great. Five or six minutes at most.'

She nodded, her face a mask of tight self control. She wouldn't crack open the champagne until the file was in her hands.

'Can the Agency trace this?' she asked.

Alex shook his head. 'Nope. This one's below their radar.' He grinned. 'See what I did there? Thought you might appreciate the military lingo.'

She didn't, and her expression made it clear.

In search of a more appreciative audience, Alex turned towards the door. 'Hey, Gregar! Come here and take a look at this, mate. This is poetry in motion!'

There was no response.

'Gregar!' Alex called out. 'Now's a bad time to be taking a shit!'

Still there was no reply. Frowning, Alex looked at his companion.

'Keep working,' Anya instructed, drawing the automatic from the back of her jeans.

'Wait. What about—?'

'Just do it!' she hissed. 'Let me know as soon as the file is downloaded.'

Saying nothing further, she turned and vanished from the room, leaving Alex to it.

Swearing under his breath, Alex turned his attention back to the download task bar, curious why the file seemed to be taking so long to download. A quick check of the system's network activity soon revealed the answer. The download was being directed to more than one place.

One stream was feeding into Landvik's computer, while the other was being beamed off to an IP address he didn't recognise.

'What the hell are you up to?' he mumbled, clicking on the link.

—

In the garage, Landvik was fumbling with trembling hands to get his key in the ignition of the big Mitsubishi 4x4. However, panic-stricken haste made his task a great deal more difficult than it should have been, and the keys slipped from his grasp.

'Fuck!' he hissed, bending down to retrieve them. Every second he delayed increased his chances of being caught.

Snatching them off the floor, he sat up, then let out an involuntary gasp at the sight that confronted him. Anya was standing directly in front of the vehicle, her weapon trained on him. At such close range she could hardly miss.

'Get out of the car,' she instructed. 'Now.'

'Oh fuck, oh fuck, oh fuck,' he groaned, reaching for the door and pushing it open. 'Please, I was only trying to—'

No sooner had he stepped out onto the concrete floor than she rounded the vehicle, gripped him by his t-shirt and hauled him forcefully back into the main part of the house, keeping the barrel of the weapon pressed against his head.

As soon as they were in the living room, the weapon was withdrawn. He felt an instant of relief, then suddenly something struck him on the back of the neck, sending lightning forks of pain radiating out through his body. A kick to the back of his left knee was enough to finish the job, and he went down with a cry of pain and terror.

Struggling to see properly, he heard the sound of footsteps on the hardwood floor circling around in front of him, and managed to focus on Anya as she stalked into view. She had a gun in one hand and a knife in the other, and he didn't doubt for a second that she was prepared to use both weapons on him.

'What have you done, Gregar?' she demanded, her voice flat and cold. Only her eyes revealed the anger she felt. 'We were getting ready to leave. Why try to escape now?'

He couldn't help what happened next. He felt a sudden surge of damp warmth between his legs, followed by the acrid stench of urine as it soaked into his jeans.

Landvik shook his head, realizing with a fleeting sense of shame that he was crying. 'I didn't... I can't...'

She took a step forward. One booted foot shot out and planted itself firmly in his flabby abdomen, sending another wave of pain through him. He felt his stomach constrict as if tying itself in knots, and immediately doubled over as a stream of bile and vomit flew out of his mouth and over the expensive flooring.

'Don't make me ask you again,' she advised him, taking a step back. 'Tell me what you have done.'

'I...' He sniffed, knowing what it would mean when he told her. 'I set off the silent alarm. I'm sorry! I thought you were going to kill me.'

The sound of footsteps in the corridor announced the arrival of the third member of their group. Landvik watched as Alex skidded to a stop at the room's threshold, staring open-mouthed at the scene that confronted him.

'Anya, what the fuck—?'

'Stay out of this!' she warned, rounding on him. 'Your "friend" has betrayed us to the Norwegian police.'

Alex's eyes turned to Landvik, who was still lying curled up on the floor. 'Mate, tell me she's wrong.'

Landvik said nothing, merely shook his head.

Alex's eyes opened wide in shock as the truth sank in. 'Gregar, what have you done? You fucking arsehole, we were almost finished!'

Anya's attention was focussed on the prisoner. 'When did you do it?'

'About... ten minutes ago.'

Her stern gaze wavered for a moment as a new threat manifested in her mind. Straight away she turned to her companion, pointing back towards the bedroom.

'Get back to work, Alex. We're leaving as soon as you have the file,' she said, striding forward and hauling Landvik to his feet. It was no easy task given his sizeable frame. 'I'll take care of this.'

Alex hesitated, his eyes flitting between the woman and his friend, hurt and cowering in terror. 'You can't kill him,' he pleaded, perhaps sensing her intentions. 'He's an arsehole, but he doesn't deserve to die for this.'

'He won't,' she promised. 'Now go. Hurry!'

Alex was just turning towards the hallway when a sudden noise overhead caught his attention. A loud, rhythmic beating, accompanied by the high-pitched whine of aircraft engines.

His gaze drawn to the open expanse of lake beyond the living room's full-length windows, Alex stared in silence as a helicopter suddenly descended into view, its blades scything the air, the downwash from the main rotors whipping up a storm of wind and spray on the calm waters. He hadn't even been aware of the helicopter's noise until it was almost upon them, and now here it was not more than fifty yards away.

The sliding door fixed into the side of the aircraft was open, and he could see movement inside. He caught a glimpse of something long and gleaming angling towards them, followed by a sudden flash as if a camera had just taken a snap.

'Get down!' Anya shouted.

The tinkle of shattered glass was followed by a curious wet crunch, reminding him of an egg breaking. He felt something warm splash his cheek, and out of the corner of his eye spotted a sudden spray of red that seemed to coat the room.

Failing to comprehend what he was seeing, Alex looked over as Landvik slumped to the floor, falling like a puppet whose strings had just been cut. But he didn't look like the Landvik he remembered. He seemed to be missing most of his head, exposing broken skull and the delicate organ that was supposed to be contained within. The blood-soaked remains of his blonde ponytail hung loose from a piece of bone and skin that had almost detached.

His mind couldn't process it, but his body was already starting to react. He could feel his heart pounding, could hear the blood rushing in his ears.

Anya was yelling something. He could hear the reverberation of her voice, even if he couldn't focus on the words. As if in a trance, Alex looked up from Landvik's body just as Anya launched herself at him, tackling him around the midsection like a rugby player.

They fell and landed hard, the impact knocking the wind from his lungs and pressing agonizingly against his already bruised ribs. The polished hardwood floor presented almost no friction against their lateral movement, and they slid several yards before finally coming to a halt in the corridor beyond.

At the same time, more shots tore through the house, shattering windows and slamming into the wall opposite. The wall-mounted television disintegrated in a shower of broken plastic and shattered electrical components, followed a moment later by one of the kitchen cupboards.

'Alex, are you hurt?' Anya asked, her face mere inches from his.

He didn't respond. He was staring around the corner at the pool of blood and brain matter that was slowly spreading out from the remains of his friend's head.

'Alex, look at me!' Anya shouted, forcefully turning his face towards her. 'I'm sorry for your friend, but I need you to focus or we both die here!'

Finally his mind seemed to emerge from the dull shock that had numbed him for the past few seconds. 'The police... just murdered him. Why?'

'It's not the police. It's the Agency,' she said, drawing the automatic from her jeans. 'They must have intercepted police communications.'

Backing up against the wall, she leaned out just far enough to survey the area beyond the shattered living-room windows. Sure enough, the chopper was maintaining station about fifty feet above the surface of the lake. Low enough to give the shooter an excellent field of fire over the house, but high enough that the aircraft's downwash wouldn't kick up surface spray and interfere with his aim.

From her extensive knowledge of such aircraft, it looked like a variant of the Bell 206. Such choppers had been exported all over the world, and were used in everything from traffic reports to police pursuits. It was a civilian rather than a military aircraft, with no armour belt or inbuilt weapons systems, but it was a perfect vehicle for moving an Agency strike team around without attracting attention.

Her USP pistol was useless against such a target. Even without armour protection, the chopper was still well beyond the effective range of the automatic, and the minute she exposed herself she'd be under fire from what sounded like a Barrett .50 calibre rifle. Such a gun was designed to take out armoured vehicles, never mind the fragile human bodies inside them.

As to remind her of this fact, the gunner perched in the chopper's doorway opened fire again, forcing Anya to duck behind cover as another heavy-calibre shell slammed into the wall mere inches away.

Guessing his intentions, she flattened herself on the floor as a second round punched right through the retaining wall above her, followed by a third, and a fourth. He was working his way methodically along the wall in case she was foolish enough to think it offered any protection.

'They have us covered,' she said, wiping concrete dust from her eyes. 'We can't escape.'

'We could wait them out,' Alex suggested. 'They can't stay up there forever.'

The woman shook her head. 'The chopper is there to keep us pinned down. Ground teams will be moving in to surround the building.'

What she couldn't understand was why the chopper gunner had decided to move in and open fire on the building in the first place. It would have been far more prudent to wait and allow agents on the ground to surround and storm the place, taking them all by surprise and subduing them without a shot fired.

Then again, perhaps he had an entirely different plan in mind. Something that would ensure none of them lived to talk about what happened here.

The aircraft outside was moving, doing a slow circuit of the building in search of a better shot. With such constant eyes in the sky, there was no chance of them escaping unseen. They were trapped here.

Alex looked at her, sensing her unease. 'What the fuck are we going to do?'

They couldn't go anywhere with the chopper overhead. One way or another it had to be dealt with. Anya chewed her lip for a moment or two, deep in thought, before finally nodding to herself.

'Does Landvik keep any weapons in the house?'

Alex closed his eyes, focussing his razor-sharp memory on his one previous visit to this house. Gregar's father was an outdoors type – very much into 4x4s, mountain biking and above all, hunting. He used to pride himself on the freezer full of elk meat that he'd killed, cleaned and gutted himself, as if the ability to point a gun and shoot somehow made him more of a man.

Regardless though, he made sure to keep the tool of this particular trade within his home, and had even shown it to Alex on one occasion.

'There used to be a hunting rifle under the stairs,' he said, though he had no idea if it was still there. 'It's the only gun I know of here.'

'All right. Get to the computer, retrieve the files.' Without hesitation she turned the automatic around and thrust it into his hand. 'Shoot anyone you see who isn't me.'

Alex swallowed, staring at the weapon as if it might explode in his hands. 'I've never fired a gun in my life.'

He saw a fleeting look of disappointment in her eyes. 'There is a round in the chamber. Just grip it tight, point and shoot; don't hesitate. That's all you have to do.' Reaching out, she laid a hand on his shoulder. 'You can do this, Alex.'

Saying nothing further, she jumped to her feet and took off down the corridor, leaving him alone.

–

Fifty feet above, Jason Hawkins surveyed the big lakeside house through his magnified sniper's scope. The Barrett M82 automatic rifle in his arms was a leaden weight that few men could have easily manoeuvred in such close confines, never mind used effectively, but years of intense training and experience had endowed him with a strength and skill that was almost unmatched.

He held the weapon steady, his face a mask of calm self control that hid the conflicted emotions vying for dominance within him. He'd felt a momentary surge of excitement and anticipation at seeing Anya again, at having her in his crosshairs and knowing he had the power to put her down.

Only her quick reflexes, and the stupid fat bastard who had inadvertently acted as a human shield, had saved her life. She was still alive and somewhere inside the house, though he was confident she couldn't escape without being seen. As well as this chopper and the ground team surrounding the house, he could also call upon a remote-controlled drone aircraft that had been tasked to the operation. Orbiting high overhead, unseen and unheard, its thermal imaging cameras were covering the entire area. Even Anya couldn't compete with the technology arrayed against her.

He had her. And one way or another, he would take her down.

There would be no arrest this time. No handing her over to a foreign government only to see her escape later. Hawkins was out to finish what he'd started six years earlier.

'Bring us around to the south-west side,' he said, indicating to the pilot that he wanted to switch position, then quickly changed frequency to broadcast a message to his ground teams. 'Alpha to all units. Tangos confirmed on-site. Hold the perimeter and don't let anyone leave.'

His radio headset crackled. 'Alpha, who's shooting?' a female, and very pissed-off, voice demanded. 'We're in position. Let us move in.'

Hawkins gritted his teeth. Mitchell, the woman who was rapidly becoming a pain in his ass. A pain he wasn't prepared to tolerate much longer. She questioned too much, thought too much, saw too clearly. People like that were liabilities he could ill afford.

'Negative, Charlie,' he replied tersely. 'Hold position. We have armed tangos inside.'

'Copy that.' Her own reply was equally hostile, but even she knew better than to start an argument in the middle of an operation. 'Standing by.'

Spotting a sudden movement in one of the bedrooms overlooking the lake, Hawkins adjusted his aim, focussing in on the window. A curtain had been drawn to hide the interior from view, but the thin fabric could do little to disguise the heat emitted by a human body – heat that his thermal imaging scope was perfectly capable of detecting.

Pressing his eye to the scope, he could make out the flickering glow of a computer or TV screen, and the red outline of a figure leaning over it. Yates.

It would be the last mistake he ever made.

'I have a tango!' he called out. 'Hold us steady.'

Tensing up, he took aim and pulled the trigger.

–

Alex was just leaning over the computer to check the download progress when he paused. The engine noise of the chopper outside had changed note, as if the pilot had made some correction to his course. He wasn't circling the building any more in search of a target; he'd stopped.

He'd found his target. But who?

Anya was too clever to expose herself, and Landvik was already dead.

That only left...

Reacting on nothing more than gut instinct, Alex threw himself to the floor just as something punched its way through the window, tearing a hole in the curtain and impacting the computer he'd just been standing over.

'Shit!' he cried out, curling into a ball as sparks and fragments of broken plastic and metal flew outward from the ruined machine.

Keeping his belly flat against the floor, he crawled backwards towards the hallway even as more shots tore through the window, destroying what was left of Landvik's workstation. And the files he'd been in the midst of downloading.

–

'Tango in the upper bedroom,' Hawkins reported. 'Possible kill.'

It was hard to tell what had happened in there, given the sudden thermal bloom as a stray round destroyed whatever electrical equipment had been running. All he knew for sure was that the figure he'd been aiming at had fallen from sight.

No sooner had he spoken than another voice cut into the radio conversation. 'Overlord has movement in the building. First floor window.'

Overlord was the call sign for the Reaper drone. Larger, faster and capable of flying higher than the Predator it was slowly replacing, the Reaper was the ultimate in pilotless aircraft. Its thermal-imaging cameras could pick out even the smallest movement, making it impossible to escape.

Some, like the one watching over them today, were even coated in radar-absorbing material, allowing them to operate in foreign airspace undetected.

Hawkins's eye was back behind the scope in a heartbeat, muscles bunching and straining as he brought the cumbersome weapon to bear on a new target.

He was a moment too late.

–

Below, Anya sat crouched by the window of the upstairs bedroom, watching the chopper as it slowly moved past her line of sight. The bolt-action rifle pressed against her shoulder was of a type unfamiliar to her, but seemed to have been designed with big-game hunting in mind. The .270 Winchester cartridges it used, popular with hunters the world over, were lethal at up to a thousand yards, and powerful enough to take down elk and moose with a single shot.

It was just as well, because her chosen prey was almost forty feet long and weighed over 2,000 pounds.

Sighting the chopper, she adjusted her aim upward to the engine housing and the delicate mechanical systems contained within. She would have preferred to take out the gunner, but the chopper itself was likely fitted with thermal-imaging equipment that was being used to direct ground units to their position. One way or another she needed to put it out of action.

Taking first pressure on the trigger, she relaxed her arm slightly in preparation for the recoil, exhaled, and fired.

The report of the weapon in such a confined space was deafening, the blast reverberating off the walls until it left her ears ringing. She let out an involuntary grunt as the weapon slammed back into her shoulder with enough force to leave bruises, the foresight jumping upward despite her efforts to hold the weapon still.

Straight away her right hand was moving, working the bolt action to eject the spent cartridge and draw a fresh one into the breech. In just over a second she had chambered her second round, sighted the engine housing once more and loosed another shot.

–

Hawkins almost smiled as his sights came to rest on Anya's head. With the power of the Barrett .50 cal, a hit just about anywhere on the body would cause catastrophic damage and deal a disabling if not a fatal injury, but he wanted a head shot.

He wanted to look into her eyes in that final moment before her skull disintegrated.

'Bang, you're dead,' he whispered as his finger tightened on the trigger, taking first pressure.

Suddenly the helicopter shuddered as the round impacted above him. Before he had time to react, the aircraft yawed violently to port, pulling the barrel of the gun upward just as he squeezed the trigger.

The Barrett discharged with a thunderous boom, sending its projectile sailing harmlessly off into the woodland beyond the house. Abandoning the cumbersome weapon, Hawkins grabbed hold of a restraining harness to steady himself as the deck tilted beneath his feet, threatening to pitch him right out the open doorway.

'What the fuck's going on up there?' he snarled as the surface of the lake lurched and swayed dangerously beneath them. It was as if the chopper had become caught in the funnel of a tornado.

'We've been hit,' the pilot replied, fighting with the stick as if it had a mind of its own. 'I'm losing hydraulic pressure.'

Hawkins ground his teeth. No way was he abandoning the attack now. 'Bring us back around and get me another shot at this bitch.'

'Working on it, sir,' he said, frantically trying to stabilize their erratic, lurching flight.

Chapter 26

In the house below, Alex started at the sharp crack of two gunshots coming from the upper floor, followed moments later by a sudden change in the high-pitched whine coming from the chopper's engines, as if they were labouring and straining somehow.

Chancing a look, he leaned out just far enough to see across the lake. And to his amazement, he watched as the chopper peeled away and retreated, struggling to maintain its course as wisps of smoke trailed from the engines.

In the comparative silence that followed, he could hear footsteps on the stairs. Turning with the weapon at the ready, he almost sighed in relief as Anya hurried over to him, clutching a heavy-looking bolt-action hunting rifle.

'The chopper is out of action, for now,' she informed him without emotion, as if it were no more than a minor inconvenience easily dealt with. 'Get the file. We're leaving.'

At this, Alex shook his head. 'They fired on me when I went in there. The computer's fucked. I lost the download.'

Anya said nothing for a moment or two, her jaw clenched, then shook her head and turned away. 'Come on, we have to go.'

'Fuck that. If we leave now, this is all for nothing.' Alex was already moving towards the bedroom, seized by the desperate notion that he could remove the hard drive from the shattered casing and perhaps salvage the file later. Getting to it would take precious time, but it had to be worth a try at least.

Anya caught his arm and pulled him to a stop, spinning him around to face her. 'We have no time for this.'

He tried to pull away, but her grip was surprisingly strong. 'Let go of me!'

In response, she pulled him close and fixed him with a hard glare. 'Listen to me, Alex. The file is no use to us if we're dead!'

Releasing her grip, she moved over to a window overlooking the driveway and the woodland beyond. The evergreen forest created a dense canopy that virtually blotted out the sun, but also resulted in few bushes or other forms of ground cover.

With her keen eyes scanning the area, it didn't take her long to spot movement in the shadows. Four operatives converging on the house in a loose skirmish line, armed with MP5 submachine guns and ready to support each other in the event of a pitched fight. An Agency fire team moving in to finish what the sniper had started.

'They're coming,' she said, her voice low and urgent. 'I can't hold them off for long.'

Alex glanced at the long barrel of the hunting rifle. 'What are you going to do?'

Her answer was simple. Her intentions weren't. 'Buy us some time.'

Reversing her grip on the weapon, she slammed the butt against the window, shattering the glass, then angled the barrel out through the jagged hole.

–

Hawkins clung on tight as the chopper's deck pitched and rolled wildly beneath his feet, the pilot working hard to gain some altitude and stabilize their course, fighting the sluggish controls of an aircraft crippled by loss of hydraulic power.

The attempt to kill Anya with a clean, surgical sniper attack had failed. Hawkins was still seething over his failure, but knew that self-recrimination would have to wait. In any case, he had other means of taking Anya down.

Gripping a restraining harness with one hand, Hawkins keyed his radio with the other. 'Alpha to Overlord.'

'Go, Alpha,' the pilot of the Reaper drone replied.

'You are weapons-free. Authorisation Bravo, Zulu, Niner. Roll in strike package on previously identified coordinates.'

The Reaper wasn't just there to observe the assault. If surveillance wasn't enough and the situation warranted it, the drone's payload of air-to-ground Hellfire missiles could reduce virtually any standing structure to rubble in seconds.

'Be advised, Alpha. This is a civilian area,' Overlord cautioned him. 'Mission will be compromised.'

'Understood. This is my call.'

There would be repercussions from this, of course. A single woman found dead in a remote house could be covered up, but a drone strike against a civilian target was a whole different level. Lies about terrorist activity would have to be spun. The Agency's reputation would take a hit, but he knew it would be worth it. Cain would see to that.

'Roger that, Alpha. It's your call. Overlord is weapons free.'

Hawkins felt a fleeting sense of disappointment as he imagined the building disintegrating under the impacts of several Hellfire missiles. Such an impersonal way to kill someone.

'Overlord to Alpha, be advised we have friendly units inside the kill area,' the terse voice of the drone pilot informed him. 'Aborting strike run.'

'Say again, Overlord?' Hawkins demanded.

'We have friendlies in the vicinity of the house. Looks like ground teams are moving in to breech.'

It took no small measure of self control to stop himself yelling in anger. There was only one person he could think of who would have ordered the ground team to move in. Mitchell had taken matters into her own hands.

Unfortunately for her, she had no idea what she was getting into.

In an instant, he made his decision. 'Swing us around, take us back toward the house,' he called out to the pilot.

'I can't, sir.' He glanced around at Hawkins, the fear in his eyes making it plain they were in serious trouble. 'That shot took out our hydraulics. I can barely keep us level.'

Hawkins had heard enough of this shit. He hadn't come halfway around the world to give up when he was mere yards away from his prize. Reaching into his jacket, he drew a Beretta automatic and jammed it against the pilot's face.

'You take us back around,' he said through clenched teeth, pressing the barrel in a little tighter. 'Now.'

Few men would argue about something like this with a gun to their head, and the pilot wasn't one of them. Wrestling with the controls, he brought the stricken chopper around in a wide, clumsy arc, swinging the nose around towards the house.

'I can't hold it steady for a shot,' the pilot warned.

'You don't need to,' Hawkins replied, holstering his weapon and moving closer to the open doorway. 'Just get us in low, close to the shore.'

–

Gathering herself up, Mitchell leapt over a fallen log as she pounded through the woodland towards the lakeside house. The MP5 submachine gun was a familiar, reassuring weight at her shoulder, and as she glanced left she saw Argento about twenty yards away, armed in the same fashion.

Two other operatives were also converging on the house from either flank, all armed and able to support one another in the event of a fire-fight.

She was under no illusions about the effectiveness of the Kevlar vest covering her torso, having seen similar armour easily defeated by the 7.62 mm rounds fired by Afghan insurgents. Of greater value to her was the GPS transponder fixed to the shoulder pads of the vest, which broadcast a coded signal identifying her as a friendly to the remotely piloted aircraft overhead, essentially allowing the operators to distinguish Mitchell and her comrades from whomever else might be in the area. Without it they would all appear as identical white blobs of heat on the drone's thermal cameras, making it impossible to tell friend from foe.

Still, all this technology was nothing more than an aid; it could help them but it couldn't protect them. Mitchell and her team still had to cross the open ground between the house and the treeline, and no drone or spy satellite could change that. Assaults like this always carried an element of risk, as she had learned from hard experience.

Her thoughts were interrupted by the sudden crack of a gunshot from the direction of the house. Instinctively she threw herself to the ground just as something whizzed by on her left side, burying itself in the trunk of a nearby tree in a shower of splinters and fragments of bark.

'Contact front. Sniper!' she called out, backing up against a low boulder surmounted by tangled tree roots.

Another gunshot echoed through the woods, followed by a third.

'Anyone got eyes-on?' she asked, reluctant to expose herself. She'd felt the slight change in air pressure as the first round zipped by dangerously close, and guessed the shooter had her position zeroed in.

'I saw movement. Ground-floor window, second from the end,' Argento replied. 'They might have relocated.'

It made sense. No sniper worth their salt would remain in the same place after giving their position away. The question was what to do now.

Their own weapons were ineffective at such range. They could spit out a high rate of fire, but they were designed for close-quarters fighting. Advancing on the house might well cost them heavy casualties, and there was no telling how difficult it might be to clear the place out room by room.

Still, they would achieve nothing by sitting here waiting. The sounds of the brief gunfight would have been heard at other properties nearby, and it wouldn't be long before local police arrived on the scene to investigate. They had to act now.

Reaching up, she pressed the radio microphone at her throat. 'This is Charlie. Bravo, on me. Delta and Echo get ready with suppressing fire. We're moving in.'

The only logical approach was the cover-and-advance method. With two operatives watching the house at all times while the others moved, they could at least respond if they came under fire again.

She was just getting ready to move when her radio crackled in response.

'Delta to all units. I got vehicle noises coming from the garage on the west side.'

Catching her breath, Mitchell strained to listen. Sure enough, she could hear the deep rumble of a big engine echoing from the house's integrated garage, revving hard as if someone was stamping awkwardly on the accelerator. The metal doors were still closed, however, prompting a quizzical glance from Argento.

'What the—?'

Suddenly the noise rose to a crescendo, and the garage doors buckled and threatened to give way as something slammed into them from inside. A moment later the thin metal split and tore free, revealing a big civilian 4x4 that rocketed out of the garage, heading for the road leading away from the house.

'Target dead ahead!' Mitchell hissed, raising her weapon.

The windows were tinted, making it hard to identify the driver, but no way was she allowing them to leave. Sighting the driver's side front wheel, she squeezed off a short burst of automatic fire.

The MP5's 9 mm rounds weren't powerful enough to cause much recoil, but a sustained burst nonetheless made the lightweight weapon difficult for novices to control. Mitchell however was well used to such submachine guns, and her aim was true.

At least three of her shots found their mark, tearing through the rubber tyre walls with ease. There was a loud pop and hiss as the tyre gave way, and suddenly the vehicle slewed off to the left.

Lowering the gun, Mitchell watched as it careened off the road, bumped over a drainage ditch and finally slammed headlong into the unyielding trunk of a tree, the wheels still spinning and clawing at the dirt.

'It's down!' she called out, loud enough that she no longer needed the radio. 'All units move in!'

Without waiting for acknowledgement she closed in on the wrecked vehicle, her weapon up and ready once more. The engine was still running despite the clouds of steam billowing from beneath the hood, the wheels throwing up clods of dirt and mud as they continued to turn.

'Overlord has you covered, Charlie.' The drone orbiting overhead would have fixed its cameras on the crashed vehicle.

She wondered if the driver had been knocked unconscious by the collision, and was perhaps lying slumped over the wheel with their foot pressed on the accelerator. Whatever, they were certainly making no effort to reverse or manoeuvre around the obstacle barring their path.

'Charlie, on your nine!' she heard Argento call out as she approached the driver's door, having to yell to be heard over the noise of the engine. Mitchell felt a moment of relief that someone was there to back her up.

'Cover me,' she hissed, glancing at him to confirm he understood.

He nodded while keeping the weapon at his shoulder. 'On it.'

Gripping the MP5 in one hand and the handle in the other, she took a single breath, tensed herself up, and hauled the driver's door open.

'Shit.'

Now she knew why the 4x4 wasn't going anywhere. The accelerator had been wedged down by what looked like the snapped handle of a broom, the steering wheel tied in place with a length of bungee cord to keep the car on a roughly straight heading.

The car was a decoy. And she had fallen for it.

'Trunk's clear too,' Argento said, having popped the rear door to check the car's storage area, just in case their targets had hidden themselves away in there.

Reaching inside, Mitchell switched off the ignition and slammed the door shut.

'All units be advised, the car is a decoy,' she said, speaking the instructions into her radio through gritted teeth. 'I say again, the car is a decoy.'

But the sudden silence had afforded her a moment or two to tune into the sounds of her surroundings. In the peaceful wooded glade she could hear the whistle of birds in the treetops overhead, the distant thump of Hawkins' damaged chopper, and closer at hand, faint but unmistakable, the high pitched rattle of a small engine.

Her keen eyes surveyed the wooded area around the house, and in particular the lake beyond, its mirror-like surface reflecting the blue sky overhead. And standing at the shore not more than twenty yards from the house, was a small boatshed partially screened by trees and bushes.

'Son of a bitch,' she said under her breath, then reached for her radio again. 'All units, tangos may be trying to escape by boat. Delta and Echo converge on the lake. Move!'

Her transmission complete, she turned to Argento. 'Move in on the house. Let's go.'

Yates and the woman might be making good their escape across the lake, but she wanted to secure the house before they moved on. It was only a matter of time before the Norwegian police arrived on the scene, and she wanted to gather what evidence she could before they showed up.

He nodded, and together the two of them advanced across the wide turning circle in front of the building, their boots crunching on the gravel as they sprinted across the open space. Here they split up, with Mitchell heading for the now open garage and Argento taking the front door. When they breached, they would go in from two directions simultaneously.

Despite the twisted and crumpled doors lying strewn across the ground outside, the house's integral garage was a neat, well-ordered work space, with rows of tools hanging from racks along the walls. There were no real hiding places in there, so Mitchell was content to bypass it as she closed in on the door leading into the house itself.

Backing up next to it, she checked her weapon and hit the radio transmitter at her throat. 'Charlie in position.'

'Bravo good to go,' Argento replied a second later.

Taking a breath, Mitchell nodded to herself. 'In three, two, one... go!'

One look at the solid door barring her way was enough to forestall any notions of kicking it in. Without a breaching shotgun, it would be both messy and time-consuming to make a forced entry. In any case, Yates or his companion must have come through this door to start the car up, which meant it was unlikely to be locked.

Reaching out, Mitchell gripped the handle and turned it. As expected, there was a click as the lock disengaged. Now free to enter, she shoved the door open and advanced inside.

The open-plan kitchen facing her looked like it had come straight out of a catalogue; all expensive granite worktops, polished floors and stainless-steel units. However, this particular kitchen bore the scars of a recent firefight. Several of the units had been punctured by high-velocity rounds fired from the chopper, and a wall-mounted television had been reduced to so much broken scrap by another hit.

Jesus, what the fuck had Hawkins been thinking?

She could see something in her peripheral vision, and turned right to survey the living room. There she caught sight of the first casualty, and moved closer to investigate.

One look was enough to tell her it was a fatality. He'd taken a direct hit to the head, the catastrophic damage rendering him almost unidentifiable. For a moment she wondered if it might be Yates, but his overweight frame bore no relation to the lightly built young man she was hunting for.

She could see no weapons on or near the body, suggesting he'd been caught in the crossfire somehow. He must have been a civilian, perhaps a resident of the house.

Catching movement in the corridor directly ahead, Mitchell raised her weapon and tightened her grip on the trigger, but relaxed a little as Argento crept into view. His expression was focussed and alert, but also tight with anticipation. This was his first house assault, and he was nervous.

It had been the same for her the first time.

'Hallway clear,' he hissed. She saw his eyes linger on the dead body.

'Check the other rooms,' she instructed, knowing she needed to keep him focussed. 'I'll take upstairs.'

As Argento moved deeper into the house, Mitchell hurried forward, heading for the stairs leading to the upper level.

She hadn't covered more than a few paces before a blur of movement erupted in the corridor. Turning right, she caught sight of a figure emerging from one of the bedrooms with something small and red clutched in one hand.

There was a sudden loud whoosh, and in a flash Argento was consumed in a cloud of white smoke. His startled cry was cut off abruptly by a loud metallic clang, followed by the soft thump of a body hitting the floor. Belatedly Mitchell realized her companion had just had the contents of a fire extinguisher sprayed in his face, before being beaten unconscious by the unit itself.

She had no idea how seriously he was hurt, and in an instant she knew there was no time to think about it. With her senses now painfully sharp and the brief smoke screen beginning to clear, Mitchell sighted their attacker and raised her submachine gun to open fire, her lips drawing back in a snarl as her finger tightened on the trigger.

At the same moment, her enemy turned and hurled the small extinguisher straight at her. Reacting instinctively, Mitchell twisted aside to avoid the improvised missile as it whirled through the air, though doing so forced her to turn the weapon away as well, disrupting her aim.

Exploiting the opening, the lone attacker rushed straight at her, covering the five or six yards separating them with terrifying speed. Knowing she would have no time to bring the weapon into the fight again, Mitchell let go of the submachine gun and allowed it to clatter to the floor, raising her fists to defend herself against the sudden onslaught.

She barely had time to block a hard strike aimed at her vulnerable windpipe, and her attempt to retaliate with a knee to the stomach was easily deflected. Anger and adrenaline surging through her veins, she lashed out with a stinging right cross, but her opponent twisted aside with such graceful ease that it was as if they had known what she was going to do before she'd even thought of it.

A heartbeat later she felt her outstretched arm seized in an iron grip, and suddenly her adversary had used their momentum to twist it behind her back. She could feel muscles and sinew straining beyond their limits. Instantly she knew what they were trying to do, and in desperation she lashed out with her elbow, feeling it make contact, with a satisfying thump that jarred her arm but nonetheless caused the grip to slacken.

Tearing herself out of the hold, she turned away, spotted a knife block on the kitchen counter and drew the first blade she could get her hands on. Thus armed, she whirled to face her enemy once more, swinging the knife around in a wild swipe.

But her attacker was ready again, and before the blade could find a target, her wrist was once again seized in a brutally strong grip. Mitchell had at last come face to face with her enemy, the tip of the knife poised mere inches from their throat.

For a heartbeat, the two enemies remained locked in that silent battle for dominance, their muscles straining, their strength perfectly balanced. Their eyes met during that brief moment, and Mitchell found herself staring into two infinite pools of ice, their depths unknowable, the will behind them indomitable.

The moment passed and her enemy's weight suddenly shifted, twisted down and away, pulling her with it so that she was pitched forward, landing hard on her back, the knife stolen from her grasp. Through bleary eyes she looked up to see her opponent looming over her, the knife now raised to finish her off, her face betraying no hint of emotion.

'Anya!' another voice called out. 'Stop!'

From the corner of her eye, Mitchell saw a young man standing a few yards away. A young man she recognized straight away as Yates. He was holding one of the MP5s that had been dropped during the confrontation, and to Mitchell's disbelief seemed to be pointing it at Anya.

Her attacker hesitated, apparently weighing up how seriously to take his implied threat.

'Don't kill her,' Yates went on. 'Please.'

Glancing back down at her, Anya let out a breath. Mitchell saw her booted foot rise up, then come rushing down towards her. There was an explosion of light followed by gathering darkness as her consciousness departed.

Chapter 27

Once more the house lurched into view as the damaged chopper swung and pitched its way across the lake in sluggish rolls that barely stopped short of completely stalling it.

'Lower!' Hawkins called out, gripping his harness tight. Strapped across his back was an MP5 submachine gun that he'd taken up in favour of the heavy and cumbersome sniper rifle he'd tried to use earlier. He wouldn't be able to unfasten the weapon until he was on the ground, but he intended to put it to good use when he did.

With the nerve that only a direct threat to his life could impart, the pilot brought them in closer to the surface of the water, so close that spray from the engine downwash rose around them like an artificial cloud.

The shoreline was approaching rapidly, the pilot lacking enough control to slow their velocity. The landing was going to be rough, but Hawkins was prepared for that.

Another slow roll brought the lake into full view, and he knew this was the best chance he'd get. Unclipping his safety harness, Hawkins threw himself out the open doorway without hesitation.

Several seconds of tumbling, sickening weightlessness followed as he plummeted through the air towards the lake. Clearly the pilot hadn't brought them in as low as he'd instructed.

This thought was followed a heartbeat later by a thundering, crushing impact as he slammed into the water and disappeared beneath the surface. With a million icy pinpricks assailing him as the cold seeped into his muscles, Hawkins quickly recovered his sense of orientation and kicked for the shimmering light above him.

Emerging with a gasp and a spray of chill water, he found himself about twenty yards out from the rocky shore, the sound of the stricken chopper already receding into the distance. Wasting no time, he strove towards it with sure, powerful strokes, and soon felt stony ground beneath his boots.

–

Tossing the knife aside, Anya knelt down beside the unconscious woman and began to undo the clips holding her body armour in place.

'What the hell are you doing?' Alex asked, puzzled by her behaviour.

'They may have air assets watching this area. They'll see us the moment we try to leave,' she explained, deftly removing the armour, followed by Mitchell's radio unit. 'These vests have transponders that let them tell friends from enemies, so put this on.'

Tossing the vest to him, she rose to her feet. The look in her eyes was enough to make him back off a pace. 'And unless you intend to pull the trigger, *never* point a weapon at me again.'

With that she brushed past him to retrieve the second vest, snatching the MP5 out of his grasp as she went. Alex knew better than to protest.

Donning the unfamiliar Kevlar vest, Alex followed Anya as she headed for the front door. She had armed herself with the MP5 taken from her erstwhile adversary, and quickly swept the open area beyond with the weapon.

'It's clear,' she judged after a few moments, leading him outside.

They hadn't made it more than ten yards before the radio earpiece she was wearing sparked up with an incoming transmission. 'Overlord to Charlie. Sitrep.'

Anya was very familiar with such devices, and immediately hit the transmit button strapped around her neck. 'Charlie copies. House is clear, no sign of tangos. Moving outside.'

Alex stared at her, startled by the sudden shift in her voice. She'd managed to perfectly replicate the accent, and even the timbre of Mitchell's voice. Heard over the pop and crackle of a radio network, it was unlikely anyone would be able to tell the difference.

'Roger that. Be advised you have police units inbound. ETA seven or eight minutes.'

Anya smiled at their good fortune. 'Copy. Recommend Overlord with-draws. We're moving to evac.'

'It's your call, Charlie. Good luck. Out.'

Switching off the radio, Anya looked down towards the lake. There was no sign of the remaining team members, but it was likely they were still in the area. 'They will realize their mistake soon. We must hurry.'

'Where do we go?'

'Anywhere but here.'

With Anya leading the way, they took off through the woods, running as only people fleeing for their lives can run. Adrenaline and fear charging through his veins, Alex sprinted through the shadows beneath the dense evergreen canopy, paying little heed to the direction they were heading. His only concerns were putting as much distance as possible between himself and the house, and keeping pace with his companion.

To her credit, Anya did at least slow down occasionally and glance over her shoulder, though he couldn't say for sure whether she was checking on him or looking for signs they were being followed.

Alex made it a few hundred yards before shock and exhaustion caught up with him. Stumbling against a tree, he doubled over, coughing and retching and clutching at the trunk for support.

Coming to a stop, Anya undid the tabs holding her Kevlar vest closed and tossed it aside. The GPS identification system built into the vest had served them well during their escape from the house, but it wouldn't take long for the Agency to figure out what had happened and turn that same technology against them.

This done, she turned to look at Alex. 'Get rid of your vest. We must keep moving.'

Moving was the last thing on his mind at that moment. Over and over he saw that image of Landvik falling to the floor, his head blasted apart by the powerful sniper round. His friend; a man who had allowed them in his home, who had agreed to help them (albeit reluctantly) and who had paid for it with his life.

'I killed him,' Alex whispered, tears stinging his eyes. 'Jesus Christ. He's dead because of me.'

It was one thing to have ruined what was left of his own life and put himself in danger, but this was completely different. An innocent man had died today because of Alex's stupidity and arrogance.

'We don't have time for this.'

He sank to his knees, staring down at the muddy ground as despair and grief pressed down on him like a physical weight. 'What's the point in running? We lost the download. We're fucked.'

Suddenly he felt himself seized by a strong grip, and looked up to find Anya kneeling beside him, her eyes locked with his. 'Alex, listen to me. I know he was your friend, but his death was not your fault. He killed himself when he triggered that alarm. You can grieve for him later if you must, but for now we have to leave this place. Now get up!'

Her words had done little to assuage his guilt, but they did at least kindle a small fire of resolve within him. Wearily he pulled himself to his feet and fumbled to undo the tabs on his vest. Gratefully shedding the cumbersome and restrictive body armour, he allowed Anya to lead the way once more. She was still moving quickly, but at a more measured pace than before, to give him more of a chance to keep up.

Their course ran parallel to a small stream at the base of a shallow creek for the next hundred yards or so, allowing them to remain more or less hidden from view as they retreated. Only when Anya spotted a trail winding through the woodland up ahead did they change direction.

She halted for a moment and knelt down to examine some markings in the ground. It had clearly been raining since the tracks were made, but even Alex was able to discern tyre marks in the dirt. The nature of the vehicle that had left them was lost on him however.

'This way,' Anya said, leading him down the trail.

'Olivia! Olivia, wake up!'

Mitchell's eyes opened a crack, her conscious mind struggling to reassert itself as confused thoughts and images whirled through her head. Then suddenly she saw an image of the woman named Anya standing over her, saw her boot come crashing down, followed by an explosion of light and a great gulf of darkness that seemed to swallow her up.

In that moment, her eyes flew open and she sat upright, almost knocking Argento off his feet. 'Woah! Easy,' he cautioned, taking her by the shoulder and easing her back. 'You took a blow to head. I was starting to wonder if you'd come round.'

She was starting to wish she hadn't. Waves of pain radiated through her head like ripples in a pond, and she had to swallow hard as a surge of nausea threatened to overwhelm her. Gingerly she reached up and touched her left temple, which seemed to be throbbing in time to her pulse. A swelling the size of a boiled egg seemed to have risen beneath the skin.

'How long was I out?' she managed to say.

Argento made a face. 'Search me. I've been out a while myself.'

It was only then that she noticed his dishevelled state. Bruising and cuts marked one side of his face, and his hair was matted with congealed blood. Then again, taking a fire extinguisher to the head was likely to cause a fair amount of damage.

'You okay?' she asked, ashamed for not noticing before now.

'I doubt I'll be doing any modelling for a while, but I'll live.'

'Any sign of Yates and the woman?'

He shook his head. 'They must've split after they took us down.'

'Shit.' The rest of her team needed to know about this. Reaching up, she felt around for the radio transmitter that linked her into the other ground units, then frowned when she realized it was gone.

'Mine too,' Argento confirmed. 'And our vests and weapons.'

'God damn it.' Mitchell could hardly believe that one unarmed woman had taken them both down and escaped with such brutal ease. It was as if they'd presented no obstacle to her.

'Listen, there's something you need to see,' the young man went on. 'I swept the house after I came round. They've got some kind of computer terminal set up in—'

'Quiet!' Mitchell hissed, straining to listen.

She could hear something outside; something above the persistent ringing in her ears and the pounding of her heart. A long, sustained wailing sound, rising and falling in pitch. Police sirens.

Argento heard it too, and immediately reached the same conclusion.

'We need to evac,' he said. Whatever he had to tell her could wait for now. 'Can you walk?'

166

'Can *you*?' she fired back, struggling to get to her feet. The world seemed to be spinning around her and the nausea was back with a vengeance.

'Guess we'll find out,' he said, helping her up.

–

In the woods not far away, Hawkins was busy following the trail left by the two fugitives in their desperate bid to flee the area. His clothes and hair were still soaking from his recent plunge into the lake, but the cold barely troubled him as he pushed relentlessly forward.

Anya, well trained as she was at escape and evasion, left a barely discernible trail amidst the pine needles and damp soil of the forest floor. The same could not be said of her companion however. Even an untrained eye could have followed his deep and uncoordinated trail with ease, and Hawkins was far from untrained.

Spotting something on the ground up ahead, Hawkins gripped the submachine gun tighter. As he approached, he reached up and pressed his radio.

'Alpha to all units. Possible contact in the forest west of the house,' he whispered. 'Anyone copy?'

Nothing. Not even static.

'Fuck.'

He'd suspected his dive into the lake wouldn't do his tactical radio unit any favours, but there had been little choice at the time if he still expected to play a meaningful part in this action. In any case, he had little faith in Mitchell and her fellow agents to do anything except absorb bullets for him.

Keeping a wary eye on the quiet woodland around him, he knelt to examine the pair of Kevlar vests that had been seemingly discarded at the base of a tree. These vests had come from his own assault team, and it didn't take long for him to guess why.

Anya had proven herself a worthy adversary once again, taking out two armed operatives and using their identification tags to clear the area without arousing the attention of the Reaper drone overhead. Leaving the body armour where he found it, Hawkins rose to his feet and prepared to pick up the trail.

She had done well to make it this far. But she would definitely pay for it.

Chapter 28

Their progress was easier on the relatively flat path, and soon the trees gave way to an expanse of open lawn. Perhaps fifty yards away stood a house of similar design – albeit smaller size – to the one they had just left. Alex realized then that they'd stumbled into a neighbouring property. The lakeside location might have been remote, but there were still other houses here, no doubt all occupying prime vantage points overlooking the water.

Both of them crouched down at the edge of the woodland to survey the area. There were no cars visible in the driveway and no outward signs of activity. It was possible the occupants were either out at work or that this place was only a weekend residence. Either way, it seemed unlikely they would find transportation here.

Signalling Alex to hang back, Anya angled left, heading for a wooden outbuilding about thirty yards from the house. It looked like a small garage or storage shed of some kind; quite well maintained, judging by the freshly treated timbers and unmarked felt roof. The double doors at the front were secured by a simple bolt-and-padlock combination that was probably all the security one needed in these parts.

Anya paused long enough to study the ground leading up to the doors. Satisfied she'd found what she needed, she reached into her pocket and produced what looked like a couple of thin pieces of metal.

Armed with these simple tools she went to work on the lock, quickly and efficiently disabling its pin tumbler system. In under ten seconds the formidable looking device fell away, allowing her to haul the door open.

'Alex, come here,' she hissed.

Hurrying across the open space and feeling exposed the whole time, Alex gratefully slipped through the door and into the cool darkness of the shed. The interior was like most small garages the world over – lots of tins of paint, plant pots, old tools, garden furniture and a hundred other things that the owners probably never used but weren't ready to part with.

The thing that marked this one out as different however was the battered but rugged-looking motorbike propped against one wall. Lightweight and durable, and splattered with dried mud, it looked like a scrambler rather than a long-distance road cruiser. The sort of vehicle that was perfect for roaring along narrow forest trails.

Wheeling the bike into the centre of the shed, Anya mounted it, leaned forward to check the fuel tank, then gave the starter lever a single powerful downward stroke. Straight away the small engine leapt into life, its high-pitched rattle sounding almost toy-like in the confined space. Still, it was ready and clearly willing.

'Get the door,' she said, nodding to the door that had swung shut.

Creeping over, Alex reached out and eased the wooden door open to survey the open ground beyond.

At the same moment, he felt the strange sensation of something whizzing past his face at high speed, moving so fast that it seemed to create a shock-wave of disturbed air in its wake that made his ears pop. An instant later, Alex flinched as the door next to him exploded in a spray of broken wood fragments, a fist-sized hole punched in its frame.

'Down!' Anya cried out.

Even as he dropped to the ground, moving more on instinct than in obedience to her instructions, he was aware of more holes suddenly appearing in the door and walls around him. Only then did the distinctive, terrifying crackle of automatic gunfire reach his ears.

Anya too had abandoned the bike and thrown herself down, recognizing the meagre protection offered by the building in which they found themselves. Broken splinters of wood rained down on them as more shots tore into the shed, shattering old plant pots and bursting apart tins of paint.

'Stay flat!' she warned, hoping a stray round didn't find a soft human target.

Crawling forward on the dirt floor, Anya drew her weapon and squinted through one of the bullet holes that now riddled the shed's wood panelling. Sure enough, she could just make out the figure of a man in dark combat gear crouched behind a tree trunk at the edge of the woods with a weapon at his shoulder. He wasn't in any hurry to advance on them yet, because he knew he had the upper hand.

With a fully automatic weapon and an apparently plentiful supply of ammunition on his side, he could afford to keep pouring fire into the shed until sooner or later he scored a fatal hit. And where there was one operative, there were likely to be more just like him. The longer he kept her pinned down here, the greater the chance that others would close the net around her. And surrounded by open ground, there was nowhere she and Alex could flee to.

Even she couldn't fight her way out of a trap like this singlehanded. If she was to escape this with Yates, she had to act now.

Gripping the MP5 she had stolen earlier, she took a rough aim and squeezed off a long burst of automatic fire in response, attempting to shoot through the holes their attacker had already made and perhaps score a lucky hit on an unprotected limb. However, her shots were too inaccurate and her target too well protected for the burst to have much effect.

Before she could squeeze off more than a dozen rounds, the priming handle snapped backward and locked in place, jammed by a stoppage. Either a defective round that hadn't cleared the breech, or a spent casing lodged in the ejection port. Either way, clearing it would take time she didn't have.

Outside, Hawkins adjusted his aim downward, squeezing off another sustained burst at the storage shed. The MP5 kicked back into his shoulder with each rhythmic thud, the working parts clicking as they drew a fresh round into the breach while ejected shell-casings pinged to the ground around him.

The shed, constructed of soft wood panelling around a basic framework, presented no resistance whatsoever, the rounds punching cleanly through and out the other side. Pausing only a moment to eject the spent magazine from his smoking weapon, he drew a fresh one from his webbing and pushed it home in a single smooth motion before rising to his feet and advancing towards his target.

In lieu of cover provided by fellow team mates, he would have to rely on nothing more than raw firepower to tip the scales in his favour.

Anya might have evaded him back at the house, but she wouldn't get away this time. The shed was surrounded by open ground, making escape impossible. He had the advantage of both armour and firepower, and he intended to make use of both.

Keeping the weapon trained on the shed, he dropped to one knee and reached for the fragmentation grenade fixed into a pouch on his chest. A messy and inelegant way to kill someone, but nonetheless effective. And perhaps Anya would survive the blast long enough for him to look into her eyes as her life faded away.

It was at this moment that he spotted the distinctive blue flash of police lights out of the corner of his eye, accompanied by the roar of a powerful engine at high revs.

Swinging the submachine gun around, he was just in time to see a Volkswagen Passat come tearing across the open ground towards him, its chassis painted in the distinctive blue and white livery of the Norwegian police service. No doubt they were responding to reports of shots fired at the lakeside house. There was no siren; the two officers onboard must have been savvy enough to disable it rather than announce their arrival.

This was a new and entirely unwelcome problem that needed to be dealt with right away. Norwegian police weren't usually issued with firearms when walking the streets, though every police cruiser kept a cache of weapons locked down in the trunk for dealing with armed criminals. Hawkins had no idea if this pair had stopped to unlock the cache, and he wasn't about to find out.

He cursed their sense of timing as he trained his weapon on the driver. If they'd arrived a couple of minutes later he could have avoided unnecessary casualties, but his actions were as necessary as they were brutal. With a fleeting sense of disappointment, he squeezed off a burst that punched straight through the windshield. Blood splattered the inside of the glass and the car slewed sideways, confirming he'd scored a good hit.

Realizing she was about to suffer the same fate as her partner, the second officer ducked down in her seat as Hawkins opened fire again. Rounds howled against metal as ragged bullet holes began to appear in her door.

In the shed, Anya had heard the sudden commotion outside and guessed the cause right away. She doubted a police cruiser would stand much chance against a highly trained operative armed with an automatic weapon, and felt a twinge of remorse at the needless deaths that were taking place at that very moment.

Still, their sacrifice might just buy her the momentary distraction she needed. Dropping the jammed submachine gun, she leapt to her feet and heaved the bike upright once more, its engine still ticking over despite being dropped on its side.

Leaving it running like that might have caused the engine to suck oil into the combustion chamber, which wouldn't do her any favours if she tried to push it hard. The last thing she needed was for the casing to rupture and spray her legs with scalding hot oil, but it wasn't as if there was a spare bike she could choose.

'Get on!' she cried, beckoning Alex forward.

The last time Alex had ridden a motorbike had been when he'd borrowed a friend's moped in high school. Even then, he'd almost lost control and crashed into a stand of bushes. But too physically and emotionally exhausted to protest, he clambered on behind Anya and slid his arms around her waist.

'Hold on,' she advised.

With little option, Alex braced himself as she opened the throttle up all the way. The bike, though weighed down by two riders, nonetheless shot forward with surprising power, leaving a cloud of grey exhaust smoke and dust in their wake.

Rocketing out through the doors, Anya veered hard left immediately, carrying them away from the one-sided gun fight taking place nearby. For a moment Alex saw the armed operative who had been poised to kill them, his weapon still spitting fire at the stricken police cruiser, saw the barrel of the gun swing towards them and another burst of fire cut through the air, the deadly little projectiles eagerly seeking a target.

He saw it all in a blur of jolting motion and fear and adrenaline, and a moment later it was gone. Within seconds they had left the open lawn behind and crossed into the relative safety of the woods once more. Alex could do nothing but hold on for dear life as they weaved through the trees, bumping through dips and jumping over mounds of earth before landing with bone-jarring force.

'Jesus Christ, I can't believe that worked!' he exclaimed, having to shout in her ear to be heard over the roar of wind and engine. 'Where the hell do we go now?'

'North, away from here,' Anya replied, her voice carrying an edge of pain that caught him off guard. 'We stick to the forest as long as we can. That should get us out of the immediate search area.'

Alex could feel something warm and wet on his hand. Glancing down, he was shocked to find it slick with blood, and he was quite certain it wasn't his.

'Shit, you're bleeding,' he exclaimed, realizing that last burst of gunfire aimed their way hadn't gone as wide as he'd thought. 'Are you all right? How bad is it?'

She said nothing to this, instead tightening her grip on the throttle.

Chapter 29

Hawkins was in a foul mood as he strode down the plush carpeted corridor of the embassy building to his makeshift office. A pair of diplomatic aides heading in the opposite direction quickly moved aside, exchanging anxious glances as he stormed past.

The operation to take down Anya and Yates had ended in complete failure, and on some level he was aware that it was partly down to him. He had allowed emotion to cloud his normally cold and clinical decision-making, and had very nearly paid for it with his life. As it was, they had left a pair of dead police officers and one Norwegian civilian in their wake.

They had failed, and it wouldn't take long for news of that failure to reach Cain back at Langley.

These thoughts had scarcely entered his head when he felt the unwelcome buzz of the cell phone in his pocket. Slowing his pace, he reached in and fished the phone out. Sure enough, the caller was Marcus Cain.

'Yeah,' he answered, his normally confident voice robbed of its power.

The reply, when it came, was direct and no-nonsense, as one might expect from the Deputy Director of the CIA. 'I assume you have an explanation for what happened?'

Hawkins winced inwardly, sensing the veiled rage and menace in his voice. There were few people in this world who could make him sweat with a single sentence, but Cain was one of them. He had the power to end careers or even lives if he chose, and even favoured associates like Hawkins weren't safe from his wrath.

He would have to choose his response carefully.

'She was ready for us,' he said, his tone calm and even. 'She took down two of the strike team and compromised our comms net.'

'And where were you when all this was going on?'

Hawkins swallowed down his own anger, knowing it wouldn't serve him now. 'There was interference from local police. I couldn't get to them in time.'

There was a sigh on the other end of the line. The weary resignation of a man struggling with the incompetence of subordinates. 'You were chosen for this job because I believed I could trust you to get this done. I'd hate to think I was wrong about you, Jason.'

'I've never let you down before.'

'But you have today,' Cain cut in. 'I don't need to remind you what's at stake here. The longer she's out there, the more of a threat she becomes. This has to end *now*.'

'I can get her,' Hawkins said firmly. 'I did it once already.'

'She wasn't expecting you then.'

Hawkins clenched his fist. 'She wasn't expecting the team I led against her. I need those same men again.' He paused for a moment, allowing it to sink in. 'Give them to me, and I'll give you Anya.'

Silence greeted him. Strained and uncomfortable. Cain was weighing up what was clearly a difficult decision. The men he was referring to were part of an elite unit known only to a select few; their identity and purpose shrouded behind veils of secrecy and subterfuge.

Each member was perfectly trained, hardened by long years of unforgiving experience and undoubtedly worth more than an entire squad of regular soldiers. Such was their value and limited numbers that they operated almost exclusively alone, going about their grim and deadly work like the assassins they were. Only in times of greatest need were they called together to serve as a unit.

Hawkins's request would mean pulling these operatives from active duty all across the world and placing them at his command. It was no small thing, even for a man with Cain's power and influence.

But for Anya, Hawkins knew he would do anything.

'I'll see what I can do,' Cain said at last. 'In the meantime, I suggest you get your house in order out there. I hope I've made myself clear.'

With that, the line went dead.

–

'Ow! Christ, watch it, will you?' Argento snapped as a medic finished applying a dressing to the side of his head.

Mitchell, seated on a bed opposite, said nothing. The ice-pack pressed against her temple was doing a good job of reducing the swelling, while the bottle of painkillers she'd been given was helping with the pounding headache.

As for the anger and frustration she felt, however, no drug could help her.

She and the rest of the team had barely made it away from the lakeside house as Norwegian police units began to arrive in force. As a clandestine unit attempting a covert snatch-and-grab operation in a sovereign country, their discovery would have turned a failed op into a full-blown international incident. As it was, they had made it back to the US embassy with their tails firmly between their legs, leaving behind a dead body and a house full of bullet holes. Not a great day's work by anyone's standards.

Worse, Yates and Anya, the two targets they had been sent to recover at all costs, were still out there somewhere. Just another failure to add to the growing list of fuck-ups today.

Her thoughts were interrupted when the door to the medical centre was thrown open and Hawkins breezed in. She hadn't seen him since her return to the embassy, though she'd known he was here. One didn't have to be a mind-reader to guess his thoughts, and this was confirmed when his baleful gaze rested on Mitchell.

'Could we have the room, please?' he said, his voice deceptively quiet and controlled.

Argento opened his mouth to protest, but Mitchell cut him off. 'It's okay, Vince,' she said. 'Give us five minutes, okay?'

Argento's eyes didn't leave Hawkins for a second. 'That's not sitting well with me.'

'Doesn't matter. Go.' There was no point in delaying what was about to happen. She might as well get it over with.

Reluctantly Argento rose from his bed and vacated the room, followed by the medic who had been tending him. The door behind them closed, leaving Mitchell alone with Hawkins.

For a moment or two, they just stood there staring at each other across the expanse of white linoleum flooring, neither one speaking or moving. The tick-tock of the clock mounted above the door was the only sign of the passage of time.

'Tell me something, Mitchell,' Hawkins said, finally breaking the silence. 'You remember that conversation we had when I took over this investigation?'

She said nothing. He wasn't looking for answers.

'I only asked two things from you – to be straight with me, and to trust me.' She could see his fingers flexing and clenching, the solid muscles of his arms tensing. 'What part of that didn't you understand today?'

'Look, what I did—'

'What you did was blow our one chance at taking down a priority target!' he shouted, his voice echoing around the small room with frightening power. If she'd thought him daunting enough under normal circumstances, he was an entirely different man now that he'd been roused to anger. 'You disobeyed orders and moved in without authorisation. You put lives at risk, your own included, and you allowed our target to escape.'

'Are you fucking kidding me?' she retorted, jumping to her feet. 'We could have breached that place right from the start, we could have taken Yates and the woman alive without a shot being fired. Instead *you* ordered us to stay back while you used innocent civilians for target practice. *You*, Hawkins! Then when you couldn't finish the job, you tried to order a fucking drone strike against a civilian target. Are you out of your goddamned mind? Is that your idea of a covert operation?'

'It's my idea of keeping people alive.' He shook his head, chuckling with grim humour at her misplaced confidence. 'You really don't have a clue what you're up against, do you? The woman we're hunting isn't just some rogue case-officer with a chip on her shoulder. She's a predator, trained to overcome absolutely anything that gets in her way. She's fought and killed on every continent on earth, and she survived two decades in a profession where a single moment of weakness can end your life.'

'You sound like you admire her.'

He shook his head. 'I don't. But I'm afraid of her, just like you should be.'

'Bullshit!' she retorted, in no mood for such bogeyman stories. 'You're just trying to cover your own ass. You had us stay back because you wanted her dead, and guess what? You fucked up. She's gone, and an innocent civilian got caught in the crossfire. Don't you even care that a man died today because of you?'

If she was expecting her scathing criticism to break through his mask of self-control, she was to be disappointed. Instead Hawkins folded his arms and stared her down for several seconds, his cold eyes that had seen too many dark things over the years reflecting not a trace of regret or doubt.

'People die every day for no reason at all, Mitchell. You should know that.'

Mitchell took a step closer, lowering her voice. 'What are you talking about?'

'Pretend for a second that I'm not as dumb as most of the people you work with. We both know I've read your file. US Army Criminal Investigation Division... a decorated investigator with commendations coming out your ass. Then one day you decide to beat a man half to death, put him in a coma he never woke up from. Maybe you should think about that before you go lecturing me about excessive force.'

Mitchell let out a breath, stunned by what she'd just heard. There was no pretence of cold detachment now, no standing her ground and refusing to show weakness. Hawkins had found the chink in her armour, and was ready to exploit it.

'But hey, I can't say I blame you,' Hawkins went on. 'Might've done the same thing in your position. I would have been a little smarter about it, though. Tell me, what made you do it in front of a dozen witnesses?'

Mitchell took a step back, her eyes reflecting the full depth of the pain and remorse – and the anger – she still felt. Part of her wanted to turn and run, to retreat from this daunting, frightening man who served an agenda she didn't understand and who seemed to know everything about her.

'How do you know all this?' she managed to say. Her service record, as well as the details of her summary dismissal, were supposed to be sealed and restricted. No one but executive-level Agency personnel could access it.

Again that mocking, knowing smile. 'I make it my business to know who I'm working with. Just like I know you were drinking hard the night before I met you. I could still smell it leaking out of your pores. I bet your little boyfriend Argento could smell it too, even if he pretended to ignore it.' He leaned in a little closer. 'Drinking to forget, huh? If you think a bottle of wine will make it all go away, you're wrong.'

She glanced away, unable to meet his withering gaze.

'That's what I thought,' Hawkins concluded. 'You'll have plenty of time to think it over on your flight back to England.'

Mitchell felt like a fist had just been driven into her stomach. 'What?'

'You and the rest of your people are being sent home,' he informed her coldly. 'You didn't honestly think I'd trust this whole op to a bunch of barely trained field agents and one alcoholic has-been, did you?' He shook his head with something akin to pity. 'My own team will take it from here. As of now, consider yourself relieved of duty.'

Mitchell had no words. Like all his dealings with her, Hawkins's revelation had been abrupt, cold and delivered with absolute authority.

'And in case you're thinking about making an issue of this, keep in mind that I was able to read your classified file simply because I wanted to. So think about what I could do to you and your "friends" if you really pissed me off.'

His devastating news delivered, Hawkins turned and swept out of the room, slamming the door behind him and leaving a stunned Mitchell alone to contemplate her fate.

Chapter 30

'How bad is it?' Alex asked as Anya sat down at the base of a sprawling pine tree, weary and pained, her clothes stained with dust and dried blood.

Reaching up, she gingerly removed her bloodstained jacket to reveal a ragged bullet wound that snaked across the skin of her upper arm. It was still oozing blood, though the bleeding seemed to have slowed as her body worked to form a clot.

She flexed the fingers of her injured arm a few times, then slowly curled and straightened the limb, wincing slightly as torn flesh was pulled apart by the movement of muscles beneath.

'It's not,' she said, though there was a resigned, almost indignant tone to her words. 'Just a scratch. I was luckier than I deserved.'

The dirt bike was standing nearby, its engine ticking as it slowly cooled. After making good their escape, they had ridden for more than an hour through the dense woodland, following winding forest trails and occasionally cutting straight across the rough terrain. The bike's suspension seemed to be an afterthought, and by the time they'd finally come to a stop with their fuel running low, Alex felt like a broken man.

He could only imagine how she was feeling after riding all that way with a hole in her arm. But like most things in life, neither the injury nor the rough ride seemed to have troubled her. The only evidence that she'd even tackled the demanding physical task of navigating the bike through dense woodland was a light coating of sweat and dust on her face.

'First time I've ever heard someone call it lucky to be shot,' he remarked. 'Don't you think we should get you to a doctor or something?'

She glanced at him only for a moment. 'Doctors ask questions, Alex.'

'They also stop you bleeding to death. Or is this like in *Rambo* where you've been trained not to feel pain?'

Anya said nothing to that, concentrating instead on tearing away a portion of her t-shirt to use as an improvised bandage. Much as she would have preferred a suture kit and a sterilized field dressing, this would have to do for now.

A pool of rainwater had formed in a natural depression in the ground nearby, and after soaking the strip of cloth in it, she set about cleaning the dried blood from her arm. Even she couldn't quite suppress a gasp of pain when she reached the gunshot wound itself.

'Let me help,' Alex said, taking a step towards her. Seeing her injured in this way had stirred an unexpected pang of guilt in him, as if she had somehow taken a bullet that was meant for him.

'I can do it myself,' she snapped, immediately causing him to back away. 'I have done it enough times before.'

'I'm sure you can. I just meant, you don't have to.' Sensing his words weren't making much of an impact, he shook his head. 'Never mind. Forget it.'

Despite her stoic silence and seemingly unlimited endurance, she was hurting, tired and defeated. She was angry, he realized, but not at him. She was angry at their failure today, angry at being forced to flee empty-handed, angry at possibly having met her match in the people now hunting them.

Anya sighed and looked away for a moment, perhaps sensing she needed to reach out to him but unsure how to do it. She reached up and ran a hand through her hair, staring off into the distance as she searched for the right words.

'I'm sorry, Alex. About your friend,' she said at last. 'He did not deserve what happened to him. And... you did not deserve to be shouted at for trying to help.'

Alex swallowed, replaying Gregar's death yet again, but nodded acknowledgement. It was about as close to an emotional reconciliation as he was likely to get with someone like Anya, and that meant something to him.

'About the file,' she went on. 'You were able to download it once already. Can you do it again?'

Alex shook his head slowly. 'The CIA didn't know what to look for last time. When they get into that house and find Gregar's computer, sooner or later they'll figure out how I got in.' He looked up at her, his eyes reflecting the immense disappointment he felt. 'I'm sorry, but it's hopeless.'

Anya chewed her lip. 'There must be another way. Come on, Alex. You're smart, and good at solving problems like this.'

He managed a weary smile. 'That's literally the nicest thing you've ever said to me.'

'I meant it,' she assured him. 'Now think. How else can you get to it?'

Alex closed his eyes, thinking once more about the complex deception he'd set up to gain access to the CIA's network. He had neither the time nor the resources to stage something like that again, and it would be impossible to recover Landvik's hard drive now.

So what was he missing?

Then, unbidden, another thought leapt into his head. A memory.

A memory of how slow Anya's file had been to download, and his discovery of the mysterious web address that the information was being routed to. It had in effect downloaded twice, resulting in two copies on different machines.

And at last he understood why.

'A ghost drive,' he said, the realisation finally coming to him. 'Gregar, you clever little shit.'

She regarded him curiously. 'What do you mean?'

'When we were downloading the file, I noticed it was being directed to two places – Gregar's hard drive, and an IP address I didn't recognise. I was in the middle of tracking it down when I heard you shouting in the other room, so I never got a chance to finish, but I think he was using a ghost drive. It's like... an online duplicate of your own computer,' he said, searching for layman's terms he could use to explain it to her. 'We used them all the time back in the day, in case our houses got raided by the police or burned down or whatever. At least all our work would be safe and backed up. I think Gregar had set one up to run automatically.'

Clearly his explanation had worked, because he saw the dawning comprehension in her eyes. 'So you're saying the file is still out there somewhere.'

He nodded.

'So how do we get it?'

'Well, we can't download it over the internet, if that's what you mean,' he said, quick to shut down that line of thought. 'The CIA will know what we were after now, so they'd know what to look for. The minute we tried to move it, they'd be on us. But...'

This prompted a raised eyebrow. 'But?'

Alex let out a weary breath. 'Well, this is purely for the sake of argument, but in theory you could get to it the old-fashioned way – find the building and even the machine the file is stored in, and manually copy it to a laptop or whatever. The CIA would never know about it, because the file would never move online. It would be like someone on the other side of the planet trying to see what you're doing in your living room with the curtains drawn, and they don't even know where you live.'

Clearly this sounded too good to be true. 'There is a catch, I presume?'

'The catch is you'd have to physically enter the building where the servers are kept, and these places are sealed up tighter than a duck's arse. Even the smaller ones have got security guards, cameras, the whole *Mission: Impossible* routine.'

Anya however didn't seem to share his bleak appraisal of the situation. 'Nothing is impossible, Alex. If I could get you in, for the sake of argument, could you do the things you've described?'

He looked at her with a mixture of disbelief and burgeoning hope. 'Probably. But—'

'This is no time for probabilities,' she interrupted. 'Can you do it or not?'

Alex suppressed a sigh of exasperation. 'Yes, I can do it.'

'And do you know where this building is?'

'I know the IP address is in Turkey, probably Istanbul, since that's where most of their service-providers are based.' The random series of numbers that made up the address would have been lost on most people, but they were imprinted on his memory like the lyrics of a favourite song.

She eyed him dubiously. 'You memorized it?'

'Trust me, remembering things isn't a problem for me,' he assured her. 'Are you actually suggesting we break in?'

'I will get us inside.' There was clearly no doubt in her mind about that. 'I only need you to download the file.'

'Great, but how am I supposed to get there? I'm a wanted man. Plus I don't have a passport.'

She nodded, her expression suggesting she had anticipated this problem. 'Then we will need help.'

'Who the hell would want to help us now?'

Anya rose to her feet. 'The man who got you involved in this.'

Chapter 31

Mitchell was in a bar around the corner from the US embassy, nursing her second vodka on ice, when Argento finally caught up with her.

'There you are,' he said, pulling up a stool next to her. 'I was beginning to wonder if you'd gone AWOL.'

He'd called three times before she'd at last relented and answered, reluctantly confirming her location. Whatever he wanted to discuss, she could only assume it was important. Not that she cared much at this point.

'Doesn't make much difference now,' she said, taking a sip of her drink. The ice clinked in her glass as she tilted it back. 'We're shut down, Vince. Hawkins pulled the plug.'

Argento winced. 'Yeah, I got the memo. The guy's a piece of work, that's for sure.'

Mitchell smiled grimly. 'A piece of work with friends in high places.'

One of a bar staff, a plump woman in her forties with dusty blonde hair, wandered over to take his order. After ordering a Heineken, Argento waited until the beer had been delivered and she'd gone off to serve another customer before turning his attention back to Mitchell.

'You never asked why I left CID to join the Agency,' she prompted, looking at him searchingly. 'Why not?'

He shrugged, taking a mouthful of beer. 'I figured it was your business, not mine. You'd tell me when you were ready.'

The woman sighed and looked down at the ice floating in her drink. It was some time before she was able to speak, but Argento made no effort to prompt her.

'I beat a man almost to death,' she finally said. It came out so fast, so easily, that she even surprised herself. 'Ended his career, and mine. It happened two years ago, when I was on my third tour in Afghanistan. You ever serve out there yourself?'

'Haven't had the chance.' His voice had lost some of its usual confidence. His was an admission of inexperience, of having missed out on something that many of his comrades had been through over the past seven years.

'It's a lonely place,' Mitchell said, her voice quiet and pensive. 'The training prepares you for almost everything. The heat, the terrain, the people. But it's the loneliness that gets to you. It creeps up on you slowly, so that at first you're not even aware of it. But it's always there, following you around every minute of every day, until eventually you forget what it's like to feel anything else.'

She exhaled slowly and took another drink.

'I was put in charge of a unit investigating crimes committed by ISAF troops against local civilians. Hearts-and-minds stuff; you get the picture. Anyway, it was my first command and I took it seriously, handled a lot of the cases myself. Probably too many. That's when I was given my first sexual-assault case – a girl, fourteen years old, who claimed she'd been arrested by one of our patrols, taken into an abandoned building and raped. It was some private military contractor called Horizon. She even identified the man who'd done it by his name tag.' She glanced up at Argento. 'I guess he assumed she couldn't read.

'Anyway, I reported it, brought charges against him and the other men involved, tried to get them prosecuted. But her family wouldn't let our medics examine her or take forensic evidence, and when I tried to push them they clammed up, refused to let me speak to her. The army didn't want the bad publicity either, not against one of their biggest contractors, so the case collapsed. Insufficient evidence. Pretty useful phrase, huh? Covers a whole lot of dirty secrets.' Her lips parted in a faint smile that was more of a grimace. 'The thing of it is, I actually saw the son of a bitch as we were leaving the hearing. He looked at me, gave me this little smile like he'd known all along he was going to get away with it. Maybe he did.'

'So what did you do?' Argento asked.

She shrugged with feigned indifference. 'Not much I could do. The justice system had made its ruling. All I could do was pick up the pieces. I went out to visit the girl they'd raped, hoping I could get her counselling or something to help deal with it. That was when I found out she'd hanged herself. She couldn't accept the shame of what had happened to her, so she took her own life.' Her grip on the glass tightened, and she blinked to rid herself of the tears forming in her eyes. 'Fourteen years old.'

Argento said nothing to this. He could see the toll this was taking on her, but he sensed she had to get it out. She'd kept this bottled up inside for a long time, and it had been eating away at her ever since.

'That was it for me,' she went on. 'I went back to my room, had myself a few drinks. More than a few, I guess. I looked at myself in the mirror... looked for a long time, and I realized her death was on me. If I hadn't pushed so hard, if I hadn't been so tired and strung-out and fucking arrogant, I could have won her family around. I could have gotten her to testify. That's when I decided to go looking for my smiling friend. It took a while, but sure enough I found him in a mess hall having dinner with his buddies. He had a lot to celebrate, I guess.'

Her breathing was coming faster now, her pulse quickening as the emotions she'd felt that day stirred within her once more.

'I had my sidearm with me, so I drew it, walked up on him from behind and clubbed him across the back of the head. He went down right away, and I… I didn't mean to keep hitting him. I thought once would be enough, but I just couldn't stop myself. It's like I was watching someone else, someone I didn't recognise. I hit him with that gun again and again, until he stopped trying to fight me off, until I could barely move my arm. Even when his buddies tried to stop me, I turned my weapon on them and threatened to kill them. And I swear to God I would have pulled the trigger. I would have done it without a moment's hesitation. That's when a couple of MPs showed up and forced me to drop it. That's when I realized what I'd done.'

With a trembling hand, she raised the glass to her lips and took a deep pull on the vodka. She needed it now.

'He didn't do much smiling after that,' she finally said. 'Didn't do much of anything, in fact. Last I heard, he's still lying in a coma in some veterans hospital, probably never gonna wake up.' She exhaled slowly, raising her chin as if facing up to her actions. 'And as for me, I got the trial he never did. A closed trial – the kind they don't keep too many official records of. They offered me a simple deal: leave CID and never talk about what had happened, or spend the next twenty years in jail for attempted murder. They were giving me a way out, or so they said, but it was a cover-up and we all knew it. A cover up of the rape, the mistrial, even me. And I went along with it, because I was too much of a fucking coward to stand up to them.'

Taking a final mouthful, she drained her drink, set the glass back down on the bar and turned to look at her companion.

'I drink almost every night, Vince,' she admitted. 'Not because I regret what I did – I don't. And not because I threw away my career – it wasn't worth shit if it was built on lies anyway. I drink because of *her*. Every night I see her face, and every night I know her death is on my hands. That's what I have to live with… forever.'

And there it was at last. The truth finally laid bare, without alterations, without omissions or exaggerations, without any attempt to paint herself in a more favourable light. She had told him exactly how it all came to pass, and she was glad of it. No matter how he judged her now, she felt better that he knew the truth, as if a weight had lifted from her.

'You never told me any of this before,' Argento said, his voice quiet and subdued. She could feel his eyes on her without having to look. 'Why now?'

Mitchell sniffed and wiped her eyes, regaining her composure with difficulty.

'This'll be my last posting, Vince,' she said, facing up to another truth she knew was inexorably closing in on her. 'No matter what I do now, Hawkins is going to end what's left of my career after what happened today. And believe me, he can make that happen. But before I go, I wanted you to know the truth. I wanted you to know who I really am.'

She didn't see him reach out, but she felt his hand on hers, warm and reassuring against the cold hardness of the glass.

'I know who you are,' he said. 'You're an impatient, condescending pain in the ass. You're terrible with authority. You manage to piss off just about everyone who has the misfortune of working with you.'

Despite herself, Mitchell couldn't help but laugh at this. It was just like him to choose such a moment to list her faults, of which there were admittedly plenty to choose from.

'And… it pains me to say this, but you're one of the finest people I've ever worked with,' Argento added, his voice taking on an uncharacteristically serious edge. She felt him squeeze her hand a little tighter. 'What happened to that girl wasn't your fault any more than it was hers. But it happened anyway… and you did your best for her. You tried to help her, you gave up your career trying to get justice for her. Nobody could ask more of you. Punishing yourself for it won't change that.'

Mitchell closed her eyes and let out a ragged, shuddering breath. The grief, the anger, the pent-up frustration and pain threatening to overflow now that it had at last found an outlet. Argento said nothing while she fought to regain control, merely sat beside her, offering what comfort he could just by being there.

'Thank you,' she said at last, pulling her hand back. It wasn't a rejection of his attempt to comfort her, merely an acknowledgement that he'd done what he could and that no more was expected of him. 'I mean that.'

'Hey, that's my good deed for the year,' he remarked with a wry smile. 'Now I'm gonna be a complete asshole to balance it out.'

'Makes a change,' she said sarcastically, though in truth she was relieved he'd opted to lighten the mood and return to his more playful, provocative nature. It was a tacit acknowledgement that things hadn't changed between them in the wake of her revelation, that he still saw her as the same person as before. And it was what she needed at that moment.

She turned to look at him. 'So tell me, what's gotten you so riled up that you had to speak to me so bad?'

The young man shook his head. 'It's nothing. I mean, it doesn't matter now.'

'Sure it does.'

'This is the last thing you need to be dealing with now—'

Mitchell held up a hand to silence his protest. 'Vince, just because I told you a few things about myself, doesn't mean we're soul mates now. I'll decide what I can and can't handle, so say what you came to say. I'll take it from there.'

Clearly he knew when he was fighting a losing battle.

'Fucking waste of time trying to argue with you anyway.' Glancing about to make sure no one was within earshot, Argento leaned closer and lowered his voice. 'Okay, like I said back at the lakeside house, I managed to clear the place before we pulled out of there. There was a computer in one of the bedrooms, a real serious looking rig, and I don't think they were using it to watch YouTube.'

Mitchell frowned, failing to see where he was going with this. 'So what was it for?'

'No idea. Hawkins had put a sniper round through it, and I'm pretty sure it wasn't down to bad aim. But I managed to remove the hard drive before we left, and sent the contents to a friend of mine back at Langley. Her name's Frost – she does a lot of technical work with the shepherd teams there.'

That said a lot about her credentials, Mitchell thought. The shepherd teams were an elite amongst the Agency's field teams, tasked with finding and retrieving operatives who went missing in the most dangerous and difficult environments on earth. Only the best in their respective areas were put forward for selection, and not many made the grade.

'How the hell do you know someone like her?' she couldn't help asking.

'Let's say she owes me a favour or two,' Argento went on, the look in his eyes hinting that there was more history there than he was prepared to get into. 'Anyway, from what she could tell, our friends had been downloading a file from the Agency's secure network. The file itself was damaged beyond repair – I guess a fifty-calibre round will do that – but she did find something interesting about the download. It seems everything was being backed up in an online ghost drive, probably as a security measure. She was able to trace the IP address to Istanbul, Turkey.'

The bartender was approaching to refill her drink, but Mitchell waved her off. Her attention was very much on Argento now. She found it hard to believe Yates would risk so much by taking another shot at cracking the Agency's network. Then again, if men like Hawkins were prepared to kill to protect its secrets, it made sense that others were prepared to go just as far to uncover them.

'So what's his play now?' she wondered.

'According to Frost, there are two options. One, he tries to set up another download. The downside is he knows we're onto him now. We've seen the program he's using, so we'd know what to look for if he tried again. For what it's worth, she'll keep a lookout for this just in case. Option two, he goes to the server building where the ghost drive is stored and manually retrieves the file without us knowing. What would you do if you were him?'

Mitchell couldn't believe what she was hearing. If Argento was right, they might well have been granted a sudden and startling insight into the intentions of Yates and his female accomplice. This was a game-changer; an advantage they simply couldn't afford to pass up.

The only question now was what to do with it.

'Does Hawkins know about this?'

He shook his head. 'I've got the only copy of the hard drive.'

'And this Frost back in DC. Do you trust her?'

Argento made a face. 'She's a pain in the ass at times – you'd like her – but she won't compromise us. I'd stake my life on it. Right now, the three of us are the only ones who know about this.'

'Then that's how I want it to stay,' Mitchell decided.

'I can live with that. But there's something else you should know.' His smile faded a little as he continued. 'Don't get pissed with me, but I also had Frost run a covert personnel search on our friend Hawkins. I was hoping she might dig up some dirt.'

'Let me guess; there's no record of the guy.' She might not have worked with the Agency for long, but even she understood that such men were kept strictly off the books. Hawkins, if that was even his real name, was most likely part of a black-ops unit that didn't officially exist, even within the Agency itself.

Argento feigned a look of surprise. 'Actually there is. At least, there's part of one. And here's where it gets interesting. Hawkins was US Army, part of Delta Force. A decorated special-forces operative with a bunch of successful ops under his belt. Then in 2001 his record stops.'

She frowned, beginning to wish she hadn't drunk so much. Her normally keen mind had been dulled by the vodka. 'You mean he was discharged?'

'No, you don't follow. His record just ends right there. No discharge papers, no information about new postings or transfers. It's like he just disappeared.' He looked at her searchingly. 'My guess is he was inducted into some kind of black-ops unit, off the books, maybe a joint venture between the army and the Agency.'

'You come up with that all by yourself, Vince?'

'Kiss my ass,' he retorted. 'The point is, there's definitely something dirty about our buddy Hawkins. I don't know what his agenda is, but it sure as hell isn't about protecting national security from computer hackers.'

She wasn't about to argue with that.

'The woman with the blonde hair is his real mission,' Argento went on. Now that his conspiracy-theory mind was in full flow, there was no stopping him. 'You saw how personal he made this during the house assault. I think she and Hawkins were in the same unit together. Maybe she turned against him, got sick of his bullshit and went rogue. Can't say I'd blame her, to be honest…'

'Okay, calm down,' Mitchell said, stopping him before things got out of hand. Once ideas like this took hold, it was easy to lose sight of the facts that had spawned them. 'All we have right now are missing service records and unproven theories. Let's stick with what we know.'

His grin was conspiratorial. 'We know where Yates and his friend are likely to head next. And we know that if we want to find out what this is really about, we won't get another chance like this. The question is, what's *our* play?'

She hadn't missed his choice of words, or their implication. '*Your* play is to follow orders and go home. I'll decide what to do with this.'

'Well, we both know I'm not going to listen to that,' he said, his cocky smile returning. 'We also know that if you're heading to Istanbul to take on this woman, you're going to need help. That's in pretty short supply these days.'

Mitchell looked at her comrade in exasperation. Argento was intelligent and enthusiastic to be sure, but he was also young and far too confident for her liking. The course of action he was suggesting had the potential to end careers, perhaps even lives if it went wrong. She wondered if he truly appreciated the dangers.

'Look, this isn't a game we're playing here. You've got a good record and a promising career ahead of you. Why risk it on something like this?'

His grin broadened. 'I'm a sucker for a good conspiracy. Plus Hawkins is an asshole and I'd like to see him take a fall. And... I hate to admit this, but I think you deserve a second chance.'

Mitchell sighed and looked down at her empty glass. 'You know there are no guarantees with this?'

'Of course. That's what makes it fun.'

There was nothing else she could say. She'd given him every chance to back out, but still he insisted on coming with her. And if she was honest, deep down she appreciated the help he was offering. She had a feeling she'd need it.

Pushing her empty glass away, she rose from her seat. 'Then let's get to work.'

Chapter 32

Standing at the edge of a lay-by near the small town of Råholt, about twenty miles north of Oslo, Alex stamped his feet and wrapped his arms around his chest. It was growing cold with the onset of evening, a chill breeze rustling the trees around them.

The dirt bike that had carried them this far before finally running out of fuel lay abandoned in the woods behind. It had served its purpose now anyway.

He glanced down at his watch for the third time in as many minutes, unable to help himself. 'He's late.'

Anya, crouched atop a low mound of rocky earth that had probably been bulldozed aside to make way for the road years earlier, didn't stir from her vigil. Her attention was focussed on the main highway, her intense gaze following each car that cruised past.

The improvised bandage around her injured arm was hidden by her jacket, which she'd also done her best to clean of blood and dirt, but it was clear even to him that the woman had been through the mill. It was unlikely she'd be able to move around a town or city without attracting attention, and they both knew it.

'He'll be here.'

Alex wished he shared her conviction. But after everything that had happened over the past few days, he was less inclined to put his faith in others.

'What if he isn't?'

She turned her head slowly to look at him, saying nothing. The dangerous glimmer in her eyes however warned him she was tiring of such questions.

'Fair enough,' Alex conceded. His companion wasn't big on providing reassurance in tense situations, or making small-talk in general. She spoke when she had something to say, but otherwise felt no need to fill the silence.

For him, however, the opposite was true.

'How is it you know Kristian anyway?'

She didn't reply for a few seconds. It was the kind of pause he'd come to recognize when she was weighing up the value of answering against the risk he'd ask a more probing question next time.

'When I defected from the Soviet Union, I came through Sweden and hiked over the border into Norway. That was where I handed myself over to the authorities. Kristian was the intelligence officer assigned to debrief me.' She shrugged. 'I suppose you could say he was the first friend I made in the West.'

Alex frowned. All this talk of the Soviet Union meant her defection had to have happened nearly twenty years ago, if not longer. 'How old were you?'

'Eighteen.'

Alex's eyes opened wider in surprise. It was certainly enough to put his own life into perspective. 'Jesus Christ. I was playing *Tomb Raider* and downing Jägerbombs when I was that age.'

While she was risking her life to make the perilous journey through the Iron Curtain.

He felt rather than saw her eyes on him in the gathering darkness. The eyes of someone who had endured hardships, made decisions and committed acts he would never understand. More than ever, he sensed the immense gulf that existed between him and his enigmatic companion.

'You must think I'm a bit of a joke, eh?' he asked, guessing her dark thoughts. 'I've pissed around my entire life, wasted time, never taken much responsibility for anything.'

'Actually, I was thinking the opposite,' she said. Much to his surprise, there was a strange undertone of sadness and longing in her voice when she spoke next. 'I envy you.'

Alex was about to reply, but the glow of headlights on the main road prompted him to hold his tongue. Crouching down beside Anya, he watched as a vehicle slowed and pulled into the lay-by. It was a black saloon of some kind, probably a BMW judging by the general outline, though it was hard to tell in the gathering dark.

The vehicle sat there for a few seconds, the idling engine venting steam from the twin exhausts, before the driver finally shut it down. Alex heard the click of a door opening, and moments later the figure of a man emerged.

Neither Alex nor Anya moved a muscle as the driver stood there, allowing his senses to tune in to the environment and his eyes to adjust to the dark.

'I'm here,' a familiar voice called out. 'I've come alone and unarmed. You might as well show yourself.'

Alex almost jumped when he felt a hand on his arm. 'Stay here,' Anya instructed.

He nodded, saying nothing. He was more than happy to let her take the lead.

Reaching for the sidearm at her waist, Anya drew the weapon and rose up from her vantage point. The driver spotted her the moment she broke cover, though he made no move to advance or retreat as she approached him with the weapon in plain view.

Kristian Halvorsen was one of the very few people in this world whom Anya had trusted enough to make contact with after her break away from the Agency. Always a large, heavy-set man with a fleshy, expressive face, he hadn't changed much since she'd first met him two decades earlier. Perhaps his swept-back hair was a little thinner now, his face a little fuller and more deeply lined, but all things considered he wore his sixty years of life far more comfortably than she expected to if she lived that long.

'My cell phone is switched off,' he said, holding his arms up to show he wasn't holding anything. 'And I was not followed.'

Anya said nothing as she briskly patted him down, checking for concealed weapons while keeping the automatic trained on him. He was wearing a woollen overcoat to guard against the falling temperature, and she made sure to search the inside pockets before stepping back a pace, at last allowing her guard to lower a little.

'You're late,' she said, her tone accusatory.

He shrugged. 'So shoot me.'

Anya kept the weapon trained on him a moment longer, then finally lowered it.

The tension broken, Halvorsen smiled, reached out and embraced her. 'It is good to see you again, Anya.'

Anya returned the gesture, more relieved than she was prepared to admit to be around someone from the world she was so familiar with. She felt like she was in her comfort zone again.

Halvorsen looked her up and down, his smile fading. 'Now tell me, what the hell have you been up to? I'm hearing reports of shoot-outs, Norwegian citizens and police officers being murdered, and then you show up just hours later. This is not how you used to operate. Or has that changed as well?'

Anya knew better than to rise to this rebuke. In truth, Halvorsen had every right to be angry. She was far from pleased at how things had turned out herself.

'I need your help,' she said instead, deciding to be honest about it.

'Clearly, or you wouldn't be here.' He sighed and glanced around, seeking the young man he knew was hiding nearby. 'I presume your partner in crime is here too. You might as well bring him out.'

Anya nodded and turned towards the mound of bulldozed earth she'd just come from. 'Alex, you can come out.'

Rising up from his hiding place, Alex shuffled down the steep earthen incline and approached them, eyeing Halvorsen with a mixture of wariness and hostility.

The older man nodded in greeting. 'It has been a long time, Alex. I'm sorry we couldn't meet under better circumstances.'

'Yeah, thanks, Kristian. That makes me feel a lot better,' Alex fired back with surprising heat. 'I'm about as popular with the CIA as Osama Bin Laden right now, but what the fuck, eh?'

Halvorsen looked from Alex to Anya, apparently lost for words after his outburst.

'Forgive him,' Anya said by way of apology. 'The last few days have been... difficult.'

'No fucking shit they've been difficult. I've been arrested, beaten up, tasered, shot at, nearly drowned, and watched my friend murdered right in front of my eyes. So yeah, it's been a bit of a rough one.' His accusing eyes were focussed on Halvorsen. 'Why didn't you tell me?'

Halvorsen had recovered from his surprise and was looking at him like he was ready to get back in his car and drive off any second. 'Tell you what?'

'Oh, I don't know. Your favourite ice cream flavour, maybe? How about that you're a fucking spy for starters? Or that you were secretly vetting us to be your fucking cyber-mercenaries? Or that the "client" you recommended to Arran was some kind rogue ex-CIA nut-job – no offence, by the way,' he added, sparing Anya a glance. 'Didn't you think any of this was worth filling us in on?'

Halvorsen took a step closer, his voice low and dangerous when he spoke again. 'You and Arran were stealing other people's secrets for your own gain long before I met you, Alex. Did you really think this wouldn't catch up with you in the end?'

Alex opened his mouth to speak, yet found himself unable to. He had no argument for that, much to his frustration.

Satisfied that he'd silenced the young man, Halvorsen turned his attention back to Anya. 'You said you needed my help.'

Giving Alex a brief look that suggested they'd be having words about this outburst later, Anya nodded. 'It is complicated.'

'Then you'd better come with me,' he said, gesturing to the car. 'I know somewhere we can talk.'

Chapter 33

An hour later, Alex let out a low whistle as the door in front of him opened to reveal a plush, ultramodern apartment with big floor-to-ceiling windows overlooking the brightly lit buildings of central Oslo. With expensive chrome fixtures, polished wood floors and marble worktops everywhere, it looked like the sort of place where Hollywood movie stars would hang out and congratulate each other on being awesome.

'Nice place,' he remarked, looking around in awe. The monthly rent on an apartment like this was probably more than he made in a year.

And yet, looking closer there was an oddly sterile look about the place. No stacks of books or magazines in the living area, no jars of herbs or decorative bottles of olive oil in the kitchen, no clutter or personal effects of any kind for that matter.

The place was as empty as it was elegant.

'This is a safe house, reserved for Norwegian security services,' Halvorsen explained, tossing his overcoat on the breakfast bar in the kitchen. 'It is used from time to time for meetings, or witness protection. Mostly it stands empty, except when one of our officers decides to take a lady friend somewhere impressive.'

The look on his face suggested this had happened more times than he approved of.

'Taxpayer's money at work, eh?' Alex remarked with a derisive snort.

Halvorsen shrugged. 'It serves a purpose. We can talk freely here without worrying about eavesdropping.' He gestured to a dining table set off to one side of the room. 'Come, sit.'

He took one side, with Alex and Anya sitting opposite. He eyed them both, like a chess playing sizing up his opponent.

'So tell me, what has happened?'

It was Anya who did most of the talking. Halvorsen listened while she briefly outlined her deal with Arran, his disappearance and Alex's subsequent arrest, her improvised rescue mission and their escape to Norway, then finally their rendezvous with Alex's friend Landvik and the shootout at his home.

'The Agency are after us, and they will use every resource at their disposal to stop us recovering the file,' she finished. 'We have one chance left to get it, but for this we need help.'

Halvorsen said nothing for the next few seconds, though his mind was clearly working overtime as he processed everything he'd heard.

'This file,' he began. 'What does it contain?'

'Does it matter?'

'We both know it does. You want my trust, then you must extend some my way.'

Glancing at Alex for a moment, Anya sighed, recognizing she'd have to give the man something. 'It is a directory of all covert operations, units and people used by the Agency, accessible by executive-level employees only,' she explained. 'Only the most dangerous and sensitive information is held on it. Every dirty secret they choose to forget, every operation they deny knowledge of; it is all there, all carefully catalogued and stored away on this file. We call it the black list.'

Alex frowned in confusion. The very existence of this black list seemed in contradiction to its purpose. 'I don't get it. Why write down stuff that never happened?'

Halvorsen leaned back in his chair, his expression making it clear he understood all too well the purpose of such a list. 'Shared responsibility.'

Sensing her companion still didn't understand, Anya elaborated. 'As the saying goes, nothing is truly secret if more than one person knows about it. There is always a chance that someone may betray the rest of the group for their own gain, or take matters into their own hands without fear of reprisal. The black list was created to prevent both of these things. It is what binds them all together and prevents any one of them from turning against the others.'

Now Alex was starting to get the picture. 'Mutually assured destruction,' he said, referring to the Cold War theory that it was impossible for one side to destroy the other without in turn being wiped out by the counterstrike.

Anya shrugged. 'If that is how you choose to describe it.'

One thing however still puzzled Alex. 'If it's super secret and designed for high-rankers only, how do you even know about it?'

There was a dangerous look in her eyes at this implied insult. 'Because I created it, Alex. Myself, and a man named Marcus Cain, back in 1989 when I returned from my work in Afghanistan.'

Alex saw something then at the mention of the man named Cain. A waver in her composure, a chink in the armour. A warrior feeling the twinge of an old wound. He wondered what hold this man had on her, but knew it wasn't the time to interrupt.

'I had been disavowed by the Agency after I was captured by the Soviets. I was a ghost. As far as they were concerned, I no longer existed, and it was only because of Marcus that I was able to return to duty. He had just been promoted to leader of the Agency's Special Activities Division, and I convinced him that we had to change how things were done. There could be no more cover-ups, no denial of knowledge, no more lies and betrayals of our own people. The black list was supposed to represent shared responsibility, to hold us all to a higher standard.' The anger in her eyes faded, replaced by a look of sadness and guilt; the look of someone reflecting on old failures. 'It did not work as I'd hoped.'

Her expression told its own story. 'So what do you expect to get from this list now?'

'Six years ago I was ambushed and captured by Russian agents during a mission in Iraq.' Anya looked away and chewed her lip, saying nothing for a few moments. Clearly this wasn't a comfortable topic for her. 'I spent a long time in one of their prisons because of it. But the ambush was no random accident – they knew where and how to find me, which means someone in the Agency told them. Someone made the decision to betray me.'

The look of absolute, cold-blooded conviction in her eyes told him there would be no mercy shown for those responsible. 'Not many people even knew I existed then, never mind where and how to find me. Such a decision could only have been made at the highest levels of power.'

'What do you mean? The White House? The president?'

She let out a derisive snort that might have been a grim laugh.

'Presidents change. Administrations come and go. The men I am talking about are far more… permanent than that. They have held onto their power for so long, fought so hard and sacrificed so much for it, that they would never give it up. They no longer answer to the White House or anyone else, because no politician who holds that office for a few years can hope to control them. Most presidents don't even know they exist.'

'So who the hell are they?'

'I don't know,' she admitted. 'I never met them directly. At least, none of the top members. Apparently I was not considered… reliable enough. Only Marcus seemed to know who and what they really were. He called them the Circle, said they were made up of senior men from nearly all branches of the government, even the military.'

Alex had heard conspiracy theories about secret organisations like this a million times before, from documentaries about the Illuminati and the Freemasons to movies with shadow government agencies as the antagonists. Even coming from someone like Anya, his innate cynicism wouldn't allow him to accept it outright.

'So you're saying there's some secret group of power brokers secretly controlling the government?' he scoffed. 'Meetings in impractically dark rooms, all that stuff?'

'Is it really so hard to believe that there are men in positions of power who prefer not to have their own Wikipedia page?' Halvorsen asked him. 'The world we live in is more complex than you could imagine, and what you see on the surface doesn't always reflect the reality beneath.'

Alex looked to Anya, hoping she could shed more light on it. 'Let me guess – they're trying to take over the world, right?'

She shook her head with the weary resignation of one who had long anticipated such doubts. 'They have no interest in taking over the world, as you put it. And they don't meet in dark rooms. They rarely gather in one place at all, in fact, because there is no need. Their purpose is to preserve the world, at least as they see it, by keeping it in balance. They can do this not just because they are powerful, but because they are free. Free to act, to do what has to be done without worrying about media reaction or opinion polls or congressional hearings. They are free, because as far as the world is concerned, they don't exist.'

Alex frowned, surprised by the tone of her description. 'You sound like you admire them.'

'I believed in their purpose, at least for a while,' she admitted. 'Because I knew well enough that doing the right thing was not the same as doing the popular thing. Some people had to be there to do what others were not prepared to. I believed in them, even believed I could become one of them. For a while.'

Alex was stunned by what he'd heard. Never had he imagined the complex history behind her actions, or the scale of what she was attempting. Not only was she talking about taking on one of the most powerful and dangerous agencies in the world, but a group of men so influential and secretive that even she didn't know their true identities or the full extent of their influence.

Halvorsen however was more concerned with their present situation. 'You said you had a way to recover this file. How?'

Anya nodded and gestured to Alex. 'Tell him what you told me.'

He took a breath, trying to compose his chaotic thoughts and express the complex technical problem facing him in simple terms. Halvorsen didn't look like the kind of guy to understand the complexities of server-gateway access protocols.

The older man listened patiently while Alex did his best to describe his hacking attempt earlier in the day, his breach of the CIA's system and his attempt to download the Black List, and finally his discovery that the file had been backed up automatically online.

'The only way to get our hands on the Black List without being detected is to physically go to the server where the file is stored, connect to it and manually download. It's ugly, but it's pretty much our only option at this point.'

The Norwegian intelligence officer rubbed his chin, pondering what he'd said. 'And if you do this, the Agency will know nothing of it?'

'Assuming we do it properly, and quickly,' Alex agreed. 'Sooner or later they'll figure out the ghost drive just like I did. And we've got a few... hurdles to overcome.'

'Such as?'

'Well, first of all the server building is in Istanbul. Second is physical security on-site. I can give you the IP address to find the building, but we'll need as much information as possible about the place to plan a way in. Security protocols, staff on duty, even the keycard system they use for internal doors. Three, we need a way of getting into the country without being arrested.'

'Alex's identity is compromised,' Anya explained. 'He has no passport, no entry visa, no driver's license. He needs a whole new identity, and I don't have time to create one for him. We also need transport to Istanbul that avoids customs and border checks, which means diplomatic identities for both of us.' She eyed Halvorsen hard. 'That is where you come in.'

Halvorsen chuckled, his hands resting on his ample stomach. 'You don't ask for much, do you? Basically you want me to give you all of the resources and intelligence to mount your own covert operation.'

Anya spread her hands in a gesture of reluctant acknowledgement. 'You know I wouldn't ask if there was another way.'

'And tell me, what exactly do I get in return?'

At this, Anya raised an eyebrow. 'What do you want?'

His smile broadened. 'Come now, Anya. You're asking me to commit resources, time and effort to this, not to mention put my own career at risk. If I do this for you, I want something in return.'

Alex's gaze flicked to the woman, looking for a reaction to Halvorsen's demand. But there was nothing. She could have been a professional poker player, such was her self-control.

However, her response left him in no doubt where she stood on the matter. 'I can't give you the Black List.'

Halvorsen shook his head. 'You misunderstand. I don't need it all, but I want information about any operation concerning my country. Anything the Agency has been doing here that it shouldn't have, I want to know about it.'

'And what will you do with that information, Kristian?' Anya asked, her tone faintly challenging. 'Threaten? Blackmail? Profit from it?'

'Hardly,' he said, looking almost insulted by her accusation. 'But the relationship with our friends at Langley is rather... unbalanced these days. They take what they need, and give us only what they see fit. With the Black List, I might just be able to redress the balance.'

Anya said nothing for several seconds. She just there opposite Halvorsen, her piercing blue eyes focussed on his. Alex could practically feel the tension hanging in the air as the seconds stretched out.

Then at last she seemed to reach a decision.

'Agreed.'

With that, Halvorsen seemed to relax. 'Then I'd better get moving,' he said, rising from his chair. 'I have some phone calls to make. Stay here until I come back, and do not open the door for anyone who isn't me.'

Anya didn't need to be told twice. Drawing the USP from her jeans, she laid the weapon down on the table with a heavy *thunk*.

'Any chance of a takeaway?' Alex asked without much hope, having searched the fridge and cupboards and found them as disappointingly empty as the rest of the apartment. 'I've got a real craving for a kebab.'

The Norwegian spared him a glance as he donned his overcoat, but said nothing.

'Thought as much,' Alex grumbled.

Halting by the door, Halvorsen looked at them both. 'With luck, I'll be back soon.'

With that less-than-promising farewell, he departed, leaving Alex and Anya alone.

Chapter 34

I dream.

A confused dream, jumbled thoughts and images tumbling through my head.

I'm standing in Tim Dixon's cubicle of an office, waiting while he reads through a report on everything I've done so far. The expression on his face tells me the news isn't good.

'Oh dear, Alex. This really doesn't make for good reading, does it?' he asks in his most patronizing tone, looking up from the document. 'You can't honestly believe you're cut out for this, can you? I mean, you've barely done a thing right since this all started.'

I look down at my feet, unable to look at him.

Sweating, I stammer a reply. 'I-I didn't know what—'

'Shut up, you useless bastard,' Dixon snaps. 'And look at me when I'm talking to you.'

Reluctantly I drag my eyes up to look at him, except he's not Dixon any more. He's Gregar. Sitting behind the desk, with the top of his head blasted apart, blood dripping down his face onto his neatly pressed work shirt.

'Look at me, Alex,' he says.

But I can't, because his eyes have already rolled back into his head.

I open my mouth to scream in horror, but no sound comes out. Instead I stumble backwards, groping blindly for the door handle as Gregar rises from his chair on dead legs.

'Look at me, Alex!' he yells, rounding the desk and coming right for me, arms outstretched to grasp at my clothes. 'Look at me!'

—

Alex awoke with a start from an uneasy sleep, his heart pounding and his skin coated with a faint sheen of sweat. The pain from his injured ribs at the sudden movement barely troubled him, the urgency of the moment overriding such minor discomfort.

For several seconds he sat upright in bed, staring into the darkness around him as if hidden terrors waited to spring at him from every shadow. Gradually however the clawing fear of his nightmare subsided, allowing him to think more rationally.

It was just a dream. He was safe here. Well, as safe as one could be as a wanted fugitive in a foreign country, spending the night in an apartment controlled by an intelligence officer of dubious intentions, with a woman he neither understood nor trusted.

He was tired and his injured body was keen to remind him of everything it had been through over the past few days, yet he had no desire to go back to sleep. The dreams that seemed to find him were no better than the reality that surrounded him.

He lay in bed for a few minutes more, unsure of what to do but reluctant to make a move. Finally however he'd had enough.

'Shit,' he muttered, throwing the sheets aside and pulling himself out of bed.

Trying to be quiet, he crept down the hallway towards the living room, pausing for a moment outside Anya's door and straining to listen for any sounds within. There was nothing. No snoring, no breathing, no movement of a body on the mattress.

He wondered if she was even in there, and briefly contemplated opening the door to check, before abandoning the notion. Still armed with the automatic that he was sure she kept under her pillow, there was no telling what she'd do if someone tried to enter her room in the middle of the night. Being shot and killed by his only ally would make for a disappointing way to go out.

Instead he carried on towards the big open-plan living area, crossing the room before coming to a halt in front of the main windows. There he stood and stared out across the brightly lit skyline of central Oslo. With a population of just over 600,000 people, Norway's capital city could hardly be considered a sprawling metropolis, but from this height the view was nonetheless impressive.

Leaning forward, he closed his eyes and allowed his forehead to rest against the cool glass. It was so quiet up here, he realized. The apartment's triple-glazed windows filtered out all noise from outside, leaving the interior bathed in tranquil, meditative silence.

Seen but not heard; he wished he'd had that option back home in London, where the blare of car horns, the rumble of trains, and his neighbour's love of heavy metal music had been a constant intrusion into his life.

Not that that was much of a concern now, he reminded himself with a flash of grim humour. He was a fugitive now. Home for him no longer existed. Perhaps it never really had.

He heard the soft tread of bare feet on the wooden floor, and opened his eyes as Anya appeared beside him. She said nothing, just stood there at his side staring out across the city. Some people might have considered such behaviour odd, but for him it was starting to make sense. Words weren't always necessary; sometimes it was enough just to be there. She seemed to understand that better than most.

'Couldn't sleep either?' he asked.

She gave him a sidelong look, a hint of humour in her eyes. 'You do not move as quietly as you think, Alex.'

It was a minor jibe, but he sensed no offence was meant. 'I'm new to this,' he said without apology.

'So I noticed.' Anya surveyed him for a long moment, no doubt sensing his tension and unease. 'You have something on your mind.'

'Lots of things, actually.' He sighed and ran a hand through his hair. 'The man you mentioned earlier – the one who helped create the Black List. Cain, wasn't it?'

He stole a glance at her just as he said the name, and saw that same look as during their earlier conversation with Halvorsen. The same moment of recollection, the same flicker of pain.

'What about him?'

'He means something to you, doesn't he?' Alex asked. 'Or he meant something once. I saw that look when you mentioned him before, and... I see it again now.'

'You notice things,' she conceded, looking none too happy at his observation.

'I remember things,' he corrected her.

She elected not to follow up on that one.

'Why do you want to know about him?'

He shrugged, deciding to give her the only thing she ever expected – the truth. 'Because you don't want to tell me. Which means he's important, and you don't like to give away things that are important. I understand that, but I'm asking anyway because I want to know what I'm risking my life for. I think I've earned that right by now. You can tell me it's none of my business, or that I'm safer not knowing, or a hundred other versions of the same bullshit if you like. I don't care, and I can't make you talk. But you asked, so... there it is.'

The woman stood beside him in brooding silence for a time. It was hard to tell if she was angry or conflicted by his persistent questioning, yet she made no move to leave. And he began to wonder if he'd been wrong.

Perhaps she did want to tell him after all. Perhaps this had been festering away inside her for longer than she cared to admit.

'Marcus was... my mentor.' She said that word with some reluctance, as if acknowledging an unpleasant truth. 'He brought me into the Agency, guided me through the world he lived in, even helped me understand the men who ran it. He made me believe that I could be like them one day – we both could. We could make the decisions that truly mattered, change the world for the better. One day.' She cocked her head and frowned, as if intrigued by the memory. 'But we had to fight for it. Marcus made me fight. Not against the men, but against myself. Against the fear, the smallness, the weakness. Against everything that could hold me back. Until eventually I became what he wanted me to be... for a while.'

It was hard to describe the change that had come over her as she spoke. It was as if the layers of armour that she had built up around herself had begun to fall away. The hardness, the coldness, the hostility were being discarded little by little with each word, revealing a glimpse of the soul that lurked behind them.

'What went wrong?'

He heard a sigh then. The weary sigh of someone replaying old mistakes.

'I wish I knew,' she said, and never had he been more certain that she meant it.

Coming from someone who always seemed to have the answers, who always had a plan or a way out of any situation, such an admission of fallibility was nothing less than shocking to him.

'So now you're on the run from him. Cain?'

A faint, sad smile. 'From Cain. From the Agency. From the Circle. From everything.'

'This is my life now as well, isn't it?' he asked in a moment of frank honesty. 'Even if we get the Black List and you find the answers you're looking for, it'll never be over. I'm going to be hunted for the rest of my days.'

Anya said nothing to this. There was no need.

'How do you live like this?'

How long could one exist on that knife-edge between life and death, waking up each day not knowing if you were going to see the next? Alex knew she had already survived far longer than he ever could.

She thought about it for a moment. 'Day by day. I suppose it has always been that way for me.'

'Didn't you ever have a... normal life?'

He didn't mean it as an insult, and he hoped she understood that. He was merely seeking, whether he knew it or not, some kind of common ground on which to base his understanding of this woman.

'What is normal?' She turned to look at him, her eyes betraying deep sadness and regret. And he could guess why – because she really didn't know the answer.

'No CIA, no running, no hiding. Even you must have had that once.'

She thought about that, as if genuinely trying to remember a life without all of this.

'I don't often think about before,' she admitted with some reluctance.

He frowned, struck by her odd choice of words. 'Before what?'

He saw a flicker in her eyes then, a moment of hesitation, as if she'd just said something she hadn't intended to.

'You were right about me, Alex. I had a life once, a family, even a future. And I was very different from... what you see now. Quiet, gentle, a daydreamer. But it all changed. Everything I thought was so safe and permanent was taken away from me, and I knew I couldn't be that person any more if I wanted to survive. I had to be someone else. Someone without fear or weakness or regret. Like… an actor playing a role. And I've played that role, been that person, for so long now, I don't… know how to be anyone else. But I see it sometimes in my dreams. Always the same dream.'

'What do you see?'

The woman shrugged, reached up and moved a lock of blonde hair away from her face. It was an instinctive gesture he'd started to notice when she was stalling for time. He made no move to press her, knowing she would either speak or remain silent as she alone decided.

'It's evening, the sun is just touching the horizon. I'm lying in the long grass near my home, staring up the sky. A perfect sky. One that… seems to flow from day into night, from horizon to horizon. You know this?'

Alex nodded. He had seen evenings like that, and even recalled the strange sense of longing and wistfulness they could provoke in him.

'I breathe in, and I can smell earth and pine needles and wild flowers. I feel safe, content – the way you only can when you're a child. And it feels good.'

She smiled a faint, bittersweet smile, and once more he was offered a glimpse of the person beneath the armour. The woman who still grieved for a life of mistakes and failures far greater than he could understand.

'And then when I look up, I see the contrail of an aircraft cutting across the sky. I watch the sun glinting off it, the endless blue of the sky beyond, and… I smile. And I know, somehow I understand then, that it will be the last thing I ever see.'

'What do you mean?' Alex asked, his voice hushed.

She blinked, dismissing the memory. 'It's a dream, nothing more. The little girl who saw and felt those things… she is gone now.'

Alex looked at her, struck by the sadness and longing in her tone. It was as if she was mourning someone who had passed away.

'No she isn't,' he said, not sure whether it was appropriate to challenge her on something like this or not. All he knew was that it was what he wanted to say. 'She's standing here next to me. She's just… waiting for a chance to get out.'

Anya met his gaze only for a moment.

'Try to get some rest,' she said, moving away from the window. 'We have a long day ahead of us tomorrow.'

Alex watched in silence as she quietly retreated from the room.

Chapter 35

I didn't know what to think as I watched her leave. She'd told me more about herself in those five minutes than she had in the past five days, and yet I felt like I had more questions than ever before. It was as if I had the pieces of a jigsaw, but no idea how they fitted together.

Who was she really, beneath all the armour she'd built up around herself? Why did the CIA, the Circle, even this Marcus Cain, really want her dead? What was driving her to risk everything for the Black List, and what would happen to me when she got her hands on it?

I was caught up in something I couldn't begin to understand, something much bigger than me, and maybe even her. Something that could easily end lives, including my own.

And yet, for the first time in my entire life, I actually felt like I was doing something meaningful. I doubted they'd write songs about me or enter my name in the history books, but maybe, just maybe, I'd live through this and know I'd been able to help someone.

That was the plan, at least.

–

Alex awoke to the smell of coffee and cooking food. Intrigued, and very much aware that he hadn't eaten a proper meal in some time, he slipped out of bed, pulled on his jeans and t-shirt and padded through to the living area.

Anya was there already. And so, it seemed, was breakfast.

'You are having a laugh,' he said, eyeing up the plates of scrambled eggs, toast and bacon laid out on the dining table as only a starving man could. After going to bed on an empty stomach, he'd scarcely beheld a more welcome sight. 'Where the hell did all this stuff come from?'

Anya shrugged as she poured herself a cup of coffee. 'There is a convenience store not far from here. They open early.'

He frowned, remembering Halvorsen's words of caution last night. 'I thought Kristian said not to go outside?'

'I have spent enough of my life being hungry,' she said. Had such a statement come from another person he might have dismissed it, but the look in her eyes told another story. 'Anyway, we have a lot of work ahead of us today, so sit and eat.'

He wasn't about to argue with that. Taking a seat at the table, he picked up his cutlery and took his first bite. Straight away his face contorted in a grimace. 'Jeez, the bacon's a bit underdone.'

Anya's eyes shot up from her plate, and he grinned in amusement.

'Just kidding. Don't shoot me.'

Again he saw that faint half-smile he'd come to associate with moments like this. 'No promises.'

Unsure whether she was serious or not, he attacked his breakfast with the kind of focussed determination that only comes with prolonged hunger. Not only had he barely eaten over the past few days, but he'd expended great amounts of energy at various times in evading their pursuers, trekking through rough woodland or swimming against fast-flowing river currents. Being a wanted man was apparently enough to work up quite an appetite.

If he made it out of this alive, maybe he could market it as the next fad diet.

Only when he'd destroyed most of his plate did he turn his attention back to the woman sitting opposite. 'So what's our plan?'

'We wait for Kristian to return,' Anya decided. 'If there is no word from him by midday, we leave and take our chances.'

'Sounds... less than promising. You think he'll live up to our deal?'

Anya took a sip of her coffee. 'I've known him a long time. He would not let us down on purpose.'

That didn't exactly inspire confidence. Just because he didn't consciously betray them didn't mean the man couldn't fuck things up. Then again, as with so much that had happened over the past few days, the matter was beyond his control.

Finishing her food, Anya rose from the chair and carried her plate into the kitchen. She was wearing only jeans and a plain white tank top, leaving her neck and shoulders exposed as she turned away. Her injured arm was plainly visible, the wound now bound up with a clean and properly applied dressing.

But there was something else that caught Alex's attention; something marring the tanned and otherwise unblemished skin across her upper back. Straight and silvery-white, it looked to him like old scar tissue. Several such lines appeared to crisscross each other, as if she'd been deeply cut or scratched somehow.

'What happened there?' he asked before he could stop himself.

'What do you mean?' She was busy running the dishes under hot water.

'Those scars on your back.'

Just like that, she stopped what she was doing and turned to face him, as if to hide what she hadn't realized she had revealed. The expression on her face was quite different from the look of cool composure he'd become accustomed to. Instead she looked almost embarrassed, as if he'd just seen her stepping out of a shower.

But there was something else there too. Something deeper and stronger than mere embarrassment. Pain, old pain, as a long-buried memory was dragged to the surface once more.

'It was a long time ago. I made a mistake.'

'What sort of mistake?'

'I trusted the wrong people. And I paid for it.'

Alex was about to speak again, fascinated by what he was hearing, but the click of a key in the front door told him someone was about to enter. He saw Anya unobtrusively reach for one of the knives in a chopping block next to sink as the front door swung open to reveal Halvorsen.

He had clearly been busy since their last meeting. If possible, he looked even more tired and haggard than Alex. Dumping a pair of canvas holdalls that he'd been carrying, he surveyed the apartment's two occupants.

'The arrangements have been made,' he announced. 'I had to call in a few favours to make this happen at short notice, but I have new passports for you both.'

He tossed one to Alex, who barely managed to catch it after setting down his cup of coffee. Opening it up, he studied the photograph ID page for several seconds. Apparently his new name was James Williams, and he was now a Canadian citizen. It looked legitimate enough, though he wondered if immigration officials would be so easily fooled.

'Really?' Alex asked, slipping the passport into his back pocket. 'Do I sound Canadian to you?'

'Right now you look and sound like shit to me.' Placing his foot behind one of the holdalls, Halvorsen shoved it across the floor to Alex. 'I had to guess your size, but there are clean clothes and washing kit in there. I suggest you use both.'

Unconsciously Alex reached up and scratched at the stubble that coated his jaw. It had been a couple of days since his last shave; a fact he was becoming increasingly aware of. 'Nice of you to notice.'

Kneeling down, he unzipped the bag and was surprised to find a folded, neatly pressed business suit inside. He was far from an expert in men's fashion, but even he could tell that it was high-quality and expensive.

'The three of us work for an engineering consultancy firm,' the Norwegian explained. 'We are in Istanbul to advise on stabilizing the foundations of a mosque that is being restored. You two are my personal assistants. I have made sure you pass through Norwegian border controls without being detained, but the cover story will be needed once we arrive in Turkey.'

Anya hadn't missed the intent behind his brief summary of their roles. 'I did not agree to you being part of this.'

'You said you needed my help,' he reminded her. 'Well, here I am.'

'I needed information and resources, not a hired gun. You haven't been a field operative in a long time.'

'Neither have you.'

'That's different. I'm still trained for it. But you are...' She trailed off, unwilling to finish that line of thought.

'Old and fat?' He smiled, perhaps amused that he might have succeeded in embarrassing her. 'Anya, I'm not talking about infiltrating that building with you. But a job like this can't be done with just two people, only one of whom is a trained operative. You will need my help in Istanbul, whether you're ready to admit it or not.'

Anya eyed him hard. Alex could guess she didn't like being strong-armed into anything. Still, even she couldn't deny the merits of what he was saying.

'Fine,' she conceded with sour grace, kneeling down to open up her own holdall. 'Just remember that this is my operation.'

'As if I could forget.'

Seeking to dispel the tension, Alex interjected with a question of his own. 'Not to sound like a naysayer, but how exactly are we supposed to get out of Norway?'

The Norwegian smiled. 'You will see.'

Part IV

Completion

Rafael Nuñez aka RaFa, a notorious member of the hacking group World of Hell, is arrested following his arrival at Miami International Airport for breaking into the Defense Information Systems Agency computer system on June 2001.

Chapter 36

Istanbul, Turkey

Six hours later, Alex braced himself as the Gulfstream III executive jet touched down with barely a bump on the tarmac at Istanbul Atatürk Airport, the engines roaring with increased power as the pilot applied reverse thrust. Outside, the hot afternoon sun beat down from an almost cloudless sky.

The past several hours had passed like a hectic, stressful dream. After quickly washing and donning their new clothes, he and Anya had departed the safe house in a car with blacked-out windows, heading out of Oslo. Rather than make for Oslo Gardermoen Airport, the main commercial hub serving the city, they had travelled further east to a smaller, private airfield at Fornebu.

And there, parked in a private hangar some distance away from the Cessnas and other light aircraft that populated the small field, the Gulfstream had been waiting for them. There had been no passport or identity checks, no searches by immigration officials, not even a glance from the lone security officer manning the main gate. They had simply exited the car and walked right onto the plane, the engines already starting to power up, and five minutes later they'd been airborne.

'Not a bad old job you've got here, mate,' he'd remarked to Halvorsen at the time, awed and a little envious that the man had been able to summon up private jets and fake identities seemingly at the drop of a hat.

Halvorsen had made a face at this remark, guessing his meaning. 'Believe me, there will be a lot of explaining to do when my superiors learn of this. Hopefully I can show them something in return for this "investment".'

Alex had never even been inside a private jet before, never mind flown in one, but after passing away several hours in this one, he was quite convinced that commercial air travel was no longer for him. The seats alone probably cost more than he made in a year, and as much as he would have liked to sample the champagne in the onboard drinks bar, he knew he couldn't afford to indulge with so much work ahead of them. Anyway, Anya would likely have kicked his arse from one end of the plane to the other if he'd tried it.

The woman herself had spent most of the flight immersed in the laptop computer she'd set up on the small folding table in front of her, poring over the information that Halvorsen had been able to supply. The Norwegian intelligence officer had come through for them in more ways than one, providing design blueprints, personnel lists and even satellite images for the target building yielded up by Alex's IP trace. He assumed that, armed with this information, she'd been busy formulating some kind of plan for getting them in and out without being arrested or killed.

That had been Anya's homework for the flight, and she had taken it as seriously as a heart attack. The only time he'd even seen her leave the computer had been to get a glass of water. It was just as well, because in a few short hours they would be putting everything she'd learned to the test, and this was one test that didn't permit second chances.

Turning off the main runway, the Gulfstream taxied for a couple of minutes before turning into a smaller arrivals area set aside from the main terminal.

'How's it looking?' Alex couldn't help asking, as Anya powered down her computer and packed it away. 'Are we in with a chance?'

She glanced up at him, her eyes a little unfocussed from staring at the screen for so long. For the first time, he sensed that her physical and mental reserves weren't quite as inexhaustible as he'd once thought.

'We'll talk soon,' she replied, unwilling to say anything further on that matter.

With that less-than-glowing assessment fresh in his mind, Alex unbuckled himself and rose from his seat. He was about to leave behind the expensive, air-conditioned cocoon of relative safety that had been his home for the past several hours. Whatever else awaited him today, he had a feeling it would be far less enjoyable.

'Let's go,' Halvorsen said, gesturing to the forward hatch as the co-pilot unlatched it and swung it open. 'We have a rental car standing by once we clear immigration.'

Following him as he squeezed his sizeable frame down the narrow aisle, Alex paused for a moment at the door as the first gust of warm air sighed through the cabin, carrying with it the scent of traffic fumes and the faint tang of sea salt. It was a stark and, he had to admit, welcome change from the cool, sterile air inside the plane.

Occupying the same line of latitude as Madrid, and bordered by the Black Sea to the north and the Sea of Marmara to the south, Istanbul was well known for its hot, humid summers, and today was no exception. The sun beat down from a flawless blue sky, a faint breeze carrying warm, moist air from the south. Even though it was early May and well short of the hottest months of the year, the afternoon heat was still intense enough to raise a faint sheen of perspiration as Alex descended the aircraft's built-in stairs.

Halvorsen, leading the way, slipped on a pair of sunglasses. 'The arrivals area is this way,' he said, indicating the main terminal building about a hundred yards distant. 'Follow me.'

A covered walkway led from the aircraft ramp to the terminal, just in case any passengers should feel like taking a stroll into restricted areas.

'Make sure you have your passport and identity cards to hand,' the Norwegian advised as they entered the walkway. 'Tell me, what is your name, nationality and date of birth?'

This was one aspect of their little clandestine mission that Alex excelled in. After all, committing information to memory had never been a problem for him.

'My name's James Williams. I was born in Halifax, Nova Scotia on April 16th 1979,' Alex replied, easily reeling off the fake background he'd been given.

'And why are you in Istanbul?'

'I work for FLS Construction. We're an architectural firm specializing in structural engineering, and we're here to consult on repair work to a mosque.'

'Which mosque?'

Alex almost smiled. Halvorsen was trying to put him under pressure, but it wouldn't work. He'd memorized every word of the dossier given to him. 'The Molla Çelebi Mosque in the Findikli district.'

'What are your parents' names?' Anya asked suddenly.

So taken aback was Alex by this question that he said nothing for a good couple of seconds. In his mind, this was a break from the information that had been given to him, a disconnect between fantasy and reality that he couldn't immediately resolve.

Sensing his difficulty, Anya halted and turned to face him. 'Your memory will only take you so far, Alex. Sometimes you have to improvise. Be prepared for the questions you *don't* expect.'

Leaving him with that terse advice, she turned and resumed her march towards the arrivals lounge, and Turkish immigration control.

'Thanks, Obi Wan,' Alex said under his breath.

Arriving as they had on a private jet, there was no sudden rush of disembarking travellers to become caught up in. However, both Halvorsen and Anya, as if by unspoken consent, managed to stall and waste enough time to allow the next planeload of foreign tourists to disembark ahead of them, creating a large crowd that they were able to slip into virtually unnoticed.

The intention was obvious. The dull routine of processing dozens of foreign travellers would hopefully erode the immigration officials' focus, and the prospect of many more to come might make them less inclined to thoroughly check each passenger.

Alex wasn't exactly a seasoned international traveller, but even he recognised that some countries were more stringent than others when it came to border security. The United States might have interrogated anyone foolish enough to enter their country, but for most places a simple passport scan and visual confirmation was often enough.

Alex could only hope such a mood was prevailing today as he filtered into one of the lanes. The passport-control booths were lined up two at a time, with the officers manning them calling the next passenger forward as soon as they'd finished with the last one. Which officer one encountered was determined by simple timing.

In Alex's case, the booth on the left was operated by a grim, overweight man in his fifties, with thick-framed reading glasses balanced on a long, disapproving nose. He seemed to be taking longer and asking more questions than the others. A jobsworth; the kind of guy who diligently followed every rule and procedure to the letter, regardless of circumstance. The kind of guy who would take those extra few moments to thoroughly check a forged passport.

His comrade in the other booth was, by contrast, a woman in her late thirties or early forties. Relaxed and genial judging by her body language, she seemed more focussed on getting people through as quickly as possible.

Come on, give me the woman, give me the woman, Alex silently pleaded as he edged forward. The odds were in his favour. The woman was processing three passengers for every one by the opposite booth.

Soon Alex found himself at the head of the line waiting to be served. It was just a question of which officer would finish first.

The man was busy frowning over some detail he'd spotted in the travel documents of the couple in front of Alex. They looked torn between boredom and concern, as well they should have. He seemed like the kind of guy who would happily keep them tied up in red tape for hours if everything didn't add up perfectly.

Opposite, the female officer was just finishing up with her latest passenger. Alex almost let out a sigh of relief as she handed the man's passport back.

He took a step towards her, eager to cement his place in her line, only to stop suddenly. Her passenger, some old bed-wetter in his eighties who looked like a strong breeze would blow him over, apparently wasn't ready to move on. He was leaning forward, asking her for directions, clearly not understanding something that was blindingly simple to everyone else.

Come on, piss off, you old bastard, Alex silently cursed. Just go now and let me get through this.

But his octogenarian friend had no intention of moving on. By the looks of things, he didn't give a shit if there were fifty people in line behind him waiting to be served. Alex imagined it was a particular brand of casual indifference to the world that only sheer age could bestow.

As the female immigration officer pasted on her most patient expression while she tried to explain where he needed to go next, Alex spotted movement in the other booth. The male officer had finished with his pair of passengers, and was beckoning Alex forward.

He hesitated a moment, hoping against hope that the woman's patience would prevail, only to find the old man looking even more confused and befuddled.

Shit.

The male customs officer was beckoning him forward again, more emphatically this time. The look on his face betrayed mounting impatience that someone wasn't doing what was expected of them.

Now Alex had pissed him off, he'd be even less inclined to show leniency.

With a sinking feeling in the pit of his stomach, Alex shuffled forward on unsteady legs and presented his passport for inspection. The immigration officer snatched it with a large, hairy-knuckled hand and quickly ran it beneath the terminal's barcode scanner.

Nothing happened. The officer frowned, and for a second or two Alex could have sworn his own heart stopped beating.

He ran the passport through again, and somewhere in the terminal Alex saw a green light flash. That had to be a good thing, he told himself. Green was always good, right? At least no alarms had started blaring.

Studying the passport a moment longer, the officer glanced up at Alex, regarding him over the rim of his reading glasses as a disapproving librarian might look at someone who had just returned a book six months late.

'Canadian?' he asked.

Alex's own reaction had been much the same when he'd first laid eyes on it.

'Yeah,' he replied, trying to inject some kind of accent that sounded vaguely Canadian into his voice.

'How long in Turkey?'

'A week. I'm here on business.'

The officer was typing something on his computer. Alex had no idea whether that was a good or a bad thing, but there wasn't much he could do either way. So he just stood there with a bland smile on his face, his heart pounding as the seconds crawled by. Was he sweating? He felt uncomfortably warm. Could the man tell? Was he typing out a report flagging him as suspicious?

With a final few keystrokes that seemed to be hammered down a lot harder than necessary, he thrust the passport back to Alex.

'You can go,' he said, his tone one of gruff indifference. And just like that it was done. He was free to leave.

Saying nothing, Alex simply nodded and walked away, somehow managing to keep from crying out in relief and exhilaration.

He almost expected it to be a ruse of some kind; that the minute he turned away, armed police units would swarm in and arrest him. But no such thing happened. He walked through the arrivals corridor to baggage reclaim, and nobody showed the slightest interest in him.

Halvorsen and Anya were waiting for him there. Spotting his flushed complexion, the Norwegian fished a handkerchief from his pocket and held it out.

'Wipe your brow,' he said, his voice hushed. 'You're sweating.'

'Really? Hadn't noticed,' Alex lied, his heart rate finally settling down to something approaching normality.

Halvorsen wasn't convinced. Still, there was little point in belittling him. Instead he glanced at his watch. 'We need to get to that car,' he decided. 'Follow me.'

Chapter 37

Occupying the narrow strip of land that marked the geographical and cultural boundary between Europe and Asia, the city now known as Istanbul had a rich and eventful history stretching back more than two and a half thousand years. Founded in the sixth century bc as Byzantium before being re-established as Constantinople seven hundred years later, it had finally attained its present name of Istanbul when the Ottoman Empire captured it in 1453.

Standing at the crossroads of Europe and the Middle East, and occupying the only sea link between the Black Sea and the Mediterranean, this vital trading hub had been fought over, conquered and rebuilt countless times by countless different empires, each new period of occupation leaving its own cultural and architectural mark.

These days it was a thriving metropolis, and one of the largest urban conglomerations on the face of the earth. This ancient city now covered more than 2,000 square miles and was home to some 14 million people; almost three times the entire population of Norway.

None of these facts were lost on Alex as he sat in the back seat of the rental car, watching the curious mix of ancient Roman, Byzantine and Ottoman architecture slide past outside. The fingerprints of lost civilisations set amongst fast-food restaurants and souvenir shops.

Halvorsen was at the wheel, manoeuvring them with confident precision through the heavy afternoon traffic that crowded the city's narrow roads. Alex was quite content to leave him to it, his thoughts instead turned inward as he pondered what lay ahead for him.

Their route was taking them into the Fatih district, located deep within the ancient centre of the city. Once a prosperous and affluent part of the old town located near the thriving harbour, it was now a densely populated working-class area. Classical domes and archways of the Ottoman period stood in stark contrast to 1960s high-rise residential buildings festooned with satellite dishes, all crowded in close to the narrow streets.

It was into a small courtyard at the back of one of these dreary apartment blocks that Halvorsen turned and brought the car to a halt.

'We have an apartment prepared on the top floor,' he said, pointing upward. 'I hope you are feeling energetic, because the elevators are out.'

Alex stifled a groan. The last thing he felt like doing at that moment was ascending the Mount Everest of apartment blocks. Still, there wasn't much choice if he wanted to reach their makeshift base of operations.

Six flights of stairs later, a sweating and out-of-breath Alex found himself in what clearly passed for a safe house in Istanbul. It couldn't have been further from the plush, spacious, modern apartment they'd left behind in Oslo that morning.

Cramped, hot and with faded 1970s decor that made his own place back in London look like the height of good taste, it certainly wasn't the kind of place he'd want to set up shop. Shafts of bright afternoon sunlight filtered in through cracks in the shuttered windows, highlighting tiny insects flitting around in the dusty air.

With his injured ribs throbbing each time he took a deep breath, Alex loosened his tie and gratefully flopped down on the threadbare floral-patterned couch set against one wall. The overtaxed springs sagged beneath his weight but somehow held on.

'I suppose you spent most of our budget on the plane, eh?' he remarked, eyeing a peeling patch of wallpaper opposite.

Halvorsen shrugged. 'We needed somewhere anonymous. If you think you could do better, be my guest.'

'This will be fine,' Anya said, the look in her eyes warning Alex against further criticism. Turning away, she unlocked the shutters barring the main windows and pushed them open, allowing bright sunlight to flood the room. With his eyes now accustomed to the gloomy interior of the room, Alex was forced to avert his gaze from the harsh glare.

'Better,' Anya decided, then turned her attention to Halvorsen. 'Did you arrange the package I requested?'

The Norwegian smiled and nodded. Opening a cupboard beneath the sink, he retrieved a leather sports bag and laid it on the cheap wood-veneer kitchen table.

Anya was on it right away, unzipping the bag and lifting out what looked like a set of drab brown shirts and trousers, complete with boots and the kind of equipment belt that a police officer or security guard might wear.

'These are a match?' she asked, glancing at Halvorsen.

He nodded. 'As far as our people could tell, yes.'

That seemed to satisfy her, for now at least.

Next out were a pair of Kevlar vests that Alex had come to recognize quite well after their improvised escape from the lakeside house in Norway. He understood the rationale behind them, but hoped fervently they wouldn't have to put the body armour to the test.

The last item to emerge from the bag was something more offensively minded. Carefully Anya lifted out the dark, sleek form of an automatic handgun. Alex wasn't much of a firearms aficionado, but even he recognised the distinctive shape of the Colt M1911 from countless movies and TV shows he'd watched throughout his life.

Better known as the Colt .45 for the ammunition it used, the M1911 was a rugged, reliable 8-shot automatic that had been in service for the best part of a century, and was still favoured by police and special-forces units even today. Like the great white shark, it had reached the apex of design long ago and had no need to evolve further.

'Still favouring the .45?' Halvorsen remarked as Anya carefully fitted a suppressor to the weapon's barrel. 'Some things never change.'

The woman glanced at him, flashing something that might have been a smile. 'It has never let me down. And that is a rare thing.'

Halvorsen said nothing to this as she laid the weapon down on the table.

'So what's the plan, Rambo?' Alex asked, eager to know how she intended to get them inside.

Glancing at him, Anya replaced the contents of the bag and laid it on the floor, then gestured for him to sit. Both men took a seat while she powered up her laptop and called up the file she'd been working on.

'If what Alex has told me is correct, the Black List is being held on a server in this building,' she began, showing them an overhead shot of a large office block set in amongst other buildings of similar construction. 'It is one of the main facilities for ISS Communications, a Turkish internet provider.'

Next she brought up a detailed building blueprint which Halvorsen's colleagues in Oslo had managed to obtain from the Istanbul central planning office.

'Given the location of the building, and the time and resources available, a tactical assault is out of the question,' Anya went on. 'Our only feasible option is to infiltrate the building at night, when most of the office staff have left for the day. To do this we will need to gain access to the main entrance, neutralize any physical security measures on site and disable the building's surveillance system. According to the blueprints, all of this is controlled from a central security station located just off the entrance lobby, so locking down this room must be our highest priority. Once the system is down and outside communications have been cut, Alex and I will make our way to the server room in the basement where he will find and download the Black List. As soon as he has it in his possession, I will escort him back upstairs and outside, where Kristian will be waiting to pick us up.'

It sounded simple enough, but then Alex supposed most plans did when one was seated around the kitchen table talking it over.

'You really think you can do all this?' he couldn't help asking. 'Get us inside, take out armed guards, disable security systems?'

Anya glowered at him across the table, her blue eyes smouldering. 'I used to infiltrate fortified Soviet outposts for a living, Alex,' she reminded him. 'You only need to concern yourself with downloading the Black List. I'll take care of the rest.'

Alex leaned back in his seat, feeling like an unruly student who had just been chastised by the teacher.

Halvorsen, briefly amused by the interplay, soon turned his attention back to more practical matters. 'As far as we could tell, there are only two security personnel on duty at night. One is on roving patrol throughout the building, and the other is on duty in the security room at all times. The room is locked and secured with an encrypted card reader, and has protected hard-line communications to the outside world. If we must go in, it would make sense to hit them in the early hours of the morning.'

'No,' Anya countered, speaking with the firm confidence born from long experience. 'This must happen during shift changeover, when the night security staff are logging in.'

Halvorsen frowned, but didn't argue. Likely he knew better than to debate with her over matters like this.

'This all sounds lovely,' Alex chipped in. 'But if the doors are locked and the security men can trip the alarm at a moment's notice, how do you plan to get inside the building in the first place?'

The look in her eyes somehow put him in mind of a hawk that was sizing up its prey. 'Like I said, you worry about the Black List. Leave the rest to me.'

Reaching into the sports bag, she retrieved the Colt .45, inserted a magazine into the open port and pulled back the slide to chamber the first round.

'Stay here. I'll be back soon.'

Chapter 38

Burak Karga glanced up from the TV, disturbed from the football game he was watching by a knock at the door.

'Get lost, I'm busy,' he mumbled, turning his attention back to the game. Galatasaray were leading 2–1 against bitter local rivals Fenerbahçe, with Fenebahçe pushing forward in search of an equaliser in the dying minutes. No way was he leaving this to deal with some beggar or travelling salesman – two things which were roughly synonymous in his opinion.

Especially not when he was facing a tedious eight-hour overnight shift, working security in a building that nobody in their right mind would want to break into. Unless they had a real thing for circuit boards and copper wire.

The knocking continued, more urgent this time. Whoever was out there wasn't about to give up.

'All right!' he snapped, rising from his chair and stomping towards the door of his small but fastidiously clean apartment. One thing he prided himself on was his sense of order and discipline. 'What is it?'

Leaning close to the spy hole, he was startled to find himself looking out at a woman. A Western woman, with tanned skin, short blonde hair and striking blue eyes. She was dressed in a sharp business suit, the blouse unbuttoned just far enough to reveal a subtle glimpse of cleavage. Who was she, and what was she doing here?

'Burak Karga?' she asked.

'Yes. Who are you?'

'My name is Anna. I work for ISS,' she explained, speaking in accented but fluent Turkish. 'Something has come to our attention, and we need to talk. Can I come in?'

Karga felt a knot of fear tighten in his stomach. If the company had seen fit to send an official representative to his home, it couldn't mean anything good. What was it about? His mind was in overdrive, churning through any minor infraction he might have committed while on duty that had somehow been discovered.

'O-okay,' he called. 'Just give me a minute.'

Turning around, he rushed into the bedroom and grabbed a fresh shirt from his wardrobe, quickly buttoning it up as he returned to the door. Running his fingers through his hair a couple of times to smooth it down, he took a deep breath, reached out and unlocked the door.

219

Of all the unpleasant possibilities that had leapt into his mind in the past thirty seconds, none of them came close to what happened next.

The instant he undid the lock, the door flew inwards, propelled by a hard kick that sent it crashing against him. Karga grunted in pain and shock as his head took much of the impact, and fell to his knees with stars dancing across his eyes. He could feel something warm and wet dripping down his face, and realized with vague comprehension that he'd been cut.

These were the least of his problems however. Quickly slipping into his apartment, the woman in the suit pulled the door shut and knelt down beside him, drawing something from behind her back.

Karga froze as the cold barrel of a weapon was pressed against his forehead.

'If you cry out, you die. The weapon is silenced, so nobody will hear it,' the woman hissed, her voice frighteningly calm and controlled. 'Nod if you understand.'

With no choice but to comply, Karga nodded.

'I am going to ask you some questions. If you answer fully and truthfully, I give you my word that you will live through this unharmed. I will leave and you will never see or hear from me again. But if you lie to me or withhold information, I will know about it. Believe me, I am very good at discovering liars. I will kill you, then I will kill both your parents and your brother. They live in Izmir, right?'

Karga could feel tears forming. How did she know so much about him? 'Please, I don't want—'

'I don't care what you want,' she cut in. 'When someone has a gun at your head, all that matters is what you do. If you do the right thing, you and your family will live. If not, you die. Now, are you going to cooperate?'

There was no choice for him to make. How could any man withstand such a threat?

'Yes,' he finally said.

She nodded, and the gun barrel was withdrawn a little. 'First you are going to give me your access card for the ISS building, then you are going to tell me everything you know about the security system. Pass codes, patrol routes, access protocols, everything. So, let's begin.'

Chapter 39

Anya was feeling a little more optimistic about their chances when she returned to the safe house about an hour later. Karga had, to his credit, lived up to his end of their agreement, telling her everything she needed to know about the building's security system, and more besides. In the end it was all she could do to shut him up.

Satisfied that he hadn't lied to her, she had left him bound and gagged in his bath tub before departing with his access card and security pass codes. Karga was single, based on both her own observations and the brief dossier that Halvorsen's people had put together on him, meaning it was unlikely anyone would visit him in the next few hours. Likely he'd make his predicament known sooner or later, but she planned to be long gone by then.

Halvorsen was seated on the couch, thumbing rounds into the magazine for his own automatic. Though he would be armed like her, his part in this operation was confined to the role of getaway driver, partly because she was dubious of his skills after two decades away from field work, and partly because she wanted operational control to stay with her. She might be short-handed when they went in, but at least she'd only have Alex to worry about.

He glanced up as she entered. 'How did it go?'

Anya held up the access card. 'It could have been worse.'

'He didn't give that up willingly, I suppose?'

She shrugged. 'I can be very persuasive.'

At this, he smiled knowingly. 'So I remember.' He gestured to the kitchen, where a coffee urn was steaming away. 'There is coffee left if you want some. Tastes like shit but it does the trick.'

She shook her head, preferring to stay away from caffeine now that they were soon to go into action. The kind of jittery, nervous energy that came with it was of no use to her, particularly when she was about to attempt a hastily conceived raid on a high-security building in a foreign country.

'Where is Alex?' she asked instead.

He pointed towards the narrow balcony beyond the shuttered windows. 'Said he needed some air.'

Which was clearly untrue, she knew. Nobody went outside simply for fresh air, particularly in a crowded urban area like this. Alex was out there because he wanted to be alone. He was afraid of what was coming, and the more time he spent alone with that fear churning over in his mind, the worse it would become. She'd seen it happen many times in the past, often with disastrous results.

She needed him focussed and motivated, not frightened and indecisive.

Leaving Halvorsen in the living area, she pushed open the shutters and slipped out onto the narrow balcony clinging to the side of the apartment building.

Whatever shortcomings this place might have had in terms of space, utilities and decor, one area where it did at least excel was the view. From this high vantage point she was able to see right across the dense and chaotic urban sprawl of central Istanbul to the glistening waters of the Bosphorus Strait. Ships and boats of all descriptions ploughed across the narrow body of water that linked the Black Sea with the Mediterranean, while on the far side stood the eastern half of the transcontinental city.

Closer at hand, six immense minaret towers rose high into the evening sky, surrounding the countless domes and high walls of the Sultan Ahmed Mosque, the largest of its kind in the country. Another reminder of Istanbul's conflict-ridden past. Anya recalled reading once that in ancient times a heavy iron chain had been hung across the sultan's entrance to the mosque, forcing him to bow as he rode inside on horseback. The intention was clear: even all-powerful rulers had to learn humility from time to time.

It was a shame today's crop of world leaders hadn't learned that lesson, she thought.

As Halvorsen had said, Alex was out there leaning on the railing, staring out across the city without really seeing anything. He was holding a packet of cigarettes, though he hadn't lit one yet.

He didn't look around as Anya slipped in beside him, sharing the view in companionable silence for a time.

It wasn't like him to be so taciturn, and for a moment Anya caught herself wishing he would say something to break the silence. At first she had found his constant questions and inane banter both irritating and draining, yet she had to admit that over the past few days she'd grown accustomed to it, perhaps even learned to like it. Maybe because when he was speaking, she didn't have to say anything herself.

At this moment, however, things were different.

'It is a good evening,' she said at last, watching a young couple sauntering along hand in hand on the street far below. Not a care in the world, Anya thought with a fleeting tinge of envy. 'When I was young, my mother used to call this the magic hour. She believed there was purpose to all of our lives, and that at moments like this, we were given a glimpse of it. She said anything was possible at such a time.'

Alex said nothing in response. His eyes continued to survey the city, though his thoughts were clearly turned inward.

'I know the last few days have been... difficult for you, Alex,' she said, groping for the right words. Conversations like this always left her feeling uncomfortable and strained, as if she didn't have the vocabulary to express herself properly. 'I know, because the same thing once happened to me.'

At last this seemed to stir his interest. He blinked, and slowly turned to look at her.

'I told you once about my life before,' she said, the muscles in her throat working as she swallowed. 'I was young then, and I was different. Gentle, naive, a daydreamer who used to lie in the long grass staring up at the sky, wondering what might be.'

She shook her head, dispelling the memory.

'That all changed one evening, not unlike this one. I was outside in the field overlooking our home when police and men in official cars arrived. I was told that my parents had been killed. There was an accident, their car ploughed into a tree, and they were gone. Just like that. Everything I had known, everything I was and might have been, was taken away from me that night. I had to change very quickly, let go of my fear and weakness, let go of who I had been. That's why I call this time "before", and why I can barely remember it. I *chose* to forget that little girl, Alex. I did this, because the memory of who I was would stop me doing what I had to do to survive. So I let her go.'

Alex was listening to her now. She could feel his eyes on her, even as she stared out across the glistening waters of the strait, though in truth her thoughts were turned inward. She was thinking about the frightened little girl she'd chosen to leave behind, the life she'd chosen to forget. She wondered, in a fleeting moment of doubt, whether it could ever be hers again.

Alex sighed and turned his gaze back out across the city. 'I'm sorry, Anya.'

She blinked, returning to herself. 'For what?'

'For a lot of things. Mostly for making this happen.' He shook his head. 'It's my fault we're here now, my fault you don't have the Black List. I'm sorry you had to go through all of this, and I'm grateful for what you've done for me. I know that doesn't mean much, but... I wanted you to know anyway. Might not get another chance to say it, know what I mean?'

She did know. He wanted to make things right with her.

Moved by a sudden impulse, Anya reached out and gently laid a hand on his arm. It wasn't often that she felt the need for physical contact, and if she was honest, overt displays of affection had always left her feeling strangely uncomfortable. But just this once it felt right.

Alex Yates was a good man, she knew then. Maybe he wasn't the sort she normally associated with, and she doubted they'd be seeing much of each other once this was all over, but he was a better person than many she had encountered over the years. And perhaps deserved a second chance.

'It does mean something,' she allowed.

That seemed to satisfy him, and for a time he was silent and pensive.

'I saw you, you know,' he said at last. 'At Trafalgar Square, the day I met with Arran. I saw you watching me.'

She blinked, regarding him with surprise. 'You remember that, out of all the people you saw that day?'

He shook his head. 'You don't understand. I remember all of them, every face, every piece of clothing, every car and bus and bike on the road. Forgetting isn't an option for me.'

Her brows drew together for a moment as she assessed the meaning behind his words before arriving at the logical conclusion. 'You have a photographic memory.'

He nodded, offering a weary smile. 'That's an understatement.'

'Has it always been this way?'

Again he nodded. 'All my life. When I was little, I found I could remember just about anything I saw or heard. It made learning things... well, easier. My teachers at school were convinced I was cheating on my exams somehow; they couldn't understand how I could remember entire textbooks word for word.'

His skills with computers were beginning to make more sense to her now, and his ability to find loopholes that others couldn't. He didn't see what others missed, he simply remembered what others forgot.

'That is a gift,' she said, wishing her own memory were as infallible. She had trained herself over the years to commit important information to memory, but of course there were limits to what she could accurately recall.

'A gift?' he snorted. 'Yeah, right. More like a curse. Imagine never being able to turn it off. It just keeps piling up, every day, every minute. My head gets so filled up with useless shit, sometimes I feel like I'm drowning in it. I even end up forgetting things that are supposed to be important. So no, all things considered, I'd rather I hadn't inherited this "talent".'

Anya said nothing, perhaps a little surprised by the vehemence of his sentiment. She would never know the turmoil that existed within his mind, the sea of random thoughts and memories that he had to constantly manage and keep under control, the sheer mental energy he had to expend just to get through the day.

'But it is yours anyway. You can either spend your life wishing it wasn't there, or you can use it. I know you can do that.' She glanced at him, comparing the man before her with the frightened, hesitant weakling he'd been only a few short days earlier. 'You are stronger than you look, Alex. Maybe even stronger than you realize.'

Alex didn't say anything to this, though she sensed her words had struck a chord in him. Maybe he would listen to her.

'Are you going to smoke those?' she asked, nodding to the cigarettes in his hand.

Alex smiled wryly. 'Thought you didn't approve?'

224

'I think you have earned it.'

He looked at the packet for a long moment before slipping it back into his pocket.

'When you have the Black List and we're on a plane out of here, then I'll celebrate,' he decided. 'In the meantime, we have work to do.'

'Fair enough,' she conceded. 'Are you ready?'

Alex nodded, summoning up the deeply buried reserve of courage that she knew he possessed. He was frightened and intimidated by what lay ahead, but he would see it through. She would make sure of that.

She gave him what she hoped was a reassuring smile. 'Then let's finish this.'

–

So there we were, about to make our final play. Like gamblers on losing streaks the world over, we were betting everything on one last roll of the dice.

It sounds insane when I think about it now. The idea that somehow we'd actually get away with it, that they wouldn't be expecting what we were about to do.

Maybe it was overconfidence getting the better of me again, or maybe I just wanted to believe there was still a way out. If I didn't still have that to hold on to, then what else was there?

Either way, I went into it with my eyes open. Seeing nothing.

Chapter 40

As the sun sank below the distant western horizon and darkness fell on the ancient city of Istanbul, office buildings, shops and factories slowly emptied as workers began their long commutes home for the evening.

But two people who had no intention of going home tonight were Olivia Mitchell and Vince Argento. Encamped on the roof of an apartment building about a hundred yards from the ISS Communications office, they had been observing it with a pair of high-powered binoculars since their arrival earlier in the day, looking for any sign of Yates or Anya. Such static observation was a mind-numbing task at the best of times, and so far one that had yielded no results.

Getting into the country without Hawkins' knowledge had been no easy task, forcing both operatives to pull in more favours than they were owed to get onto a commercial flight under false identities. As far as he was concerned, they were both on a flight back to Langley. The illusion was unlikely to last long, especially considering the extent of his influence, but perhaps it would buy them enough time to get to the truth of this whole operation.

A gamble. All or nothing, with little more than gut instinct to guide them.

'Shift-change,' Argento said, focussing the binoculars on a new arrival at the main entrance. 'Looks like night security. Jesus, he looks about as happy to be here as me.'

'Duly noted. But if this is your play for sympathy, forget it. You chose to be here,' Mitchell replied, taking a sip of coffee. The temperature was falling with the onset of night, and the steaming black liquid was as useful for keeping them warm as it was for maintaining concentration.

'Wouldn't dream of it.' Argento held out a hand without taking his eyes away from the binoculars. 'Send some of that my way, would you?'

'Tastes like ass,' she warned.

'Nothing wrong with a piece of ass.'

Mitchell duly poured him a cup and placed it in his hand. In truth, she didn't mind his occasional grumbling about the cold or the boredom or the fact that the air vent he was sitting on was giving him cramp in his legs. Long periods of observation like this were often a test of endurance, but having another person on hand to share the load made it infinitely more bearable.

Argento took a sip and laid the cup down on the ground by his feet. 'You know there's every chance they're not even going to show, right? They'd have to be pretty goddamned stupid to try something like this.'

She had scouted out the perimeter of the four-storey office building earlier in the day, checking for possible entry points or hidden ways in.

A modern, well-constructed facility laid out in a rough U-shape, with a courtyard and parking area set between the two wings, it was well covered by security cameras at all angles. These very security measures had necessitated a quick withdrawal on her part, lest she draw suspicion on herself.

Still, even a cursory glance made it plain the building was taller than those around it, making access from adjacent rooftops impossible. The only other entrance besides the front door was a loading dock at the rear, but it was securely locked down and could only be opened from inside.

Security personnel patrolled the building at all times, with at least one in a locked panic room manning the CCTV cameras. All in all, it was a pretty airtight operation. A determined assault team could certainly breach the building, but doing so without raising an alarm would be nigh on impossible.

'Stupid's about all we've got right now.' Mitchell exhaled, staring out across the brightly lit city. 'Anyway, they'll show. I know they will.'

'This a female intuition thing?'

She knew him well enough to take that remark in the spirit it was intended. 'Anya already risked her life for this file; she's come too far to back down now. It's just a question of when she makes her play.'

'And we're the only thing standing in her way,' he reminded her. 'Can't make up my mind if this is heroic or fucking stupid.'

'Neither. You saw what happened in Norway.' Mitchell unconsciously reached up and touched her temple, feeling the tight knot of pain and bruised skin that reminded her just how dangerous an adversary they'd pitted themselves against. 'She could have killed us both without breaking a sweat, but instead she let us live. Why?'

'Gunfire would have drawn the rest of our team in.'

Mitchell shook her head. 'Come on, Vince. Think. There are plenty of ways to kill people without firing a weapon. No, she spared our lives because we were no threat to her. That sound like the action of a crazed killer?'

'How the hell would I know? Isn't that the point of crazy people – they're unpredictable?'

For Mitchell, insanity didn't factor into it for one second. In Anya, she saw a resourceful and capable operative pursuing a goal with ruthless determination, overcoming any obstacle that stood in her path and yet somehow still managing to show restraint and compassion.

'She's not crazy. I'd bet my life on that.'

Suddenly Argento tensed up, moving his binoculars a few degrees to the right to focus on a new arrival approaching the building.

'You might just have to,' he said, all trace of humour vanishing from his voice now. 'I think we've got some action here.'

Abandoning her coffee, Mitchell jumped up and hurried over. She was by his side in seconds, her own binoculars quickly sighting the potential target.

'Blue panel van approaching from the south-west. Looks like its slowing down,' Argento reported.

Sure enough, a delivery van was approaching, slowing down and pulling to a halt right in front of the main entrance. The passenger door opened and a lone figure jumped down onto the pavement.

She was wearing the same uniform as the building security guards, but unlike the others Mitchell had seen come and go during shift changes, this one was definitely female. She could make out the lighter physique and the swell of breasts beneath the brown shirt, though her face was turned away and partially covered by a baseball cap.

'You got a positive ID?' she asked, wary of getting fired up over a false alarm.

'Couldn't tell for sure. I only saw her for a second, but she fits the description.'

And then, just like that, the target turned her head, glancing at something on the other side of the street and at the same time revealed herself to Mitchell. Straight away she knew the face in her field glasses matched the one burned into her memory after their brief confrontation in Norway.

'It's her,' Mitchell said, feeling her heartbeat soaring.

'Son of a bitch,' Argento breathed. 'What's she gonna do? Waltz right in through the front door?'

She seemed to be doing just that, making straight the main entrance. As she did so, the van pulled away and turned into a service alley running down the side of the building, leading to the loading bay at the rear.

'I'll bet you twenty bucks Yates is onboard that van.'

Mitchell said nothing, her face tight with concentration as she watched Anya stroll confidently up to the main entrance, reach into her pocket and swipe an access card through the reader next to the glass doors. There was a brief flash of green light, after which Anya typed in an access code of some kind, and that was it. The doors opened automatically, and with barely a glance over her shoulder she slipped inside.

'I'll be damned,' she said under her breath, impressed by the woman's audacity if nothing else. Where on earth had she obtained the card and code needed to get inside?

'We've got them,' Argento said, his voice rising with growing excitement. 'One call to the cops and we've got them trapped in there.'

'No,' Mitchell said, lowering the binoculars. 'We're not calling anyone.'

'Huh?' Argento looked at her as if she were mad. 'Why the hell not?'
Her response was simple. Her reasons weren't.
'Because I want her to succeed.'

Chapter 41

The ISS building's security room was little more than a small office with a locked reinforced door and a bank of digital monitors set along one wall, allowing the sole occupant to access any one of the two dozen CCTV cameras carefully placed around the facility. If no specific camera was selected, the monitors cycled through them at five-second intervals, the order constantly changing to prevent would-be intruders exploiting the pattern.

To say that manning this room for an eight-hour night shift was a dull job would be a gross understatement. In the three years that Emre Sahin had been working night security here, there had been not a single break-in attempt; no suspicious activity, not even a couple of co-workers caught fucking in the toilets. The most exciting thing he'd ever had to deal with was a pair of drunken foreigners arguing in the alley leading to the rear service entrance. That had been two years ago.

Tonight however things were different. Burak Karga, the man who, according to the duty roster, was supposed to be on this shift with him, had failed to report in. He should have been here for changeover ten minutes ago, but there was no sign of him.

Sahin was hardly a stickler for punctuality under normal circumstances, but the rules of their job strongly warned against having only one guard on duty at a time. The guards from the previous shift had offered to stay on until Karga arrived, but they all knew it had been a half-hearted gesture at best. Naturally he'd told them to be on their way, believing Karga would arrive at any moment and not wishing to inconvenience them.

It had seemed like a sound and fair decision at the time, but as the minutes ticked by he became less and less confident. He was the supervisor – it was his job to get things like this right. If it was discovered that he'd knowingly breached this most fundamental regulation, he'd be in the shit.

It took him another minute or so to make his decision.

'Lazy bastard,' he said, reaching for the phone to his left. He stabbed at the buttons, punching in Karga's cell phone number, and waited impatiently while it rang out.

And carried on ringing.

'Come on, what the hell are you up to?'

He knew Karga was a football fanatic, and that his favourite team had been playing a big match tonight. If the man was late and had turned off his phone just to watch a penalty shoot-out, they would be having words.

Still the phone carried on ringing without response.

Sahin slammed the phone down a little harder than necessary. He was just pondering whether or not to report the issue to his own boss when the internal buzzer sounded to inform him the main door had been opened. A glance at his computer terminal confirmed that Karga's swipe card had just been used.

Relief surged through him, though it was tempered with annoyance.

'About time,' he mumbled, rising from his chair. He fully intended to give his tardy co-worker as hard a time as possible for the stress he'd caused.

The security room's door buzzed once as Karga swiped himself in.

'Burak, what time do you...?'

Sahin's words trailed off as he stared at the woman who had suddenly appeared in the doorway, armed with an automatic that was levelled at his head. A Western woman, tanned but clearly of Caucasian origin, with pale yellow hair and piercing blue eyes. She was dressed in the same uniform as himself, but it was clear that protecting the security of this place was the last thing on her mind.

For a brief, ludicrous moment, instinct took over and he reached for the panic button fixed to the underside of his desk.

'If you try it, you die,' she warned, her pale blue eyes glinting with merciless resolve.

Her stark warning was enough to cut through whatever thoughts of resistance he'd entertained, however brief. This job paid pretty well as far as it went, but nowhere near enough to lay down his life. Heart pounding and throat dry, he quickly backed away from the desk and raised his hands to show he was unarmed.

'Lie down on the ground with your hands behind your head,' she instructed.

'Are you going to kill me?' he asked, lowering himself to his knees.

'I will certainly kill you if you don't obey.'

Having to fight a sudden urge to retch, Sahin lay down on the cold linoleum floor and placed his hands behind his head. He heard footsteps as she moved, and felt something narrow and plastic pulled tight around his wrists.

Working with the quick efficiency born from long experience, Anya secured his wrists with plastic cable ties, followed by his ankles. A third loop of plastic bound both sets of limbs together behind his back, making it impossible for him to stand up or even move more than a few inches.

Kneeling beside him, she holstered her weapon and looked into his eyes. They were dark and frightened, though to the man's credit he wasn't whimpering or pleading for his life. That was good.

'Are there any other security guards in this building?' she asked, speaking calmly now that he was no longer a threat. 'If you lie to me, I will know.'

'No. Just me.' He wasn't lying.

'Any building employees? Anyone else scheduled to arrive tonight?'

He shook his head.

'Good. I'm going to gag you now,' she informed him. 'Breathe normally and don't struggle, and you will live through this. Nod if you understand.'

He did.

Unrolling a strip of duct tape, she fixed it to his face, sealing his mouth shut. It wasn't unknown for people in such situations to panic and choke to death, or to suffer asthma or even heart attacks. For his sake, she hoped he wasn't the panicking kind.

With the guard taken care of, Anya turned her attention to the bank of monitors. They seemed to be cycling through various sections of the building, and in at least one of them she spotted a dimly lit room filled with rows of black computer cabinets, each illuminated by a few minimal indicator lights.

The server room.

Another camera was focussed on the courtyard at the rear of the building. As planned, Halvorsen was waiting patiently in a blue panel van near the loading bay, the exhaust venting small clouds of steam into the night air.

Beneath the monitors was a simple computer terminal governing electronic door locks throughout the building. Scrolling through the options until she found the loading-bay doors, she hit the button to open them.

–

Up on the rooftop nearby, Argento stared at his colleague in disbelief. 'Run that by me again?'

'Come on, use your head. This whole investigation felt dirty the minute Hawkins showed up, and it's been getting worse ever since. A guy with no official record, no past, who doesn't belong to any recognised directorate but has unlimited access to Agency resources? That's a heavy dose of bullshit right there.'

'Hey, I don't like the guy any more than you do, but who's to say Yates and his new best friend are any better?' Argento challenged her. 'For all we know, they could be fucking terrorists.'

Mitchell shook her head. 'This isn't about terrorism, for Christ's sake. This is a cover-up. Hawkins wasn't sent to arrest Yates or Anya, he's out to protect whatever secrets they're trying to uncover, and he's willing to kill anyone who gets in the way. Even innocent civilians. That sound like the kind of people you want to work with?'

Argento clenched his jaw. He didn't like what she was saying, but nor could he dispute it. 'So why come here, Olivia? Why even bother to make the trip if you're not out to stop them?'

'Like I said, I want them to succeed. And I want to know what's on that file. If I've allowed myself to be part of a cover-up, I want to know why.' She laid the binoculars aside and rose to her feet. 'That van parked round back is our ticket in.'

Before Argento could reply, however, another voice cut into their conversation. A voice that Mitchell had come to know all too well.

'Thanks for the advice.'

Startled, Mitchell whirled around, instinct prompting her to reach for the sidearm concealed within her jacket.

'Don't,' Hawkins warned, raising the barrel of his silenced M4A1 assault rifle to draw attention to the fearsome weapon. Capable of spitting out close to a thousand rounds a minute and with an effective range of over 500 yards, he could scarcely miss her if he opened fire now.

Standing not fifteen yards away, he was dressed in full night-assault gear and body armour. Two other men flanking him were dressed and armed in similar fashion.

He smiled, knowing he had her at his mercy. 'Couldn't have got here without you.'

Mitchell closed her eyes and let out a slow breath, realizing now how foolish she'd been to come here. Hawkins's sudden dismissal of her from the investigation hadn't been some whim born in the heat of the moment or the result of a festering rivalry. Sensing she might know more than she was letting on, he'd cut her loose and patiently watched while she carried on the investigation herself.

And when the time was right, he'd closed his trap.

Chapter 42

Clutching the canvas satchel that held a laptop and various other cables and components he might need to complete his task, Alex swung the rear door of the panel van open.

'Good luck,' Halvorsen called out from the front seat.

Alex glanced at the older man for a moment, saying nothing. Their success or failure rested on him now. His companions had played their part, but now it was up to him.

Never in his life had he felt that responsibility more keenly.

Jumping down from the rear of the vehicle, he slammed the door shut and gave it a slap with his hand to confirm that Halvorsen was good to go. The Norwegian wasted no time gunning the engine, easing the van out of the parking area and back down the alleyway to the main road beyond. It would have been easier for him to linger close to the building, but the danger of discovery was too great.

Alone now, Alex hurried forward and ducked beneath the rolling metal shutters that had been raised about three feet off the ground, finding himself in a small loading dock of sorts. The floor was bare concrete, the light coming courtesy of several cheap fluorescent strips fixed to the ceiling. Boxes, filing cabinets, spare desks and chairs, and all the other paraphernalia that accumulates in a busy office building were stacked along both walls.

Alex recognized this sort of area well enough, because there were plenty of rooms like it in his former workplace. It was the kind of back-room storage space where all the barely usable crap was dumped in the mistaken belief that it might come in handy one day.

And as he'd expected, Anya was waiting for him.

'The security room is neutralized. I've cut the hard lines outside,' she said, leading him deeper into the building. 'This way.'

With luck, it would be some time before anyone realized something was wrong. At least, Alex fervently hoped so. He had no idea how difficult it might be to locate the Black List amongst the millions of other files stored on the servers here, or the kind of difficulties he might encounter retrieving it.

Don't be an arsehole and doubt yourself now, he thought, giving himself a mental slapping. Just concentrate on not fucking up.

Spotting a stairwell leading down, Anya headed straight for it. 'The servers are down there.'

The heat and noise generated by such a vast collection of highly stressed electronics made their storage and maintenance problematic to say the least. For this reason, most server rooms were located underground.

As she moved, Anya keyed the small radio unit fixed to her shoulder. 'Kristian, we're inside. Heading for the server room now.'

'Copy that,' came his grainy reply. 'Standing by.'

Keeping her weapon to hand, Anya shoved the door open and hurried down the steps, with Alex close behind.

–

Up on the rooftop, Mitchell could do nothing to resist as one of Hawkins's men reached into her jacket and withdrew her weapon. Argento was given similar treatment, though his attempt to shove his captor away was promptly rewarded with a rifle butt to the stomach that dropped him to his knees, coughing and gasping for air.

It was the kind of foolish bravery that seemed to come so naturally to young men.

'Keep pushin', son,' the operative advised, apparently relishing the opportunity to put him down for good. 'You'll get there.'

Mitchell would have happily torn out the man's windpipe in that moment, though such an effort would have been suicidal. He could kill her a dozen times over with the assault rifle in his arms, not to mention his two companions.

'How you doing, Vince?' she asked, feigning only casual interest.

'Having… the time of my life,' he replied, struggling to raise himself off the ground. He looked up at their captor and flashed a defiant grin. 'Our friend here hits… like a faggot.'

That was all the excuse he needed. Taking a step back to allow himself more room to build momentum, he planted a kick square in the young man's side, delivered with enough brutal force to snap ribs. Argento was sent rolling across the rooftop by the force of the impact, coming to rest several yards away in a limp sprawl.

'You son of a—' Mitchell began, taking a step towards him.

She never got a chance to finish. Taking a step between them, Hawkins swung a lightning fast right hook that caught her just above the left eye. The impact was like a grenade going off in her head, and immediately she hit the ground, blood pounding in her ears and her vision swimming in and out of focus.

There would be no fighting back from this, she knew. She'd never had the pleasure of being knocked out before, but even she could tell that blow had come perilously close to sealing the deal. If clandestine operations didn't work out for him, Hawkins could have had a hell of a career as a professional boxer.

'I'm pissed at you, Mitchell,' she heard Hawkins say. 'You could have been a real asset to us. Instead here we are. Shame, really.'

She was going to die up here on this rooftop, she realized then. So was Argento, assuming he was still alive. On reflection, she felt worse for him than she did for herself.

He didn't deserve it.

'Didn't think you had a problem killing people,' she said, breathing hard and struggling to focus on the ground in front of her. Her fingers clawed at the gravel-covered rooftop as she tried to lift herself up.

'Never did,' he admitted. 'It just means more paperwork.'

It was then that her vision snapped back into focus and she saw him. Argento, lying several yards away after being beaten down by one of Hawkins's men. He was alive, after all, and he was looking right at her.

He was lying beside the low parapet wall from where they'd been observing the target building. She'd assumed the sheer force of the impact had sent him rolling across the rooftop, but now she realized otherwise. He'd baited that man into hitting him so that they'd no longer consider him a threat. He'd intended to end up there, so that he could reach for something that might help them.

Or rather, help *her*.

Buy her a few precious moments of distraction, at the cost of his own life.

His gaze flicked beyond her, to the other side of the rooftop. From her position it seemed to be just a continuation of the parapet wall, with a fifty-foot drop down to street level on the other side, but she knew otherwise. She knew what he wanted her to do.

No. She couldn't allow this to happen. Not now. Not him.

She shook her head. A meagre gesture, easily overlooked by the men poised to kill them, but utterly heartfelt in that moment.

She saw a flicker of a smile on the young man's face, and a tiny nod of encouragement as he reached for the steaming cup of coffee still sitting on the ground where he'd left it. He was going for it no matter what she did, no matter whether she was even able to take advantage of his distraction.

Vincent Argento, stubborn and defiant to the end.

'This is all on you, Mitchell,' Hawkins said, raising his weapon. 'I wanted you to know that.'

The moment had come. Snatching up the cup of coffee, Argento twisted around and hurled it at the man who had attacked him. Instinctively he turned away in an attempt to avoid the improvised missile, but it was far too late. Argento's aim was true, and the Styrofoam cup disintegrated under the impact, showering the left side of the man's face with its steaming contents.

It took another second or so for the pain to register, but when it did he growled in pain and clutched at his face, stumbling to his right.

Argento, rising to his feet and making to grab for the injured man's weapon, was allowed a single moment of satisfaction that he'd paid his adversary back for what he'd done. A heartbeat before Hawkins dropped him with a quick, efficient burst of silenced gunfire.

Mitchell was oblivious to this however. The moment Hawkins and his comrade started to turn towards the source of the noise, she had clawed her way to her feet and launched herself at the parapet. Her legs were unsteady beneath her and she almost expected them to give way, but somehow she remained upright.

She heard shouting from behind, heard the distinctive thump of a silenced weapon opening up on automatic. She forced herself not to think about Argento as she reached the edge of the roof, gathered herself up and leapt.

Having dispatched Argento, Hawkins turned his weapon towards Mitchell. Resourceful but foolish. The only way off this roof was the single-access door he'd emerged from, and he stood firmly in the way.

She was in his sights. He could barely miss from this range. His finger tightened on the trigger, and the weapon kicked back into his shoulder as the first round discharged.

But his target was no longer there. She had vanished, leaping right over the edge of the building and into the dark void beyond. Only when he heard a loud metallic thump followed by a cry of pain did he realize what had happened.

'Shit,' he snarled, sprinting for the parapet.

Ten feet below, Mitchell landed hard on the top level of the fire escape, the impact against the unyielding metal framework feeling like it had broken half the bones in her body.

She had landed at the top of the stairs leading down to the next level, and with desperate strength threw herself down them, trying to get some form of protection between her and Hawkins.

There was no thought of leaping down the steps or controlling her descent in any way. All she could do was grit her teeth and brace herself as she tumbled down the steel stairway fixed to the side of the building, each collision adding to the growing list of cuts and bruises she seemed to be accumulating.

When at last she landed in a heap on the level below, superficial pain had almost become irrelevant. The wild, desperate instinct for survival was what now drove her to pick her battered body up from the floor, to launch herself shoulder-first against the door leading back into the building, to ignore the bruising force of the impact.

The door, old and weathered, gave way under her frenzied assault, and she forced her way through just as another burst of deadly automatic fire scythed down from above, the rounds howling through gaps in the upper platform to ricochet off the steelwork below.

She no longer cared. She was inside, and hurtling down the corridor towards the nearest stairwell, oblivious to the pain and the blood leaking from her right side. She might have avoided the deadly burst that should have killed her, but one round had nonetheless found its mark.

On the rooftop above, Hawkins leaned back from the parapet and lowered his weapon. 'God damn it,' he said under his breath, then reached for the tactical radio fixed to his throat. 'Alpha to all call signs. We've got a runaway. Mitchell's heading down the main stairwell. Anybody have eyes-on?'

He had two more men stationed downstairs in plain clothes, partly to keep an eye on the ISS building and partly to guard against any unwelcome distractions while he dealt with Mitchell.

'Negative. Foxtrot is Oscar Mike, preparing to intercept.'

'Copy. Find her and fucking kill her.'

There was no hint of emotion in the man's voice when he replied. 'Roger that.'

Satisfied, Hawkins turned his attention back to the two men who had accompanied him. One, Rodriguez, now bore the marks of his brief lapse in concentration. Though hardly boiling when thrown, the coffee had still been hot enough to leave the skin down one side of his face angry red, even in the wan light cast by the street lamps.

He'd regained his composure by now, but his jaw was still clamped tight against the pain.

'Want me to go after her, sir?' he asked.

Hawkins shook his head. Much as he would have enjoyed hunting Mitchell down and making her suffer for the trouble she'd caused, he knew they had more important matters to deal with first. He couldn't afford to split his team any further.

'Mitchell can wait,' he said, glancing towards the ISS building. Their real objective was in there somewhere, waiting for them. 'Converge on the target building. Let's get this done.'

—

Mitchell tore down the stairs, leaping them two at a time as she made her way down, desperate to get out onto the street. This building was nothing but a trap, and the longer she remained here the more time Hawkins would have to seal it off.

It took her all of five seconds to realize he was way ahead of her.

The pounding of boots on the bare concrete stairs told her that someone was on their way up in a hurry, and it didn't take a genius to work out that Hawkins had men stationed outside. Mitchell couldn't hope to fight her way through. She was alone, unarmed, battered and bleeding, and starting to feel the pain of the gunshot wound. Instinctively she reached down and touched her side. Her hand came away slick with blood.

She couldn't go back up to the roof, and neither could she go down. The only option was to retreat into one of the residential floors, though even that was only delaying the inevitable.

Stopping at the nearest landing, she shoved open the door and staggered through, leaving a smear of blood on the door as she did so.

One floor beneath her, Frank Crichton, better known by his call sign Foxtrot, was ascending the stairs at a more cautious pace now, eyes and ears straining to locate any sign of his target. He'd heard movement on the stairwell above, followed by the creak of a door opening. Mitchell was here somewhere.

Reaching the next landing, he paused, staring at the dark spots marking the concrete floor. He inhaled, tasting the faint scent of a woman's perfume, then knelt down and touched one of the spots. As he'd thought, it was blood.

She was hurt.

His eyes travelled upward, to the door leading to the next floor. And sure enough, he saw a bloody handprint marking it.

Clutching her side, Mitchell staggered along the short corridor running the length of the building, desperately searching for anything she could use either as a weapon or a means of escape. There was nothing but doors leading into the residential apartments, all of them no doubt securely locked.

'Shit,' she gasped, teeth clenched tight against the mounting tide of pain.

Picking a door at random, she limped over and hammered against it with her fist, leaving a bloodstain on the painted wooden surface. The muted thump of the impact echoed in the apartment beyond, but there was no response.

'Please,' she gasped, tears stinging her eyes. 'I'm hurt. Please, help me.'

She heard a shout coming from inside. A man's voice, rough and angry, probably telling her to get lost. She didn't blame him. If she'd been in his position, she doubted she'd have opened up either.

Her brief bid for freedom was going to end here, she realized. Hawkins's men would see the trail of blood she'd left in her wake, and track her here like hounds following a wounded fox. Even an untrained civilian could have worked out where she'd gone.

They would see her standing alone and unarmed in this corridor, and they would drop her without a second thought.

Her strength draining away along with her hope, she fell against the wall and sank to the floor. Argento's sacrifice had been for nothing. Another pointless death that she should have prevented. Maybe it was best that it ended here for her; at least then she couldn't inflict any more suffering on others.

She almost didn't hear the click of a door being unlatched nearby. Only when it swung open, causing bright electric light to spill out into the hallway, did she look up, finding herself staring at a young and very pregnant woman wrapped in a thick dressing gown.

She stared back at Mitchell, her expression a mixture of alarm and quick, calculating intelligence. Her gaze swept down the corridor and, seeing nobody else there, she turned her attention back to the injured woman lying on the opposite wall.

'Come,' she said, beckoning her inside.

With a final surge of strength, Mitchell heaved herself up off the cold floor, staggered across the hallway and practically fell inside the apartment. No sooner was she inside than the pregnant woman closed and locked the door behind her.

–

Easing the door open, Crichton crept into the corridor, his weapon up and ready. The blood trail was leading him onward, though he was careful to keep constant awareness of his surroundings. He wouldn't put it past Mitchell to use the trail to try to lure him into a trap.

There was no sign of her in the straight, narrow corridor. And, as far as he could tell, there was nowhere for her to hide either.

Glancing down at the spots of blood, he carried onward, advancing past one door, then another, then another, until at last he came to a larger stain down one wall. A body, bleeding and damaged, had collapsed against it before sliding down to floor level.

And beside this stain, a bloody handprint on the nearest apartment door.

Crichton hesitated only a moment before raising his weapon and putting a silenced round through the lock, destroying it with a single shot. Shoving the door open, he advanced into the apartment beyond.

His first contact was a man emerging from the cramped kitchen to his right. Mid-fifties, balding and overweight. He opened his mouth to shout something, but never got the chance. Crichton took aim and put a round through his forehead, the spray of blood from the exit wound coating the cheap tiled floor and worktops, then turned away before the man had even hit the ground.

A woman's voice was calling out from the living room at the end of the short corridor, probably wondering what the unusual noise was. It wouldn't take her long to realize something was wrong. Walking with fast, deliberate strides, Crichton advanced down the hallway and opened the door.

The woman just rising from the couch looked to be about the same age as her husband. Short and plump, and still wearing the hotel-cleaner uniform he assumed she'd come home in, she froze immediately at the sight of an armed man in her living room.

'Tell me where the woman is, and you live,' Crichton said, giving her a chance.

She stared back at him, her expression blank and uncomprehending.

He didn't have time for this. Raising the gun, he dispatched her in a similar manner to her husband, then turned his attention to sweeping the remainder of the small apartment for Mitchell. There was still a chance she was hiding somewhere.

'Foxtrot to all units. No sign of her,' he was obliged to report a minute or so later, much to his chagrin. 'What are your orders?'

'Just get over here, Foxtrot,' came the terse reply. 'We'll deal with her later.'

Crichton gritted his teeth. His failure might have been overlooked for now, but it wouldn't be forgotten.

'Copy that.' Leaving the two dead occupants in his wake, he turned away and retreated from the apartment.

Chapter 43

'It's here!' Alex called out, pointing at the sealed security door up ahead.

Anya was on it immediately, striding ahead of him and swiping her stolen card through the electronic reader. There was a single crisp beep, and just like that the bulky fire-resistant door slid open on hydraulic hinges.

Anya was first through the doorway, her silenced automatic sweeping the room beyond. The place was in total darkness, with only rows of green indicator lights trailing off into the distance. However, as soon as she set foot in the room, the overhead lights blazed into life.

'Motion activated,' Alex explained, sensing her unspoken question. No sense in keeping lights burning when nobody was here to need them.

He followed her inside, and straight away was hit by a waft of chill, dry air. The smell of ozone made his nose wrinkle, while the low hum of countless cooling fans filled his ears.

Occupying most of the room's internal volume were rows of computer racks, eight feet high and surmounted by thick bundles of cables and duct-work. Each of these racks contained a server unit; a dedicated machine set up for the storage and movement of large volumes of data. The amount of information circulating in this one room was likely greater than the entire contents of the US Library of Congress.

'It's cold,' Anya said, her breath misting in the cool air. There was an eerie quality about this strange underground world of data cables, blinking lights, air ducts and whirring fans that made the hairs on the back of her neck prickle.

'It has to be. These units generate so much heat they'll melt down if they're not constantly cooled.' Glancing about, he started down the nearest row. 'Follow me.'

'What are we looking for?' Anya asked as she followed close behind, watching his back and clutching the weapon tightly.

'A way in,' Alex explained, eagerly scanning the ranks of imposing looking machines.

It wasn't until he'd reached the end of the row that he found what he was looking for. Reaching out, he pulled open the metal cover protecting the server access terminal, then opened his satchel and reached inside for his laptop.

'I can access the network from here,' he explained, waiting a few moments while the laptop booted up. 'Once I'm in, all I need to do is find the Black List and download it.'

'How long will it take?' she asked, keeping a wary eye on the doorway.

'Not sure.' He was distracted, busy connecting a serial cable between his laptop and the access point, and didn't notice the look she gave him.

'That's not what I want to hear.'

'That's not what I wanted to say either,' he said, crouching down with the laptop resting on his knees. 'But this isn't like logging into Hotmail. There are a hundred different factors outside my control.'

He was staring at the screen intently as the laptop and server access system tried to establish a connection. They were essentially two different systems speaking in different languages, but Alex was prepared for that. The customized program on his laptop was there to act as a translator, hopefully allowing him to bridge the gap between the two systems.

'Come on, come on,' he whispered, watching as the dialogue box flickered several times, the program behind it working to make the connection.

Finally the status changed to *connected*.

'We're in,' Alex hissed, tapping in a rapid series of commands. 'Right, access server routing grid, locate file and... God, I'd kill for a cigarette right now.'

'Bad idea,' Anya said, nodding towards the fire sensor mounted in the roof nearby. 'It will set off the Halon extinguishers.'

With fire an ever-present threat in a room filled with highly stressed and expensive computer equipment, a powerful extinguisher system was vital. The moment any of the sensors detected heat or smoke, they would flood the room with Halon gas designed to chemically neutralize any fires while leaving the rest of the equipment undamaged.

Alex glanced up at her. 'We really need to work on your sense of humour when this is over.'

—

Armed with the most sophisticated tools of the trade available, it took one of Hawkins' men less than thirty seconds to run an electronic bypass of the magnetic lock on the building's main door, disabling the system and allowing Hawkins to stroll right into the lobby area beyond.

'Secure the room,' he said, gesturing left and right. Straight away two of his men peeled off to take flanking positions, covering him while he advanced towards the security room located behind the front desk.

A similar effort from his technical specialist disabled the electronic lock barring his way, and he swung the door open to find what he presumed was one of the building's security guards gagged and hogtied on the floor.

'Anya, you're getting soft in your old age,' he remarked, shaking his head. The woman he'd once known would never have left this man alive.

Ignoring the guard for the moment, Hawkins surveyed the rest of the room. The data-storage units for the CCTV system had been removed from their racks and now lay in a smashed pile on the floor, which was just fine with him. Neither he nor Anya wanted any record of what happened here tonight.

The recording system might have been disabled, but the cameras themselves were still broadcasting their signals to the bank of monitors. Searching through the displays, he finally fixed on one showing a young man crouched down beside an equipment rack with a laptop balanced on his knees. Standing guard over him with a silenced automatic – an M1911, naturally – was a woman with short blonde hair.

'Well, hello gorgeous.'

Leaving the monitor blank, he knelt down beside the restrained guard, reached out and ripped the duct tape away from his mouth. The tape took a few hairs and a layer of skin with it, and the guard let out a grunt of pain.

'Hey pal, you speak English?' Hawkins asked.

Licking his lips, the guard glanced at Hawkins's weapon and nodded.

'Cool.' Hawkins gestured to the monitor showing Yates and Anya. 'Know where those two are?'

'The... server room. Basement.'

Hawkins smiled and nodded. 'Thanks, buddy.'

Rising to his feet and stepping back a pace to avoid the resultant blood-splash, he took aim and put a single round through the man's head, then left the room to rejoin his team.

'They're downstairs,' he said, heading for the stairwell. 'Let's get them, boys.'

Chapter 44

Breathing hard and clenching her teeth against the pain of the ragged wound that was still oozing a steady stream of blood, Mitchell looked up at the young woman who had unknowingly saved her life.

She couldn't have been more than twenty-five, if not younger. Short and petite – save for the swollen abdomen – with the dark hair and olive skin characteristic of people in this region, she looked as unlikely a saviour as Mitchell could have wished for.

She surveyed the injured woman lying on her floor for several seconds, as if trying to work out whether she'd made a mistake by letting her in. Despite her diminutive size, there was a confidence in her posture and a shrewdness in her gaze that suggested this wasn't the first time she'd encountered someone injured and bleeding.

'American?' she said suddenly.

Such was the directness of the question, Mitchell could do little but answer in similar fashion. 'Yeah.'

The woman's gaze rested on the wound in her side. 'Wait here.'

Turning away, she swept off into what Mitchell assumed to be the kitchen, moving with surprising speed given her advanced pregnancy. She returned only moments later clutching a white hand towel.

Kneeling down beside Mitchell, she moved the woman's jacket aside and peeled away the blood-soaked t-shirt beneath to expose the injury.

'Hold this here,' she instructed, pressing the towel hard against the wound. Mitchell winced in pain, having to bite her lip to keep from crying out. 'It hurt. But pressure will slow bleeding.'

Mitchell simply nodded, unable to say anything.

'What happen?' the young woman asked. Her English was accented but perfectly understandable.

She swallowed hard, trying not to think about Argento. Trying not to think of another life lost because of her. 'I was attacked. By a man. I ran in here looking for help.'

'He rob you?'

If that had been the worst thing that had happened to her tonight, she'd have been dancing a jig at this point. 'Something like that.'

The young woman looked at her with that shrewd, calculating gaze. 'Then why he shoot you?'

Mitchell's eyes snapped up to meet hers. 'What?'

'I see this kind of wound before. At hospital. I treat many myself.'

Suddenly her calm, no-nonsense demeanour made a lot more sense. 'You're a doctor?' she asked, sitting up a little. The wound in her side blazed with pain.

'A nurse. At Alman Goz hospital. At least, I was. Soon I am mother.' She was leaning in a little closer, examining the position and size of the wound.

'What's your name?' Mitchell asked.

'Sevde.' She glanced up for a moment. 'And you?'

'Olivia.'

'You are lucky, Olivia,' she concluded. 'Bullet miss vital areas. Towel will slow bleeding until you get to hospital.'

Already she was rising slowly to her feet, no doubt about to reach for the nearest phone and call an ambulance.

'No,' Mitchell implored her, grasping her slender forearm. 'No ambulance. No hospital.'

The young woman's expression of professional medical concern was rapidly giving way to doubt and suspicion. 'Why not? You need help.'

Perhaps, but she certainly wouldn't get any at a hospital. By law, any patient admitted with gunshot wounds had to be reported to the police, in which case Hawkins would be on her before they could administer the first shot of morphine.

'You've already done enough for me,' Mitchell said, trying to rise to her feet. 'I'll go now, leave you alone.'

'You not go,' she said firmly, exerting surprising force given her petite frame. Then again, Mitchell supposed it said more about her current condition than it did about Sevde. 'Get help. You need it.'

'Listen to me, Sevde,' Mitchell pleaded. 'The men who attacked me tonight will find me if I go to hospital.'

'They have guards, police,' she countered.

'It won't matter. They'll find me and they'll kill me.' She bit her lip and looked away for a moment, blinking back tears as the reality of the past few minutes at last caught up with her. 'They already murdered my friend, right in front of me. And if I don't do something they're going to kill other good people tonight.'

Sevde stared at her, torn between suspicion and compassion. 'What can you do?'

There was only one thing that came to mind. It was stupid, hastily conceived and more than likely to result in her own death, but that no longer mattered. They were into the endgame now, and she wanted Hawkins. She wanted him in her sights, to look into his eyes the moment she pulled the trigger.

If that was how she had to go out, she could accept that.

She looked at Sevde, her eyes hardening with cold-blooded resolve. 'You got a gun in this place?'

–

He was getting close, he could sense it. His search program was trawling the server's vast online storage space, searching the thousands of directories and folders for the one file that could mean the difference between life and death for him. It was in there somewhere, it was just a question of time.

Clearly Anya was harbouring similar thoughts. 'How much longer?'

'A lot sooner if you didn't keep—' He paused as the computer chimed once, the search alerting him that it had returned a result.

1 Result found: D1189 – Download Y/N?

'Well, fuck me!' Alex cried, clenching his fist. 'Got you, you little bastard.'

He couldn't hit the Y key fast enough. Straight away a progress bar appeared on screen as the data was transferred into a memory stick on the side of his laptop, giving an estimated download time of thirty seconds. With a direct connection like this, there was nothing to slow it down.

'We're almost there,' he said, barely able to conceal his excitement. 'Twenty seconds and we're out of here.'

Anya nodded. She was a long way from opening the champagne yet. 'Get ready to move. When we leave, I'll lead. You stay close to me.'

'Whatever.' At that moment he would happily have formed a conga line and danced his way out of the building.

Reaching for the radio at her shoulder, Anya pressed the transmit button. 'Kristian, we'll be outside in sixty seconds. Stand by to pick us up.'

She was expecting an acknowledgement, but instead her call was met with nothing but the faint pop and hiss of static.

Frowning, she hit the button again. 'Kristian, do you copy?'

Nothing.

'It's the walls,' Alex explained, nodding to the thick concrete shell that encased the room. 'They're shielded against interference. Your radio won't work in this room.'

'You could have warned me.'

'Would it have changed your mind?' he asked rhetorically.

Anya looked at him disapprovingly. But before she could speak, the lights in the room suddenly went out, plunging them into darkness. Only the glow of Alex's computer screen and the green indicator lights on the rows of servers provided any illumination.

'Anya, what the—?'

'Hush!' she implored him, slowly lowering herself into a crouch just as the electronic locks on the main door disengaged with a buzz and a metallic click.

Clutching the automatic tight, she leaned her head out a few inches to survey the long computer-lined avenue stretching out before them.

Her movement was answered by a rhythmic thumping sound coming from the far end of the room, and she hurriedly ducked back behind cover as a trio of 5.56 mm rounds slammed into the thin metal sheeting beside her. A shower of sparks and fragments of broken circuitry rained down on them as one server unit was blasted apart by the impacts.

'Tangos in sight!' a male voice called out. 'Centre aisle.'

'Copy. Move in!'

Alex curled into a ball, trying to make himself as small a target as possible while his mind screamed at him in blind panic. 'Oh fuck, oh fuck, oh fuck! They've found us!'

'Jesus, what do we do?'

Anya however had more pressing matters to attend to. Flattening herself against the floor, she leaned out just far enough to bring the automatic to bear and opened up.

Whatever Alex had seen in the movies about the effectiveness of silencers was clearly way off the mark, because the loud, booming thud of each shot was enough to leave his ears ringing. In such close proximity, he could even feel the vibrations through the server rack as the pressure wave passed through them.

Her flurry of gunfire was answered by a shouted command. 'Cover! Cover!'

She had bought them a momentary respite, but in the near-darkness her shots were unlikely to find their mark. In any case, the defiant hail of fire couldn't be sustained for long. The M1911, for all its stopping power and impressive history, held only eight rounds in a single-stack magazine. There was no way it could compete with the firepower arrayed against them. After loosing one last shot, the slide flew back and locked in place to expose an empty breech.

Her adversaries seemed to seize upon this immediately, and no sooner had she ceased firing than they returned the favour, spraying automatic fire down the room towards her. It was suppressing rather than lethal fire, intended to keep her pinned down while they closed in.

Crawling back behind cover herself, Anya ejected the spent magazine from her weapon and placed it in her pocket, then hurriedly slapped a fresh one home. Already the air reeked of burned cordite.

'Is the file downloaded?' she asked, her voice low and urgent.

Trembling, Alex looked at his computer screen. Sure enough, the Black List had finished downloading. Not that they were likely to live long enough to benefit from it.

'Yeah.'

Anya nodded, her jaw clenched as she weighed up her options. It took her all of two seconds to make her decision. Raising her weapon, she took aim at the smoke detector mounted in the ceiling and fired a single, well-aimed shot.

Straight away the darkness of the room vanished, burned away by the bright red emergency lights that blazed into life. As the room was submerged in their crimson glow, a warning klaxon blared out, sounding the activation of the fire-suppression system.

And a moment later, it came.

Alex had never experienced Halon gas before, though he'd heard it was widely used in situations like this where traditional sprinklers would cause more harm than the fire they were supposed to extinguish.

Whatever the technical theory behind its operation, the reality was that Alex suddenly found himself enveloped in clouds of thick white smoke that were suddenly ejected from vents in the ceiling. It carried no scent that he could detect, and seemed to be breathable, though he did notice a strange sense of disorientation and light-headedness after the first few seconds. With nowhere for it to disperse, the strange, dense mist rapidly filled the room, reducing visibility to only a few yards.

'Go now!' Anya yelled over the blare of the alarms.

Alex fumbled to disconnect the laptop from the access port but, unable to make his fingers cooperate with his brain, simply yanked out the little USB memory stick plugged into the side of it. He had what he needed now anyway.

'Come on!' Anya practically hauled him to his feet and pulled him towards the main door, which had opened automatically when the fire-suppression system kicked in.

They had made it about halfway down when a figure suddenly loomed out of the mist, the long barrel of an assault rifle out in front of him.

Anya reacted with the speed and aggression born from years of experience. Ducking down low to present a smaller target, she rushed in against him, closing the distance before he could bring the weapon to bear, and jamming her own sidearm against his body armour. The M1911 thudded as a round discharged, quickly followed by a second.

Even the best armour in the world couldn't protect him from such lethal close-range fire, and he began to fall. A third round to the head was enough to put him down for good. Letting him drop to the floor, Anya quickly disengaged from him and hurried onward, with Alex leaping over the fallen man and trying not to look at the gruesome results of her work. He'd already seen enough things over the past few days that he knew would revisit him late at night for years to come.

A muted thumping sound from behind told him that at least one of their pursuers had circled around behind them and was spraying fire indiscriminately down the corridor. Instinctively Alex threw himself to the floor as several rounds whistled overhead, impacting the far wall and gouging deep holes in the concrete. As he landed, his injured ribs blazed with pain.

Once more Anya reacted. Swinging around, she dropped to one knee and opened fire into the chemical fog.

'Alex, get out of here!' she hissed, loosing another shot. 'Get outside.'

Alex ducked down as another burst whistled by so close that he could feel the change in air pressure as the rounds passed him. 'What about you?'

'I'll hold them here.'

The look in her eyes told its own story. She wasn't planning to leave this place.

'Fuck that! I—'

Suddenly she turned to look at him, her eyes blazing with fierce anger and, most of all, desperation. She needed him to do this. 'Trust me, Alex,' she pleaded. 'Go now!'

There was no time to argue, no time to ponder the alternatives and reach a compromise. It was do or die.

Gritting his teeth, Alex stumbled to his feet and rushed headlong for the door. His last sight of Anya before she faded into the mist was of her rising to her feet and snapping off another shot, keeping their enemies at bay, buying him the time he needed to escape.

At the cost of her own life.

Slipping through the door and into the stairwell beyond, Alex knew he could do nothing to help her now. Nothing except survive.

–

Crichton was already in a foul mood after his failure to recapture Mitchell, but as he sprinted into the lobby of the ISS building and heard the distinctive blare of fire alarms, he sensed things were rapidly going from bad to worse.

Pausing by the reception desk, he keyed his radio. 'Foxtrot to all units. Sitrep?'

The reply, when it came, was garbled and inaudible. Too much interference, probably from the subterranean vault in which the building's servers were stored. That told him everything he needed to know about his comrades' position, if not their situation.

Wasting no time, he abandoned the desk and sprinted through a set of double doors into a service corridor beyond. The corridor seemed to encircle the core of the building, giving access to offices and repair rooms along each side. A sign for stairs pointed to a door about halfway along, and straight away he made for it.

However it seemed someone else had the same idea. Crichton skidded to a stop as the door flew open and a man stumbled out into the corridor. A young man of slender build, holding something in one hand.

Yates.

For a heartbeat the young man stood rooted to the spot, staring at him as if failing to comprehend what he was seeing. Crichton had no such difficulty. Instinctively he dropped into a firing position and raised his weapon, taking aim at his target's centre mass while his body readied itself for the recoil.

In a flash, reality seemed to snap back into place for Yates, and he stumbled backward into the stairwell, the door swinging shut just as Crichton squeezed off a shot. The round tore through the door's wooden veneer before ricocheting off the steel frame beneath.

'God damn it,' he hissed, jumping to his feet and taking off in pursuit.

He covered the fifteen yards to the door in mere moments, kicking it open and advancing into the stairwell with the weapon up and ready. The clatter of feet on the metal stairs above told him that Yates was heading up, which made sense. He couldn't go back down without running into Hawkins and the others.

But even this desperate course of action was nothing but a temporary respite. This was the only stairwell, and with no other way down Yates was effectively trapped.

Realizing he had the young man trapped, Crichton leapt up the stairs in pursuit. As he did so, he keyed his radio again. 'Foxtrot has Tango in sight. It's Yates. He's heading for the roof. I'm on him!'

Having made his report, he tightened his grip on the handgun and pounded up the stairs. Mitchell might have eluded him, but no way was Yates leaving this building alive.

Chapter 45

Gripping the M1911 tightly, Anya edged along the wall, her senses painfully alert as she strained to discern any movement in the red-tinted haze around her. The warning klaxons had ceased now, as had the vents spewing out Halon gas into the server room, but visibility was still severely limited.

At least here the odds were even, and her opponents' superior numbers counted for little. It was just as well, because she was almost out of ammunition. By her count, only two rounds remained in the M1911 – one in the mag and one in the chamber. Not much to take on a heavily armed Agency kill team.

She was running out of time. The fire alarm had undoubtedly triggered some kind of automated request for help, and it wouldn't be long before emergency services arrived. She could only hope Alex had used the time she'd bought him and made good his escape, because he was beyond her help now.

Her thoughts were interrupted by the hiss of hydraulic pistons, followed by the buzz of an electronic lock engaging.

'You're not going anywhere, Anya,' a male voice called out. American, smooth, confident and arrogant. Not the voice of a man fighting for his life at all. 'I've sealed the door and destroyed the lock. It's just you and us now.'

She continued edging along the wall, sticking to the outer edge of the room so there was less chance of being taken from behind.

'Real heroic of you to sacrifice yourself for Yates, by the way,' the voice taunted. 'I'm impressed. The Anya I used to know wouldn't have given him a second thought.'

Anya said nothing to this. She knew far better than to give away her position by rising to such bait, though she felt her heart rate increase. What did he mean by 'the Anya he used to know'? Who was this man who had been sent to kill her?

'Waste of time, of course. We nailed the little bastard the minute he tried to leave the building.' She heard a snort of amusement. 'You really think you could get by us? You tried the same thing in Iraq, as I remember. Didn't work out so well.'

Despite herself, despite everything she'd been taught, everything that had been drilled into her about never losing focus, Anya let out an involuntary gasp of shock.

For an instant she found herself in that winding river valley near the border, injured and beaten down, surrounded by the strike team sent to capture her. Once more she felt the pain and the despair of knowing that her hastily conceived mission, her last chance at redemption, had failed.

Back then she could scarcely have imagined the ordeal that awaited her. Four years of imprisonment in a Russian fortress deep within the icy wastes of Siberia. Four years of torture, beatings, deprivation, isolation and most of all, the utter, agonizing knowledge that no one was coming for her. She had endured many hardships in her life, but that was the only experience that had truly come close to breaking her.

And it had all started the day they captured her.

How could he know about Iraq?

She could hear movement off to her left, snapping her mind back to awareness. One, possibly two operatives moving to outflank her.

Reaching into her pocket, she withdrew the empty magazine she'd ejected from her weapon earlier, took aim and hurled it against the far wall. In the deathly silence following the shutdown of the alarms, the clatter of the magazine against the concrete wall sounded like a bucket of scrap metal falling off a shelf.

More movement, closing in on the source of the disturbance, two men covering each other. They were too professional to give away their position by speaking. More than likely they'd operated together enough times to guess each other's intentions.

Taking a deep breath, Anya pushed herself off the wall and rushed straight at them. Sure enough, the first figure materialized out of the red haze just a few yards away. Hearing her approach, he swung his weapon around to open fire.

But Anya was ready. Shifting her balance, she threw herself to the ground, her momentum causing her to slide across the smooth concrete floor just as he squeezed off a round.

Raising her own weapon, she took aim just as she passed beneath him and fired upward, putting a round straight through his head. Good kill – no way could he survive that.

Leaping to her feet, she spotted the barrel of an assault rifle emerging from the mist, its muzzle coming to bear on her. Reaching out with her free hand, she grasped it and jerked it upwards just as its owner opened fire. The first round missed her head by mere inches, and she could feel the heat on her face from the excess gasses escaping the muzzle.

Keeping her grip on the weapon that was now spitting fire into the ceiling, she thrust her own sidearm upward, felt the silencer make contact with something hard, and pulled the trigger. There was a dull crunch, a burst of warm fluid that coated one side of her face, and suddenly her opponent was falling away, his weight and momentum finally yanking the assault rifle from her grasp.

Anya let out a breath, trying to calm her wildly beating heart. Two rounds, two men dead. By her reckoning that left only their leader to deal with now.

No sooner had she thought this than a fresh burst of gunfire erupted from the far end of the room. Instinctively she twisted aside and threw herself behind the nearest server rack, but the long sustained burst was throwing a lot of rounds in her direction, and inevitably one of them found its mark.

Anya's first impression was of a giant fist slamming into her chest, knocking her backward as surely as if she'd been hit by a freight train. Caught off balance, she landed on the floor in a painful heap, barely managing to crawl behind cover as more rounds ricocheted off the ground around her. The gas was slowly clearing, but visibility wasn't yet good enough for her attacker to take proper aim. That was likely the only reason she was still alive.

Her Kevlar vest had stopped the round, barely, but the sheer kinetic energy of the impact would have caused severe bruising and perhaps even cracked a rib or two. Grimacing against the pain and trying to draw the breath that had been knocked from her lungs, Anya tossed aside her now useless weapon.

Nearby, she heard the distinctive clatter of a spent magazine falling to the floor, followed by the click as a fresh one was inserted and locked in place. Clearly her opponent had no shortage of ammunition, and he would expend every round of it to take her down.

Even now she could hear his footsteps on the floor, slow and measured, heading in her direction. He was closing in to finish her off.

–

Alex pounded up the stairs, gasping for breath, adrenaline coursing thick in his veins as he took the steps two at a time. He almost didn't care where he was running to, couldn't think about anything but the next flight of steps.

His pursuer was somewhere below him, tackling the ascent with both greater determination and greater ability. He was gaining, despite the frantic burst of speed that fear had imparted.

Somewhere in the back of his mind he knew he was only delaying the inevitable, that sooner or later he would either run out of stairs to climb or find himself shot in the back by his opponent. But fear and panic drove him onward, forced him to keep climbing even as his muscles ached and his lungs burned.

And then, sure enough, he found himself at the top of the stairwell, confronted by a door leading out onto the building's rooftop. Barely breaking stride, he hit the release bar to open the door and staggered out.

Straight away the breeze hit him, cool and refreshing compared to the sterile air in the stairwell, and carrying the faint tang of sea salt. The rooftop, like those of most office buildings around the world, was crowded with air vents, aerials and satellite dishes, none of which provided much cover.

Rushing over to the nearest aerial, he yanked it free from its fixture and wedged it in place against the door. The sturdy metal rod was enough to hold it closed, for now at least. He had no idea how effective a barricade it might be, but perhaps it would buy him the time he needed to act.

With this in mind, Alex sprinted across to the edge of the roof in search of another way down.

Built as it was in a heavily urbanized area, the ISS building was sandwiched in between two other structures, both of which were a floor lower and separated by perhaps ten or twelve feet. Enough to allow vehicles to drive along the service alleys between and make deliveries at the rear.

Sweating, heart pounding, Alex surveyed the yawning gap stretching before him, the terrible drop below and the cluttered rooftop that was now his only way out. Twelve feet of open air lay between him and salvation. Twelve feet that might as well have been twelve miles. Below, maybe seventy feet down, a narrow service alley ran between the modern office blocks.

It would be a rough fall if he reached the other roof, and there was a fair chance he'd break bones or even fail entirely and rag-doll all the way down to the street below.

But it had to be worth a try.

He backed up a pace, trying to draw on the mental and physical reserves he'd need to make the jump, to put aside the danger and just go for it.

He couldn't do it, he realized straight away. He couldn't do it in London several days earlier, and he couldn't do it now. Even now with his life hanging by a thread, he just didn't have it in him.

A rapid series of muted thumps followed by the crunch of shattered wood behind warned him that his makeshift barricade had just been blasted apart.

'Freeze!'

And just like that, it was over. His one chance to escape, to justify the faith that had been shown in him, to prove he wasn't completely useless; it all vanished in that moment.

'Turn around!'

Letting out a breath, Alex reached up for the little USB memory stick hanging around his neck, and turned slowly to face his adversary.

Just as he'd expected, the man standing a few yards away was dressed in casual clothes that belied his deadly purpose. Jeans, hiking boots that had no doubt served him well on the frantic chase up the stairwell, and a loose blue shirt that didn't quite hide the bulky body armour underneath.

He was breathing a little harder, and a faint sheen of sweat coated his forehead. That gave Alex some small measure of satisfaction, as if he had somehow scored a point by making his opponent work for the kill.

And killing was certainly what was on this man's mind now. His weapon was trained on Alex's head, his finger tight on the trigger.

'Give me the memory stick,' he instructed, his voice cold and commanding. He might have had to work a little harder than usual to catch his prey, but he was firmly in control of the situation now.

Yanking the memory stick free from his neck, Alex suddenly thrust it out behind him, dangling it over the gap by its plain canvas necklace. Such an innocuous little piece of technology – the kind of cheap storage device used by everyone from office workers to teenage music fans. But appearances could be deceptive. The information stored within its digital pathways, carefully coded and encrypted, was what really mattered.

That was what he had travelled five thousand miles around the world for. That was what he had risked his life for. That was what he was about to die for.

'You shoot me, I drop this, the police recover it,' he warned. 'They'll find the Black List. Everything you were sent to cover up. It's all on you.'

His soon-to-be killer smiled. The fierce, predatory smile of one used to taking lives without mercy or hesitation. 'The police? You think we can't get to *them*?' he taunted. 'We can get to anyone. So do yourself a favour. Lay it down on the ground and back away, and we both walk. That's it.'

Alex might have laughed if he hadn't been so crushed by his failure. No matter what he did, no matter how compliant and cooperative he was, only one of them was walking away from this, and it wasn't him.

Alex was just another target to this man. Just another loose end to be taken care of. A stupid, clueless civilian who had only made it this far because he'd had someone far smarter and more capable watching his back. Someone who might well have given her life to buy him time to escape.

You fucked up, an accusatory voice in his mind told him. Just like everything else in life, you fucked this up. You might as well give him what he wants. Just back down and give up like you always do.

Then Alex did something; something even he didn't expect until it happened.

'No,' he said, his voice surprisingly calm given the frantic pounding of his heart. 'Not this time.'

Taking a step back, he mounted the low parapet encircling the perimeter of the building's roof. A gaping, terrifying chasm lay beneath him. An armed man intent on ending his life stood before him.

And all around, lit by the orange glow of uncountable lights that glimmered off the dark waters of the Bosphorus Strait, was the ancient city of Istanbul.

Not a bad place to end up, Alex thought as he took a step back into the abyss.

The crack of a single gunshot caused him to flinch, and instinctively he tensed up, waiting for the gut-wrenching penetration as a bullet tore into his body.

But no such thing happened. Instead, he watched in disbelief as his adversary staggered forward a pace, blood leaking from the exit wound on the right side of his forehead, then crumpled to the ground in a lifeless heap.

Alex let out a breath, struggling to process what had just happened, hardly able to comprehend the reprieve he'd just been handed. It had to be Anya, he reasoned. Somehow she must have fought her way out of the server room and made her way up here to help him.

Watching his back even now.

His heart swelling with relief, he looked up from the body, expecting to see his companion looking at him, probably pissed off that he'd failed to escape by himself. If so, he could live with that.

But Anya wasn't there. His brief surge of elation vanished as he found himself staring at a woman with dark hair and blood-stained clothes. The same woman who had tried to capture them in Norway.

It might have been the same woman, but she bore little resemblance to the uniformed tactical operative she'd been then. Her civilian clothes were torn and ripped, her skin cut and bruised, while a blood-stained dressing covered the right side of her torso.

She was armed with a short-barrelled revolver; the kind of antiquated weapon a 1930s New York policeman might have wielded. And yet there was no denying its deadly effectiveness, as the body lying between them proved.

'You're Alex Yates?' she began.

Alex had no answer for her. He was still trying to understand everything he'd just witnessed, and coming up short.

'It's okay,' the woman said, lowering her weapon. 'I'm here to help. My name's Olivia. I'm... a friend.'

Alex stood his ground, though he was uncomfortably aware that one strong gust of wind might well blow him right off the parapet to his death. 'You didn't look like a friend back in Norway.'

She nodded grimly. 'Things change,' she remarked, pointing to the bloody improvised dressing at her side. She was clearly in pain from the injury, and breathing hard after her ascent up the stairs, but remained defiantly on her feet.

'What happened to you?'

'The people I work... *worked* for, aren't who I thought they were. Neither are you, if I'm right.' She glanced at the ledge on which he was now balanced precariously. 'You might want to step down from there. Be a shame if I went through all this for nothing.'

He eyed her dubiously. 'Why should I trust you?'

Her answer was as simple as it was heartfelt. 'Because I want to kill those sons of bitches as much as you do.'

Chapter 46

Advancing down the row of now silent servers with the assault rifle up at his shoulder, Hawkins glanced down at the two dead bodies of his men. He spared them only a glance as he picked his way between them, feeling no grief at their loss. He'd expected casualties, taking on an operative like Anya, and he could always find replacements.

The years spent in prison apparently hadn't dulled her skills, not that it made much difference now. The discarded M1911 lay nearby, its empty breech confirming she had run out of ammunition. And judging by the spots of blood on the ground, she was injured.

One of his shots must have hit home.

The blood trail was leading towards the end of the row. She couldn't get far without him seeing or hearing her. He had her trapped.

'Just you and me now, Anya,' he said as he edged forward, his senses now painfully alert. The gas was slowly dissipating, allowing him to perceive his surroundings more clearly. Her advantage of concealment was almost lost. 'This is what you live for, isn't it? Honour amongst soldiers and all that shit.'

As he crept forward, he became aware of something. A noise, crackly and distorted. A radio receiving an incoming transmission, coming from the same direction the blood was leading. Hawkins backed up next to an equipment rack, taking a deep breath to calm and focus his mind.

'You know, I almost feel sorry for you. You worked so hard to get the answers you were looking for, it's a shame you were asking all the wrong questions. You're so desperate to find out what happened to you, you never thought to question why it happened.' He smiled, imagining what his next words were going to do to her. 'You wouldn't believe what the Russians gave us to get their hands on you.'

Rounding the corner, he raised his weapon to open fire, his eyes eagerly probing the crimson gloom for a target.

None presented itself. But he did see the source of the noise. A portable radio unit was lying on the floor just a few feet away, its transmit button held down by a piece of duct tape to create a low, crackling hiss of static.

Bait.

Crouched in the narrow space between the server racks and the basement ceiling, Anya looked down on the man intent on ending her life. Blood dripped from her arm where she'd intentionally pulled open the bullet wound she'd received in Norway, creating the blood-trail her enemy had been so diligently following. So focussed was he on tracking her down that he'd failed to anticipate the trap she'd set.

It would be the last mistake he ever made.

Gathering herself up, she leapt down from her hiding place to finish him. She possessed no weapons other than her bare hands, but that would suffice. She had killed armed men with them before and would do so again today.

But even as she landed on the ground behind him, he whirled around to face her, reacting with the speed of a man who had been expecting this very thing. Dropping the unwieldy assault rifle that would only slow him down in a close quarters fight like this, he swung a crushing left hook that she barely managed to raise her arm to block. The impact caught her off balance and sent her crashing against one of the server racks. Plastic shattered and the metal framework buckled as she hit.

Ignoring the pain of the impact, she pushed herself off the rack and circled her opponent, her fists raised and her body tensed up, ready to throw herself back into the fray.

'You didn't really think I'd fall for that, did you?' he taunted, smiling at her. He was just standing there, making no move to attack. 'Come on, you can do better than that, Anya.'

Only then, facing off against him, was Anya at last afforded a proper look at her adversary. Only then was her subconscious mind able to compare his face to the vast reservoir of identities stored away in her memory and deliver a single, chilling conclusion.

She had met this man before. A long time ago.

A potential candidate for the clandestine field unit she had once led, he had sailed through every physical and mental test they could throw at him. In most respects he'd been the perfect soldier, the perfect addition to her task force, but she had overruled the selection process and reject him.

She had done it because she'd long since learned there was more to being a soldier than the ability to hit a certain target, run a certain distance or solve a certain problem. It needed something more – a certain restraint and understanding of the grave responsibility they wielded, the ability to be more than just a weapon, but to think and question. She had sensed this was one trait the promising but arrogant young recruit would never possess, would never understand. She had no place for such people.

Little had she known at the time that this same man would find a new home where such traits were actively encouraged and sought out, and that he would one day return to take bloody revenge on the woman who had once shamed him with her rejection

'Jason,' she gasped, her mask of focus and self-control slipping aside.

'So you *do* remember. Been a long time. About… six years, as I recall.'

Such was her shock and disbelief that it was almost possible to forget she was fighting for her life against this man. The possibilities and implications

259

whirling through her mind were a maelstrom of different emotions that she couldn't begin to control.

'The Agency... *they* sent you to capture me in Iraq?'

His look was that of a teacher regarding a slow-witted student. 'What do you think?'

Her breath was coming in gasps, her heart beating wildly as the implications sank in. 'Why give me to the Russians? Why not just kill me?'

At this, Hawkins chuckled in amusement and shook his head. 'You still don't get it, do you? You weren't a target, you stupid bitch. You were a trade. You and your task force.'

A trade for what? her mind screamed. What had her life been worth? And who amongst the Circle had made the decision to give her up?

'For what it's worth, I'd much rather have killed you myself back then. I guess nobody expected you to come back from Russia. Then again, nobody expected you to come back from Afghanistan either.' Hawkins rolled his shoulders, preparing himself for the attack that he knew was about to come. 'Lucky for me they're taking no chances this time.'

–

'How the hell did you end up in this?' Alex asked as he leapt down the stairs, heading for the building's security room. It was the only place he could think of that might allow him to help Anya.

'I was... part of an investigation team,' Mitchell replied, struggling to keep pace with him. Her breathing was laboured and her steps heavy. She was forced to clutch at the railing for support. 'When...those agents were murdered in the UK... we were brought in to find the killers. We thought... you were a terrorist.'

'How did you know I wasn't?' he asked, unable to help himself.

Despite the obvious pain she was in, she managed a dry, brittle laugh. 'You don't look like the type. Anyway, Hawkins, the man... sent to catch you, was as bad as any terrorist. When I questioned him... he had me thrown off the investigation. I tried following my own leads... but he turned on me, killed my partner, tried to kill me too. The man doesn't care how many people... have to die... to end this.'

It seemed that killing innocent people was becoming a habit for this Hawkins, Alex thought as he shoved open the door at the base of the stairwell and hurried along the corridor to the security room.

The first thing he saw when he unlocked the door was the guard lying in a pool of blood on the floor. By the looks of things, he'd taken a round to the head.

Strangely, Alex felt almost nothing on beholding such a gruesome sight. He'd witnessed so much death over the past few days that his mind felt like it had reached saturation point. He just didn't have anything left.

'I'm starting to see what you mean,' he remarked grimly as Mitchell entered the room behind him. She was really struggling now, swaying on her feet and trembling with exhaustion. The arduous climb up to the roof must have taken it out of her, and the descent had only made things worse.

Still, Alex could do little for her right now. Turning his attention to the bank of computer monitors, he selected any available cameras in the basement and brought them up on screen. It didn't take long to find what he was looking for.

'There she is!' he exclaimed, pointing at one monitor in particular.

It was a black-and-white wide-angle shot, but nonetheless he was able to make out Anya's distinctive silhouette. Somehow she was still alive and on her feet, though how long she would remain that way was dubious at best. By the looks of it, she was facing off against a far larger and more physically powerful opponent.

'Hawkins,' Mitchell managed to say, her voice heavy.

'We have to help her,' he said, abandoning the monitor bank and heading for the door. 'If you want to kill this arsehole, now's your chance.'

Mitchell tried to follow, but her strength was failing. She managed one unsteady step before her legs gave way and she sank down to the floor with a painful, exhausted groan.

Alex hurried over and knelt down beside her. The dressing around her torso was soaked with blood which was now leaking down her side, smearing the floor.

She shook her head, teeth clenched against the pain. 'I can't... I can't go any further,' she managed to say. 'Get out of here... Alex. Take the files... release them across the internet if you have to. Just don't... let Hawkins get them.'

The young man hesitated, torn about what to do. 'What about Anya?'

'She was... willing to risk... her life for this. It's worth more... than all of us. Take it... and get out of here.'

Deep down he knew that her suggestion was the prudent, logical course of action. If he left now he could escape into Istanbul's maze of backstreets, make his way to safety and release the Black List to the world's media. Encrypted or not, someone would eventually find a way to open it, and then all the dirty secrets that men like Hawkins were willing to kill to protect would be exposed to the world. The Circle, the Agency... all of it would come crashing down.

At least then, all of this wouldn't have been for nothing. At least he'd survive. Perhaps one day he'd even be able to make a new life for himself.

But Anya would still be gone.

Just for an instant, his mind flashed back to that day years earlier. The day he'd walked away from a childhood fight he shouldn't have. The day he'd allowed a good friend to take a beating to save his own skin. The day he'd never stopped regretting all his adult life.

I don't even have the good grace to feel guilt or remorse. All I feel is relief.
Relief that it isn't happening to me.
Relief that I'm safe.

It took him all of three seconds to realize he could never live with that. Not this time. Not after everything he'd been through. Anya had risked her life on countless occasions to protect his, and he'd done nothing in return but get in the way and disappoint her. She needed his help now, and even if he was unprepared and untrained, he was all she had.

For once in his life, he couldn't walk away.

'No. I won't leave her behind,' he said, easing the revolver out of her grip. He'd never fired a weapon in his life, but this one looked so simple that even he couldn't fuck it up. 'I'll take care of it.'

She tightened her grip on the gun. 'Hawkins is a killer,' she warned him. 'Are you sure you want... to do this?'

'Nope, but I have to.' Alex swallowed hard, rallying what meagre reserves of courage remained to him. 'Just... stay here and get your breath back.'

'What... about you?'

Turning his attention to the dead body on the floor, Alex rolled him over and removed the walkie-talkie from his belt, then helped himself to another unit that was plugged into a charging station on the desk.

'Take this,' he said, handing one to Mitchell and attaching the other to his belt. 'If you can, watch me on the cameras. I'll need you to open the security doors from this station. Can you do that?'

The woman nodded, her eyes hardening with fierce resolve. She would see this through no matter what.

'I'll come back up and get you once Anya's safe,' he promised.

Mitchell hesitated a moment, then reached out and gripped his hand. It was an unexpected but nonetheless genuine expression of respect.

'Good luck.'

Alex simply nodded, not knowing what else to say. Never in his life had he felt so unprepared, so overwhelmed, so alone.

Taking a breath and rallying whatever reserve of strength and courage remained to him, he rose to his feet, adjusted his grip on the weapon and hurried out into the corridor beyond. Leaving Mitchell alone.

Chapter 47

Ignoring the pain of her growing list of injuries, Anya pushed herself off the wall and launched herself at Hawkins once more, trying for a kick to the stomach that would double him over. Yet again he seemed to be ready for her, and twisted aside so that his flank absorbed most of the force of the hit.

Hawkins was unlike any opponent she had ever faced before. True, he was bigger and stronger than her, but she had faced and overcome larger adversaries in unarmed combat before. It was more than that.

She couldn't read him.

Anya had been born with an ability that few others could understand. An intuition, a heightened sense of perception that allowed her to notice tiny shifts in posture, movement, even facial expressions that most others were blind to. It was this same ability that warned her when someone was deliberately trying to deceive her, and more importantly it gave her a distinct advantage in hand-to-hand fighting.

In essence, she could sense what people would do before they did it, could sense the tiny muscle twitches that signalled the beginning of a punch or a kick. But not with Hawkins. He was different, and that difference had robbed her of her advantage.

Before Anya could recover, he had seized her leg with one arm, preventing her from breaking free, while his other hand yanked a knife from a sheath across his chest and swiped it at her throat. Reacting on instinct, Anya leaned back, allowing the deadly blade to sail past her exposed throat by mere inches.

Attempting to use his strength and momentum against him, she gripped his hand before he could reverse his swing, and shoved it even harder in the direction of travel, causing the blade to lodge in the narrow space between two server racks.

She had to take the knife out of play.

Exerting all the force she could command, in one sudden, violent heave, she yanked the knife towards her. There was a moment of taut resistance as the steel blade flexed with the tension, followed by a dull snap and a sudden release as it sheared off.

Releasing his grip on the now useless weapon, Hawkins snapped out a short, vicious punch to the face, hoping to break her nose and disorient her. It took all of Anya's strength to parry the short-ranged strike and twist his arm aside, though doing it left her head unprotected.

She saw him lean back, saw his head come rushing forward to meet hers, and suddenly a lightning flash exploded across her eyes. She was no stranger to taking hits, but even the toughest fighters in the world can still be knocked out with a single well-placed blow.

Such was the case now. Vaguely, through the fog that seemed to have enveloped her brain, she was aware of being lifted off her feet and thrown backward through the air. There was a moment of curious weightlessness, and then suddenly the concrete floor rushed up to meet her. Her world was engulfed in pain once more as she landed hard, sliding several yards across the smooth surface before bumping against an equipment rack.

Anya was in trouble and she knew it. She'd underestimated Hawkins, believing she could overcome him like any other opponent. Never had she expected a fight like this.

A fight she was losing.

'You know, this almost makes it worth the trouble it took to get you here,' Hawkins said, closing in to finish her off. He was taking his time, making his fun last a little longer. 'Almost.'

–

Alex was verging on exhaustion by the time he staggering to the bottom of the stairs, his breath coming in strangled gasps that brought a fresh stab of pain with every inhalation. The fatigue of ascending and descending the full height of the building, combined with the various injuries he'd sustained over the past few days, was taking a heavy toll on his already depleted reserves of strength.

Leaping down the final step, he found himself confronted by the only door leading into the server room. Huge and indomitable, constructed of solid steel, with only a single reinforced-glass viewing port permitting a glimpse of the room beyond.

Alex crossed the last few yards and peered through the small window. The room beyond was still shrouded in gas from the Halon system, but even through the crimson-coloured haze he was able to make out Anya locked in desperate combat against Hawkins.

She was fighting, and she was losing. Alex watched in horror as Hawkins butted her full in the face, picked her up bodily and hurled her like a rag doll across the room.

Gripping the door handle, he turned and pulled it. Nothing happened. The door remained firmly closed. It was sealed and locked, the electronic access panel at the side glowing red to indicate the security locks had been engaged.

'Shit!' he hissed, watching as Hawkins closed in on Anya to finish her.

Fumbling for the radio at his belt, he yanked it free and hit the transmit button. 'Olivia, I'm in the basement. Open the server-room door.'

There was no response.

'Olivia, if you can hear me, open the door now!'

—

In the security room above, Mitchell found her mind hovering in a curious space between reality and fantasy, between wakefulness and gathering darkness. Vaguely she was aware of the blood still seeping from the wound at her side; the wound that had been made so much worse by her frantic sprint up to the roof, by her refusal to give in to the pain and the growing exhaustion.

She had resisted for a long time, but now knew she was approaching the end of her strength. She was losing too much blood, her thoughts growing confused and muddled, her eyes heavy. If only she could close them and rest, just for a few minutes...

And then, just like that, a voice reached her. Faint and crackling, and yet somehow cutting through the fog that was enveloping her brain.

'Olivia, please tell me you're still there!'

Frowning, she looked around, wondering at the source of the voice. Only when she spotted the radio unit lying on the ground by her left hand did it begin to make sense.

'Olivia, listen to me. If you don't open this door now, Anya's going to die. It's all on you; I need you *now*! Please.'

And just like that, the confused and jumbled thoughts coalesced into a single purpose. She had to get up and open the door. She had to get up.

Get up.

Gritting her teeth, she reached up for the edge of the desk, managed to get a good grip on it, and pulled. She pulled until her muscles trembled, until her vision blurred and she threatened to black out. She pulled until she felt herself rise up from the floor, until she was on her knees staring at the console laid out in front of her.

Though she had no experience of this system, she'd worked in secure facilities most of her adult life and understood how such things were controlled. By her reckoning, the security control system consisted of nothing more than a series of switches governing the electronic locks on all major doors, grouped by floor number.

And there, at the far end of the panel, was a single switch marked B1.

—

Forcing her mind back from the brink of unconsciousness, Anya found herself lying against the side of an equipment rack. Something was seeping into her left eye, blurring her vision, and with a vague sense of disorientation she remembered Hawkins's skull making contact with her own, remembered the blinding flash of the impact that had nearly knocked her out cold.

He was still with her, standing just a few yards away, watching her feeble efforts to get up with what she presumed was amusement. He was toying with her, drawing out the inevitable, but this reprieve wouldn't last long. The moment she showed signs of recovery, she knew he'd close in to finish her.

Her eyes turned away from him, looking for anything she could use to defend herself from the inevitable attack. The assault rifle he'd discarded during their earlier confrontation was still lying where he'd dropped it, though to get to it she'd have to go through him first. No good.

The computer drives fixed into the racks around her might serve as primitive shields, but they were held in place with bolts and tangled bundles of cables that she had neither the time to disconnect nor the strength to break. Keep looking.

Only then did she see it. Lying just beyond her reach in the narrow space between two metal frames, its polished steel glinting in the crimson light overhead, was her one chance to defend herself.

She had to get up. She had to reach it.

An instinct, deeply etched into her mind and reinforced by decades of hard-won experience, screamed at her to get up, to fight back before Hawkins could finish her.

With a supreme effort of will, Anya rolled over and began to drag herself to her feet, breathing hard, trying to get more air into her lungs. Chilled, dry air clawed at her throat while blood dripped from the gash over her eye, staining the concrete floor beneath as she slowly extended her arms.

But Hawkins wasn't about to let her rise up again. With deliberate care he took a step forward and kicked her in the ribs. Anya shuddered under the blow that seemed to radiate through her very bones, but managed to hold herself defiantly up.

There would be no withstanding the next blow however. His second kick struck almost exactly where she'd been hit by a stray round, and was delivered with all the force that his considerable frame could command. Even Anya couldn't hold in her cry of agony, and collapsed onto her side.

But the pain of his blows had been worth it. Even as Hawkins reached down and closed his fingers around her neck, she grasped the broken blade of the knife she'd deliberately snapped to protect herself. Straight away the wickedly sharp edge cut into her hands, but the pain was almost irrelevant now. Pain no longer mattered; she was fighting for her very life.

Somewhere behind her she heard the hiss of hydraulic pistons working, but paid it no heed as Hawkins leaned in close, his grip tightening mercilessly. Already she could feel her windpipe constricting as he crushed the life out of her.

He was staring right into her eyes. He wanted to be the last thing she saw as her vision faded and her life finally ended.

With a defiant cry, Anya swept the broken blade upwards, aiming for the face that was now so terrifyingly close to hers.

There was a spurt of red, a spray of warmth that coated her face, and suddenly Hawkins let out an almost bestial howl of pain. Releasing his grip on her, he stumbled backward clutching at his face.

Taking advantage of the momentary distraction, Anya scrambled to her feet, still brandishing the improvised weapon in bloody fingers. She was hurting and tired after their brutal confrontation, yet through some great effort of will and sheer resilience she was standing.

Hawkins meanwhile had overcome the shock of her sudden attack and rounded on her once more, his face twisted in rage and hatred. A deep gash traced a gory path from cheek to forehead, bleeding profusely and narrowly missing his right eye. Such a wound would leave a prominent scar, but it was unlikely to cause any lasting damage. It certainly wouldn't be enough to stop him now.

Nothing would stop him.

Hawkins took a step towards her, his fists clenched, the muscles of his formidable body marshalled behind a single purpose. There would be no toying with her now, no hesitation or mercy. He was out to destroy her.

Anya raised her hands and gripped the knife blade tighter, readying herself for what could well be the last fight of her life. She had spent her life fighting in one way or another, never submitting, never hesitating, never retreating. That was how she had lived, and if the time had come, that was how she would die.

Hawkins closed in on her, his lips pulled back in a snarl, one side of his face a bloody ruin. His eyes glimmered in the crimson light overhead. The feral, wild eyes of a predator. A killer.

But before Anya could react, a crack like thunder echoed around the room, and suddenly Hawkins was knocked backward a pace as if by an invisible blow. He hesitated, his expression uncertain, as if failing to understand what had happened, only for a second shot to slam into him.

A third shot finally knocked him right off his feet, and he toppled backwards, crashing to the ground with an audible thump. Two more shots followed even as he fell, though his collapse caused the rounds to sail right over his head.

Hardly believing what had just happened, Anya whirled around to face the mysterious shooter. Alex was standing in the doorway, clutching a revolver in his hands, wisps of smoke still trailing from the barrel.

'Alex?' she gasped, for once unable to contain her surprise.

Before she could say anything more, however, Alex shouted out a warning. 'Anya, run!' he cried, beckoning her towards him.

Glancing over her shoulder, Anya saw Hawkins scrambling to get up. The soft lead slugs that Alex had fired at him might have been enough to knock him off his feet, but his body armour had protected him from any real injury. Already he was reaching for the assault rifle he had dropped earlier, no doubt intending to hose down both of his targets with a single deadly burst of automatic fire.

Abandoning any thoughts of finishing him, or of questioning how Alex had made it back down here, Anya turned and sprinted for the door, summoning up whatever reserves of energy she still possessed in one final burst of speed.

'Move your fucking arse!' she heard Alex scream, backing away from the door to let her pass. Dropping the empty revolver, he raised a portable radio to his mouth. 'Seal the door, now!'

She heard the distinctive hiss as hydraulic pistons went to work, causing the door to swing inward. Covering the last few yards with the kind of speed that only comes when one's life is at stake, Anya twisted her body sideways to squeeze through the rapidly closing gap. A second later, the door slammed shut, the electronic locks automatically engaging.

No sooner had the locks clicked into place than the door resounded with heavy impacts from the other side. Both Anya and Alex watched as a deformation suddenly appeared in the centre of the steel frame, followed by another, and another. Hawkins was firing on it, trying to force it open, though his efforts were wasted. Nothing short of explosives would break through that door.

Staring through the observation port, Anya watched as he hurled the weapon aside and strode right up to the door, glaring at her in silent, brooding hatred. They remained like that for the next few seconds, their eyes locked with one another in a silent battle of wills.

'Come on,' Alex said, pulling at her arm. 'He's not going anywhere.'

Even as Anya allowed him to lead her towards the stairs, Hawkins silently mouthed a single sentence just for her.

I'll find you again.

It had been a long time since Anya had felt afraid of another human being, but she felt it at that moment, like a snake twisting around in her guts. Somehow, even though he was trapped in an underground prison with police closing in, she believed what he said.

The thought lingered with her even as she followed Alex up the stairs.

–

They were out. Despite the pain and the darkness that seemed to be closing in around her, Mitchell allowed herself a weary smile of triumph. Somehow both Alex and Anya had made it out of that room, while Hawkins, the piece of shit, was trapped. She had watched him empty an entire clip into the door, venting his fury and impotent rage the only way he knew how. But he wasn't going anywhere as long as she remained in control of the door locks.

Not that that was likely to be for long, she thought, as she surveyed the monitors before her. One of the cameras mounted at the front of the building showed the glare of flashing blue lights. Fire trucks and Turkish police cruisers had pulled up moments ago, and already uniformed officers were trying to force their way in through the front door.

It wouldn't take them long to get in here. But perhaps long enough.

Suddenly Alex's crackly voice filled the room. 'Olivia, can you hear me?'

With a trembling hand she reached for the radio beside her. 'I'm here.'

'Bloody good timing, mate! We're on our way up to get you now. I'll buy you a pint of whatever crappy beer Americans drink when this is over.'

She smiled, though it was the bittersweet smile of a promise that would never be fulfilled. 'Maybe... some other time.'

'What do you mean?'

'The police are here, out front.' She turned her gaze to the cameras at the rear. 'The loading dock still looks clear. You should make it out if you hurry.'

'Fuck that!' Alex retorted. She could see him on one of the monitors, could see the anger in his face. 'We can't just leave you here.'

'Yeah, you can. I wouldn't make it more than a block in this shape.'

'So I'll carry you.'

'Don't argue with me!' she snapped, knowing she had to make him understand. 'This is... what has to happen. Go, while you still can.'

Pausing for a moment, Alex looked up at the nearest camera, knowing she could still see him. Even in the grainy image, she could sense how conflicted he was. It gave her some measure of satisfaction to know she'd been right about him, that he was a good man in his own way.

'You're sure this is what you want?' he asked.

'It is.' Swallowing, Mitchell raised her chin. 'Go, Alex. Don't let this... be for nothing.'

She watched his shoulders sag a little as he let out a sigh, then turned away and headed for the loading bay with Anya close behind. He didn't say anything else, and she didn't expect him to.

Mitchell watched them manually crank open the bay doors and slip outside, and for the first time in a long time felt at peace with herself. Whatever mistakes and shortcomings she might have had in life, she could at least feel proud of what she'd done here.

Those were her last thoughts as the radio slipped from her grasp and she allowed the darkness she'd been holding back to finally envelop her.

–

Emerging tired and hurting into the parking lot at the rear of the building, Alex glanced around. He could hear sirens on the main road, and see the distinctive blue flash of lights. The fire alarm would have triggered an automated call to the emergency services, though it was unlikely they understood yet the full scale of what had happened here tonight. If they had, the place would have been swarming with SWAT teams and police choppers.

Reaching up, Anya pressed the transmit button on her radio. 'Kristian, please tell me you copy.'

Silence, broken only by the crackle of radio static. Alex's heart sank.

'I copy. Good to hear from you at last!' Halvorsen's scratchy, grainy voice replied. Even over the radio net, his relief was obvious. 'The police are everywhere. Had to circle around to the main drag north of you. Can you make it?'

'We'll make it,' she replied. 'Stand by.'

Releasing her grip on the radio, she turned to Alex and pointed across the parking lot to a narrow alleyway running between two larger buildings to the rear. Alex had no idea where it led, but it seemed to be going directly away from the ISS building, and that was good enough for him.

'This way. Follow me,' she gasped, leading the way.

Picking their way around rusted, overflowing dumpsters, they ran with whatever speed and strength they could still summon up. Both were very much aware that they were unarmed and totally vulnerable if they happened to encounter police units, or worse, more of Hawkins's men.

Alex couldn't say how long it took to negotiate that maze of back alleys and side streets as they fought to reach the main road, every passing moment increasing their chances of being intercepted. His heart was thundering in his chest, his legs burning, fear and adrenaline driving his weary and battered body onwards.

Stumbling out of the alley and onto the main road beyond, Alex blinked and tried to get his bearings, the harsh glow of street lights and passing traffic almost blinding in its intensity.

'Where the hell is he?' he asked, glancing around. Every pair of headlights streaming past looked the same to him. Surely every passing driver would be staring back at the battered, dishevelled-looking foreigners who had just lurched out of an alleyway.

'We're on the main road,' Anya spoke into her radio. 'Where are—?'

She was cut off by the screech of brakes as another pair of headlights shuddered to a halt just yards away. Halvorsen? Police? CIA?

Alex tensed up, his weary heart pounding with renewed urgency, ready to make a run for it. Even exhausted as he was, there was no way he was surrendering now.

'Wait,' Anya said, sensing his thoughts.

Alex frowned, wondering what she was thinking. Only when a door opened and a silhouetted figure stepped out of the van did he understand.

'What took you both so long?' Halvorsen asked. 'Hurry up and get in!'

Part V

Reflection

In 2011, elite hacker *sl1nk* released an extensive account of his penetration of the US Department of Defense, Pentagon, NASA, NSA, US Military and UK government websites. His account is widely believed to be authentic.

Chapter 48

The sun was just creeping over the horizon, its golden rays spilling across the glistening waters of the Black Sea, when Halvorsen finally brought the van to a halt in a deserted parking lot just yards from the beach. At such an early hour, theirs was the only vehicle on the road.

They had been driving for the past few hours, putting a decent distance between themselves and the scene of their crime.

Neither Alex nor Anya had said much. Indeed, they had passed most of the journey in thoughtful and companionable silence, each contemplating everything that had happened.

Somehow, through some combination of improvisation, determination and sheer good fortune, they had made it. Alex had imagined he'd be celebrating at this point, but he could no longer dig up such an emotion. After everything that had happened, after the struggles and hardships he'd endured, after the loss of Arran and Gregar and Mitchell, he simply felt exhausted.

Opening the van's rear door, he stepped out onto the tarmac parking area, grateful to be outside. Grateful to be free. Grateful just to be alive.

Ahead of him stretched a white expanse of sand that seemed to stretch all the way to the horizon. A fresh breeze blew in from the sea, carrying with it the scent of salt and life, the roar and crash of breaking waves mingling with the shriek of gulls overhead.

Never had he seen a sight so splendid in all his life.

He smiled, struck by a thought that had popped into his head almost at random. Reaching into his pocket, he fished out the packet of cigarettes he'd kept with him since their arrival in the country. Still unopened.

'You said you would celebrate once we had the Black List,' Anya prompted, having stepped out to join him. 'Now seems like the time.'

'Yeah.' He handed her the packet. 'Here, take these.'

She frowned, looking down at the crumpled packet in her bandaged hand. 'I don't smoke.'

'I know. I want you to do me a favour and get rid of them.' He grinned sidelong at her. 'These things will kill you.'

That was when he saw it. That smile. That small, almost grudging smile she gave when he'd said something she liked but wouldn't admit to liking. Just another little thing he'd come to know, had come to appreciate, about her.

Another little thing he knew he'd miss when this was over.

'Now I remember why I retired from field work,' Halvorsen said, easing himself out of the driver's seat and arching his back. 'It's a young man's game.'

'Don't kid yourself, mate,' Alex countered. He was a good thirty years younger than the Norwegian officer, yet he felt just as pained and weary. 'Count me out of the next one.'

Halvorsen snorted in grim amusement.

'What happens now?' Anya asked.

'We change vehicles here, and make our way to the airport.' He glanced at his watch. 'Our new car should be along any time now.'

'You did well, Kristian,' she said, giving the older man a grateful nod. 'I have a lot to thank you for.'

Halvorsen glanced at her, but instead of his usual wry smile, he seemed oddly troubled by her words.

However, before he could say anything, Anya's posture tightened, her battered and weary muscles tensing as she stared off down the road.

'A car is coming,' she warned, her eyes suddenly wary.

Alex followed her gaze, and sure enough spotted a silver BMW heading in their direction. Not hurrying, but travelling at a fair speed nonetheless.

'Our changeover,' Halvorsen explained. 'Be calm.'

And sure enough, the vehicle began to slow as it approached, then turned into the parking lot and came to a halt no more than fifteen yards away. The windows were tinted, making it difficult to see the occupant, but judging by the way it was sitting on its suspension, Anya guessed there was only a driver on board. Halvorsen watched the big BMW in silence as the driver shut down the engine, opened the door and stepped out.

The moment Alex caught sight of the tall, deceptively strong frame, the unruly blonde hair and the lean, chiselled features, his heart leapt and his stomach constricted in a tight knot of fear. His mouth seemed to open of its own accord as shock and disbelief overwhelmed him.

'What's the matter, mate?' Arran Sinclair asked, flashing the same cocky grin that Alex had once known so well. 'You look like you've seen a ghost.'

Alex felt like he was about to throw up.

It was a lie, he realized now. All of it. The crash, the disappearance, the desperate letter addressed to him. All faked. Arran; his friend, the man he trusted, had played him.

'The car crash,' Alex managed to say. 'They said you'd been killed.'

Sinclair's look was almost apologetic. 'I had to do something to get *her* off my back,' he said, nodding to Anya. 'I knew she'd be following my every move once we'd made our deal. The only way to get rid of her was to die. Shame I had to write off a perfectly good car to do it.'

–

The narrow, unpredictable road would slow the vehicle following him, the steep river gorge to his right acting as a deterrent to all but the boldest of drivers. Sinclair almost smiled as he pressed harder on the accelerator, knowing there was a long straight coming up. He'd grown up around this area, had learned to drive here and knew every bend and corner of this road like the back of his hand.

He held the advantage over the car following him.

No sooner had this thought crossed his mind than he saw something on the bend up ahead, something that made his heart leap and adrenaline surge through his veins.

A single piece of coloured ribbon tied around one of the trees by the side of the road. He had marked it there several days earlier, and used it now as his point of reference. This was where he had to do it. This was where the slope on the other side of the crash barrier was steep enough and sufficiently free from trees to allow the car to tumble all the way down into the river below.

This was where he was about to die.

Straight away he slammed on his brakes and turned the wheel hard over. Tyres skidded on slick tarmac and the low metal crash barrier at the edge of the road swung into view as the car fishtailed.

Sinclair tensed up, bracing himself for what was coming, then opened his door and threw himself out.

The impact was harder than he'd expected, the rough tarmac rushing up to greet him with enough force to bruise flesh and tear clothes and skin. The car had lost much of its momentum by this point, just as he'd calculated, but the pain of his fall prompted an agonized groan as he rolled over and finally came to a stop. Mercifully, he didn't seem to have broken any bones.

Gritting his teeth against the pain, he looked up just in time to see the car barrel into the barrier, crash through it and plummet over the edge.

Pulling himself up, Sinclair limped over to the edge of the road and looked down, watching as the car flipped over onto its roof, rolling and crashing down the steep brush-covered slope to the fast-flowing river far below.

By the time it impacted the surface, the chassis had been reduced to a mass of twisted and buckled metal. With nothing buoyant enough to support it, the wreck quickly filled with icy cold water and disappeared beneath the surface within a matter of seconds, leaving only the wreckage-strewn slope behind as testimony to the violence of its final moments.

'Perfect,' he whispered.

—

'Why?' Alex implored his friend. 'Why go through all this? What was the point?'

'Why?' Sinclair repeated, an edge of irritation in his voice now. 'I wouldn't have had to do any of it if you'd just taken my offer back in London.'

Anya was glaring at the tall young man with barely restrained hatred. 'Why Alex?' she demanded.

'Because he needed me. He couldn't do it by himself.' Alex closed his eyes as the impact of his friend's revelation sank in. 'You needed my help, but I wouldn't give it to you. So you did all of this to force my hand.'

Sinclair, the charismatic and visionary leader, had always been the driving force behind their group, but none of that could change the fact that Alex had always been the man who made it happen. His skills had been unmatched by any of the others, and without him, Sinclair had been unable to complete the ambitious task that Anya had handed him.

'I meant what I said then, Alex. I would have made you rich if you'd helped me. It would have been just like the old days, but you were too much of a fucking coward to go for it.' He sighed and shook his head. 'That was always your problem – you never had any vision. No imagination, no backbone. You just follow instructions, go along with anyone who looks like they know what they're doing. Well, that being the case, I gave you some instructions to follow. And in the end, you did exactly what I wanted.'

'I trusted you, Arran,' Alex said, clenching his fists. 'We were friends. Now I'm a wanted fugitive. How could you do this to me?'

Sinclair looked at him with something akin to pity. 'Wouldn't be the first time.'

And then, in a flash, Alex's earlier confrontation with Landvik came rushing back to him.

He swallowed, searching for the right words. 'I didn't do it, Alex. I know you don't believe that, but it's the truth. For a while, I wished I had thought of it. I was so pissed at you and Arran for shutting me out, and I wanted to get back at you. But I'd never take it that far. We're friends, Alex. Or… we were friends once. No matter how angry I was with you, I wouldn't turn you in to the police.'

'It was you, wasn't it?' he gasped, staring at Sinclair in disbelief. 'You gave me up to the police three years ago. You told them where to find me.'

His former friend said nothing. There was no need to confirm what Alex plainly knew already.

His mind was in turmoil. Two years in jail. His life destroyed, his relationship in tatters, his future stolen from him. All because of Sinclair.

'For Christ's sake, why?' Alex asked, almost pleading with him.

'You just don't get it, do you?' Sinclair taunted. 'You were all about doing the right thing and going legitimate, as if we could all spend our lives wearing ties and working in some shitty office like the rest of the fucking losers in the world. I knew you didn't have the balls to go after the big prize. It was a way of getting rid of you and Gregar at the same time. Once I blamed it all on him, he was out of the picture. And I could use the rest of our group for what they were meant to do. And little Alex did exactly what *he* was meant to do – stay quiet and do his time.'

That was it for Alex. Something snapped inside him at that moment, as all the pent-up emotions of the past week suddenly coalesced into a storm of pure rage. Balling his fists, Alex rushed at the man who had twice destroyed his life, fully intending to beat the skinny, arrogant bastard into the ground for what he'd done.

But suddenly he caught a movement to his right, and just like that everything changed. His pace slowed, his rage daunted by the barrel of an automatic now trained on him.

'Don't,' Halvorsen warned, staring down the sights of the weapon at him. However rusty he might have been as a field operative, there were few ways for him to miss at this range.

Alex faltered and came to a halt, while Sinclair offered an apologetic shrug. 'Like you said to me once, any system can be beaten. All you need is skill, planning and patience.'

–

Stirlingshire, Scotland – seven days earlier

Glancing up from the wrecked vehicle at the bottom of the gorge, Sinclair watched as a pair of headlights approached. The car that had been tailing him since he'd left his home about half an hour earlier. The car whose arrival he'd anticipated almost to the second.

Easing to a stop beside him, the driver opened his electric window and leaned out to survey him.

'It worked as planned?' Kristian Halvorsen asked.

Sinclair nodded. 'This river leads all the way out to sea. The police will assume my body was swept away by the current.'

The Norwegian nodded, satisfied with that. 'That should get Anya off your back, for now at least. Now get in before someone passes by.'

Sinclair wasn't about to argue. Wincing a little as his bruised body protested, he slipped into the passenger seat.

'What if she doesn't believe it?' he couldn't help asking.

'You worry about your friend Alex,' Halvorsen said as he accelerated away from the scene. 'I'll take care of Anya.'

–

'Now, Alex. Give me the Black List,' Halvorsen said, his voice icy calm. 'Don't do anything stupid.'

Alex stood his ground, staring at the older man. Only now did he realize the full magnitude of his failure. 'You were working with Arran the whole time.'

'Think bigger, mate,' Sinclair said. 'Kristian recruited me the day we broke into his company's website. It was a test, and one that we passed.' A

277

faint, knowing smile. 'Of course, there were a few conditions. We had to cut out some dead wood before he'd take us on full time.'

Alex felt like he'd been punched in the stomach. Sinclair had given him up to the police all those years ago on Halvorsen's orders, knowing Alex would never condone the idea of becoming his own personal cyber-terrorist.

'Why, Kristian?' Anya demanded, the anger and pain in her eyes plain to see. Sinclair's betrayal was one thing, but she had known and trusted Halvorsen for the best part of two decades. 'We had a deal. I was going to share it all with you.'

'Isn't it obvious? I'm not taking it, Anya. I'm returning it.'

Only then did his true intentions, or rather his true allegiance, at last become apparent.

'You work for the Circle,' Anya said, crushed by this final, shattering betrayal.

'Like you said, they are powerful and dangerous men. Far more so than even you can imagine. How do you think they held on to that power for so long? They anticipated all of this, and they were ready for it. You should think yourself lucky they chose me for this operation, otherwise you would both be dead.' His eyes focussed on Alex once more. 'Now, give it to me.'

Alex did nothing. The memory stick in his pocket was his only means of salvation. Surrendering it now would mean a life on the run, a life with no future.

Lowering the weapon, Halvorsen squeezed off a single round. The crack of the gunshot, and the sudden explosion of sand and broken stones at Alex's feet, made him jump with fright.

'The next one's in your stomach. Believe me, it's a bad way to go,' Halvorsen promised, raising the weapon so that it was pointed at his abdomen. 'Give me the Black List, and we all walk away from this. You're a smart man, so do the smart thing, Alex.'

Alex sighed and closed his eyes, knowing that further attempts to stall would be futile. Reaching into his pocket, he lifted out the little plastic memory stick, held it in his hand a moment as if to savour the victory that was almost his, then tossed it to the older man.

Halvorsen caught it out of the air, then deftly slipped it into his jacket pocket.

'If you think you can trust the men who created that list, you're making the biggest mistake of your life,' Anya warned him. 'I know you are doing this because you're afraid of them, but you don't have to be. I can protect you. I'm giving you a chance to help me stop them forever, Kristian. Give us back the list, and I promise we can do this together. Don't let it end this way. Don't let them use you like they use everyone else. Please.'

There was a moment of hesitation, of doubt that showed in his eyes as the force of her words sank in. Even he wasn't immune to the sheer emotion and desperation in her voice.

But just as quickly as it appeared, it was gone. Halvorsen smiled and shook his head, his mind made up. 'You were a good operative, Anya. The best, but you're short-sighted. That was always your downfall.' He gestured to the road stretching off into the distance. 'You'll have a long time to think about that.'

Alex watched as he removed the keys from the van's ignition, then used a small penknife to slash both front tyres, rendering the vehicle unusable. 'You're going to leave us out here?'

He shrugged. 'My orders were to recover the list. The Circle want no part of your vendetta against Marcus Cain, so consider this a warning. I suggest you listen to it. And for what it's worth, I hope your luck holds — both of you. But if you ever come looking for me, the Circle will make sure it doesn't.'

With those parting words, he settled himself into the driver's seat of the BMW. Sinclair followed a moment later, pausing briefly to look at Alex one more time. He said nothing, though the look in his eyes conveyed far more than mere words.

For his own part, Alex regarded his former friend with absolute disgust. 'If I were you, I'd hope we don't meet again.'

'We won't.' Giving Alex a mocking salute, Sinclair slipped into the passenger seat and slammed the door shut.

With that, the sleek saloon took off and roared back onto the main road, leaving only dust and tyre marks in its wake.

Alex and Anya were, once more, alone.

Chapter 49

The journey had passed more or less in silence. Neither Sinclair nor Halvorsen had much to say to one another. In truth, Kristian Halvorsen was racked with guilt over what he'd done to Anya. He had known the woman for more than twenty years, could still remember the day he'd sat down to debrief the tired, bedraggled teenager who had walked right into the central police station in Oslo to claim political asylum.

Never could he have imagined then that it would lead them to this.

But it was worth it, he told himself as he patted the memory stick in his pocket. Whether she hated him or not, he had saved her life by retrieving the Black List today. The Circle, who had remained largely neutral in this conflict so far, would not tolerate such a threat to their anonymity.

It was worth it, he told himself again. To protect Anya, it was worth it.

'I need a piss,' Sinclair said, breaking the silence. He was sitting with his seat tipped back, feet resting on the dashboard, his blonde hair streaming in the breeze from the open window.

'The plane is only a few miles away. Hold it in,' Halvorsen advised him. The same private jet that had delivered himself, Alex and Anya to this country was now waiting to take him back to Norway, parked at a small airfield near the Black Sea.

'I've been doing that for the past half hour,' the young man protested. 'Come on. Somehow I doubt they'll catch up to us now.'

Rolling his eyes with impatience, Halvorsen turned off the road and drove a short distance down a bumpy dirt track until they were out of sight.

Sinclair sighed, staring thoughtfully out at the dusty, scrub-covered hill-side in front of them. 'Tell me something, Kristian. Is there anyone you won't fuck over to get ahead?'

Halvorsen glared at him. 'Watch your tongue, boy. You've been useful so far, but don't push it.' He shifted position in his seat, the automatic in his jacket digging uncomfortably into his hip. 'Now get on with it. Make it quick.'

'It will be,' Sinclair promised him.

Then, in a sudden darting movement, his hand leapt out. Before Halvorsen could stop it, the automatic had been yanked clean out of his pocket. He whirled around, making to grab for it, only to find the barrel staring him in the face. A pair of wild, remorseless eyes stared back at him.

His last thought before Sinclair pulled the trigger was that at least he no longer had to worry about Anya's vengeance when she finally caught up with him. Perhaps he even deserved what was coming.

Exiting the car with his ears still ringing from the crack of the gunshot, Sinclair wiped a splash of blood off his face, then used a handkerchief to wipe down the gun. Circling around to the driver's side, he opened the door, gripped Halvorsen under the arms and heaved him out; no easy task considering the man's size and weight.

Nonetheless, with some effort Sinclair managed to drag him a short distance, then placed the gun in his meaty hand.

Reaching into his pocket, he fished out the memory stick and held it up. The Black List, the file that Anya, the Circle, even Halvorsen were willing to kill for, and it was all his. A world of power in the palm of his hand.

He smiled, pocketed the memory stick and returned to the car, already reaching for his cell phone and dialling a number from memory.

'It's me,' he said simply, eager to keep the call as short as possible as he started the engine up once more. 'I have what you need. Meet me at the agreed place.'

–

'It was all for nothing,' Anya said, staring absently off into the distance as traffic rumbled past on the main road nearby, engine fumes mixing with the smell of manure, human bodies and cooking food. The glass of ice water on the table in front of her sat untouched, despite the intensity of the midday sun beating down on them.

After leaving the crippled van behind, the two of them had started the long walk along the deserted coastal road, largely staying out of sight lest a police car pass by and notice them. At last, tired and wilting in the hot sun, they had decided to chance their luck and flagged down a passing station wagon that looked like it was older than Alex.

Miraculously the elderly couple onboard had bought their story of being lost tourists, with Anya explaining away the cuts and bruises on her face by claiming she'd been mugged a couple of days earlier. The woman had cast a suspicious glance at Alex, no doubt harbouring her own thoughts on that matter, but nonetheless had allowed them to collapse gratefully into the back seat.

Despite some misgivings on the part of their hosts, their rusty and dilapidated ride had brought them as far as the small town of Corlu, where they had stopped at an outdoor cafe for a much-needed drink, and to plan their next move.

Anya however seemed to have run out of plans. Indeed, Alex had never seen her so despondent. She looked beaten, plain and simple. Everything she'd risked so much for had come to nothing.

He on the other hand was harbouring quite different emotions.

'Cheer up, mate. It could be worse,' he said, taking a gulp of his beer. The ice-cold liquid tasted better than he'd imagined, and before he knew it he'd drained the entire glass. Closing his eyes, he let out a sigh of absolute satisfaction. 'Bloody hell, that was worth waiting for.'

Anya regarded him with a mixture of curiosity and irritation as he motioned to the waiter to bring over another. 'I don't see why you're so happy.'

He couldn't help but grin. 'Oh my God, I think this is the moment,' he exclaimed. 'Right here, right now. Knowing something the other person doesn't. This is what it must feel like to be you.'

Her blonde brows drew together in a frown. 'What are you talking about?'

Reaching into his back pocket, Alex laid something down on the table. Something that prompted a wonderfully satisfying look of disbelief from his normally stoic companion.

'Is this what I think it is?'

Alex nodded, then thanked the waiter as he laid another bottle of Efes Pilsen down in front of him.

Anya was oblivious as she gently picked up the memory stick with the reverence of a sacred relic. 'How can this be?'

Alex shrugged, taking a sip of his beer. 'I just did what Kristian said – the smart thing. No way was I giving that fat prick the Black List after everything we went through. I'm just glad he didn't have a computer with him.'

That was when he saw it. The smile. The smile so rarely seen, but so welcome when it finally came.

Leaning back in her chair with a weary sigh, Anya shook her head in amusement, though there was something else in her eyes as she regarded him across the table. Something he hadn't seen before – respect.

'I will say one thing for you, Alex Yates. You never cease to surprise me.'

He grinned and held out his bottle in a toast. 'I'll drink to that,' he said as they clinked glasses.

Clearly however one thing still troubled his companion. 'But if you didn't give Kristian the Black List, then what was on that memory stick he took from you?'

At this, Alex merely smiled and took another sip of his beer.

–

Samsun, Turkey

It was a beautiful evening in the port city of Samsun, a warm breeze sighing in from the Black Sea across the wide harbour crowded with yachts, speedboats and countless other pleasure craft.

Glancing out the window, Arran Sinclair watched a motor launch filled with young men and women heading out to a much larger vessel moored out in the bay, no doubt to party the night away before heading off to their next destination. All were tanned, all good-looking, all rich.

He caught himself wondering if he might find himself in such company before too long. With this heartening thought in mind, he turned off the main road and into a small private airfield overlooking the coast.

As he'd expected, there was only one plane sitting parked beside a small hangar at the far end of the runway. A private jet, sleek and expensive.

Its owner was waiting for him as he pulled Halvorsen's car into the hangar, flanked by a pair of stocky bodyguards. All were dressed in civilian clothes, though Sinclair knew well enough that they were anything but civilians. They were Pakistani intelligence operatives, but more than that, they were rich Pakistani intelligence operatives, who were willing to part with 3 million US dollars to get their hands on the Black List.

Not bad for a few days' work.

Bringing the car to a stop, Sinclair killed the engine and stepped out. The inside of the hangar was just as warm as the balmy evening air outside, but the steel shell overhead provided at least some respite from the sun's glare.

'You are late,' his contact remarked, checking his watch.

Sinclair shrugged, affecting an air of nonchalant confidence that stood in stark contrast to what he was feeling at that moment. 'But I'm worth waiting for.'

'We shall see.' Vizur Qalat was a tall, neat-looking man in his mid forties, with dark hair swept back from a high forehead, and clean-cut features that somehow made him seem younger than his years. His English was impeccable, perhaps the result of a higher education in the UK, making it almost possible to forget the sinister agency he represented.

But there was an edge to him. Something hidden beneath those suave good looks that put Sinclair on edge, warning him this was not a man one ever wanted as an enemy.

'I assume you have brought it with you, Arran?' he prompted.

Reaching into his pocket, Sinclair held up the memory stick for inspection.

At a nod from Qalat, one of the bodyguards strode forward and plucked the device from his hand, while the other unpacked a laptop from a carry case and set it up on a small work table nearby.

'You'll forgive me if I verify the contents,' Qalat said, clearly unconcerned whether Sinclair approved or not.

'No problem,' Sinclair assured him. 'When will my money be transferred?'

Qalat didn't look at him as he waited for the laptop to start up. 'As soon as we have confirmation, you'll get your reward,'

283

In the tense moments that followed, Sinclair found his thoughts drifting back to Alex, and particularly his female companion. It was a shame that Halvorsen had insisted on leaving her alive, perhaps clinging to some mistaken belief that she would one day understand and forgive his betrayal. Although he knew little of her, Sinclair was troubled by that woman. He had faith in his own ability to disappear and leave no trail, but he'd sleep better at night knowing she was out of the way.

On the other hand, he felt a twinge of genuine sympathy for Alex. His former friend had been a great asset, and was undeniably skilled at what he did. But for all his great abilities and intellect, he'd remained a naive and trusting fool right to the end. Perhaps now he'd wise up.

He let out a breath as Qalat waited a few seconds for the contents of the memory stick to load up. Straight away the computer's automatic virus-checkers went to work, sweeping the memory stick for any sign of malicious code, then promptly advising that it was clean.

Smiling, Sinclair watched as his benefactor clicked on the file to open it. However, his smile soon vanished as the laptop froze for a moment, a dialogue box appearing on screen to inform him the file couldn't be opened.

Sinclair felt his heart beat faster, his palms growing moist with perspiration. Qalat tried to open it again, only to meet with the same result.

Turning on Sinclair, the Pakistani intelligence officer regarded him with an almost disappointed look. 'Would you care to explain this, Arran?'

'Let me see it,' Sinclair said, hurrying forward and attempting to open the file himself. It didn't take long to confirm that his efforts were wasted.

Only then did the realisation finally hit him. Only then did he realize that it was Alex who had scored the final point in their battle of wits. He had been duped in the most pathetically simple way possible.

'Alex, you bastard.'

The conditional access module, the very same piece of software he'd mailed to his friend when this all started, was now running on this computer. The same tool used to entrap and manipulate Alex had now been used against him.

He reached out and closed down the laptop with trembling hands, knowing it was a futile gesture since the damage had certainly been done, then backed away and turned to look out of the hangar.

'I'm annoyed with you, Arran,' Qalat remarked, though Arran barely heard him. Just as he barely heard the click of a safety catch being disengaged. 'I had such high hopes for you.'

Once more Sinclair stared out across the sunlit bay, watching the distant pleasure craft and the holidaymakers and the rays of the evening sun glinting off the water. The world was as it had been before, but not for him.

Not now. Not ever.

He closed his eyes for the last time as the dull thud of a silenced gunshot shattered the peaceful silence of the hangar.

Chapter 50

'Are you sure you're ready for this?' Alex asked, holding the memory stick containing the Black List at the ready. The laptop computer they had purchased less than an hour earlier from a budget electrical retailer was humming away, awaiting a command.

Anya raised her chin a little, squaring her shoulders as if she were facing up to a firing squad. The answers she'd sought for so long, as difficult and potentially devastating as they might have been, were now at her fingertips. She had but to reach out and take them.

'I'm ready,' she replied after a moment.

Alex took a breath. He had disabled the laptop's wireless communications system, ensuring there would be no repeat of what had happened to him in London if the Black List had somehow been booby trapped, but nonetheless he was nervous.

After everything they'd been through, he almost refused to believe they finally had what they needed.

'Here goes nothing.'

Inserting the stick, he waited a few seconds while its contents were scanned and read. Then, sure enough, a window popped up on screen with a single file.

D1189

Hovering his cursor over the file, Alex sent out a silent prayer, then clicked to open it. Anya leaned in close, her eyes staring intently at the screen. He could almost feel the tension and anticipation radiating out from every taut muscle in her body.

Then, at last, the file was opened, allowing them both to view its contents.

'Oh my God,' he groaned.

There were no secret dossiers contained within it. No incriminating pictures. No mission reports or debriefings. No signed presidential orders.

All that was displayed on screen was a single line of numbers.

Straight away Alex's heart sank. He closed his eyes and sank back in his chair, his short-lived triumph destroyed. He felt utterly and crushingly defeated.

'I don't understand,' he whispered, holding his head in his hands. 'A fucking number. All this for a number. I don't understand it.'

'I do,' Anya said, her voice heavy. 'It's an invitation.'

Alex looked up at her. 'For what?'

'For me.'

Reaching into her pocket, she fished out a cell phone. A cheap burner not unlike the one she'd given him in London.

Pausing a moment to read the number on screen, she punched it in, took a breath, then waited for the call to connect.

It rang for nearly ten seconds before it was answered.

'Hello, Anya,' a voice said, showing not a hint of surprise or alarm at her call. An American voice. A man's voice.

Marcus Cain's voice.

Anya closed her eyes for a moment and let out a breath. It had been a very long time since she'd heard that voice, and despite everything, despite all that she'd been through in the intervening years, the sound of it was enough to evoke something in her. A shadow of the young woman she'd once been. The memory of the way she'd once felt when she'd known the owner of that voice.

'Relax, I'm not tracing this call,' Cain went on. 'It's just you and me now, like it should be.'

'You set me up,' Anya said, her tone accusatory. 'You let me go through all of this for nothing.'

'You didn't really think I'd leave the Black List unguarded, did you?' he chided her. 'I had the real list deleted a long time ago. But... I had a feeling you'd come looking for it one day. I guess it still served a purpose.'

Anya turned away from Alex, not wanting him to see the look in her eyes. 'Why, Marcus?' she whispered. 'What do you want?'

'I want to make you an offer. It'll only come once, and if you refuse then there's no coming back from it, so I suggest you think very carefully before you answer.' He paused a moment; a breathless, agonizing moment. 'I want you to give this up, Anya. Whatever revenge trip you're on, whatever you think you're going to achieve... give it up and walk away. Say you'll do this, and I'll believe you. I'll stop looking for you, I'll call off any searches the Agency or anyone else is making, I'll end this whole thing today. It'll be over for good. I promise.'

Anya said nothing. Somehow she managed to keep her composure, but the look of turmoil in her eyes was impossible to hide.

'I can't change the things that have happened,' Cain went on. 'God knows I wish I could go back and do it all differently, but I can't. Neither of us can. But the two of us, right now, can change how this plays out. You've spent most of your life fighting, running, hiding... I can't imagine the loneliness you must feel, or how tired you must be. But you don't have to do it any more. It's over. It's time to let it go.'

Anya let out a ragged, shuddering breath. Cain, the master strategist, the man who so keenly saw the true nature of others, perceived all too well who she really was.

'You can still have a life, Anya. You can live out the rest of your days in peace, because you deserve it. It's yours. All you have to say is yes.'

The woman closed her eyes for a moment, her once iron resolve wavering in the face of his impassioned plea. He was telling the truth. She couldn't rationally explain it, but deep down in the very core of her being she knew that his offer was genuine.

She could leave this all behind. This life of fighting, of pain and heartache and loss and sacrifice. She could let go of it all. All it took was a single word.

And then, unbidden, the old words that had been drilled into her a lifetime ago surfaced from the depths of her mind.

I will endure when all others fail. I will stand when all others retreat. Weakness will not be in my heart. Fear will not be in my creed. I will show no mercy. I will never surrender.

'Do you remember the day I came back from Afghanistan, twenty years ago?' she asked suddenly.

'Anya, what are—?'

'Do you remember, Marcus?' she cut in, a harder edge in her voice.

She heard him sigh. 'I do.'

'I was hurting when I woke up in that hospital in Peshawar. And I was weak. So weak I could barely lift my arm. But I saw you sitting at my bedside, and I felt… I felt like I had come home. For the first time in a long time. I thought you would be happy to see me, but… that wasn't what I saw in you. You were looking at me, but not seeing me. It was as if you couldn't bear to look at me.'

She could feel a tiny warmth on her cheek. The warmth of a tear trickling down her skin. 'At the time, I thought you were… ashamed of me, like I was tainted and ruined. I thought that when you looked at me, you could see only the things they had done to me, and it disgusted you. I… disgusted you.' She swallowed hard, maintaining her self-control only through a supreme effort of will. 'But I was wrong. It wasn't me you were ashamed of; it was yourself. Because you knew where they were holding me – all along, you knew. You could have found me, but you didn't, because I wasn't meant to come home. And when I did, my life, my survival, became an endless reminder of your own weakness, your own failings.'

'Anya, you don't understand—'

'No,' she said, her wavering resolve suddenly blazing to life once more. 'I do understand. You're not interested in saving me, Marcus. Just as you weren't twenty years ago. You're interested only in saving yourself. Well, this is one fight you can't run away from.'

She heard a sigh on the other end of the line. The weary, resigned sigh of a man finally acknowledging a painful truth.

'You know what this means,' he warned her. 'You know there's no going back.'

Anya reached up and wiped away the tear that had so briefly stained her cheek, pushing aside the weakness and the doubt. She was herself again. Strong, capable, determined, and set on her course no matter what.

'I hope you're ready, because I'm coming for you,' she promised. Tossing the phone on the ground, she brought her booted heel down on the device, crushing it.

Chapter 51

'You are sure you want to do this?' Anya asked, nodding towards the winding mountain road stretching out before them. Somewhere up ahead, perhaps ten miles or so, lay the border with Austria.

She had driven him up here in a battered old 4x4 that she'd bought at a local dealer for less than the price of a new TV back in the UK. The vehicle might not have looked pretty, but its rust-streaked chassis was still solid and the engine rumbled with a throaty growl that defiantly belied its age.

Alex followed her gaze, his eyes hidden behind a pair of dark sunglasses.

'Nope,' he admitted. 'But isn't that what makes it fun? Not really knowing.'

Anya said nothing to that. No doubt she entertained her own thoughts on such matters and felt no need to share them, but he was used to that now. Indeed, he'd grown used to a lot of things about her since the tumultuous events in Istanbul a week earlier. They had travelled together, lived together, even fought to survive together. He wouldn't exactly call their relationship a friendly one, but somehow it seemed to work.

Their journey had taken them from Turkey across the border into Bulgaria, through Romania and into Hungary. There, Anya had been able to provide him with a new passport and identity, courtesy of a forger she had known and worked with many times before. As far the European Union was concerned, he had everything he needed to travel from Lisbon to Helsinki.

And now that he had his new identity, the time had come for them to part ways.

'Where will you go now?'

He shrugged. 'I was thinking of taking a career break. Never really got around to travelling, but... maybe now's my chance.'

He certainly wouldn't be going near a computer for a while. With warrants still out for his arrest in the UK and US, he intended to lay low and live 'off the grid', as they were so fond of saying in cheap action movies.

'Will you be all right?' Anya asked, looking and sounding a little less sure of herself. It was the same thing that always happened when she had to deal with any of the interpersonal stuff that so rarely entered into her normal life.

'Well, let's see. I've got no job, no home, no friends, no money and no prospect of changing that any time soon.' He grinned at her. 'I don't think I've ever felt better.'

It might have been a facetious remark, but there was nonetheless a grain of truth in his words. He felt more alive, more optimistic, more determined now than he ever had in his so-called life before this all began. He didn't know what the future held for him, but it was a hell of a lot better than what it had offered before.

And for once, he felt ready for it.

Anya shook her head in bewilderment. 'And I thought only Americans were lunatics,' she remarked. 'Still, maybe I can help you with one of those things.'

Reaching into the glove compartment, she handed him a plain brown envelope, thickly packed. Opening it, Alex found himself confronted by a large wad of euros; far more than he could easily count.

'What's this?' he asked.

'Payment for services rendered.'

'You don't have to do this,' he said, feeling like he'd taken far more from her than he'd given in return.

'That was the agreement I had with Arran,' she informed him. 'One hundred thousand pounds on completion of the deal. I would say you've earned it.'

Alex sighed, her generosity only serving to highlight their failure. Halvorsen's betrayal had weighed heavily on both of them since that day in Istanbul. His only consolation was the knowledge that the man apparently hadn't lived long enough to celebrate his achievement. An online news report from Turkey had confirmed that Halvorsen had been found dead in a patch of waste ground just off the man highway, apparently having committed suicide.

As for Sinclair, there was no sign. For now at least, the man had vanished.

'Thanks,' he said, not sure how else to phrase it. In truth, he wasn't too proud to take the money. It would at least buy him a place to stay for a while, and perhaps the time he needed to get himself together. 'What about you?'

She looked away, staring off into the distance but seeing nothing. 'I started this looking for answers. I will find them, even if I have to do it alone.'

'Not alone,' he corrected her, though unaccountably he felt himself blush as he said it. 'Well, what I mean is, if you ever need a hacker with bad aim and worse taste in films, let me know, yeah?'

He guessed she wouldn't have much trouble finding him if it came to it.

He didn't imagine such an offer would mean much to someone like Anya. And yet, to his surprise, her face lit up with a smile. The kind of smile that seemed to wipe away the years of care and pent-up anger she carried with her, and that once more offered a glimpse of the woman he'd watched peacefully sleeping that morning in Norway.

He watched as she reached out and took his hand, her grip strong and her gaze searching. 'Remember what I said to you on the balcony in Istanbul?'

You are stronger than you look, Alex. Maybe even stronger than you realize.

'Yeah, I remember,' he said quietly. Those words would stay with him for the rest of his days. However long that turned out to be.

'I meant it.' Releasing his hand, she settled herself in the driver's seat once more. 'Good luck to you, Alex.'

And that was all she had to say; all she needed to say. As with everything else in her life, there was no desire for emotional farewells. Alex watched as she swung the car around and drove off back down the road at a steady, unhurried pace, leaving only a faint cloud of dust in her wake that was soon carried away by the fitful breeze.

As the throaty rumble of the engine receded into the distance, he caught himself wondering if their paths would ever cross again. Anya's arrival in his life had changed him beyond all recognition, had destroyed nearly everything he'd once had. And yet, part of him hoped he would see her again.

Adjusting the straps on his rucksack, he turned and surveyed the road ahead. It was a long walk to his next resting place, but that was just fine with him. Plenty of time alone with his thoughts.

As he started forward, his boots crunching on the little rocks underfoot, the sun beating down on him, an unknown future lying ahead, Alex couldn't help but smile.

–

Anyone who saw me walking along that dirt track must have thought I was a lunatic; a man walking alone in the middle of nowhere grinning like a fool. Anyone who knew me before this all started would have questioned what on earth I had to smile about.

But none of that mattered any more. For the first time in my life, I was making my own way, following my own path.

I'm not a normal guy. I don't have a job, or a car. I don't pay taxes, I don't even know where my next meal is coming from. And that's fine with me.

This is happening.

This is me. This is who I am now.

Strange the things that flash through your mind when you realize you have a reason to live.

Epilogue

She was alive.

She was alive, and she was moving.

Even through the haze of painkillers and sedatives, Mitchell was vaguely aware of movement. She could feel the bounce and rattle as her hospital gurney was wheeled down a busy corridor, slowing down occasionally as it was steered past staff and patients.

She was surrounded by sounds. Ringing phones, beeping life-support machines, whirring printers and most of all the clamour of voices. Voices everywhere; so many of them merging and blending together that they became little more than a background hum, no more distinct than the drone of a thousand bumblebees.

And yet even amongst this background din she was able to discern a conversation close at hand. A conversation in English.

'I have told you, the patient is still in a dangerous condition. She can't be moved yet.' A doctor's voice, tense and agitated, filled with concern.

'I understand, sir.' This voice was cold, precise and clinical. To her surprise, it was a woman's voice. 'But she isn't secure here, and we have our own team of doctors on standby. She's to be extradited to the United States. As of now, you're relieved of professional responsibility for this patient.'

With some effort she forced her heavy eyes open, seeing nothing but the hospital's cheap, intense overhead lights sliding by. She blinked, tried to reach up and rub her eyes, only for her hand to be jerked back.

Something cold and metal was shackled around both wrists. Handcuffs.

With a fleeting sense of disappointment, she at last realized what was happening, who her mysterious new carers were. The Agency had come for her.

She'd known it would happen of course. The moment she awoke for the first time several days earlier in a clean and sterile hospital room, she had felt that same disappointment. Disappointment that the doctors had fought so hard to save a life that was doomed anyway, disappointment that she couldn't have slipped away peacefully on her own terms. Disappointment that they would be the ones to end her life.

The trip didn't last long. An ambulance was waiting for her in the parking lot outside. Mitchell made no effort to protest or cry out for help as she was loaded onboard. It would do no good anyway.

The doors slammed shut, and the woman who had helped load her into the ambulance took a seat. A young woman, Mitchell noted with vague surprise. Couldn't have been more than thirty years old. Short and slender, with spiky dark hair, pale skin and a nose piercing.

Christ, I'm going to be interrogated and executed by a fucking kid, she thought.

'If you're going to kill me, you might as well get it over with,' she said, straining to sit up straighter in her gurney. 'I don't regret anything I did.'

To her surprise, the young woman with the piercing smiled at her. There was no animosity, no hint of malice in her smile. 'Relax, Mitchell. We're not here to kill you.'

She frowned, a little less sure of herself now. The effort of holding herself upright was starting to tell. 'So what do you want?'

As she watched, the ambulance's driver twisted around in his seat, his vivid green eyes flashing in the afternoon sunlight. 'It's lucky for you we have a mutual friend,' he explained. Bizarrely, he spoke with an English accent. 'We're here to get you out. We'll take you to a safe place until you're recovered enough to travel. That all right with you?'

Mitchell's heart was beating faster now. She had resigned herself to the ignominious fate that awaited her, had made peace with it, but this sudden and unexpected change in her fortunes had shocked her into silence. More than that, it had kindled the wild, inexplicable hope that he might be telling the truth.

'Who are you people?' she managed to say.

'My name's Drake, but you can call me Ryan,' he said, then nodded to the young woman sitting in the back. 'And this is Keira Frost, part of my team.'

'Team?' The name Frost was familiar, but in her confused state she couldn't place it.

'Shepherd team,' he explained, and suddenly a big piece of the puzzle fell into place. 'You're in good hands, Mitchell. For now, at least.'

'And after that?'

'Well, that's up to you. You can run and hide, and hope none of this catches up to you.' He shrugged. 'Or... you can stand with us, and maybe do something about it.'

With that, he turned around and started the engine.

'Like what?' she asked, unable to help herself. 'What can you do against people like that?'

She caught those intense green eyes in the rear-view mirror once more, set with a resolve that was almost frightening.

'We're going to war, Mitchell.'

Printed in August 2021
by Rotomail Italia S.p.A., Vignate (MI) - Italy